Born in Dublin in 1969 and now living in Canada, Emma Donoghue is a writer of fiction, history and drama for radio, stage and screen. She is best known for her international bestseller *Room*, shortlisted for the Man Booker and Orange Prizes.

For more information, visit www.emmadonoghue.com.
Follow Emma on Twitter @EDonoghueWriter

Praise for *Frog Music*

'The novel is brilliant as historical fiction and crime thriller, but it succeeds best by showing the everyday things that don't change with time . . . As a chronicler of motherhood, Donoghue remains hard to beat' *Independent on Sunday*

'A gripping tale of a woman's struggle to survive in the anarchic, near lawless world of a frontier city . . . shows what a wonderfully talented and versatile writer Emma Donoghue is' *Daily Mail*

'A subtle inquiry into the possibilities of motherhood, love and sexual freedom . . . Blanche's fraught journey to independence is artfully structured through flashbacks, fast-forwards and moments of stillness . . . Children's rhymes are potent and hard to forget. *Frog Music* is the same' *Daily Telegraph*

'*Frog Music* is a roiling, simmering brew of a novel: dramatic, unexpected' *Spectator*

'With *Frog Music*, a literary crime novel fixated on human darkness, Donoghue proves herself endlessly inventive . . . This is the kind of book that will keep you up at night and make you smarter' *Cosmopolitan*

'This is another smart and finely wrought consideration of parenthood, further proof of Donoghue's significant skill as an author' *Observer*

'Reminiscent of Anaïs Nin at her most filthily exuberant . . . nuanced sexual politics' *Financial Times*

'This wild ride of a novel shakes, rattles and rolls its way along, throwing off sparks of sensuality and intrigue and transporting the reader through the steamy demi-monde that is the city by the bay in 1876 . . . for *Frog Music*'s swelter and helter-skelter, its regard for the presentness of the moment as well as for the drives that see us through, and above all for its irresistible readability, the only word is *formidable*' *Irish Times*

'Emma Donoghue's last novel was the gripping *Room* and there is the same sense of tension, of suppressed panic in this highly charged, elegant murder mystery . . . Donoghue's enthralling narrative zips from the past to the present, revealing the heartbreaking secrets behind Jenny's stance . . . *Frog Music* soars with the raucous melodies of the street and, even as doubt and darkness creep ever closer, the novel remains thrillingly alive to the possibilities of change and transformation' *Sunday Express*

'Lively, entertaining and well-written' *Evening Standard*

'*Frog Music* keeps us captivated because Donoghue has filled the foreground and background of this wild tale with irresistibly captivating characters . . . First-rate historical fiction' *Washington Post*

'A riveting literary thriller revolving around a brief, unlikely friendship that ends with one dead and the other transformed' *O, The Oprah Magazine*

'Alive, brimming with sin and music' *New Yorker*

'Heartfelt, affecting, and real' *Chicago Tribune*

'Ebullient mystery . . . Donoghue cross-cuts between Blanche's desperate present-time search and scenes from her Technicolor past with show-stopping aplomb . . . Call it a mind-bendingly original crime novel, or a dazzling historical mystery, but in the end, this is a really a book about love – a mother's love for a strange child, for an exotic friend and finally, for herself' *San Francisco Chronicle*

'Is it literary fiction, a whodunit, a historical novel, fictionalized biography? Actually it's all of those things but also that relatively rare beast, at least these days – feminist fiction . . . The weight of fact and detail doesn't prevent the story bouncing off the page. All the colour and grit of the era is here. *Frog Music* is shocking in parts, explicit in others, touching and witty' *New Zealand Herald*

'Sexy, mysterious and full of courage'
New Indian Express

ALSO BY EMMA DONOGHUE

Astray

Room

The Sealed Letter

Landing

Touchy Subjects

Life Mask

The Woman Who Gave Birth to Rabbits

Slammerkin

Kissing the Witch: Old Tales in New Skins

Hood

Stir-fry

FROG MUSIC

EMMA DONOGHUE

PICADOR

First published 2014 by HarperCollins Publishers, Toronto, Canada
First published in the UK 2014 by Picador
First published in the UK in paperback 2014 by Picador

This edition published 2015 by Picador
an imprint of Pan Macmillan, a division of Macmillan Publishers Limited
Pan Macmillan, 20 New Wharf Road, London N1 9RR
Basingstoke and Oxford
Associated companies throughout the world
www.panmacmillan.com

ISBN 978-1-4472-4976-4

1 3 5 7 9 8 6 4 2

A CIP catalogue record for this book is available from the British Library.

Printed and bound by CPI Group (UK) Ltd, Croydon, CR0 4YY

For Margaret Lonergan,
friend and muse for a quarter of a century

CONTENTS

FROG MUSIC

I

DARLIN'

Sitting on the edge of the bed in the front room, Blanche stoops to rip at the laces of her gaiters. " '*Dors, min p'tit quinquin—*' " Her husky voice frays to a thread on the second high note. She clears her throat, rasping away the heat.

A train hurtles north from San Jose. The light from the locomotive's headlamp jabs through the long gap between the peeling window frame and the green blind, illuminating the room for Blanche: the shabby bureau, the bedstead, and Jenny, lolling against the scarred headboard. The Eight Mile House shakes like cardboard as the freight cars rattle by. Here at San Miguel Station, they're right at the southern boundary—the last gasp—of San Francisco.

Two days Blanche and Jenny have been boarding with the McNamaras, *auld acquaintance* to Jenny but still virtually strangers to Blanche. How much longer will Blanche be stuck in this four-room shack, she wonders, on the parched outskirts of the outskirts of the City? And how will she decide when it's even halfway safe to go back?

Blanche has got the left gaiter off now, and the boot below it, but the laces on the other one have snagged, and in the light of the single candle stub she can't find the knot; her long nails pick at the laces.

Dors, min p'tit quinquin,
Min p'tit pouchin,
Min gros rojin . . .

Sleep, my little child, my little chick, my fat grape. The old tune comes more sweetly now, the notes like pin-pricks. A silly Picard rhyme her grandmother used to sing to Blanche in the tiny attic in Paris.

" '*Dors, min p'tit quinquin, min p'tit pouchin . . .*' " Jenny slides the refrain back at her like a lazy leaf in a river.

It still amazes Blanche how fast this young woman can pick up a song on first hearing.

"How does the rest of it go?" Jenny asks, up on one elbow, brown cheeks sparkling with sweat. Her flesh from nose to brows is puffy, darkening. She'll have a pair of black eyes by morning.

But Blanche doesn't want to think about that. Jenny never harps on what's past, does she? She wears her bruises like parade gear, and they fade fast.

Blanche sits up straighter on the edge of the bed and sings on.

Te m'f'ras du chagrin
Si te n'dors point qu'à d'main.

" 'Shut your trap, little baby, before I shut it for you,' " Jenny translates very loosely, nodding. "Guess most lullabies boil down to that."

And Blanche is suddenly winded by an image of P'tit, wherever he is. A stern hand coming down to shut his trap. If only she knew the baby was all right: just that much. Has Jenny ever in her life stopped to think before opening her own goddamn trap?

But her friend's eyes are half sealed already, feline as she settles back on the limp pillows. Above the nightshirt borrowed from McNamara, Jenny's battered face is flattening toward sleep.

Blanche hauls up her skirt and sets her right ankle on her left knee to get a better look at the tangled lace. The gritty canvas of the gaiter clings to her calf like skin that won't be sloughed. Mud flecking the floorboards, the dingy sheets; the whole shack is probably crawling with fleas and lice. Blanche bends closer to make out the knot. Another few seconds and she'll have it undone. Her lungs fill, stretching rib cage, skin, corset, bodice, as she croons again: " *'Te m'f'ras du chagrin—'* "

The cracks come so hard Blanche takes them for thunder. The hot sky must have finally exploded, forking its blades into the eaves of the Eight Mile House. Oh, she shouldn't have been singing, she thinks with a superstitious shiver; she's brought on a storm.

"*Qu'est-ce—*" Is that the start of a question from Jenny, or just a gasp?

The candle's out, and it's so dark here in the hinterlands. "Wait," Blanche tells Jenny, lurching to her feet with her right boot still on. A sulfurous tang on the air—she's never known a thunderstorm to smell like that. Fireworks? But what is there to celebrate on the fourteenth of September? Outside, the dogs of San Miguel Station bark in furious chorus. What can blow out a candle? Knock it over, spatter its burning wax—is that what's running down her jaw?

"John!" That's Ellen McNamara in the back room, bawling for her husband.

A thump, something falling near Blanche. Has the little washstand toppled off the bureau?

"John!"

Blanche's right cheek is dripping as if with scalding tears, but she's not crying. She swabs it and something bites—some monstrous skeeter? No, not an insect, something sharp. "*Merde,* I've been cut," she cries through the stifling dark.

No answer from Jenny. Behind the thin bedroom wall, in the saloon, a door bangs. McNamara, only half audible, and his wife, and the children, shrieking too high for Blanche to make out the words.

She's staggering now. The boards crunch under her bare sole. Glass: that must be what's cut her cheek. The lightning's shattered the window and made a hole in the blind, so a murky moonlight is leaking in. Blanche pants in outrage. Will those dogs ever shut up so she can hear herself think? She squints across the bedroom. "Jenny?" Kicking shards off her foot, Blanche clambers onto the bed, but Jenny's no longer there. She couldn't have got past Blanche without opening the door, could she?

The sheets are sodden to the touch. What can have wet them?

Blanche's eyes adjust to the faint radiance. Something on the floor between bed and wall, puddled in the corner, moving, but not the way a person moves. Arms bent wrong, nightshirt rucked obscenely, skinny legs daubed with blood, and wearing a carnival version of a familiar face.

Jenny!

Blanche recoils.

A second.

Another.

She forces her hand down toward—to feel, to know for sure, at least—but the geyser spurt against her fingers sends her howling back to the other side of the bed. She clings to the foul sheets.

Light smashes in the doorway from the saloon: McNamara with a lamp. "Miss Blanche, are you shot or what?"

She blinks down at herself, scarlet all over.

*

Not quite a month ago, at the House of Mirrors in San Francisco's Chinatown.

From the piano, the soft opening chords of a waltz. In the very center of the little stage, rising like the stigma of a flower: Blanche. All in white tonight, true to her stage name. She begins very slow and stately, as chaste as any ingenue in her first role; that's the trick of the skirt dance. With delicacy, with wonder, as if she's only just discovering the sleek waterfall of white satin spilling from her waist to her toes, Blanche circles the platform. She enfolds herself in the glossy material (forty-four feet around), lingers in its caress.

She makes sure to act as if she hasn't noticed the men in the tight rows of crimson velvet chairs, as if they aren't even there. The Grand Saloon is already packed early on this Saturday evening in the middle of August. Lamplight ricochets from the floor-to-ceiling looking glasses, and the red walls and matching tufted carpet seem to pulse with heat. Inside her frilled bodice, sweat is trickling down Blanche's sides. But she holds herself as serene as any swan spreading its milky wings. She makes a screen of the vast silk skirt to silhouette her curves. The *michetons* must be leaning forward by now, eager to peer through the fabric, but she doesn't so much as cast them a glance.

Delibes's sweet melody gives way to the bolder theme, and Blanche starts to hop, glide, spin. She pushes every pose to its precise extreme. Face dipped to one knee, she raises the other leg behind her, pointing her toes at the gilt-coffered ceiling. The skirt slithers down her thigh, catching a little on the gauzy tights, threatening to turn inside out, and a few gasps erupt from the audience, even though they can see nothing yet—what thrills them most, Blanche knows, is what they can only imagine—but she rights herself and starts waltzing again as the music returns to the calm opening tune. Her face still cool and virginal.

Michetons who pay this much to watch a dance have complicated cravings. They need to be roused and refused at almost the same moment. Blanche is an expert tease, an *allumeuse* who lights the flame and snuffs it, lights and snuffs it.

She knows this routine so well, and the famous "Swanhilde Waltz" it's set to, that she can let her mind wander. What was that slip of an Italian called, the first Swanhilde, at the premiere of *Coppélia* they attended, back in Paris? Five, no, six years ago; Blanche remembers being dazzled by every pirouette. Arthur came home one day during the siege with the news that she'd died, the little Italian. Even top ballerinas had had their wages frozen while the Prussians were at the gates of the city, and this one half starved, it was said, and succumbed to smallpox on her seventeenth birthday.

Goddamn it. Blanche has been trying to keep it outside the walls of her mind, the pestilence that began infiltrating San Francisco back in May. Smallpox: the very word makes her itch.

She almost stumbles. Then strikes a pose, very classical: a fleeing nymph metamorphosed into marble. As the music darkens in the final section of the waltz, Blanche bends back, all the way back, till her fingers are almost stroking the boards, and she starts to spin, her whole body the trumpet of a white lily revolving helplessly on its stem.

The accompaniment spirals upward, frantic, and Blanche whips upright, her swirling skirt engulfing the stage. Thunderous, triumphant chords. At the crescendo she touches the secret tape at the small of her back and the whole thing flies free, creamy satin swooping toward the audience and landing, albatross-like, on a pair of old millionaires.

The men's whoops break the tension, but that's all right. It wouldn't be burlesque without a few laughs.

Blanche, now wearing only her bodice and a pair of shirred white pantaloons over her translucent tights, sucks one fingertip. As if she's an innocent, discomfited by the greedy stares. The Professor, at the piano, knows to wait. She sings the first verse a cappella, like some creamy-skinned beggar girl on a street corner:

Darlin', better love just one—
Darlin', better love just one.
You can't love more than one,
And have all the fun—
Darlin', better love just one.

Now the piano takes up the tune, adding some sauce. " 'You can't love two,' " Blanche warns the crowd, wagging that wet-tipped finger, " 'and keep me true to you—' "

The minute she first heard this song, crooned off-key at the back of a streetcar, she knew she could make an act of it. She does a different little dance after each verse. Blanche is gaining in knowledge, ripening before their eyes. By the fourth verse her strut behind the footlights grows impudent. " 'You can't love four, and come knocking on my door—' " *Can't,* she insists, but her dance is saying *Can, can, can, can.* Her hips respond to imaginary handling. Blanche moves as dancing girls have moved for as long as there've been dancing girls, through the whole sweaty history of the human race.

You can't love five,
And eat honey from my hive—
Darlin', you can't love five.

A surge of heat goes through Blanche. She's counting: fifty dollars from this performance, plus whatever she'll make from a private rendezvous afterward. Every dip, sway, pout, wiggle, grind, she converts into greenbacks in her head and that gives extra vim to her movements, burnishes the shine of her eyes. " 'You can't love six, and teach me any tricks—' " she scolds the crowd, flicking a couple of hats off their front-row wearers with rapid-fire toe kicks. One red-faced visitor squeals with such delight, she fears he might drop down in an apoplectic fit.

At the back of the Grand Saloon stands a nunnish figure in gray, the proprietor: Madame Johanna Werner. She gives Blanche a sober nod of approval.

Jump splits now, panting just enough to make it interesting:

You can't love eight,
And get through my pearly gate—
Darlin', you can't love eight.

Did Blanche forget the seventh verse? Who cares. Down on her hands and knees, shaking her hips as she taunts the *michetons* over one round shoulder. " 'You can't love nine, or you'll run out of time!' " She jerks as if rammed by an invisible lover. " 'You can't love ten, and do that to me again—' "

At the twelfth verse, Blanche shuts her eyes and belts it out as urgently as she can.

Darlin', you can't love twelve—
Darlin', you can't love twelve.
You can't love twelve,
Or I'll have to manage by myself—

She lets her voice crack with desperation. One hand slips inside the waistband of her pantaloons; now the other. Men are groaning, writhing in their velvet chairs.

Every *cigare* in the house is smoking now. And Blanche is excited too. Her genius for this job is that she doesn't have to pretend, because every throb of her salty little crack is real.

Flat on her back now. Legs thrashing in the air. Assailed by an unseen crowd of thrusting incubi. Blanche gasps: " 'You can't love thirteen, or it's gonna start hurting . . . ' "

Later that evening, as she steps out of the International Hotel, her sleeves instantly glue themselves to her arms. The ink-black porter holds the door, and the quarter she drops into his pink palm is sticky from hers.

The organ-grinder at the corner is cranking out the Triumphal March from *Aida,* the same barrel he was playing more than an hour ago when a cab brought Blanche to the hotel. The man has stamina, she'll grant him that. His organ must weigh a hundred pounds, and despite the spindly hinged leg it leans on, its strap is pulling his shoulders down like a millstone. His wife gives her tambourine a listless smack on every fourth beat, and their spaniel capers in a joyless, practiced way.

Twilight now, and the light is dimming but the warmth has only thickened. *L'heure bleue,* they used to call it at home, "the blue hour," when the sky turns that serious azure and the jagged horizon blackens. Not that this cockeyed metropolis is a patch on Paris, to Blanche's mind, even if some call it the Paris of the West. The Capital of the West, maybe, but San Francisco is a tenth the size of the City of Light, and it hasn't a smooth boulevard, a promenade, even an avenue worth the name. The City, the locals call it, as if it's the only one. All hills, like some feather bed that a giant's shaken and left a crumpled mess. Blanche has been marching up and down these slopes with all the other human ants for a year and a half, since she arrived from France, but she'll never get used to the dizzying gradients.

She's tired now. It's not the leg show at the House of Mirrors, or the quick glass of champagne at the International with the *micheton* she's just left winded on the hotel's fine sheets. (He wasn't a regular of hers but a silver millionaire passing through town for the night who begged Madame Johanna to bump him to the top of Blanche's line. Actually, Blanche rather prefers the fly-by-nights, since it's easier to make a spectacular impression if it's one time only.) No, it's this strange heat that's wearing her out. The summer began civilly enough, with warm breezes whisking away the morning fogs, but now, heading into the second half of August, the City can't breathe. The air's a stinking miasma of all the steams and soots San Franciscans can produce. One newspaper's dug up an odd little fellow who's been noting down what his thermometer tells him every day since he arrived in '49. This summer of 1876 is the hottest season in his records, with the mercury hitting ninety every afternoon.

Half a block down Jackson, that same opera seems to be dragging on at the Chinese Royal Theater, all screeching strings, drum and gong. Blanche shakes her head to clear it. She gathers speed as she marches down Kearny, fuchsia skirt swaying lankly, heels knocking puffs of dust out of the wooden sidewalk. She'll be back at her apartment in ten minutes. Then she can get out of these sticky clothes, and maybe have a drink with Arthur, if he's home.

The Pony Express Saloon is already advertising September's grand-prize-gala dogfight. Spotting a yellow smallpox flag nailed over the door of a dress shop, Blanche holds her breath and veers away. Red dots on face, hands, or feet, that's what you look out for, according to the so-called experts. Not that they can agree on how you catch it, whether by poisonous vapors leaking from the ground or invisible bugs jumping from the sick to the well. And really, who can bear to stay shut up indoors holding their breath all summer?

Past the Bella Union Theater, where what sounds like a full house is chanting for the variety show to begin. The Ice Cream Boudoir is stuffed to the gills, but City Hall's deserted—except for a prisoner in the lockup who clangs on the bars of the basement window as Blanche walks by, making her jump. Portsmouth Square is fenced with iron spears dipped in gold. Confetti of limp flower beds. Snoozers stacked like war dead under every canopied tree. In the fountain, two drunks wrestle for a chance to lie full length under the spout. Children hover out of range, gathering their nerve to dash in for a faceful of water. The sight makes Blanche thirsty, but she doesn't fancy pushing her way through the bums and *gamins* to take a drink.

The streets are filling up now the sun's gone down. Folks burst out of their stifling rooms. When Blanche stares west, past Nob Hill, she catches the last of the light sinking into the Pacific. On the corner of Clay, she spots that old one-eyed woman dragging her stained valise. To avoid her, Blanche pivots to cross Kearny but has to wait for a horsecar to rattle by. The fist-shaped cobbles release all the stored heat of the day into her shoes' thin soles. She steps out in the streetcar's wake, watching for fresh dung in the uncertain dusk—which means she doesn't see the thing till it's on top of her.

Black antlerish handlebars, that's all she has time to glimpse before the gigantic spokes are swallowing her skirts. Her scream seems to break the bicycle in two. Machine explodes one way and rider another, smashing Blanche to the ground.

She tries to spring up but her right leg won't bear her. Mouth too dry to spit.

The lanky daredevil jumps up, rubbing one elbow, as lively as a clown. "*Ça va, mademoiselle?*"

The fellow's observant enough to read Blanche's nationality from her style of dress. And the accent is as French as Blanche's own. But the voice—

Not a man's, Blanche realizes. Not a boy's, even. This is a girl, for all the gray jacket, vest, pants, the jet hair hacked above the sunburned jawline. One of these eccentrics on whom the City prides itself—which only aggravates Blanche's irritation, as if the whole collision were nothing but a gag, and never mind who's left with *merde* on her hem.

A cart swerves around Blanche, hooves close enough to make her flinch. She gets up onto her knees, but she's hobbled by her skirt.

The young woman in pants holds out a hand, teeth flashing in a grin.

Blanche slaps it away. For this female to run her down and then smirk about it—

A long screech of brakes: another horsecar at the crossing, bearing down on them. The stranger offers her hand again, with a theatrical flourish. Blanche grabs hold of the cool fingers and wrenches herself to her feet, hearing a seam rip under one arm. She staggers to the sidewalk, her skewed bustle bulging over one hip.

As she shakes out her aching right leg, she realizes she's alone. The daredevil's run half a block up Kearny and is roaring in English at some *gamins* who've seized their chance to make off with her fancy machine. Serves her right if it's gone!

But by the time Blanche has hauled her bustle straight and slapped the dirt from her skirts, the rider's back. Perched above the gigantic front wheel, she glides down the street to Blanche, then swings one leg over, hops down, and hits the ground running. "Jenny Bonnet," she announces as if it's good news, the accent thoroughly American now even if she says her surname in the French way, with a silent *t*. She tips her black hat to a natty angle. "And you are?"

"None of your business." Blanche blows at the strand of hair that's stuck to her damp lip and summons her crispest English, because what she lacks in height she can make up for in hauteur. "Listen, you he-she-whatever, the next time you get the notion to make the street your playground—"

"Yeah, this thing's the devil to steer," interrupts Jenny Bonnet, nodding as if they agree. She has only about six inches on Blanche, up close. "Didn't hurt you, though, did I?"

Blanche bristles. "I'm bruised from head to toe."

"No bones sticking out, though?" The young woman makes a show of looking her up and down, mugging for a laugh. "No actual bloodshed per se?"

"You might have killed us both, imbecile."

"If it comes to that, I might have fallen off a steamer to Lima this morning, and you might have caught your death," says Jenny, jerking her thumb at a smallpox flag on a tobacconist's just behind them.

Blanche jerks back and takes a few steps away.

"Instead, it appears we're both safe and sound, and so's my high-wheeler." Jenny lets out a cowboy whoop.

And oddly enough, Blanche's wrath begins to lift a little. Maybe it's the whisper of a breeze rising off the Bay, where the masts of the quarantined junks and clippers seem to be swaying a little, unless that's a trick of the dusk. Or the soft trill from a flute player in some apartment overhead. The lights are flaring on in the cafés and shops along Kearny, and soon Chinatown's border will be as glittering as a carousel.

"Let me buy you a drink," suggests Jenny, nodding toward Durand's brasserie.

Blanche always likes the sound of that. "As an apology?"

"If you like. Never found them worth the candle myself."

Blanche hoists her eyebrows.

"If you're sorry, folks can tell," remarks Jenny. "No use piling on the verbiage." She lays her bicycle flat outside the brasserie's door and beckons a boy over to guard it.

"Do you reckon this kid won't run off with it as fast as the others did?" asks Blanche, sardonic.

"Ah, I know where this one lives."

That disconcerts Blanche. "I never imagine them as living anywhere in particular."

Jenny nods up at the building's rickety overhang: "He's a Durand."

As the two of them step into the garlicky fug, a couple of customers glance up, but nobody gives the young woman in pants a second glance. This Jenny must be an habitué.

Monsieur Durand greets her with a nod and clears a space at the bar with his elbows. His fat mustache is leaking wax as he comes back and slaps down their glasses and a carafe of wine. Blanche pours the wine, takes a long drink. Ah, that's better. She wipes sweat out of her eyes. "Aren't you sweltering under all those layers?"

A shrug as Jenny fills her own glass.

"September can't come too soon for me. It has to cool down by then."

"The City's the exception to any rule," says Jenny. "I've known it to be hottest in October."

Blanche groans at the prospect.

Durand returns with two bowls of *cuisses de grenouille au beurre noir* they didn't ask for. Discovering that she's hungry, Blanche rips the firm, aromatic flesh from the frog thighs. "These aren't like back in France."

"No, they're better," Jenny counters. She lets out a grunt of pleasure as she chews. "Only ten minutes dead, that's the trick. But a touch too salty. Tell him he's still oversalting," she throws at Durand.

The owner thumbs his mustache off his unsmiling mouth. "Portal," he roars over his shoulder.

"How long have you been here?" Jenny asks Blanche.

"Since the winter before last."

"So why've you stayed?"

Blanche blinks at the question. "You have no manners, miss."

"Oh, I've got some," says Jenny, "they're just not what you might call pretty. Diamond in the rough, that's me."

Blanche rolls her eyes. "And why shouldn't I have stayed, may I ask?"

"Most move on through," observes Jenny. "As if the City's just a mouth, swallowing them whole, and the rest of America's the belly where they end up."

Blanche winces at the image and pours herself more wine. California was Arthur's choice, she recalls. Blanche couldn't have found it on a map. All the French they got into conversations with on the ship were heading, like Arthur and Blanche and Ernest, to some big city—New York or Chicago if not San Francisco—where, it was said, the hospitality and entertainment trades paid well. "We came because we heard you can cock your hat as you please here," she says, "and stayed for the same reason, I suppose."

"Who's *we?*"

But Blanche has had enough of this style of questioning. "And you, when did you arrive?"

"Portal!" roars Durand again.

"I was three," says Jenny, neat teeth nibbling her last frog leg, "but even then I was choosy about my food."

"What are you now?"

"Still choosy."

"No," says Blanche, "I mean—"

A chuckle. "Twenty-seven."

Really? "Huh. That's three years older than me, and I still look pretty fresh."

Jenny grins back at her, neither agreeing nor contradicting.

"It must be your outfit," says Blanche with a sigh, nodding at the pants. "It's as odd as all get-out, but it does take years off you."

They're bantering as if they've always known each other, it occurs to Blanche with a prickle of unease. She's not one for making friends with women, as a rule.

A mournful face looks through the hatch from the kitchen, and Durand snaps at him, "Ease up on the salt, Jeanne says."

This must be Portal. The cook makes a small, obscene gesture in Jenny's direction.

"You know I'm right, *mon vieux,*" she tells Portal.

"Stick to swamp-wading." He mops his forehead with his sleeve and disappears again.

"So come on now," says Jenny to Blanche, greedily, "who are you and what's your story?"

"Hold on. Swamp-wading?" Blanche repeats.

"I caught these last night, out by Lake Merced," Jenny tells her, holding up a glistening bone.

"That's your trade? Hunting frogs?" Well, it would go some way to explain the young woman's getup. "Don't they give you warts?"

"That's pure dumb superstition." Jenny offers her small hands for examination.

They're brown but smooth. "Couldn't you work at something . . . I don't know, less disgusting?"

"Guess I don't disgust easy," says Jenny. "The City has three hundred restaurants, and all the French and Chinese ones need frogs."

"But they're such ugly, clumsy creatures."

"Clumsy? You ever seen them swim?"

Now that she thinks about it, Blanche realizes she's never seen a live frog except on sale in barrels on Dupont Street. "But the smell, the slime—"

"That's fish you're thinking of. Frogs don't smell of anything," Jenny corrects her, "and without a touch of slipperiness, you can't have it both ways."

"Both ways?"

"Live on land and in water as well. I call that crafty."

Blanche purses her mouth. "That's my glass you're drinking from, by the way."

Jenny blinks at it. "Sorry." She gestures to Durand for another.

"An apology at last," marvels Blanche under her breath, satirical.

When the proprietor slaps a clean glass down in front of her, she refills it and strips the last shred of garlicky meat from a delicate bone with her teeth. "Since you've drunk from my glass," she tells Jenny, "you should be able to read my thoughts. Except you'd probably call that more *dumb superstition.*"

Jenny furrows her brow. "Your name is Patience Vautrien . . . and you're a dairymaid."

Blanche makes a small sound of outrage. Those girls are known for their reek. "I did once work with horses," she says. A fact, if a misleading one.

"But not anymore?" Jenny presses her temples, frowning with effort. "Mrs. Hector Losange, mother of five lovely offspring, known for her charity teas?" She waits. "Arabella Delafrance, lady spy?"

"Enough!" The joke suddenly sours on Blanche. As if it's not as clear as day from her flowered bodice, fuchsia skirt, and general gaudiness that she's a showgirl, at least, and probably on the town.

Why should she care who knows? If Blanche didn't want to be recognized for what she was, she wouldn't dress this way, would she? She never exactly intended to be a soiled dove (that curious euphemism), but neither can she remember putting up any real objection. She stepped into the life like a swimmer entering a lake, a few inches at a time.

"So where did you grow up," she asks, to change the subject, "America's belly or mouth?"

"Some gristly part, anyway," Jenny jokes instead of answering.

"How much?" asks a man at Blanche's shoulder.

She decides to assume he's addressing Durand. "Have you family?" she presses on.

"Found under a cabbage leaf, I was," says Jenny, deadpan.

"I said, how much?" The American is breathing right in Blanche's ear, and she can smell the chaw in his mouth.

"I'm eating," she says without looking around.

"Only asking a civil question." The big man squeezes up to the bar between the two women, dark wheels of sweat under his arms.

"You're bothering the lady," mentions Jenny.

He turns to look her up and down. "You reckon I can't afford her?" Jingling coins in his pocket. "Because for your information, I could hire six of this slut"—jerking his thumb at Blanche—"with change to spare."

"As the fellow says," Jenny remarks, "better keep your

mouth shut and seem stupid than open it and remove all doubt."

The last thing Blanche wants is a quarrel. Across his bulk, she frowns furiously at Jenny.

"You calling me stupid?" asks the fellow after a second's delay, reddening as he shifts his quid of tobacco to the other cheek.

"A leather-headed lunk of the highest order," says Jenny pleasantly.

He presents his fist for inspection, inches from her face. "Somebody ought to teach you to keep your nose out of other folks' business, girlie."

"My friend Mr. Colt here would not concur." Jenny slides her jacket aside to show a tapering shape in her trouser leg.

Blanche is off her stool and an arm's length away, butter dripping. Absurdly, she wishes she'd picked up her napkin to wipe her mouth.

"Oh," growls the American, "you've got nothing on you that impresses me, you, you puny—goddamn morphodite!"

Durand has finally noticed what's brewing. *"Dehors,"* he roars, pointing toward the door.

Jenny hops down from the stool, a Harlequin in a pantomime.

The American follows obediently, but when Jenny holds the door for him with flip courtesy, he backhands her into the wall. The crack of the young woman's skull against a faded print of the Champs-Elysées makes even the most dogged drinkers glance up.

"Monsieur Durand!" protests Blanche.

But the owner only raises his eyes to heaven.

Jenny, with the look of a stunned calf, bends to retrieve her hat. The print falls to the floor with a tinkle of glass. And now the *connard* has her wrist behind her back and he's marching her out, using her shoulder to shove the door open.

Blanche races out after them, yanks at his arm: "Have you no shame, whaling on a female like some brute?"

The American flicks her against the wall.

Struggling for breath, clutching her side, Blanche curses her size. At times like this she feels like some fairy in a world of trolls.

The man has dropped Jenny on the sidewalk. Is he going to stave her ribs in, stamp on her head?

Blanche lets out a wail.

No, he just lands a squirt of brown juice on Jenny and slouches off down the street. Without a second glance at Blanche, she notices—which tells her it was a row more than a woman that he was itching for all along.

She leans on the windowsill of the brasserie, dizzy. The leg bruised by the bicycle wobbles under her, and her ribs throb. Nothing's broken, though. Blanche has enough experience to know that.

Kearny Street is humming around them, burners and reflectors multiplying the light of oil lamps in every store-front. Drinkers shuffle arm in arm from bar to bar, bawl-ing dirty choruses. Knots of men head for the *bordels* on Commercial or Pacific to sample Jewesses, Mexicans, black girls, Orientals (though they'll still pay highest for French, Blanche thinks with a certain satisfaction). A river of faces, festively red-eyed, as if they've given up even trying to sleep till the heat breaks. Smallpox be damned, nobody's staying in tonight.

Jenny sits up and lifts her sharp chin with an attempt at a grin. Her face is swelling already: a dark-edged cut below the left eyebrow. She turns aside and pukes her supper neatly into the gutter.

How the evening's complicated itself. Blanche should just walk away, right now, from this gun-packing jester who's caused her damage twice in as many hours. Life in the City by the Bay is demanding enough without the company of someone who runs toward risk like a child to bonbons.

But she lets out a long breath. The fact is, Blanche hasn't had so much fun with a stranger since—well, since leaving France, and farther back than that. Their little circle in San Francisco is—as it was in Paris—composed of Blanche, Arthur, Ernest, and whoever the two men bring home. Blanche can't think of another acquaintance she's formed as fast (and on her own) as tonight's with Jenny Bonnet. Such a strange sense of familiarity and ease along with the novelty. "You should slap a bit of meat on that eye," she advises.

A derisory grunt from Jenny.

"Where do you live?"

"Nowhere in particular."

What a one for secrets this young woman is. "Come on, let's get you home," says Blanche, holding out her hand.

"Fact is," says Jenny, clambering to her feet, "I'm only out a week."

Out? Out of . . . ah, doesn't that just take the cake: a jailbird. "What were you in for?"

"Oh, the usual. 'Appearing in the apparel of the other sex,' " quotes Jenny in a pompous voice.

Blanche frowns. Can that be an actual crime? "Well, if this outfit gets you arrested," she asks with a hint of impatience, "what makes you keep putting it back on?"

"It suits me," says Jenny.

So deadpan that Blanche doesn't register the pun until a second later. This young woman's spirits sure revive fast. "You must be lodging somewhere," Blanche persists.

"Been high-wheeling, mostly," says Jenny.

Zooming along on that contraption, day and night? "What, you sleep on the wing like some seabird?"

"I take naps in parks or theaters, or on a friend's sofa when I feel the need," Jenny concedes.

There's blood trickling onto the woman's collar, Blanche notices now, and a trace of vomit on her chin. Blanche lets out a small groan. After all, it was for her sake, out of some kind of misguided gallantry, that this curious female got herself beat up. "Come on. I'm just a step away, on Sacramento Street."

"Lady, what makes you think you have to—"

"Come if you're coming," she snaps.

The Durand boy, perched astride the great spokes of the bicycle's front wheel, is taking in the whole scene as comfy as if he's in the stalls at the Bella Union Theater. Jenny flicks him a small coin and leads the machine off by the handlebars down Kearny Street.

She suddenly cuts sideways, nearly knocking Blanche down again, and rattles her machine across the cobbles. She halts below a window from which a song is drifting in a scratchy voice.

'Tis you who makes my friends my foes,
'Tis you who makes me wear old clothes.

Jenny leans against the wall, her face alight as she listens to the unseen man.

He sings, " 'Here you are so near my nose—' "

" 'Tip her up,' " Jenny carols in an oddly sweet soprano, " 'and down she goes.' "

From inside the building, laughter, and several voices roar the chorus back at her.

Ha, ha, ha, you and me,
"Little brown jug," don't I love thee!
Ha, ha, ha . . .

Blanche turns away with a sudden yawn. She crosses at the flagstone strip on the corner.

" 'The rose is red,' " Jenny belts out, gliding after her, standing straight-legged on the mounting peg of her machine.

My nose is, too,
The violet's blue, and so are you;
And yet I guess before I stop,
We'd better take another drop.

Blanche leads the way west on Clay into Chinatown proper, where the streets are sinking into the patchy blackness of their accustomed night. The moon's waning C has got caught in one of those alleys so skinny that the overhanging balconies almost touch. When Blanche and Arthur came to the City, they naturally washed up in Chinatown, where the rents were low and patrolmen hardly ever penetrated the warren of passageways. Few of the businesses here can afford to hire Specials to guard the streets, so folks live more or less as they like. Passing her favorite noodle house now, Blanche breathes in hot oil, ginger, and sesame. Then rotten vegetables, from the next alley. This quarter's always filthy—mostly because the City supervisors won't fix its sewers or pay for garbage collection. Arthur relishes it, claiming that skirting piles of fishtails makes him feel like a true bohemian. The newsmen call Chinatown a laboratory of infection; if even half what they say were true, Blanche thinks irreverently, she and Arthur and all its other residents would be dead by now.

Dupont Street is littered with yellow flags that shopkeepers must have ripped off their doors so they could get back to business. "I hope you've had your scratch?" she asks Jenny, suddenly wary.

Jenny slaps her sleeve above the elbow. "Stood in line for a day, eight years back, when it hit the City last."

"I thought perhaps you'd take your chances," Blanche teases, "being so devil-may-care."

Jenny grins back. "Devil-may-care's not the same as dumb as an ox."

In the middle of the street, a spectral man in silk pants and bonnet is stooping to collect the little flags. Chinatown's a soup of these pigtailed bachelors—more and more of them stirred into the mix every month. Low Long, Blanche's lodger, tells her that's because no one will rent to Orientals elsewhere in the City.

"What do you want with those?" Jenny calls out to the man.

He blinks, doesn't have enough English to answer her.

Blanche laughs under her breath. "Word's going round this week that the flags aren't the mark of the disease, but the opposite—they scare it away."

Jenny shakes her head in wonder. "Like some old girls I met in jail, quite convinced by the scaremongers that vaccinations give you syph!"

Looking into an alley, Blanche glimpses knots of people bedding down on skinny balconies, flat roofs, even stoops—anywhere that might offer a breath of air in the suffocating night. At the corner of Sacramento Street, she and Jenny pass a metal drum full of smoldering blankets and rugs. A rubber-masked man is hammering a wet sheet over the door of a building that has steam pouring out all its windows. Another white official is herding a dozen Chinese men with waist-length braided pigtails into a wagon stenciled *Board of Health.*

Blanche and Jenny step off the sidewalk but both catch pungent facefuls of sulfur and start coughing.

"Jenny!"

Merde. It's that one-eyed wreck of a Frenchwoman whom Blanche tried to avoid earlier. She's hovering over the paraphernalia she hawks from her suitcase.

"Maria, *chérie, ça va*?" Jenny calls back, rattling her machine across the cobbles to reach the old witch and then kissing her on both cheeks.

Perhaps a cancer, or is it leprosy, eating the woman down to the bone? Blanche wonders with a shudder. She can't bring herself to look at the melted face. The rouge only makes it worse, and so does the kohl ringing the remaining eye. Breasts hanging in this Maria's bodice like thirsty tongues; she still dresses like what she must have been, though who'd pay for a piece of that? Still, no accounting for men's tastes.

"You ride this thing?" Maria's asking Jenny in a gravelly voice.

"I fly it," Jenny corrects her.

"Till you land and smash your face." She puts one yellowed nail to Jenny's swollen cheekbone.

"Nah, that was in a little scrap," says Jenny with a hint of pride. "You know my friend?" she asks, gesturing to Blanche.

Who's already shaking her head.

But Maria makes a ghastly curtsy. "Blanche Beunon, Blanche la Danseuse, top of the bill at the House of Mirrors!" Jerking her head down the block toward the brothel. "I haven't had the honor."

"Blanche la Danseuse," repeats Jenny with a grin, "the famous dancer, that's right."

To avoid looking at the woman's missing eye, Blanche examines the litter laid out around the valise as if there's something she might possibly want: a set of brass weights, a stained cravat . . .

"Is that your *mac* I've seen with you, that long string of misery, Ernest something?" Maria steps so close, Blanche gets a reek of spirits off her.

"No," she says, edging away.

"Ah, his *ami intime,* then? Albert, Arnaud?"

Blanche fights the impulse to tell the hag it's none of her business. "Arthur Deneve," she corrects her coldly.

But Maria's already turned to Jenny. "You should put some meat on that to draw out the bad blood."

"What claptrap. Blood's just blood," says Jenny.

Blanche takes her by the patched elbow of her gray jacket and hurries her west on Sacramento, the high-wheeler clattering along beside them. "Are you mad, kissing that creature?" she hisses when they're out of earshot. "These things can be catching."

Jenny giggles. "Acid, catching?"

Blanche is taken aback.

"One splash of vitriol, that's all it took to wipe out half Maria's face," says Jenny. "They didn't do things by halves back in the Rush. She was the first French dove here, or so she claims . . ."

Blanche shudders. The Gold Rush was almost three decades ago; could the one-eyed hag really have lasted that long? "I say it again: you like everything disgusting."

"You mean Maria?"

She does, but that sounds harsh. "I mean her story."

"I just like stories," says Jenny with a shrug.

Blanche insists they stop at Hop Yik and Company for some meat. Mei's face is glassy with sweat as he serves his countrymen unrecognizable things in bamboo boxes and twists of paper. He charges Blanche only two bits for a steak, though she suspects that's because it won't last another day. It has that tinge of gray, but it's cold, at least.

She badgers Jenny into holding it to her swollen eye, and she wheels the machine for her across the busy intersection with Dupont Street to Blanche's building, number 815. This block of Sacramento's so steep, the sidewalk slashes diagonally in front of the first floor, where Low Long has his living quarters, workshop, and shoe store. With one of the keys on the ring hanging from her waist, Blanche lets them into the pitch-black stairwell.

" *'Au clair de la lune,'* " she sings softly, " *'on n'y voit qu'un peu.'* " By moonlight, you can't see much.

"Can't see a thing, in fact," says Jenny. "What a deep voice you have for such a slip of a girl. Did Maman teach you that one, back in Paris?"

Blanche snorts. "She smacked me if she heard me singing."

"*Quelle salope!*"

"She said it would attract lightning," says Blanche, a little defensive. "Did you never hear that one—that a song can turn the weather?"

Jenny laughs.

"More *pure dumb superstition*, I suppose."

"Some folks just like to hit kids," remarks Jenny, "the way others like a drink."

"Oh, Maman liked that too," says Blanche under her breath as she heads up the stairs. She thinks of her bedbound grandmother who shared Blanche's mattress and taught her all the old songs sotto voce, mouth to ear. "You can leave your darling machine down here," she throws over her shoulder.

"Won't the landlord object?"

"That would be me," says Blanche, smiling in the dark.

"Huh," says Jenny behind her.

It still sounds incongruous to Blanche. She never aspired to own property until a few months back, when one of their fellow lodgers mentioned that the building's

Swiss owner was desperate for cash to pay some fine. It gives her a twinge of amusement to remember bargaining him down to fifteen hundred dollars. All that legwork at the House of Mirrors, all those bouts in hotel rooms, converted by alchemy into bricks and mortar . . .

"Don't much care for buying things, myself," remarks Jenny.

Blanche bristles a little. Remembering Arthur's laugh, the day she produced the deed with a ta-da. How he told her she'd make a good little bourgeoise. Not that he objects to the cash she collects every week from Low Long and their nine other lodgers of all trades and tints. "What about that revolver you were brandishing at Durand's?" she counters.

"Ah, my equalizer," says Jenny fondly. "Won that off a California infantryman in a poker game."

"Why's it called an equalizer?"

"Because anyone can load and fire it, easy."

"I bet it'd be easy to shoot yourself in the leg if you keep bicycling around with that thing in your pocket," Blanche tells her. "Yourself or the next innocent party you crash into, of course . . ."

"It can't go off if I haven't cocked it," says Jenny, laughing.

"Hey, if you *don't much care for buying things,* where did you get your precious high-wheeler? I can't imagine what such a fancy contraption costs."

"Me neither," Jenny assures her. "I found it last week on Market Street."

"Found?" repeats Blanche, dubiously.

"Saw the wheelman come a cropper and get toted off

on a stretcher," explains Jenny. "That little back wheel's treacherous—one rut and it flips you over the handlebars."

"So you stole a valuable machine from a wounded man!" They're on the second-floor landing now. The scent of oregano wafting down from the fourth story tells Blanche that the pickle-factory men from Corfu are cooking on their tiny stove.

"Well, I sure wasn't going to just leave it lying there for the next passerby to grab."

"The next thief, you mean," retorts Blanche as she lets them in her front door.

"Well, a toff that can afford such a toy, I figure he can afford to lose it too," says Jenny.

Blanche finds the matchbox and strikes a light.

When they first came to number 815, Blanche and Arthur lodged in a nasty chamber on the fifth floor—and then, once she'd been dancing for a month or two, they moved down to a better set of rooms on the third. After Blanche bought the building, she let the little room on the fifth to a pair of Irish hat trimmers and the one beside it to a Chinese vegetable-seller; two Scots, widow and daughter, lodge and run their photography studio on the third floor. Which means Blanche and Arthur have this roomy apartment that takes up the second story and gives them the fewest stairs to climb (which helps, when his back is bad). Air and light and space. No kitchen, but really, in San Francisco, why bother cooking if you can afford to eat out?

Jenny stands just inside the door, steak still pressed to one eye, gazing around with a child's frank curiosity.

When Blanche has lit a few hanging lamps she can see

that Gudrun's at least cleared away the detritus of lunch, though the long deal table's still speckled with crumbs. (Their help is a Swedish seamstress who lodges in the attic in exchange for light house-cleaning. Blanche and Arthur prefer this arrangement to having some live-in on top of them; Gudrun flits in and out, morning and evening, as if nervous about lingering long in such a ménage.)

Trying to see through the stranger's eyes, Blanche registers the bare windows, the motley furnishings: a fine Turkish shawl draped over the balding back of the sofa. Not so much *la vie de bohème,* it occurs to her, as life in a dump. But why should Blanche give a rat's ass what this visitor thinks? Jenny Bonnet's a vagrant just out of lockup. An admitted thief, too, whom Blanche has invited into her home for reasons that aren't entirely clear to her.

Jenny's over by the window now, apparently relishing the view of Sacramento Street.

While the woman's back is turned, Blanche undoes the top buttons of her greasy silk bodice and tugs out half the cash she earned in the International Hotel this evening. She tucks the notes into the emerald chamber pot that sits cheekily in the fireplace. (It was Arthur's brain wave, one drunken night, to stash their money where burglars were unlikely to look.) The pot's not as full of notes as it was, Blanche notices before she sets the lid back on; Arthur must have taken a big handful as his night's gambling stake.

Looking in the huge mirror, she considers her hair, a cloud of maddened bees. In lieu of an hour with hot irons and pins, she catches one honey-brown curl and thrusts it back into the hive.

Ah, there's yesterday's *Courrier de San Francisco* over

the back of a rush chair; Blanche flattens it on the sofa. "Take the weight off your feet," she orders, "but keep that steak on."

Jenny stretches herself out in a gingerly way. Shifts, then pulls her revolver out of her pocket and slides it under the sofa. The meat juice trickles down her face onto the newspaper, and her hat tips sideways, letting out her shock of black hair.

Blanche sinks into an old lion's-claw-footed armchair. She should boil up some coffee on the spirit lamp, change her butter-stained bodice. But she's spent, all of a sudden. The unending August heat, the collision with the bicycle, strong wine, that *connard* hurling her against the wall outside the brasserie . . . She lays her head back, just for a minute.

*

In the saloon of the Eight Mile House at San Miguel Station, on the fourteenth of September, Blanche huddles on one of the barrels that serve for stools. *Dead. Dead,* she repeats in her head, trying to grasp it. *Jenny's dead on the floor in there. In our—the McNamaras' front room.*

Behind the bar, John McNamara fumbles open the case of the clock. What's he doing? He clutches the pendulum, stills its tick: 8:49, Blanche sees, squinting at the clock hands. The time. He's stopping the time.

"The boy," Ellen McNamara howls suddenly from the back room. She appears in the doorway, crazy-eyed. "Where's the boy?"

Her husband only blinks at her.

Blanche's mind is moving as slowly as syrup. That wasn't thunder she heard, a matter of minutes ago, but bullets shattering the window. A hard hail that just missed Blanche where she was sitting, on the edge of the bed. Bullets winging over her head as she bent down to undo her right gaiter.

She presses her teeth together so as not to say his name: the man whose bullets have ripped her friend to pieces. She thinks she may puke.

Jenny! All that light snuffed in a single second.

The door bursts open and Blanche almost screams.

But it's not him. Only little Phil Jordan from the grog-shop next door, eyes wide, dancing from foot to foot like a featherweight. With the twelve-year-old hunched behind him. "Did you hear that?" demands Jordan.

Then his eyes take in Blanche, the butcher-shop state of her.

"Hear it?" wails Ellen McNamara. "Wasn't there gun-fire punching through the wall within an inch of my head?" She glimpses her son behind Jordan and runs over to enfold him in her arms. "John Jr., are you shot?"

The boy only yelps in her grip.

"This young fellow was sitting in the outhouse doing his business," says Jordan, patting him awkwardly on the head. "The noise put him into such a fright, he leaped up and gave his arm an awful thump on the door."

"Jenny's—" McNamara, sunken-faced, tilts his head toward the bedroom.

"Ah no," cries Jordan. "Not Jenny." *Dead?* He mouths it as if it's an obscenity.

McNamara nods.

Blanche notices, for the first time, spatters on the floor by the bedroom door.

"To think of you stumbling around in the middle of murderers," Ellen keens over her boy.

"Don't upset yourself," her husband soothes her.

"Upset myself, is it? Hoodlums roaming the countryside, or them slit-eyed gurriers from Chinatown for all we know, and I amn't supposed to turn a hair?"

"Did you see anything, son?" asks McNamara.

John Jr. shakes his head, eyes huge.

"Would you not have thought to throw something over the looking glass?" Ellen rebukes her husband, slopping whiskey as she pours herself a measure.

"Like what?"

"Anything, Mother of God, what does it matter?"

"Never mind the mirror," Jordan butts in. "John, shouldn't you and me—I reckon—" He casts a nervous look over his shoulder, toward the front door.

Suddenly stern, McNamara collects a scarred billy club from behind the bar.

"You aren't going to leave women and childer alone while there's some class of slaughterer roaming?" protests Ellen.

"Just a wee look around," John promises her, shouldering his weapon and handing Jordan a lamp to carry.

What good is a club against a gun? Blanche wonders.

The men step outside. Their voices, muffled, going round the side of the house.

Twenty-seven, Blanche thinks; that's how old Jenny was. Twenty-goddamn-seven years old, cut down halfway through a song.

In the back room, the smaller boy, Jeremiah, is still sobbing with fright. Kate and Mary Jane's voices, soothing him. Ellen goes in to them without a word to Blanche, tugging John Jr. behind her.

Blanche shudders on her stool. Her clothes seem to be tightening. She stares down; Jenny's blood is stiffening the fabric of her once-white bodice.

She makes herself picture him out there on the porch: the killer. Stepping soft and sure-footed across the rot-edged planks. Peering around the skewed green blind, through the grimy glass, into the circle of candlelight where Blanche and Jenny were chatting about a lullaby as they got ready for bed.

Ellen comes back with what looks like a mackintosh and gets up on a stool to drape it awkwardly over the big looking glass. Mumbo jumbo, that's what Jenny would call all this fussing with clocks and mirrors.

The Irishwoman gulps her drink and doesn't offer Blanche one.

Blanche keeps her eyes down. She can't let these people guess that it's she who brought the contagion trailing invisibly behind her from the City. That Blanche knows who's killed Jenny, and more: that it's all her fault.

The men thump back in. "It's dark as the pit out there," complains McNamara.

What about the moon, wasn't there a trace of moonlight? Blanche wonders. Through the saloon's caked window, she sees that the sky is wadded with clouds now. *Au clair de la lune, on n'y voit qu'un peu.*

"No sign of anything," adds Jordan.

Is he gone already, Jenny's killer? Blanche's heart

sounds in her throat at the thought of his face, the last time she saw it, gaunt with complicated rage.

Ellen is filling two glasses.

McNamara downs his in one swallow. "Miss? Miss?"

Blanche twitches, registering that her host is talking to her.

"Will you take a nerve-settler?"

She manages to nod and hold out her hand. The whiskey is harsh in her throat; just right. *As the fellow says,* quips Jenny in Blanche's head, *sometimes too much to drink is barely enough.*

"We've been round the building twice, and my grocery as well," Jordan announces importantly, "and over past the pond to the railroad track. Not a trace."

As if these fools would know the trace of a murderer if he left it painted a mile wide!

Blanche can't say his name even in the privacy of her mind, in case it shows on her face: her awful knowledge. She knows, which doesn't mean she understands—not a bit of it. How could he have discovered that she and Jenny were staying in the middle of nowhere, at San Miguel Station, of all places, eight miles south of downtown?

The two men go into the front bedroom. From what Blanche can hear, they're heaving what's left of the guillotine window up and down on its ropes. She hopes they've straightened out Jenny's poor forked body so it looks halfway human. Or thrown a sheet over her, at least, the way you might cover a chair in a vacant house? That's what Blanche would do if only she could uncurl, make herself stir from the barrel she's crouched on like some survivor of a shipwreck.

Ellen's disappeared, but the two small McNamaras emerge from the back with the fifteen-year-old, Mary Jane. Their bare toes hover at the edge of the browning shadow around the door of the front bedroom. They all stare at what the men are doing, owl-eyed. Blanche wishes somebody would shoo them away from there. She can't. She can't so much as stir.

"Shotgun, must have been," says Jordan over his shoulder as he steps out, nudging the children aside. "Ten-gauge, would you say, John?"

The Irishman comes out shaking his shaggy head and holding his hand up to the wall lamp to squint at its sticky contents. "Twelve-gauge, more like, loaded up with buckshot. Six—no, five balls we have now, Phil, with the one you pulled out of the wall, and others stuck in the headboard still. Common number-ones, by the looks of them."

"Number-twos, I reckon."

Like small boys proud of their harvest of berries. Shaking with such rage, all of a sudden, Blanche feels she might slither to the floor. Ten-gauge, twelve-gauge, where would the man have gotten a shotgun, or learned how to use it? None of it makes sense. How many days ago did he decide that the only solution—no, not solution, but the only fit expression of his fury—would be to shoot Jenny dead?

Blanche thought she knew him. She thought a lot of things that have turned out to be bunkum.

McNamara drops the bullets on the bar and wipes his hand ineffectively on a rag. He refills his glass and clinks it against his wife's so hard the liquid slops. "Rest her soul," he mutters.

"The dogs," says Phil Jordan suddenly. "How could some Chinaman have climbed onto your porch with the dogs there?"

They all stare at him.

"The smell off him, you mean?" asks McNamara.

The little man waves that away. "Any stranger from town, hatchet man or hoodlum or the Lord knows what. Wouldn't the dogs have gone mad barking?"

But didn't they? Blanche seems to remember a terrible howling.

Mary Jane steps out of the dining room with a bucket over one arm and a mop and brush held erect like weapons in the other.

"Let the girl into the guest chamber there now," says her mother, "or we'll be tracking blood and glass round the house all night."

The children scatter. But John McNamara holds up his hands. "Ah, we couldn't take it on ourselves to—'tis the police should survey the scene of the crime first." McNamara pronounces the word "*po*lis," with the weight on the first syllable, in his bog-Irish way. And "the scene of the crime"—that's the jargon of a penny dreadful.

Blanche could slap this man to the floor for his drunken slur and his saloon full of flies circling every stale drip of liquor. The lousy sheets and slick boards in the front room where something that used to be Jenny lies in the corner like garbage.

Mary Jane sets down her cleaning things, uncertain.

"Did you not send for the police yet?" Ellen McNamara barks.

"What time is it?" asks her husband instead of answering.

"How should I know?"

They all stare at the frozen clock, whose hands still stand at death: 8:49.

"Would you ever nip up to Mrs. Holt with the telegram, Phil?" asks McNamara.

His neighbor's neat hands leap, averting the notion. "Ah, now, it's not my house."

"What the hell kind of difference does it make whose—"

"I'm only saying, I'm glad to lend a hand, neighbor-like, but I don't want cops in on top of my business."

"Isn't it me sending the yoke, and paying for it too?" roars McNamara.

"Why can't you take the message up to the depot yourself?"

"Because the old harpy has it in for me," admits McNamara, lifting his glass to his lips. "Called me and mine all manner of filth a fortnight back. If I go banging on her door this late—"

It can't be very late yet. Blanche's eyes slide back to the paralyzed clock.

"What should I put in this telegram anyway?" John McNamara asks.

" 'On the fourteenth of September,' " Ellen dictates in a grand tone, " 'at my residence, to wit, the San Miguel Hotel, San Miguel Station—' "

"Ten words is a dollar, Mammy," mentions Mary Jane.

Blanche longs to get out of this room. This is some awful farce, misremembered in a dream.

"Why would the police need us to tell them today's bloody date?" objects McNamara. "All we need to say—"

" 'Jenny Bonnet has been shot by persons unknown at San Miguel Station,' " suggests his daughter.

" 'Persons unknown,' well put, girl. Will that do?" McNamara asks.

Nobody answers him.

"Ah, the City police know her well enough, don't they? 'Jenny Bonnet shot by persons unknown at San Miguel Station. Stop.' "

Blanche is swaying, dizzy.

"You don't need to put 'stop' unless there's two lines, Dadda," says Mary Jane.

" 'Dead,' " says Phil Jordan. " 'Shot dead,' you ought to say, or they might think she's only wounded, like."

" 'Jenny Bonnet shot dead by persons unknown at San Miguel Station'? '*In* San Miguel Station'?" McNamara flounders, as if this is a foreign language.

"How many words is that?" Ellen asks her daughter fretfully.

"Eleven."

Blanche clambers off the barrel like a very old woman. Her bare left foot isn't cut, she notices dully; a dancer's soles must be tough enough for broken glass. "It'll say on the form where the telegram's coming from," she points out, hoarse from all the screaming she did earlier. "Put 'Jenny Bonnet shot dead' and be done with it."

Jordan breaks the silence that follows. "Short and sweet. Shouldn't cost two bits."

Blanche lowers herself to the floor and slumps, her back against the barrel.

"The pair of us could go up to herself at the depot in a while," says McNamara softly to his neighbor, as if proposing an excursion.

"Another nip first, maybe, to steady ourselves," Jordan suggests, reaching for the bottle.

McNamara watches the level in his glass rise, then takes a long sip. "Not much the police could do in the pitch-dark, I suppose, anyway."

Sliding, sliding. Blanche is stretched on the floor now, her bustle a stone in the small of her back, her splattered bodice as tight as a straitjacket. The voices blur into a cloud. Just to close her eyes for half a minute—

She jerks to consciousness to find John Jr. taking the weight of her head in his small hands, pushing a folded flour sack underneath her hair. The boy's angular cheek almost touches hers. "Thanks," she says, so raw it's barely audible.

His sky-blue eyes have the sheen of oily puddles. How's the boy ever to forget this night? His head turns toward the front room, the speckled shadow of blood.

"Don't look," says Blanche, grabbing him.

He hisses, his hand flying up to his injured arm.

"Sorry."

Ellen McNamara is suddenly on her feet. She crosses the floor and pulls her son away, making him yip with pain. "Down on your knees, you should be, Miss Blanche, thanking the merciful that you were spared."

Spared, repeats Blanche in her head. She's been learning English since she was fifteen but still sometimes a word turns strange to her, as impenetrable as a pebble.

"Leave her be, would you," says McNamara, without lifting his head off the bar.

"Well, tell me this," Ellen demands, "how did every godforsaken bullet happen to miss Her Nibs here, but Jenny's lying in there in flithers?"

Nobody answers. Blanche can taste the hatred, like vinegar on the air. The funny thing is, these people don't know that she's the source of the bloodshed, the cause. But even so, she can tell they all wish it were the other way around, with their old friend Jenny sharing a late-night jar with them, and the other visitor's body askew in the next room.

She struggles up until she's sitting against the barrel, the room spinning around her. It's a fair question: How did every godforsaken bullet miss Blanche? She bent down, that's all she can think of to explain it. She leaned down to undo the knot of her gaiter. Mary Jane's gaiter; Blanche asked for a pair only yesterday to keep the skeeters off. Yesterday? Thursday morning. *This* morning, because this is Thursday night. Blanche stares at her single small boot with the gaiter taut over it. It feels as if her right foot's been tied into its borrowed skin for a lifetime. Must ask for a knife, a knife to cut the laces. What a fluke. To owe her life to a borrowed gaiter. Because when Blanche doubled over to pick at the knotted lace, that happened to be the very moment—

Now her heart hammers with belated panic. What if she'd stayed sitting up straight, singing one more verse—if she'd gotten her laces undone without a struggle—would there be two bodies in the next room right now, a tangle of stiffening limbs in a lake of blood? Was the gun aimed at both of them?

No. Just at Blanche.

It's all a mistake.

How stupid she's been this evening, how she's misunderstood from the moment the shots tore the air. Blanche's creamy body cut down, that's what he wanted. That makes a horrible kind of sense. Isn't it Blanche, not Jenny, he has most reason to resent? Blanche who could be said to owe him something, everything, according to the twisted logic of men? What did Jenny ever do to him except make the error of befriending Blanche?

A thought occurs to her, like a hand around her throat. Did he stay to look through the shattered window afterward? Does he know what he's done, and what he's left undone? *Christ!* Blanche wants to run straight out the door of the Eight Mile House—except that he might be waiting out there for her, half a mile up the County Road, to finish the botched job. She could let her dancer's legs carry her far away, if she had any idea where in the world she'd be safe from him. Her pulse sounds so loud, the room seems to shake with it.

II

I HAVE GOT THE BLUES

That Saturday night in the middle of August, Blanche wakes in her armchair. Her leg throbs painfully, reminding her of the collision with the high-wheeler, the thug at Durand's brasserie, and her new acquaintance Jenny Bonnet, who's stretched out on the couch, snoozing like some cat.

What's roused Blanche is the men coming in. "There's some ridiculous *con* on the sofa with meat on his face," Ernest is remarking to Arthur in the whimsical tone that means he's soused.

"Mister, the evening is over," Arthur murmurs, leaning over the back of the couch in the pose of a spread-winged angel.

As if Blanche would bring some *micheton* home. How could Arthur think that? "No, my love, it's just a girl," she tells him. (Speaking English, as has been their habit since the three of them stepped off the ship, because it's the only way to get ahead in this country.) "She needed a rest."

"Don't we all." Ernest's long jaw cracks open into a great yawn as he hangs his bowler on an empty bottle.

"What a heart you have, *chérie,*" murmurs Arthur, coming over to give Blanche an appreciative kiss.

Jenny blinks and grins at the company, pulling the steak off her eye.

"Arthur Deneve—Jenny Bonnet," says Blanche, waving instead of getting up. She savors her fancy man through the visitor's eyes: his elegant eyebrows; the slim checked pants that sit just so, even in this heat; his strong hands studded with rings (black intaglio, bloodstone, a signet *A*); those cuff links, each painted with a tiny horse and rider, she blew so much on for his thirtieth birthday last year . . . For all Arthur's love of unconventionality, he's a scrupulous dandy.

"Enchanté," he says with one of his slightly mocking bows.

"Oh, and Ernest Girard," she adds with a gesture at the younger man.

Who only nods. "Now, why don't you toss her out," Ernest suggests, "so we'll have room to sit down?"

Arthur raps the floor with his crystal-topped cane. "Where's your sense of hospitality?" he scolds his friend.

Jenny places the steak on the folded newspaper on the carpet. In the manner of a magician who's seen better days, she pulls a crumpled handkerchief from her brown-edged cuff and wipes her face.

Ernest lets out a mocking wolf whistle.

Rich purple all around her eye, the lid half shut. "Am I going to have a pirate's patch?" Jenny laughs.

"I'll say," says Arthur.

"She had a run-in with a brute chez Durand," Blanche explains, leaving herself out of it. She never lies to Arthur, but she doesn't need to tell the whole truth. Living together has much in common with horse-handling, it strikes her now: best to keep the tone soothing, the signals simple.

"So whose *pantalon* are you wearing?" Ernest asks the visitor.

"My own," says Jenny.

"She's just done forty days for those pants," Blanche puts in, figuring it's better to introduce the subject of Jenny's recent jail time in this playful way.

"Chacun ses goûts," says Arthur with a tolerant smile, " 'to each his own' and all that."

Ernest is down to shirtsleeves now. The fuzz is shadowing the young man's jaw and throat already, Blanche notices, though he always shaves before going out in the evening; Arthur sometimes calls him his gorilla. Ernest is wearing exactly the same mustache as his friend this season—a wax-stiff pair of wings—but somehow Ernest's appears stuck on. How unfair, Blanche thinks, not for the first time, that his strong features, genteel pallor, and impressive height somehow don't add up. Arthur—a head shorter, with Mediterranean coloring, past thirty—is the peacock everyone wants to stroke.

"Forty days, for such a triviality?" Ernest exclaims.

"There's nothing trivial about clothes," Arthur reminds him in a scandalized tone, taking off his jacket and folding it carefully over the back of a cane chair. "They maketh the man, and all that."

"As the fellow says, there's never been a naked president," Jenny points out, which earns her a grin from Arthur.

"Remember the old joke about Déjazet when she was doing breeches parts?" Ernest asks him. "She complained to a friend, 'Half Paris thinks I'm a man.' "

"'*Qu'importe,* don't worry'"—Arthur delivers the punch line with a leer—" 'the other half *knows* you ain't!' "

Jenny sniggers. "I heard that before—about Adah Menken, I think it was."

Jokes must be like songs, Blanche supposes: the words change when they cross an ocean. "It's funny that travesty's all the rage onstage," she says with a little laugh, "but if you step into the street, the same pants will get you locked up."

"It's usually a fine," Jenny tells her. "The cops been catching me and letting me go every month or two for a couple of years now, all very cat and mouse."

"How much of a fine?" Ernest wants to know, sitting down.

"Ten bucks—and then there's the lawyer's fee on top," complains Jenny. "Once I made mine tell the judge that I considered the whole thing an infringement on the rights of women, and the son of a bitch fined me twenty."

"How come you ended up in jail this time?" asks Arthur.

Jenny makes a face as if she has a toothache. "Sacked my lawyer and demanded a jury instead of a judge. I told them the truth, that I don't have any other clothes, and would they prefer me to walk around naked as a worm?"

Hoots all round.

"Turned out twelve good men and true didn't look any kindlier on me than one. Now, spending forty days dry," she adds ruefully, "that was the real kick in the pants—as it were!"

"Speaking of which—some cognac?" proposes Arthur, getting up.

"I can't believe you sacked your lawyer," Blanche tells Jenny. "When your Maman said not to touch the stove because it would burn you, I bet you went right ahead and touched it."

"How else was I supposed to know if she was lying?"

"Why would somebody lie about a stove?" wonders Blanche.

"Folks always lie to kids, don't they?"

"Tell me we've still got ice," Arthur calls theatrically from the passage.

"In the closet, under a blanket," Blanche calls back. "It was the coolest place I could find."

"Alaskan or Nevadan?" Ernest demands.

Blanche gives him a look. "Are you claiming you can taste the difference?"

"Got both? We could test him blindfolded," suggests Jenny.

"Well," says Ernest, conceding, "so long as it's not that machine-made muck."

"Practically a puddle," complains Arthur, coming back in with the bowl. He hands the ladies their cognacs with a few pebbles of ice in each glass.

"Any luck at the game tonight, *mon beau*?" Blanche asks him under her breath.

Arthur winks.

Well, that's a pleasant surprise. She's more used to hearing about "disappointments" or "mishaps," as the fellows of the sporting set refer to losses.

"*Heureux au jeu, malheureux en amour,*" Ernest intones lugubriously from the floor.

"Oh, I think I'm lucky in both lines, gaming and

love," says Arthur, giving Blanche another long, spirituous kiss.

She wishes they could go to bed, right this minute.

"What's your game, gentlemen?" Jenny's asking.

"Faro, of course," says Ernest. "It gives the best odds, unless the bank's rigged."

"You know a house in America where it's not?"

"My friend and I seem to make out all right," he says sleekly.

Jenny breaks into satirical song. " 'For work I'm too lazy,' " she trills, beating time on her thigh.

And beggin's too low,
Train-robbin's too dang'rous,
To gambling I'll go.

The men cackle at that. Blanche thought they'd have sent Jenny on her way by now, but they seem to be enjoying her no end. Clearly Blanche should bring strangers home more often.

"Was your *petite amie* out with you two this evening?" Blanche asks Ernest.

"Madeleine?"

"As if you ain't sure which I mean because you have so many lady friends and not just one loyal old blonde!"

A rueful smirk from Ernest. Blanche has teased him about Madeleine's age so often, it has no sting anymore. Madeleine's placid as well as lovely, and she never seems to object to the fact that her young man spends at least as much time here, in the spare bedroom of his old intimates from Paris, as he does at her place.

"No, we were a pair of lonely bachelors tonight," says Arthur, striking a mournful pose. "Is that your bicycle we tripped over in the hall?" he asks Jenny.

"Such a pleasure to study one up close," says Ernest, "if only in the dark, with our shins. I saw one just like it selling for two hundred bucks the other day," he tells Arthur.

Blanche's eyebrows soar at the price. "Jenny, ahem, *found* this one on Market Street."

"Ah, the divine workings of chance," says Arthur, blowing a kiss toward the sky. "Five foot, is it, that front wheel?"

"Four foot nine," says Jenny fondly. "It shoots down California or Sutter at about twenty miles an hour. The next best thing to being an eagle."

"And on the flat?" asks Ernest.

"Smooth as silk. The knack of it is, prop your feet in front of the handlebars so if you meet an obstacle you can jump free."

"An obstacle such as . . . me," Blanche can't resist adding.

Jenny's grin is devilish. "Well, even birds crash, the odd time. Those high buildings going up downtown, with their yards of plate glass—I've seen a gull break its neck against a window."

"Ah, you ain't a true citizen of this city until somebody's run you over," Ernest says with a yawn.

"Sounds as if you've had quite a night, *ma puce,*" murmurs Arthur to Blanche, caressing her neck.

Oh, she could ride him right here in the chair. Leaning back, Blanche straightens her stiff leg, rotating her ankle. "You owe me a spin on that machine of yours sometime," she tells Jenny.

Who grimaces. "I know you're a dancer, but I'm afraid that, to master the high-wheeler, you'd have to be something of an acrobat."

Ernest and Blanche burst into simultaneous laughter.

Blanche lets the visitor in on the joke. "The three of us happen to have forgotten more about acrobatics than you'll ever know."

"My partner here was the best flier in the Cirque d'Hiver," boasts Ernest, patting Arthur's glossy shoe.

"Ah, *les jours anciens.*" A dark edge to Arthur's voice. "Ancient history now."

How much does her man miss being the lean aerialist of those past times? Blanche wonders. Arthur's muscles aren't gone, just softened, looser on his frame, and from his perfect carriage, you'd never know about his back. Who can take their eyes off him?

"Well, I'll be damned," murmurs Jenny. "The Cirque d'Hiver in Paris?"

Blanche spreads her hands as if to say, *Where else?* "That's where we learned our English, from a pair of genuine Yankee cowboys in the troupe."

"The Cirque d'Hiver's where our master Léotard *invented* the flying trapeze," Ernest puts in, "no matter what charlatans claim otherwise."

"Hey, did you wear those skintight fleshings?" asks Jenny.

"As the maestro used to tell us," Ernest remarks, stroking his thigh, "if you want the crowd to love you, the trapeze is optional, but the fleshings are compulsory."

"Enough nostalgia," commands Arthur, cutting through Jenny's laughter. "We were always cold, underdressed, and underpaid." He gets up and stalks over to refill his glass.

"And you, Blanche," Jenny pushes on, "what class of artiste were you? Wait, you mentioned horses earlier—"

She listens, this one, Blanche notes.

"An equestrienne?"

Blanche smiles. She knows Arthur wants to drop the topic, but—

"Bareback?"

She nods. "Jumping ribbons, bursting hoops, scenic riding, Roman . . ."

Jenny lets out a respectful whistle. "The Wilson Circus came to town when I was a kid," she reminisces, "with this dazzler of a Creole rider, Mademoiselle Zoyara. Turned out after, she was actually one hundred percent man."

"Des conneries!" scoffs Ernest.

"Just telling it as I heard it. Well, I guess this is my lucky night. Genuine stars of the Cirque d'Hiver," Jenny marvels. "How high up was your trapeze hung?"

She throws the question in Arthur's direction, but he ignores it, sipping his cognac.

She persists. "What was your riskiest trick?"

"They're called passes," Ernest corrects her.

"No nets, I hope?"

He gives a snort of contempt.

"Ever fall?" asks Jenny.

The young woman doesn't know it, but she's gone too far. "Everybody falls," says Blanche, to close the subject. She means it to sound nonchalant, but it comes out shrill.

"Speaking of risky," says Arthur, staring under the sofa with his head on one side, "is that a revolver?"

"My single-action army .45," says Jenny with satisfaction. She hooks it up with one finger to show it off: reddish wood and silvery metal. Blanche reckons the thing must be a foot long.

"This is one strange class of female," Ernest remarks to Arthur.

A shrug from Jenny. "Why should your lot have all the firepower? As they say, God made men and women, but Sam Colt made them equal."

Arthur bursts out laughing. "Who says that?"

"I bet you've never fired that thing," Ernest mocks, weighing the revolver in his hand.

"Into the air, a couple times," Jenny tells him.

He sniggers. "Can't bite? Don't bark."

"The air's the best place to shoot," she insists. "A gun's for keeping trouble at bay."

Arthur holds out his hand for the Colt, takes it, and fingers its metalwork.

"Well, tonight at Durand's, it welcomed trouble in," mutters Blanche.

"Because tonight's fellow was a foolhardy loggerhead," says Jenny.

"Oh, *he* was foolhardy?" Blanche rolls her eyes. All that makes this creature halfway tolerable, she decides, is that she delivers her bluster with a wink.

"It's the weather," says Ernest, "making tempers flare all over. At the table beside ours this evening, a pair of Spaniards went for each other's throats."

Jenny grins at the image.

"Well," says Arthur, handing the Colt, butt-first, back to Jenny, "I suppose if a girl means to swagger around

Chinatown in pants, she's as well off carrying something."

Blanche snorts. "I've never had any difficulty. The neighborhood's notoriety is more than half invented, to give tourists a thrill. Ying upstairs told me the guides have taken to staging brawls in Fish Alley, paying fifty cents a man!"

"Yeah," says Jenny, jerking her head north, "the Barbary Coast dens are ten times more dangerous than Chinatown."

"Nowhere's dangerous if you know what you're doing," says Arthur silkily. "My friend and I go all over the City, wherever our affairs happen to take us."

Blanche holds her tongue. *Affairs,* he always says, as if he and Ernest are partners in some serious line when all they do, between faro games, is hand wads of cash to dodgy characters they call "business associates," money they rarely see again. Or they wine and dine richer suckers in the hopes of persuading them to share the risk of one of the schemes in which Arthur and Ernest are already entangled.

"Do you bring protection yourselves, gentlemen?"

Arthur smiles. "Americans are so gun-crazy. A knife's more reliable and won't spoil the line of a suit."

Blanche couldn't swear to whether her lover's ever used it, the stiletto he's carried as long as she's known him. She can imagine it, though. Arthur stays good-humored longer than most men, but when he finally loses his temper, it's not a pretty sight. A couple of times over the years, he and Ernest have made vague references to having to persuade a fellow of something, or teach him a lesson . . .

But Blanche doesn't ask. She does her leg shows and meets her *michetons,* and the men lay their wagers and run their schemes.

Ernest's asking Jenny what she lives on. "Frog-catcher—is that slang for something dirty?" he wonders hopefully.

"It's what it says."

"What a deliciously bizarre trade," says Arthur.

"These free spirits despise all trades," Blanche warns Jenny. "Arthur claims the only truly honest way to make a buck is by chance, whether at the gaming table or the Exchange."

Her lover grins. "There is a certain grace to speculation."

"Blanche is just not naturally indolent enough to be a true bohemian like us." Ernest sighs. "Nose to the grindstone, night after night . . ."

His graphic mime of her giving some *micheton* a below-job makes Arthur burst out laughing.

Blanche feels irritation grip her temples like the claws of a bird. It's true, and it's no secret, so why should she mind? It's just that Ernest's bobbing head is like a distorted reflection of herself in some filthy pool.

Jenny's eyes are on her, watchful.

Blanche makes herself giggle too. "Just as well I work so hard, or there are times we might have starved."

That came out wrong: not witty but biting.

Arthur's smile has faded at the edges. Then he leans back languidly as if posing for an artist. "Starving's terribly bohemian."

He's saved the moment, Blanche thinks with a rush of relief.

Ernest puts in a caveat: "So long as we've always got a bottle and a cigar!"

Without anyone noticing, the apartment seems to have filled with light. Blanche squints at the windows: another *satané* sunny day.

Hoisting herself to her feet, Jenny begins her round of thanks.

"Is that your blood or the cow's?" Arthur wants to know.

Yawning, as she buttons her jacket over her shirtfront: "A splash of each. The puke's definitely mine."

"You can't go out there looking like that," scolds Arthur. "We *Français* must maintain our reputation for chic."

"I'm hunky-dory," says Jenny, dropping her revolver into her trouser pocket.

"Find her something, would you, my sweet?" Arthur asks Blanche.

Who goes into the bedroom. First she puts the rest of the cash she earned this evening into a shabby high-heeled boot under the bed. (A little nest egg she's never felt the need to mention to Arthur.) The deed to the building she keeps tucked behind a lithograph of his favorite painting: a strange picnic in which a naked woman sits on the grass between two black-jacketed dandies.

Then Blanche opens a tin-covered trunk, still bearing its pasted labels from when they arrived on the *Utopia*. (Arthur likes to keep his things perfectly folded but refuses to succumb to anything as respectable as a chest of drawers.) She picks out one of his shirts—not the newest, because they may never run into this Jenny character again, but still an elegant one, greenish, with a flowering-vine motif.

By the time she gets back to the salon, Arthur's dusted off the steak and thrown it into a chafing dish over the flame of the spirit lamp. He's scrambling some eggs too. Jenny goes into the bedroom to change. Arthur sends Ernest out for bread, and Blanche back into the bedroom to see if their visitor needs anything else.

Blanche finds Jenny pulling the shirt on over her head; the way men do it, it strikes her.

"A little privacy," snaps Jenny.

Blanche recoils, turning her back. What the hell does Jenny think she's hiding? As if it's not perfectly clear she's got a pair of little breasts under there . . .

"Thanks for the shirt," says Jenny, her voice so civil now it's as if Blanche imagined her angry tone. "First time in a fancy-patterned one."

Blanche doesn't answer, just heads for the salon.

"Who's the baby?"

That freezes her.

Jenny's plucked the silver frame out of a litter of kohl, rouge, and jewelry on the small table.

"Our son." It sounds grand, solemn. Blanche has never had to explain the photograph before. "P'tit," she adds, diffident. She calls him that, but really it's P'tit Arthur—Little Arthur.

"I'm sorry."

"Oh no, he's not—he's being nursed out, on a farm, for his health," Blanche clarifies. "I was taken sick after he was born . . ."

Memories like flotsam looming through the fog of that dimly remembered milk fever. How the creature leaked from every aperture—emerald pus in the corners of his eyes, even—and wouldn't touch her right nipple but worried her left till it bled, and keened from five o'clock every afternoon on until the whole building seemed to shake . . . Blanche was delirious and vomiting by the time Arthur carried the infant away to ask Madame Johanna's advice. His decisiveness filled Blanche with gratitude, especially when Madame found some compatriots of her own, the Hoffmans, to take P'tit in at once. Even though Blanche hurt twice as much when P'tit was gone—her left breast swelling up like something out of a dime museum, so ugly that she refused to let Arthur set eyes on her without a wrap for a week—it was such a relief, being quiet, alone with the pain.

Jenny's scrutinizing the carte de visite. "But you said for *his* health. What's wrong with him?"

Blanche blinks at the blunt question. "Nothing." Nothing in particular, that is. True to his name, P'tit's still tiny, except for the huge eyes. There's a lassitude to him, a dullness that disappoints her. But Blanche's siblings were all older than her, so what does she know about how babies should be? At least his belly's round; when she reports this to Arthur, he always says it's proof that P'tit must be eating well at the Hoffmans'. "It's the done thing, you know, back home," she says, her voice defensive.

"Is it?"

"You wouldn't remember, because you left so young. One never sees a baby in Paris; they don't thrive in cities. And rents are so high, mothers have to work . . . We were all farmed out to country folk," she goes on, struggling to remember the name of the woman who looked after her. "I barely set eyes on my family till I was—" Three? Four? Blanche doesn't recall how old she was, the day she was brought back. Just the feeling of being deposited among strangers, in that narrow house on the urban islet of Ile Saint-Louis that, she was informed, was home.

"So how old is your P'tit now?" asks Jenny, setting the picture back on the table.

"Almost—" Blanche reckons the months in her head, and is startled. Last week. How could the date have gone right by without her noticing? Was she drunk that day—drunker than usual? "Just about a year," she says vaguely. Oh, well, never mind; a one-year-old doesn't know what a birthday is.

"Do you visit much?" asks Jenny, putting on her waistcoat.

What a talent this one has for putting her nose in other people's business. And her finger on sore points. "A nurse from the farm brings him," says Blanche, as if answering the question.

Not to 815 Sacramento Street; P'tit hasn't been back here since Arthur took him away to Madame. The nurse totes him in a basket to meet Blanche at the House of Mirrors. In the early months it was every week, without fail, even before Blanche had her health back. Of course she missed her little one; what kind of unnatural mother would she have been if she hadn't missed him? Arthur came with her; two or three times, anyway. These days, the visits have slid to once a month, more or less, without Blanche recalling who set that schedule. They bore her and leave her vaguely uneasy. Blanche smiles and nods at her son's slightly misshapen face for a quarter of an hour, privately wondering why he's got a faint reek about him despite being trussed up in layers of starched linen. She once asked the taciturn, uniformed nurse, who looked offended and told her that was how they smelled, infants. Blanche doesn't make the mistake of trying to pick P'tit up anymore; some babies just won't stand for being fussed over, according to the nurse, who should know, Blanche supposes. She always brings him a molasses stick to suck, at least.

If she weren't so busy all the time . . . It'll be different when P'tit is old enough to respond more to her company, or at least recognize her. She's just waiting till he's got some spark in him, till he could be said to be thriving. Till he's grown into the makings of a son worthy of the name of P'tit Arthur Deneve.

"What kind of farm," Jenny wonders aloud as she buttons her jacket, "dairy, poultry, tillage?"

"Why do you ask?" says Blanche, nettled, instead of admitting she doesn't know. Really, why should she allow herself to be interrogated about the finer points of the arrangement? It hardly matters whether the Hoffmans keep cows or chickens; P'tit's too young to notice. He won't remember, any more than Blanche recalls her first years. Dairy or goddamn tillage! She hasn't been out to the farm yet, as it happens. Madame vouches for the place and seems happy to arrange P'tit's visits to the House of Mirrors, so much more convenient than Blanche going out to the Hoffmans'. It all works perfectly well, so who does this stranger think she is, with her prodding and probing?

The front door; that must be Ernest with the bread. *"A table, messieurs-dames,"* calls Arthur, and they go in for breakfast.

*

At San Miguel Station, the fifteenth of September stops and starts, stops and starts. Only when Blanche notices she's twisting her neck to get her face out of a puddle of light does she realize that it's day. And then the terror seizes her again as she remembers: Arthur tried to kill her last night. It was only the wildest stroke of luck that shielded her, a one-in-a-million chance. There's not a mark on Blanche except a tiny graze on her cheek from flying glass. *It should have been me, not poor Jenny.*

"Care for a wash, Miss Blanche?" offers Mary Jane McNamara.

She looks down at her ghastly browned clothes. "Have the police—"

"Haven't seen hide nor hair of them yet," says Mary Jane. "Dadda had to send another telegram in case the first one went astray, and Mrs. Holt wanted to know if he was doubting her competence." Her tone bubbles. This murder is clearly the most thrilling thing that's ever happened in the girl's vicinity.

Blanche remembers being fifteen: the dull, shackled sensation that life is something that happens to other people. And then one day, with no warning, it begins.

He'd fly thro' the air with the greatest of ease,
A daring young man on the flying trapeze.

Blanche went to see the circus, that's all she did, a harmless way to spend a winter afternoon. And found herself gawking up at a beautiful olive-skinned man flying like a knife across the gilded ceiling. The crowd sang along to that year's hit waltz:

He'd smile from the bar on the people below,
And one night he smiled on my love.
She winked back at him and she shouted, "Bravo!"
As he hung by his nose up above.

Blanche hung around the stage door for hours, not caring that she was cold or that she was missing her supper, at least, or earning herself a beating. At last he came out, in street clothes and half drunk already, the lovely man; his greasepaint was meticulously wiped off but his face still held the eye. One arm slung around a lanky boy with the beginnings of a mustache. (That was Ernest; Blanche didn't pay him much attention at first. Didn't know how many years ago Arthur had taken this orphan on as his protégé, his circus brother.) She hung around, chattering and flirting as hard as she could, till night fell.

She came back the next day. He was a thrilling exotic to her: Arthur Pierre Louis Deneve. Twenty-two, and a man of the world; he'd read things, been places, tried everything. He boasted of being a bohemian, and Blanche didn't even know the word, but she swore she was one too. She was fifteen, and barely had a bosom yet, but it was just as well, because circus girls needed to be as light as air, and soon Arthur was persuading his Monsieur Loyal to try her out on the Shetland pony . . .

But what does all that matter now? What does it prove? That Arthur was a fine piece of manhood until this summer? Until circumstances conspired to—no, let's be honest. Until Blanche broke him. Broke his heart, his spirit. Broke the charming man Arthur seemed to be, cracked that shell and let the devil seep out. Maybe it just proves she was an idiot to fall in love with him nine years ago.

Her brain's still moving at half-pace. It must be tiredness. And shock. *If Arthur wanted me dead last night, he wants me dead today.* She'd better run for her life. But not in these clothes, Blanche decides, staring down at herself.

Like some automaton, she follows Mary Jane out of the Eight Mile House. On the threshold between the saloon and the rickety porch, her feet lock, refusing to carry her into the hard brightness. She straightens her aching shoulders and makes herself step forward, steeling herself against imagined gunfire. (As if muscles could repel buckshot!) The air's heating up already, dusty; better than the stink of blood and whiskey, at least. Blanche puts up one hand to shield her face. Where's her straw hat? Even under these circumstances, she finds—even today—she's not willing to get a freckle. Her translucent pallor is one of the things Blanche is known for, the promise in her name. Otherwise she'd just be plain Adèle Beunon again.

Blanche scans the ragged settlement of San Miguel Station for any sign of danger. There's Jordan's poor excuse for a country store, just across the baked yard to her left; his low frame building and McNamara's squat by the County Road like a pair of robbers planning to waylay travelers. Right now the road's a powdering line with not a vehicle, not a person on it as far as the eye can see. A stone's throw to the northeast stands the flat brown railroad depot, ruled by Mrs. Holt. In the distance to the southwest, the log cabin where that pair of Canadians scratch out a living—Louis, the man goes by, Blanche remembers, but whether first name or surname, she doesn't know. Farther out, a scattering of shacks; what laborers or squatters subsist there? Then nothing but sandlots, ruled by rats and fleas.

"This way," calls Mary Jane impatiently, beckoning her round the back of the Eight Mile House.

Blanche holds her breath as she follows the girl past the tiny, fetid box with a crescent cut into the door: the toilet where the twelve-year-old took fright at the sound of the shots. "How's your brother?"

"Wee Jeremiah? Sick with nightmares half the night."

"No, John Jr. His arm."

"I couldn't tell you." Mary Jane tosses her head. "That fella's always mooching off on his own."

Who'd be an eldest girl if she had a choice, really? Blanche wonders. All the mopping and potato-peeling and minding the little ones . . .

An old sheet held up with sticks passes for a screen, a pail of pond water behind it. With clumsy hands Blanche picks at her encrusted buttons. How muddy blood turns as it hardens. Now she's got the shakes, like some drunk shuddering outside a barrelhouse before dawn. "Mary Jane?" she calls hoarsely.

No answer.

She clears her throat and tries again. "Mary Jane? If you could—"

But when Blanche puts her head around the sheet, there's no one there. Only her own large carpetbag, incongruously festive with its orange arabesques. A stain on the top that's been wiped off, not carefully enough.

Well. These people met her only Tuesday. To the McNamaras, Blanche is just some stranger left behind like storm debris on their doorstep. They may even have guessed by now that it's she who brought this horror to San Miguel Station.

They're trash themselves, she reminds herself. *Down on your knees, you should be, Miss Blanche,* Ellen McNamara had the gall to tell her last night. The grandiose slattern clearly thinks herself a cut above Blanche. But didn't they all leave that kind of humbug back in the Old World? *You Frog whore,* that's what Ellen would like to call Blanche, no doubt, except that the woman probably can't bring herself to say such a word because the Irish are the prudes of Europe. (Always have more children than they can feed, then go round crossing themselves as if they don't know what fucking is.)

Blanche stares at her hands, willing them to be steady. Surely she can do this much, get her own stinking clothes off. First she tackles her right boot, finally undoing that wretched gaiter. Then the blood-spotted mauve skirt, the bodice, the sleeves so narrow she can barely wrench them over her knuckles, the stiffened corset, sweaty chemise, petticoats, and knickers—she drops them all on the sandy ground.

Blanche avoids looking down at herself. Nothing glamorous about her in this brutal light: raw, peeled, hideously bare, with the reek of death about her. Scooping the water over her shoulder fast, she scrubs herself with the rag. For all the heat of the morning she shudders as if she's scraping off her own skin. She takes the nailbrush to her long fingernails so hard that her fingertips are soon sore.

Small mercies: Blanche has an extra corset in her bag to cinch her into some simulacrum of her usual self. She rotates her bustle, checking the cotton sheath of every metal band. One brown stain, the size of a penny . . . but that can't be helped, and Blanche doesn't mean to trail around as flat-skirted as some hick, not today of all days. She tightens the tapes as if girding on armor.

The bag holds no garment quite right for the morning after a murder. She finds herself dithering between a skirt with orange and white stripes and a blue plaid one with deep matching flounces. *Hurry, hurry.* But telling herself that doesn't make it any easier to choose. This is absurd. A prickling burr of a tune dances in the back of her mind: *"Then I was gayest of the gay . . ."*

After yanking on the blue skirt, Blanche adds a yellow jacket-bodice, yellow striped stockings, and a pair of white mules with little heels. Pulls out her second-best parasol. That's all she's got, all she thought to stuff in her carpetbag before she marched away from number 815 Sacramento Street exactly a week ago. Everything else Blanche owns in the world is still there. Her apartment, her whole goddamn building; it's her name on the deed. But she can't go home, can she? Home is the last place in the world she should go if she means to stay alive another day.

She checks the bottom of the bag. Her fingers meet a bottle. A diaper. A beloved black doorknob.

Blanche stares at them with prickling eyes. She was forgetting P'tit. How—

Because I've been shot at, she wants to scream. *Because I've been caked with my friend's blood.* Of course Blanche has never really forgotten her son. All week, since she found the *macs* gone from the apartment, and P'tit with them, she's been looking for the baby, fretting over him, waiting for the moment she'll get him back safe. Right now she's just preoccupied with staying alive.

The word, like a fist in the face. *Alive.*

Blanche crouches on the dusty ground. Not sorrow, exactly, more like a weight, a cartwheel rolling across her chest and coming to a stop. A sense of her own stupidity so overwhelming that she can't draw a breath. Because what reason has she to believe that Arthur hasn't done away with the baby too?

Think it through, she orders herself. With a crazy sort of logic, like Arthur's. Say that he somehow discovered where Blanche was hiding. He bought or borrowed a shotgun and set out for San Miguel Station yesterday evening. What would he have done with the baby? Left him with Ernest? No; Ernest can't stand P'tit's *caterwauling.* Would Arthur have hired some neighbor or one of their old lodgers to keep an eye on P'tit while Papa was off murdering Maman?

Blanche would like to believe that. She really would. Even if she never sees P'tit again, if she could believe him alive and well . . .

But P'tit's his own son!

He's always been Arthur's, Blanche reminds herself, but that hasn't meant Arthur's been particularly interested in the baby's welfare, or even his existence. After having P'tit on his hands for a whole week, Arthur could well have worked up a wave of bitterness big enough to extinguish any last trace of parental feeling. After all, if Arthur's capable of firing through a window at the woman he's claimed to love for nine years, then he must be equally capable of ridding himself of the inconvenient burden of

P'tit. It would be so much easier than killing a woman. A one-year-old who can barely sit, who hasn't yet figured out how to crawl, let alone walk or run . . . it wouldn't even take a bullet.

No. Stop it. You don't know. So don't speculate.

She presses her last few bits of clean linen into the bag to block P'tit's things from her view. Her face is slick with sweat. This weather must be about to break; how much heat and humidity can the air hold? *"Then I was gayest of the gay—"* Curse it, how does it go?

Jenny would know. Would have known, Blanche corrects herself. Hundreds of songs cached in that narrow head; thousands, maybe.

A quick squint at her face in her tiny mirror tells Blanche that she can't do much except rub Jenny's blood off it with the smeary rag. Don't dwell on it. *Blood's just blood,* isn't that what Jenny told old Maria? The tiny cut on Blanche's right cheek from the window glass has formed a little scab already; how fast the living body tidies itself up. She pulls her lank brown hair into a knot, nets it, and stabs it with half a dozen pins.

Snap goes the clasp of her carpetbag. Blanche gathers her stained clothes into a bundle with shaking fingers.

The tune finally comes to her in a rush: one of Jenny's. Delivered with a stage frown, but a smirk behind it, and a few syncopated steps.

Life was a rosy dream I vow,
It seems a horrid nightmare now!
Then I was gayest of the gay,
But I have got the blues today.

Blanche puts up her parasol with a click of steel. The green silk blocks the worst of the light. Emerging from behind the hanging sheet with the rank bundle of clothes gripped and held at arm's length, she stares around for anywhere to dispose of it.

Near the pond, a tiny bonfire sends up its smoky flag. A small child beside it. As Blanche gets closer, she sees it's John Jr. With dry eyes he blinks up at her from where he squats. One hand is tucked into his belt, the hurt shoulder held high.

Paper flares and blackens: an old volume that says *Ragged Dick,* something about *A Bad Boy* . . . John Jr. leans in to stir up the fire with a long stick. Blanche recognizes the green and gold binding of *Around the World in Eighty Days.* "What are you burning her books for?" she demands.

"She gave them to me," he sobs.

Well, it's as good a way of grieving as any, Blanche supposes, even if there is something heathen about it. Jenny would have done the same. If things had gone the other way last night—if it were Blanche who'd met Arthur's bullets with her body—then Jenny would probably be chucking not just Blanche's clothes but every trace of her on a bonfire this morning.

"May I—" She gestures with the bundle instead of speaking the words.

His face turns puce. One of these boys caught in the quicksand of puberty who're mortified by everything to do with the opposite sex, Blanche decides. Ignorant about the whole business, trapped here with no girls to ogle except his big sister; the less he knows, the more his imagination bulges. A handshake from a farmer's wife could probably make this lad hard, let alone the sight of the underclothes of a genuine Parisian burlesque dancer. Not that he's likely to be aware of exactly how Miss Blanche earns her daily bread, but instinct always trumps knowledge.

There's a mongrel beside her, sniffing at the bloodstained folds excitedly. She kicks at it.

John Jr. leaps up so fast Blanche is startled into taking a step backward. But the boy's seizing the clothes with one arm, pressing the whole foul mass of them to his chest. Blanche is ludicrously embarrassed that a stripling of twelve is handling her petticoats.

He tosses the lot onto the fire. Foul smoke billows and for a moment she thinks the clothes have suffocated the flames. Then John Jr. pokes the fire with his stick and it begins to lick busily again.

Blanche stands as stiff as a fashion plate and keeps her eyes north on the distant hills that cut San Miguel Station off from the City proper. She's gripping the wooden handle of her parasol, she finds, as if its spindly frame and thin dome of silk might somehow lift her out of here. "Thank you," she says, so hoarsely that she's not sure the boy can even hear her over the crackle of the flames.

With no warning, he flings himself against Blanche, his head on her chest, so hard she can feel a button dig into her sternum, and his good arm pulls her tight. For all the clumsiness of his embrace, John Jr. is the only one in this derelict hamlet who seems to give a rat's ass about Blanche. So she hugs him back.

His words are muffled.

"What?" she says, pulling away.

"It's all right, Miss Blanche." The boy's slate eyes are raging with misery. "Going to be all right now."

An odd phrase; a remark some lost-for-words adult would make. "Oh, I doubt that," murmurs Blanche, and staggers away toward the Eight Mile House.

Strange: the bicycle isn't where she saw it last, tucked behind some dried-up bushes at the side of the building. What would have made Jenny move her high-wheeler yesterday? Blanche's eyes interrogate the desiccated leaves. The porch has a gnawed-looking patch just under the shattered front, she notices. Was that always there? The window's not a window anymore; it's a ragged eye socket.

It occurs to Blanche only now that Arthur might have had Ernest with him. Must have had, in fact; what does Arthur ever embark on without the help of his familiar, his boon companion, his comrade in pleasure and trouble?

What would they have said to each other, these two men, creeping into San Miguel Station in the dark? She pictures Arthur as he was a week ago, elegant and snide at a faro table. Would he have ranted, abused Blanche, justified his bloody plan in a whisper as he and Ernest edged along the side of the Eight Mile House? No, Arthur wouldn't have needed to say a word. Ernest, his longtime catcher on the high trapeze, would follow his old flier—his old master—anywhere.

Looking back down the years, Blanche glimpses the tiny seedling of resentment Ernest must have been nursing from the moment he laid eyes on her. At the stage door of the Cirque d'Hiver, he was only a knock-kneed trapeze apprentice and she was the milky-skinned girl who caught and held the gaze of his beloved mentor. When Ernest shot up into a muscular young man, long-limbed enough to replace Arthur's old partner in the catch trap—because the catcher has to be tall—the two friends and Blanche carried on living in one another's pockets. And really, over the nearly ten years they've spent together, knocking about in Paris and then in San Francisco, has Ernest ever thought Blanche good enough for Arthur? Hasn't there always been a jagged edge to his joking? And this summer, hasn't he come to hate her just as much as Arthur has, on his own behalf as much as Arthur's? Four days ago on Waverly Place, Ernest seized her by the jaw and called her an *infernal whore*. No, Blanche decides, he wouldn't have needed any persuasion to help Arthur pay back every slight, to rid the world of Blanche Beunon once and for all.

There's a wagon outside the Eight Mile House, she notices with a jolt. Too clean to belong to a local.

Don't be ridiculous, Blanche scolds herself, why would the *macs* come back to shoot her in broad daylight, and with a wagon?

She walks back into the saloon and has to stop her eyes from turning to the left, toward the front bedroom. A coffin sits on the exploded remains of the mattress. A plain wooden box, all angles, no handles, no ornaments. Two strangers in rubber aprons are draping a muslin sheet in it. The floor and walls are still dark with blood and pocked with the occasional hole. The baize blind hanging off its nail in the window has a missing corner with blackened edges. Jenny's body must still be there, hidden by the bed.

"No, twelve hours is worse than six any day," the thick-chested man is insisting. "Stiff as the proverbial."

"Daresay you're right," murmurs the older one, who has soft white sideburns.

"Of course I am. Going to take any amount of massaging to—"

"Miss," says the elder, loud enough to alert his colleague.

The barrel-chested one, not discomfited at Blanche overhearing them, nods at her. "You'll be the other party?" He waits. "Travel companion of the deceased?"

She manages to nod and concentrates on shutting her parasol so the green silk pleats smoothly.

"Coroner's deputy," the man says, introducing himself, "and assistant"—nodding at the older man. "The dieners will need to know what to put her in."

"The—the who?"

"Attendants in the deadhouse, don't you know."

Blanche stares at the coffin. But what's that for, if not for putting Jenny in?

"What the deceased will wear," he spells out, "when formalities are complete."

She's troubled by a vision of a ball with everyone in formal dress. "What do the, the dieners usually . . ."

The coroner's deputy rubs his hands on his smeared apron. "Well, there's day wear, or night."

"For a trip, see, or a long sleep, depending how you look at it," murmurs the assistant.

"She came in this getup?" the deputy asks Blanche, pointing in a gingerly way at the pile of clothes on the bureau with the Colt resting on top.

She gathers her strength to say yes, to tell them to put Jenny back in the clothes she chose for herself. The worn gray jacket, the baggy trousers tide-marked with the mud of Sweeney Ridge . . . what could possibly be criminal about them now? Rags, but they must have been some kind of treasure to Jenny for her to have gone through so much for them and still keep pulling them back on every morning, year after year.

Then Blanche's eye focuses on a fold of fabric: Jenny's shirt. Not quite unrecognizably dirty; the vine pattern flickers through the pall of dust. The shirt of Arthur's that Blanche picked out to lend to the crazy bicyclist that early morning in the middle of August. "No."

"She came in something else?" asks the deputy.

Blanche shakes her head. "I mean no, she can't wear those." Can't be buried in her killer's shirt.

"Wouldn't be proper," he agrees with a prim sigh. "No luggage other than the satchel . . ."

"No shoes neither," frets the assistant.

"Her boots are under the bed, right at the back," says Blanche.

They all look at the wine-dark floor. Neither man gets down on his knees.

"We'll have them lay her out in a nightshirt, then," says the coroner's deputy.

"But—" Blanche tries not to picture the punctured, soaked rag still on Jenny. McNamara's spare nightshirt, which his wife lent Jenny their first night here. Just three days ago.

"He means a special one for burial," the man with the sideburns murmurs, "furnished out of the autopsy budget."

Blanche knows he's being kind, but she thinks she may

be sick. She stumbles out of the room, lets the door slam behind her.

The clock's been reset and wound again, she notices. She watches the seconds go by.

No sign of the cops yet. Not that Blanche has any love for the authorities, but this is murder, goddamn it. San Miguel Station only feels like the back of beyond. It's no more than twenty minutes by train from the downtown terminus of the Southern Pacific at Third and Townsend. Pretty quick by road too; Jenny whizzed out here on her bicycle on Tuesday, swerving around the ruts. (Where can that wretched bicycle have got to?) And the City detectives must have their own carriage, it occurs to Blanche. What could possibly be taking them this long? She rests her head on the sticky pine of the bar.

"Miss Buneau?"

She jerks, suddenly aware that she's been dozing. Buneau? Does this American mean her?

"My condolences. *Vous comprenez?*" He can't be police: slight, even paler than her, with glasses tinted dark blue. His straw hair stays damply behind his ears as he lifts off his vast brimmed hat. "Cartwright's my name, Cartwright of the *Chronicle.*"

"And my name is Beunon." Pronouncing it as crisply as some Parisian matron.

"Pardon me, I was told Buneau," says Cartwright, lifting his notebook almost to his face as he jots down the correction. "I'm getting up a piece about Jenny for the afternoon edition."

Blanche balks at the forename. "You two were acquainted?"

"Not in person," admits Cartwright. "But the *Chronicle's* been covering her for a few years now. She was twenty-four or thereabouts, am I right?"

"She's—"Blanche swallows hard to steady her voice. "She was twenty-seven." In three more years, Blanche will be twenty-seven, too, but Jenny won't be a day older; Jenny won't be anything.

"She was mighty popular with our readers."

"She's not a character out of a serial," spits Blanche. She gets to her feet and the room spins around her.

Cartwright puts a damp hand on her arm. She flicks it off. "You could help me get the facts right, at least," he suggests.

"Help you? Who's helping me?" Blanche's voice swoops up, way up. "My friend gets blown to pieces last night and the police don't even bother showing up this morning—"

"That's disgraceful." Another pencil mark in the little notebook.

The creak of a hinge from the bedroom. The coroner's men carry the coffin out. Jenny's old satchel riding on the lid, the long nose of her equalizer sticking out of it.

Anyone can load and fire it, easy, remarks Jenny in her head.

If ever Blanche needed protection . . . "Could I keep the Colt?" she asks them.

They halt. " 'All personal property to be collected, recorded, and transferred to the City treasurer until the estate is settled,' " quotes the deputy. "Was she intestate?"

"Pardon?"

"Did she fail to leave a valid will?"

Blanche's mouth twists. She'd be surprised if Jenny had even let herself be counted in the census.

"We'll be searching her lodging, miss, if you can provide an address," says his assistant.

"She doesn't—she didn't have one."

Cartwright scribbles that down.

The men exchange a resigned look and shuffle toward the door like a pair of footsore dancers.

Blanche is left in the saloon with the reporter. The heat, she groans silently. Jenny will be ripe by the time they reach the City. Have they ice in the wagon, at least?

"The City detectives do seem a little slow off the mark this morning, but they're the nation's finest, I assure you. Captain Lees is a genuine genius," Cartwright says soothingly.

She forces her eyes back to the pale newsman's.

"Mug books of every suspicious character in California, a laboratory for scrutinizing clues . . . I've known him to make a case on the tip of a boot print!"

Blanche nods, to shut him up.

"Another scorcher," he remarks, glancing toward the azure sky framed in the dirty window. He disappears behind the bar, comes back after a minute with a brown jug.

She remembers the song: *"Little brown jug," don't I love thee*. "Don't assume I'm a dipso," snaps Blanche.

"It's water," he assures her, filling two glasses and sitting down.

She sips at the stale stuff and wishes she'd asked for cognac. The fellow's spectacles are distracting her, the heavy blue double Ds and side lenses boxing his eyes in. "Can you take those things off?"

Cartwright removes the glasses and folds the straight arms with a click. His eyes blink at her, watery blue, an unguarded quiver to the sparse lashes.

"You're—in France, we say *albino*?"

The man rubs between his blond eyebrows as if he's got a headache. "From your excellent English I deduce you've been here long enough to remark on the general relish for the strange?"

Blanche shrugs.

"Take the craze for collecting postcards of rarities, or laughing right in the unfortunates' faces at the dime museum," he comments drily. "So you'll understand if I'd rather not hang any particular label around my neck." He fits his glasses on again. The skin of his ear is fine-veined, pink where the sun shines through.

Against her will, Blanche remembers P'tit: his small ears ablaze with light. Her voice comes out in a snarl. "I understand that you'd rather be the barker of the freaks than one of them. 'Roll up, roll up, come see the trouser-wearing miss lying in her gore!' "

"Your anger does you credit, Miss Beunon," says Cartwright, "except that I ain't the proper target. You want a noose for the man who shot your friend? Somebody out there knows his name, and—"

"I know his goddamn name!"

The translucent eyebrows shoot up.

It feels as if a pit has opened up at her feet. Danger, pungent on the air. But Arthur wants to kill her, has already tried to kill her; what's there to lose?

P'tit. That's all that keeps Blanche from speaking up. The awful uncertainty. The ghostly blur that's all she can see when she tries to picture P'tit this morning, somewhere in the City. The thought that her son—*if* he's still alive—might be with these appalling men, his survival dependent on their whim. If she names them as Jenny's killers, is it P'tit who'll suffer?

And yet P'tit's most likely to be saved if the authorities hunt down his father right away. So what the hell is Blanche waiting for?

None of this makes any sense.

"Deneve," she says very fast, before she can change her mind. "Arthur Pierre Louis Deneve."

Cartwright writes it down. "You actually saw him last night?"

She shakes her head. "He's my—" Hard to choose a word. The terms in English all sound dirty. Working folk in Paris generally don't bother with weddings, and Arthur always sneered at marriage anyhow, calling it *disinfected love*. "He used to be my man."

"When did he leave you?"

Her eyes narrow.

"Beg pardon," says Cartwright smoothly, "I mean vice versa."

"He and his friend Ernest Girard, they've been making murderous threats—"

That's when boots thump on the porch, and detectives file through the door. In plain clothes, but with that thick-necked police look about them that makes Blanche's hackles rise.

"Cartwright," says the leader, "are you trying to do my job again?"

"Ah, Mr. Bohen. I'm just preparing the way, like John

the Baptist for Our Lord. This weather must be keeping you busy," remarks the journalist, jumping up and putting his notebook away.

"We're always busy," Bohen corrects him. "Guns mean corpses, and since the war, every fool in America seems to own a firearm. But these hot nights do make matters worse."

The celebrated Captain Lees is on vacation, it turns out. Bohen is his second in command. He insists on referring to Jenny as Jeanne Bonnet because that's the *name of record.* He mangles Blanche's surname, of course.

"Beu*non,* with an *n,*" she tells him frostily. "Two *n*'s," she corrects herself, "the second one said in the nose."

"Point taken, Miss Beu*non,*" honks Bohen with a hint of satire.

He sets his men to taking measurements. Cartwright hovers helpfully. "This entire case has been botched from the first," Bohen complains to him. "No proper search of the settlement last night—the porch was stampeded over, the windowsill pawed to a high polish, bullets clawed out of walls! The landlord seems to have wasted several hours drowning his sorrows before bothering to inform us—"

"And then you took even longer to turn up," says Blanche under her breath.

"There seemed no urgency in a case of presumed suicide," Bohen snaps back.

She gapes at him. *Jenny Bonnet shot dead.* That curt wording was Blanche's suggestion, she remembers now; she can see how the detectives jumped to the wrong conclusion.

"San Franciscans kill themselves all the time," he points out, "and this notorious individual—"

"Notorious for wearing pants," Blanche objects, "not for trying to kill herself."

"Well, for your information, there's a previous attempt on file."

Cartwright's notebook is up near his eyes again as he jots that down.

On file in the police station where Jenny was dragged in and charged for wearing pants over and over? A libel set down by her persecutors? Blanche doesn't believe a word of it.

Detective Bohen is peering out through the dingy window now. "These isolated roadhouses . . . a creeping fungus around the edge of the City."

"It's from the City that Arthur came last night and shot her," Blanche cuts in.

The detective stares.

Cartwright flips back a page in his notes. " 'Arthur Pierre Louis Deneve,' " he reads crisply, " 'cast-off paramour.' "

"Of Bonnet's?" Bohen asks.

"Of mine," says Blanche.

"Your *mac*?"

Her mouth hardens. What if Blanche *is* a dove—does that mean her testimony doesn't count? "I don't care what you call it. Arthur took—" *A baby,* she wants to say. *His baby. Our baby. He took away my baby and I don't know where or even if*—But the story's too complicated, too incongruous, too mortifying to speak out loud.

"This Deneve took something of yours?" Cartwright prompts her. "Valuables?"

The thread of Bohen's patience snaps. "Good day, Mr. Cartwright."

The journalist nods civilly, goes out onto the porch, and shuts the door behind him.

Bohen turns to Blanche, sits down next to her, and makes a peremptory gesture. "He took what?"

The fact is, she doesn't know how to tell him about P'tit without making herself sound like a coldhearted bitch who deserved all she got. So she'll stick to the point, which is murder. Blanche decides, all at once, not to muddy the waters by telling the detective that it would have been her who'd gotten shot if Arthur's aim had been better. That's not important, and she can't prove it; all that matters is who killed Jenny. She must focus all her efforts on convincing Bohen that it was Arthur. "He took . . . he took offense at my breaking with him," she says through her teeth, "and he thought Jenny an undesirable influence."

It sounds feeble, unconvincing. *An undesirable influence.* Like the complaint of a schoolmistress.

The detective hasn't written any of this down. He consults a little diagram. "The bullets must have passed very close to you."

"They'd have killed me too if I hadn't been bent over undoing my gaiter," says Blanche, eager to release that much of the truth.

"According to Mrs. Holt," murmurs Bohen as if to himself, "nobody got on or off any train at San Miguel Station last night. None of the residents heard horses either."

She waves that aside. The *macs* must have slipped in somehow, maybe on foot. "He—Arthur and his friend

Ernest, Ernest Girard—they've made the most bloodthirsty threats against us, against me and Jenny both—"

"Does Deneve own a shotgun?"

"Yes," she lies, but a second too late to be convincing.

Bohen's mouth purses. "You'd apprised him of the fact that you and Bonnet would be lodging down here?"

She chews her lip. "He must have found it out somehow. How else could he have tracked us down and shot Jenny?"

"Why is female reasoning so circular?" Bohen asks of the ceiling.

Resentment makes Blanche flush. But she's distracted by a thought: Madame Johanna. The Prussian was the only one who knew where Blanche was going. Could Arthur possibly have browbeaten—no, Madame's more than a match for him, but could he somehow have charmed her into letting slip where Blanche had gone?

"Another problem," says Bohen heavily, not looking up from his notes. "According to Mrs. Holt, the dogs didn't bark until after the gunshots. Those curs should have gone wild as soon as a stranger came within sniffing distance."

That stumps Blanche.

He lets his notebook drop shut.

"You don't mean to do a thing, do you?" asks Blanche. "No surprise! You're the ones who nicked her over and over for a crime so petty it shouldn't even be on the books . . ."

A small snort. "You're thinking of patrolmen on the beat," says Bohen, getting to his feet. "We City detectives are an elite force, with more important things to worry about than what folks wear."

Nothing trivial about clothes, isn't that what Arthur said the night they met Jenny?

"No known address," he murmurs. "Where did she keep the rest of her possessions?"

Blanche is about to mention the missing bicycle, then realizes it might lead to questions about how Jenny acquired it in the first place. If he thinks of Jenny as a thief, will he take even less trouble to solve her murder? "She preferred to travel light" is all she says.

"The remains are on their way to Gray's Undertakers, on Dupont," he says. "Be at the inquest Saturday—that's tomorrow—ten o'clock. Coroner Swan insists on punctuality."

"But Arthur and Ernest, they're lodging at my house on Sacramento Street," says Blanche with an urgent gesture northward. "If you hurry—"

"Your job's not to tell me mine, Miss Beunon," says Bohen. "It's to describe what you know to a jury."

After the police go, Blanche finds the McNamaras over at Jordan's letting the man from the *Chronicle* stand them to brandies.

"But I haven't seen him since yesterday," John is saying.

"Louis? He's away to San Jose," Ellen reminds him.

The newsman is taking notes.

"Then there's a couple of Prussians in a shack to the west a bit," says John. "I can never get their names straight . . ."

Nobody offers Blanche a drink. Gloom settles on her as she listens. Cartwright does seem industrious, but he's not going to see justice done by charting every outlying inhabitant of San Miguel Station. Well, if the police won't listen to her, perhaps the jury at this inquest tomorrow will.

"I'll be on my way now," she interrupts them, with a nod to the group.

Mrs. McNamara wipes one eye and asks, "What about the room?"

Blanche frowns, puzzled.

"Tuesday, Wednesday, Thursday—that's three dollars."

"Ah, now, Ellen." Her husband sighs.

"It's not as if she can't afford it . . ."

This bitch is trying to shame me. Wrath revives Blanche; her pulse bangs to life. "When you rent me a room in which I can sleep without being shot at, I'll be delighted to pay. And since we're on the subject of money, where's Jenny's high-wheeler?"

"What's that?" asks Cartwright, pencil poised.

"Her bicycle. It's worth a fortune, and somebody's pinched it." Blanche mentioned it just to put the McNamaras on the back foot, but as she watches them exchange a dull stare, she begins to wonder. Perhaps at some point in the long misery of the night it had occurred to one of the pair that Jenny wouldn't be needing the machine any longer? Some compensation for their trouble? "She left it behind the bushes, right beside your lousy shack," Blanche presses on. Had the parents sent Mary Jane out before sunrise to stash the bicycle in some abandoned outhouse? Would they wait a few weeks and then lead it into the City to sell?

"Nobody's laid a hand on anything," protests John McNamara.

"What call have you to be making accusations when

it's probably the murderer that took it?" Ellen moans. And then, after another sip: "If it's all that valuable—it might have been for the machine that she was slaughtered, I suppose."

Behind those bleary blue eyes, is that a glint? Blanche's stomach turns. Could Ellen be blaming her own crime on an imaginary stranger? Two hundred dollars would be a fortune indeed for this pitiful family. Could McNamara have crept out on his own porch last night, at his wife's urging, and shot Jenny through the window for the sake of her high-wheeler?

Ridiculous.

But is it? Folks get done to death for money every day of the week.

No. Quite absurd. If the McNamaras had coveted the high-wheeler, couldn't they simply have hidden it in a hay bale and claimed to know nothing about it until Jenny got tired of searching? They wouldn't have needed to bring the City detective force down on their heads by committing a murder. Besides, Blanche doubts this pair would have the intelligence and energy for theft, even. They can barely manage to feed their children.

No, the real reason it's absurd to try to pin Jenny's killing on this potato-faced family is that Blanche knows it was Arthur. Only his rage, only his vindictive malignity, only his need to punish her, could explain the horror of last night.

"If the yoke does turn up, we'll send it straight to Sosthenes, of course," says McNamara.

"Who's that?" asks Cartwright.

"Her father, over in Oakland."

Blanche stares. Jenny still had family in this part of the world?

"Sosthenes Bonnet, this would be?" Cartwright's gesturing to Phil Jordan to refill the four stubby glasses.

"He and the missus were bright stars back in the Rush. Comedy, tragedy, opera, the whole shebang." McNamara sighs into his brandy. "Sosthenes pushes a mop in a barrelhouse now. Jenny takes the ferry across every month or two to slip him some cash—used to," he corrects himself, fumbling a sign of the cross.

Jenny's parents, musical actors? Blanche's irritation surges. Her friend always implied she had no kin left, or none worth mentioning. Why would she have disowned a pair of former *bright stars* living close at hand by San Francisco Bay? Sometimes Blanche found Jenny to be a fascinating puzzle—but at other times, just damn mulish. Evading and prevaricating and equivocating just for the fun of it, even when there was nothing to hide.

Back in the destroyed front bedroom at the Eight Mile House, Blanche finds her straw hat in a drawer. She sets it forward on her head and lowers the limp lace, stares herself down in the mirror. She's a woman with no man, no friend, no child.

As she turns to go, her foot catches the edge of something sticking out from under the bed.

Burlap. Jenny's frog sack. Full of the creatures she caught up on Sweeney Ridge on Wednesday. Only a day and a half ago, but it feels like a lifetime.

Does Blanche's eye detect a small movement? Surely not. How could these tiny hoppers live through what happened in this room last night?

On an impulse she doesn't understand, Blanche grabs the sack by the neck; the dampened material is surprisingly heavy. She walks out the front door and around to the back of the Eight Mile House, carpetbag swinging on one elbow, frog sack held away from her skirts.

The small girl, Kate, is at the pond. Mud-colored hair pulled back in a punitive braid under a straw hat oddly like Blanche's. What is she, eight? Nine? Waltzing with her one-armed cloth doll and whispering some Irish ballad.

Blanche struggles with the knotted burlap, abrading a finger on the rough cloth.

"What you doing, miss?" asks Kate.

"Letting some frogs out."

"What for?"

She can't think of an explanation. "To go back to their people, because I don't want them."

"Frogs ain't people. Except if you mean Frenchies," Kate adds confusedly.

"Clearly I don't," snaps Blanche, fighting with the knot. After a minute she adds, "Why do you call us that—Frogs?"

"Frenchies?" Kate furrows her forehead. "Because you eat frogs, I suppose."

"We're hardly the only ones."

"Yeah, but you started it. And horses too," the girl adds with a frown.

Blanche considers that. It's true, in Paris she was raised not to be sentimental about food.

Out of the corner of her eye she spots the five-year-old, knock-kneed in the bulrushes. How long would it take Jeremiah's soused parents to notice if he never came home from the pond? It occurs to Blanche that children expire every minute unless someone's fighting to keep them alive: they sicken, suffocate, or burn. The odds against any one of them making it past a first birthday . . . "Shouldn't you pull your little brother out of there before he drowns himself?" asks Blanche, too sharply.

"He knows all right," says Kate.

The boy is squatting in the water now, slapping the green-scummed surface with pleasure.

"I don't suppose you've seen Jenny's high-wheeler?" asks Blanche.

Both children nod.

She's excited. "Where?"

"Here, when she rode it," says Jeremiah with a jerk of his head.

"No, I mean today? Have you seen it since she—"

The boy's eyes are vacant. The girl shakes her head, and then her doll's head. But then, thinks Blanche, her father and mother might have prepared Kate for that question; threatened her, to keep her mouth shut . . .

Oh, Blanche, let it go. She knows in her gut it wasn't the McNamaras.

Blanche's barely got the bag open before a biggish frog startles her by leaping through. She drops the sack. In ones and twos, the creatures spasm their way out. Some are only the length of her thumb, yet they've so much go in them, hurling themselves across the few feet of baked ground toward the water as if they can smell it.

"Can I've a few?" asks Kate with an expression Blanche belatedly recognizes as hungry.

"Help yourself," says Blanche.

The little girl seizes a fat frog and smacks its head on

a nearby rock. "Jenny said to bash 'em right away, or a knife to the neck, it's only fair. Skinning them alive, that's uncalled-for," recites Kate. Her pocketknife out already.

Jeremiah picks up a hinged pair of legs and makes a jiggling puppet of them. "If you salt them, they dance by their selves," he confides to Blanche.

She's heard of that trick but never seen it. If she's obliged to watch a five-year-old perform it this morning, the top of her head is going to explode.

Is that Cartwright's wide sun hat outside the Canadian's log cabin? This pallid mouse is thorough, Blanche has to grant him that; he clearly means to interrogate every living soul within sight of San Miguel Station. She almost pities the man for his wasted efforts in this heat. Perhaps she should tell him more about Arthur. Convince him to go up to town, to Sacramento Street, and ask around. Bohen wouldn't listen to Blanche, but can't an inquisitive newsman dig up evidence of guilt just as well as a so-called detective?

But here comes a puff of smoke on the railroad in the west. If Blanche stops to talk to Cartwright she'll miss this train, and what if this is the last one heading into the City today? She mustn't get stuck here for another night. So Blanche sets off at a run for the depot.

On the platform Mrs. Holt sits at her stall as if awaiting a horde of customers. Candies twisted into their dusty papers, misshapen apples, one incongruously bright orange . . . Blanche's mouth waters and it occurs to her to buy it, but something makes her unwilling to carry away anything from San Miguel Station.

"Second class," she says, raising her voice to be heard over the shriek of the incoming train. The engine belches out its bilious gray. She scrabbles for coins in her pocketbook. She can't quite afford second, but she never travels third. She'll need to get hold of some real cash soon, but she won't worry about that now.

Nobody gets off the train. Blanche heaves her carpetbag ahead of her into the brightly painted carriage. She drops onto a two-person seat, spreads her skirt across the thin cushion to repel any man who might think of sharing it with her. She examines her boots, rubs off the worst of the dust on the aisle carpet. Breathes in the stink of coal, watching the small litter of buildings shrink behind her. Removes a bit of smut from her eye, and San Miguel Station's gone.

*

Back in the middle of August. When Jenny Bonnet heads off across the City in the green shirt Arthur's lent her that humid Sunday morning, the other three fall into their beds.

Blanche wakes hours later, twisted in her nightgown with a head that's pounding worse than her bashed-up leg, sun stabbing her in the eye. (Arthur claims it would be intolerably bourgeois to hang curtains. He and Blanche have squabbled over it just about every morning since the heat wave began.)

Her dream comes back to her now, an endless loop from last night's conversation about the photograph. *What's wrong with your baby?*

Nothing.

What kind of farm?

It's for his health.

What's wrong with him?

Beside her lies Arthur, very still, his cheek marble. Tiny black hairs thrusting through perfect pores: a forest sprung up overnight. Blanche should keep gazing at her naked fancy man instead of brooding over some stranger's nosy questions.

Will Arthur mind if she wakes him up? Not if she does it right. Not if her hand takes its time snaking through the crumpled sheets.

Her eye falls on the little carte de visite in its frame. So much of the baby's swaddled, it's hard to get a sense of his face from it. Two weeks old, three? She remembers carrying P'tit up a flight of stairs to her Scottish lodgers' studio. Blanche was feeling almost enthusiastic that day; not yet too exhausted, because P'tit slept a lot. They may not have welcomed the news of a child, she and Arthur, but they had good intentions, didn't they? They meant to make room for the little stranger in their life somehow, to carry the metamorphosis off with grace. Family life, bohemian-style. But everything changed a little while after that photograph, when P'tit got hungrier and began to gnaw Blanche, and her breast swelled monstrously, the fever making her loco . . .

So who was that jailbird to interrogate Blanche about having him nursed out, anyhow? To make her feel negligent for not having inspected the Hoffmans' farm inch by inch, and obscurely guilty for not keeping P'tit at home in Chinatown!

On his visits to her, at the House of Mirrors, he's always so . . . limp. Blanche has a private uneasiness—so private that she's never spoken it aloud—that he may have been born a little lacking. That perhaps all those things she did with all those *michetons* while she was carrying P'tit inside her did some obscure damage. But surely someone would have mentioned it, if so—the midwife, Madame, Arthur, the uniformed nurse who brings him into town once a month; somebody would have told Blanche if he was defective. So, then, the way P'tit is must be the way babies are.

She shakes her head to banish these gloomy thoughts. And begins to sing, very faintly, to get herself back in a lewd mood, that melody that was on every woman's lips when Blanche, Arthur, and Ernest left France, and when they stepped off the *Utopia* on the other side of the ocean. "'*Voici la fin de la semaine*—' " It's the weekend, and the lady's looking for love wherever she can find it. The lines prowl up and down, feline.

Qui veut m'aimer?
Je l'aimerai.

I'll love whoever loves me, and why not? Looking down at herself this morning, as she slides closer to her sleeping man, Blanche is grateful for her white sleekness; inside her nightgown, hip and belly and breast are seal-plump and ageless. When her clothes are off, who'd know she's twenty-four? She murmurs on:

Qui veut mon âme?
Elle est à prendre.

Who wants me should take me, the singer urges.

Blanche finds Arthur's sleep-swollen *cigare* with her

hand, then with her lips, casting the lightest of spells. As cocks go, it's not particularly long, but it's the thickest she's ever encountered. She could have him jammed inside her before he even knows it. She did that all the time when she was pregnant—desperate, night, noon, and morning, and Arthur liked her that way. If you have an itch, why not scratch it?

And surely Blanche has got the right. Doesn't she treat her *mac* well, lavish gifts on him, fund every scheme he dreams up? Arthur's still asleep, but who could object to waking this way, up to the hilt in a woman's mouth as if some dirty dream has come true? Besides, what better cure for a sore head . . .

"*Putain,*" Arthur swears under his breath, eyes suddenly wide, and he smiles, because what man wouldn't? And what woman wouldn't be glad to make him smile that way with every trick her grappling tongue can invent?

It's the slight movement of the sticky air that lets her know the door of the bedroom has opened. Blanche is only half surprised when she notices Arthur's eyes fixed over her shoulder: that luxurious look of watching himself being watched. The expression he used to wear on the platform, standing very erect, waiting to catch the fly bar.

"Don't let me interrupt, *mon vieux*" comes Ernest's voice, half yawning, from the doorway.

And from this position Blanche can't see if Arthur's beckoned to his young friend or if Ernest has simply walked in or if Blanche could even be said to have invited him, by a wriggle, if ever so slight, or by simply not protesting, because her mouth is full, after all. "You don't mind, *chérie,*" Arthur murmurs, his damp hand coiling her hair, not a question but a statement, a reminder, a reassurance, because why would Blanche mind being looked at from any angle? The lovely motion of her hips under white cotton, the dip and duck and bend of her head . . . Blanche la Danseuse, known for movements so beautifully obscene that customers spill down Sacramento Street boasting of the banknotes they've thrown under her smooth heels.

So she says nothing, does nothing but carry on doing what she does best as Arthur starts to groan. Isn't she his, hasn't she always been Arthur's? And what's Arthur's is Ernest's, because that's the kind of man Arthur is: generous to a fault. He's never cared about the stupid *michetons* who lavish their cash on Blanche, and in return she doesn't care—well, doesn't much care—about other women. The *possibility* of other women, that is, because she doesn't know of any in particular. But a man so handsome—there must occasionally be other women, no? Arthur would never rub her face in it. He has manners. It's all part and parcel of being a free spirit, because if love isn't free, then, as Arthur says, it's just goddamn marriage without the name.

Ernest is a watcher; sometimes that's all he requires. But not today. When Blanche feels the younger man's fingers sliding the nightgown up over her hips, does she mind? That's the curious thing: sometimes you object and sometimes you don't and sometimes you crave it so much it makes you sick. Right now, for instance, Blanche can't tell whether she wants Arthur's friend. *Their* friend, she supposes, though never exactly *her* friend. Ernest is an ape below the line on his neck where his razor stops—one black swoop from shoulders to shins. The pelt ages him, so no one would guess he's only twenty-one. Blanche can't see him right now, can't see anything but the pale swoop of Arthur's belly, a little softer than it used to be when he was young. She mustn't get pregnant again, she really mustn't. Her little box of carbolic plugs in the bureau. "Wait," she says, "I ain't—"

"Prends-la dans le cul," he murmurs to Ernest, playing her nipples the way he might the strings of a guitar.

So Ernest does. It blurs Blanche's senses, the gentleness on her breasts and the hard insistence at her ass. Confusion swindles her into sensation. *Qu'importe;* whether or not she wants Arthur and Ernest to take her at both ends hardly matters at this point. The trampling on her will rather excites her; her body likes having its mind made up for it. So she gasps, letting Ernest in.

The rhythmic friction between desire and disgust; Blanche knows that from the little stage at the House of Mirrors where she doles it out Wednesday and Saturday evenings. Right now she's panting and aching, her jaw crammed to bursting with Arthur's hot girth, her wrists taking her weight as Ernest speeds up the terrible pressure deep inside her, but she knows there is in fact no limit to what she can take. Blanche is the conduit, the river, the rope, the electrical current. They're fucking right through her, the smooth man and the hairy man, and she's going to drink down every drop they've got, their spill one unbroken seam of gold through the shattering rock.

III

THERE'S THE CITY

Sunday's payday at the House of Mirrors, so Blanche strolls down the block to the *bordel* that afternoon in mid-August. A new red-and-white costume, but no jewelry, because she's always dressed so eye-catchingly that she needs none. Arthur's the magpie of the two of them, his fob always thick with baubles; like most men of the sporting set, he prefers to wear his gold.

She pauses to listen to a harpist pluck out a serenade. Her right leg is aching from last night's collision with Jenny Bonnet's high-wheeler, and the rest of her still throbs in a better way from what she and Arthur and Ernest got up to this morning.

Parasols and umbrellas form a flotilla along Sacramento Street, silk shields held up against the merciless flood of light. A general air of dishevelment, businessmen in shirtsleeves, women half bare and mopping at themselves with handkerchiefs. Every store Blanche passes is crammed with loiterers who'll stay in there as long as the shop boys will let them; every bar filled with whoever can afford a drink an hour.

Madame Johanna's Italianate mansion is angel blue,

with snowy paintwork; the epitome of taste. The porter's muscle-bound in his cyan livery. He's said to be Dutch, though Blanche has never heard a word out of him, nor out of the black maid who brings her downstairs to Madame's private parlor. Blanche once teased Madame about hiring mutes, but Madame told her that all of the servants came fully equipped; they just knew how to hold their tongues.

The parlor walls are a muted lavender. This could be a visiting room in a well-endowed convent instead of the City's most notorious brothel. Bookcases bulwark the walls, heavy with volumes in German, French, English. The carpet is primly patterned with lozenges—so unlike the red-tufted extravaganza in the Grand Saloon upstairs. Blanche can hear the Professor there now, practicing a crowd-pleaser at top speed, with too much pedal.

The proprietor sits at her desk, in ashy silk as always, with colorless hair as sleek as plaster; she could be any age at all. Madame holds up one finger to make Blanche wait. "'Reduced rates for parties from out of town,' " she murmurs, finishing her copperplate-script sentence, then lifting the page to check the carbon paper.

"Wouldn't it be easier to get up your circulars on a typewriter?" Blanche wonders.

"Ah, but our visitors appreciate the personal touch." Madame sets down her pen, lets her little glasses drop on their gold chain, and stands up to kiss Blanche lightly on both cheeks. "Who'd have thought this business would require so much paperwork?"

Blanche picks up a cabinet card from a stack of photographs beside the envelopes: a girl with heavily kohled eyes, bare limbs sliding out of Moorish draperies. "Sal's too skinny for Eastern," she comments. "Those matchstick legs!"

"She's got a notion to try a number with fringed tights and a hat in the shape of a horse's head," mentions Madame.

Blanche cackles. She chooses an overstuffed chair. She thinks back to her eight years at the Cirque d'Hiver: at least there the horses were real, even if the pay was much lower than what she makes at the House of Mirrors.

"Well, variety's the main thing. Though Madame Bertha is still stuffing all her girls into frilly white nightgowns," Madame Johanna adds, jerking her head contemptuously in the direction of the rival brothel down the street, "presumably to disguise the fact that half of them are over twenty."

Is that a jibe at Blanche's age? She counterattacks: "Have you any auctions coming up?"

"Oh yes," says Madame, pretending not to register the barbed tone, and she reads from her circular:

> The House of Mirrors is celebrated not only for the *range* of delights on offer but for their *utmost freshness,* notably on the first Friday of every month.

"Does it ever stick in your craw?" asks Blanche.

Madame's gaze is saintly. "Just because bidders may fancy that a girl is nine years old does not mean that's the case."

Blanche grimaces, picturing Madame's supplier; she's met the man only once, in a corridor upstairs, but that was enough to give her the creeps. "It doesn't mean she's fourteen either."

"Since to consent—legally—she must be ten, logically she must be that, at least."

"Logically! Anyhow, I bet your fellow's notion of consent is a little bottle of laudanum," says Blanche.

The Prussian shrugs her shoulders as if they're stiff. "Well. You wouldn't deny a girl her one chance to make a real killing? The fortunes some fools will throw down to stake a first claim, or to delude themselves that's what they're doing . . . The virgin trade should really be considered a way of milking money from mugs, rather like the forms of speculation on which the loafers of California spend their all. Or their lady friends' all, of course."

Blanche leans back in the chair and smiles. "I don't think I've ever come to pick up my wages without your managing to get in some dig at my fancy man."

"True," says Madame, "I've never quite grasped the point of Deneve. Talented on the trapeze once—I'll take your word for that—but what can he do on the ground?"

The funny thing is, Arthur calls Madame *the splendid Prussian;* he has no idea that she holds him in contempt. "He did bring me here," Blanche observes.

Meaning to America, but to the House of Mirrors too. Arthur brought her, watched, clapped the loudest. After a few weeks, it hadn't seemed to Blanche so very much of a step to go from dancing to sitting in the laps of the richer customers, and from that to letting one take her to a hotel for five times what she earned from a leg show. Arthur had been so encouraging. Blanche was pregnant and in what he teasingly called an overheated state. The *michetons* didn't object as her belly rounded; quite the contrary. It seemed to give some of them a perverse thrill.

"A stinking ship brought you here too," murmurs Madame, "but you managed to walk away from that promptly. Strange how girls of other nationalities don't seem to need these hangers-on. If they have pimps, the fellows take managerial roles, at least, whereas these French *macs* are the feeblest parasites."

Blanche only smiles. Parasite? For almost a decade, Arthur's been the soil she's rooted in, the rock she grips, the water that revives her. What would this widow know about men and women in the real world, outside her little puppet theater of performers and watchers?

There's no information to be had about the late Mr. Werner, so the parlor girls who live upstairs speculate that Madame Johanna poisoned him. She's never been seen with anyone who could plausibly be a lover, so they joke that her *chatte* must have sealed up by now, the way an old wound scars over.

"Why keep one sponger, my dear," Madame presses on, "when so many men pant at the prospect of keeping you? L'amant de Blanche, to name but one . . ."

Lamantia is the man's real name, and his punning pseudonym for himself—L'amant de Blanche, "the lover of Blanche"—sets her teeth on edge. The Sicilian businessman, partner in a large concern on Market Street, insists on using the assumed name when he hires Blanche—as if spending a night with a showgirl is a cloak-and-dagger business! "For the last time," Blanche snaps, "I don't want a keeper."

"But you have so very many friends to choose from, you could follow your whim . . ."

She can't stand that euphemism for *michetons* either—

friends, as if what she exchanges with these various merchants, railroad magnates, and other plutocrats bears any resemblance to friendship. "My whim has always been Arthur."

"Well." Madame throws up her bony hands. "You must be making a comfortable living from your rents in addition to what you earn here, if you can afford to keep such a pet."

Blanche smooths her scarlet skirt instead of answering. She wishes she'd never boasted to Madame about buying number 815 in the first place. The woman makes a habit of knowing too much and using it.

"Two pets, rather, if we count Ernest Girard—a matched pair of pugs," says Madame amusedly. "I imagine they take a great deal of feeding and grooming . . ."

This reminds Blanche, uncomfortably, of P'tit and of her new acquaintance's digging for information about him last night. To get Madame off the subject of keepers, she says, "By the way, these Hoffmans who're minding our P'tit Arthur . . ." Then she realizes she doesn't know how to phrase the question. "Is it far enough outside the City to be safe, would you say? Is the air"—Blanche strains for the word—"salubrious?" It occurs to her only now that while she, Arthur, and Ernest all got their scratches the last time the smallpox hit Paris, the same isn't true of P'tit. "No doubt they've vaccinated the babies."

"No doubt."

Blanche tries again. "Have the Hoffmans quite a few little ones in their care?"

The Prussian is looking into her cash box now; she licks

a finger to count a stack of notes. "Children have such a relish for company, don't they?"

Was that an answer? "Perhaps I should pay him a visit there," Blanche says tentatively.

The widow purses her pale lips.

"I know it's not our usual procedure, but these aren't ordinary times."

Madame Johanna shakes her head. "Frau Hoffman finds that parents disrupt the routines."

Blanche bristles. *Routines*—that makes the place sound more like a school or a hospital than a home for babies. How many infants could there be, lodging with one family of farmers? Blanche supposes she should have looked into these details before, but at the end of each visit, she's always been grateful to wave good-bye as the nurse totes her small burden away in his basket.

One of these days, of course, P'tit will be grown enough that everything will be different. He'll sit up, or stand, finally stretch out his arms to Maman, ready to be carried back to Sacramento Street to see his Papa, and perhaps even to stay, when the time is right. "I'm just a touch anxious, because of the heat and the epidemic," she tells Madame now.

"Naturally. But your little one's very well."

"How do you—"

"Frau Hoffman would have informed me if the case were otherwise."

This is where Blanche should accept her hundred in worn notes, pull on her lace gloves, pick up her parasol, and say her *merci*. But there's something veiled in the madam's tone . . . "Where do they live, exactly?" asks Blanche.

A hiss of breath. "If you're irrational enough to insist on putting the child at greater risk in order to set your mind at rest, I'll have him brought here this very afternoon."

"I just find it a little odd that you don't seem to want me to see this farm."

An elegant shrug of the silk-covered shoulders. "You're a free woman. But I find it equally odd," adds Madame with an implacable smile, "that you're suddenly so curious after almost a year."

Blanche is on her feet, knuckles on the carved bureau. "What's the damn address?"

Madame Johanna seems to be weighing something. "Folsom," she says at last.

Blanche has never heard of a village by that name. She stares. "Folsom *Street?*" That's right downtown, in the Mission. She's probably gone past the door a hundred times.

"I wonder how you picked up the impression it was outside the City?"

"You've always called it a farm. Whereabouts on Folsom?" demands Blanche.

"Sit down." Madame sighs. "You've proved your point: underneath that famously snowy décolletage beats a mother's heart. I'll send for him this minute, if you like."

Blanche sees red. "What number on Folsom?"

"Fourteen twenty-two."

Blanche strides toward the door, then turns back to snatch her parasol and gloves.

"I always thought we understood each other," murmurs Madame.

That August afternoon the air's unbearable, chalky with dust. The harpist is still on his stool outside the House of Mirrors but struggling with a tune from some Verdi opera now. Squinting out from under the pinked edge of her ivory parasol, Blanche waits impatiently for a horsecar—but when it comes, there's a boy hanging off the back whose pocks look moist. What's he doing out of bed? Blanche shudders and turns away, looking for a cab instead. Realizing, only now, that she dashed off without getting her wages from Madame, as impulsive as some green girl.

The cabbie spots her wave and brakes at the last moment, so the sweating horse almost tramples her. The man doesn't bother getting down. "Fourteen twenty-two Folsom," Blanche calls up to him, climbing into the little carriage. She slams the door shut herself.

They pass a crumpled brown shape in the street being winched into a cart: the third dead horse Blanche has seen this week. In the endless heat, the hills of the City are breaking the poor hacks; no circus pony she had the handling of ever endured so much. Blanche wishes this driver would slow down before his own wild-eyed bay drops in the traces. A knot of Specials at one corner are jawing and smoking pipes rather than engaging in any law enforcement. The streets are emptier than usual, she notices, but the vast white pavilion built for the Industrial Exhibition in this national centennial year is still pulling in the crowds. Maybe folks just want to be out of the sun, even if it means they risk rubbing up against the sick.

The cab turns down Tenth Street, into the Mission, and the variety of pale faces strikes her: Italians, Irish, Prussians, all living cheek by jowl. Blanche rather dreads reaching her destination. Under what conditions has her son been living? If these Hoffmans aren't farmers, what are they?

She spots a swarm of kids kneeling around an ice block that's fallen from a cart, still bristling with straw. They're all licking it. Children are said to be the most susceptible to infection. How could this neighborhood be any healthier for babies than Chinatown? Blanche was misled from the start. Goddamn Madame Johanna and her Prussian friends.

Number 1422 turns out to be next door to a Chinese laundry that sends coils of smoke in all directions. It's a wary adolescent who answers the door, not the uniformed nurse who brings P'tit to the House of Mirrors for his visits. "Doctress has just stepped out," she mutters.

Blanche is hit by the eye-watering reek of shit. "Who's this doctress?"

"Doctress Hoffman, she just stepped out. Wish to leave a message? What name?"

Blanche has been steeling her nerves, half expecting bedlam—babies shrieking—but this silence is worse. "Where do you keep the infants?"

The nursemaid's eyes flicker. "Doctress is — "

"Just stepped out, yes, but what I want to know is, where's my son?"

"What name?"

"Beunon. I mean, Deneve." Blanche pushes past the rigid girl and tries the first door on the right. It opens.

"Not—that's for appointments," says the girl. She

yanks the knob and shuts the door again, but not before Blanche catches a glimpse of a narrow bed, a sink, and a rack of instruments and realizes what *appointments* must mean.

The girl has more grit than one would expect; she takes her stand between Blanche and the second door, her arms out. "They're having their nap."

Blanche's pulse is hammering in her throat. "I pay eight dollars a week for his care and lodging, and I believe I have the right to see—"

While the nursemaid's still blinking at her, Blanche shoves past her and opens the door.

So dark—that's what strikes her first, even more than the hot distillation of the stink. Her eyes fight to make sense of the shapes. Crib after metal crib, littered with small limbs . . . "Christ, open the shutters."

"That'll only let more heat in," the girl protests.

Blanche fumbles her way to the window, forces her skirt between two cribs.

"Which is yours?"

Instead of answering, Blanche grabs a handle and winches till light slants across the room. Weak goatish cries go up. Two small ones in one crib, three in the next . . . Tear-shaped glass bottles in mouths, or gone crusty on chests, or lost in corners with their black rubber teats dribbling onto the sheets. Every baby is tangled in the same size garment, once white. Eyes closed, or blinking wetly, or open and vacant. All, big and small, strangely inanimate; with a sensation like a blow to her chest, Blanche finally recognizes the tribe her son belongs to.

One black face, one or two infants who could be

Indians, but most of them pallid. Pinching her nose to shut out the smell, her eyes sliding from crib to crib. She can't see P'tit anywhere.

The foot of a facedown sleeper flickers and curls, and with a pounding relief Blanche spots the soft sole and seizes it, then scoops up her son. He seems so much bigger since she saw him last, and she presses kisses all over his howling face . . .

"I said, that one's a girl."

Blanche is scarlet. Deposits the stranger child back in her crib, wipes the foreign tears off her own mouth.

"Upset her, so you did, picking her up that way," complains the nursemaid.

"Are you telling me they lie here all day in their own dirt with nobody picking them up?" roars Blanche, her eyes scanning the shadowy corners of the room.

"I do what I can."

But Blanche's not listening because she's recognized P'tit at last, in the end crib. She approaches cautiously, in case he turns into another changeling. But no, that's him, lying on his side, gigantic eyes sunken above patches of hot red skin. Watching her through the bars, as if she's a wild beast. A bulging forehead, but Arthur's pencil-thin eyebrows arching across it: How could Blanche not have known her baby?

He's chewing on something mushroom-shaped. Blanche holds out her hands to him with an attempt at a smile, but he doesn't stir.

She lifts P'tit carefully. His small garment is limp with sweat. He lets out a sob. Then a convulsive cough, and Blanche feels such pity that she presses him to her.

Registers a surge of warmth against her bodice. *Love,* she thinks in shock, love flaring up between herself and this sobbing baby, love so hot she can feel it on her skin. Then the heat dies away and she realizes what it is: he's pissed on her.

The girl's moving from crib to crib slotting bottles back into mouths.

Blanche can't bear this room a minute longer. She's tempted to set down the wailing, sopping bundle that is P'tit exactly where she found him. But of course she won't; she can't; she could never do that, now she knows what it's like here, and look herself in the face. So she pulls him onto her hip and makes for the passage.

"The shirt, if you please." The girl's too close to her.

"What are you talking about?" shouts Blanche over the baby's cries.

"I need the nightshirt back."

"Is this a joke?"

"Any parent that—'own clothing to be provided on departure,' see," says the girl, with the rapid delivery of a memorized lesson, "because it's the doctress's property, she's particular about it."

For a moment Blanche is tempted to pull the sodden rag over P'tit's head and throw it in the girl's face. Instead, she steps away.

But the girl clings to P'tit's hem. "The shirt or its value," she pleads, "or the doctress'll dock me."

"Here's its value." Blanche spits on the floor.

The girl's grip has shifted to P'tit's tiny foot.

"Take your hands off my son." Blanche yanks him away. P'tit is still weeping as his reddened mouth fastens onto the black thing in his fist, and he twists away from Blanche as best he can.

A mutter: "Reckon he knows my hands better than yours."

The truth of that fills Blanche with a wild fury, and her fist is coming around to club the girl to the floor—but then she hears a sound. It's a tiny one, and it catches Blanche's attention only because it's coming from the wrong room. Not from the room she just walked out of, where a couple of the babies are whining now, but from behind the door on the left. She listens hard; the sound's gone. Perhaps she imagined it. "What's in there?"

The nursemaid's face tightens.

"You've got more?" Blanche asks, incredulous.

The girl says something that sounds to Blanche like "Yours is a weakly," but that makes no sense. A weakling, is that what the girl means?

"He's a what?" Blanche asks.

"You pay by the week, see? So yours is a weekly," the nursemaid says, pointing at P'tit, whose sobs have calmed to little moans. "Through there . . ." She jerks her head toward the room on the left. "We call them the paid-ups because they're all paid up. A lump sum, paid in full at the start. You get me?"

Black spots float past Blanche's eyes and she thinks she might fall. She seizes the handle of the door on the left.

The girl's hand locks over hers.

How many will she find stacked in each crib, alive in name only, sucking on, what—milk diluted down to cloudy water? Glazed-eyed and crone-faced, tiny bones showing through translucent skin? Nobody's coming back for the paid-ups. It's not that Blanche wants to open this door; she's never wanted anything less. But she must. Somebody must.

Blanche is beginning to twist the knob, despite the girl's resistance. She's going in. That's what she'll always tell herself afterward—she's on the very point of marching in there and hurling the shutters open, letting in the remorseless light, when P'tit bursts out coughing. The patches on his cheek, as rough as split wood, flare up as if burning. He whoops wetly, writhes and flails on Blanche's hip, almost slips to the floor. Is that what her son wants most, to get away from her? Well, damn his ungrateful little hide. She lets go of the door handle and locks both arms around him.

The girl swerves across the hall and opens the front door for Blanche. "Keep the shirt," she gabbles, gesturing as if to shoo the pair of them out. "I'll tell Doctress Hoffman the laundry lost it."

"This place—" says Blanche, as if her tongue's made of iron. "Tell your doctress she could be had up on charges."

Before she knows it, she's on the step, and the door's thudded shut behind her.

But are there in fact any charges? Blanche doesn't know that a baby has what you'd call a right to anything. And what can she tell the police if she rushes off to report this doctress, and they ask how carefully Blanche inspected the house on Folsom Street before leaving her infant there for, what, more than eleven months? *Oh no, you see,* she'll have to say, *I left all the arrangements to my madam . . .*

At least she's out of that awful place; she and P'tit both are. Exhilaration pulses through her.

His coughing suddenly cuts off.

Blanche gives him a look to check if he's breathing. His eyes are squeezed tight against the daylight. Now she can see that his skin is corpse-pale. A humid rash all around his mouth, where he sucks on that black object—which turns out to be an old doorknob. What a thing to chew on! P'tit lets out a hiccup, and for a moment he resembles nothing so much as a little old dipso.

Blanche almost laughs. She'll rise above the fact that her white silk bodice is patchy with urine. She puts her son's face close to hers. Plants a kiss on his forehead, just one soft little *bisou,* the kind she's often seen mothers dropping on their babies' heads.

He howls as if her touch is poisonous.

"All right, no *bisous,*" she snaps.

Then, on a hunch, she turns P'tit halfway around so he's looking at the street, and he calms at once.

In the cab, the baby shies away from the air blowing in his face, so Blanche has to slide the window shut, which makes the cab stifling. Looking through the smeary glass, she describes the City for him, pointing at every oyster stall and cement wagon. P'tit blinks, expressionless; it occurs to her to wonder how far babies can see. He seems most interested in the doorknob he's clutching. When Blanche tries to pry it out of his slippery fingers, he lashes out, cracking her on the eye.

"Bordel!" The pain is startling.

Her mother would have smacked him right back, to teach him. But Blanche's hand falters. If the tiny fellow wants to hold on to the one plaything he's used to, who is she to take it away?

There's a Chinese funeral trailing by on Sacramento—

drums and gongs pounding, firecrackers going off, dozens of white-robed keeners, enough fuss that it must be for a man, and probably an elderly one. Blanche gets out of the cab outside number 815 with P'tit in her arms, and on an impulse she steps forward to show him the cab horse, putting them face to face. Might her son grow up to have her talent for riding? *"Regarde le beau cheval."* And then, correcting herself, because P'tit will have to be an American: "Nice horsey."

The tired animal blows out through his nostrils and P'tit bursts into shrieks of fright.

Blanche clutches his lashing limbs. *"Chut, chut,"* she hushes him. "Home to Papa now." Looking up at the second floor.

*

Where's Arthur when Blanche needs him most?

For what feels like hours, she's been carrying the whimpering baby through the empty apartment. Either with him facing out, her arm like a belt tying him to her, or with him facing in, but hoisted high enough on her ribs that he can lean over her shoulder. The important thing, it seems, is for P'tit not to be confronted with his mother's face. Any attempt at a cuddle horrifies him.

Blanche feels insulted by this, but the undertow of guilt keeps her going, pacing through the airless rooms. How could she and Arthur have left their son in that hellhole on Folsom Street for a day, let alone most of a year? *But we didn't know.* Why didn't they know? *Madame never told us. Nobody told us.* But why didn't they ask?

Jenny Bonnet's the only one who thought to put the obvious questions. A virtual stranger; an interfering jailbird. If Jenny knocked on the door just then, Blanche would have trouble deciding whether to thank her or throw something at her.

Well. P'tit is here: that's a fact. What Blanche is going to do with him tomorrow she doesn't know, but right now she's going to strip him down to his knotted diaper to cool him so he'll stop sniveling for a moment and she'll be able to think.

Even after he's bare, his mottled skin boils with heat. Searching among all the scaly patches, Blanche can't find anything like a fresh scab on either arm to suggest that Frau Hoffman bothered to have the babies vaccinated. She throws the awful nightshirt in the ashy stove so she can burn it tonight, once the evening's cooled enough for her to be able to bear a little fire. The smell of P'tit clouds around her, as rank as the cat cages at the Cirque d'Hiver. And her bodice, her new white bodice, is yellow with piss. The two of them need a bath, above all things, but there's no Gudrun to tote the water from the faucet in the downstairs hall. When Blanche hauled the baby up four flights of stairs to knock on the attic door a while ago, there was no answer. (Where could the girl be gone to all Sunday? Some endless Lutheran service?)

"Enough walking?" she murmurs to P'tit now. "Care to lie down?"

She puts him down warily, like he's a bomb that might go off, on his back in the middle of her and Arthur's bedspread. Then withdraws, so he won't be appalled by her looming face. P'tit mouths his doorknob and coughs as if it's choking him. Peers at the wall. With one claw he scratches a purple patch where his sparse hair meets his neck.

From this distance Blanche registers that her son is not shaped like any baby she's ever seen. It's not just his forehead, which swells like a turnip, something you might dig out of the dirt. His ankles are distinctly thicker than his bowed legs, his wrists thicker than his arms, and his breastbone pushes out, as sharp as the prow of a ship. She doesn't remember him looking like this when he was born. And Blanche has never noticed any of these oddities on visits, but then, P'tit was always wrapped in white linen from head to toe, wasn't he? Cap, bib, gown, little mittens and stockings . . . To mask the smell, Blanche thinks bitterly. To mask everything that wasn't right.

She can't look anymore; she turns her back to him. She must get out of this room and wash herself, put on a clean bodice at least. But P'tit's not safe on the bed because babies roll off beds, don't they? She doesn't know much about infants other than a few ways they can die. Mind you, P'tit doesn't seem able to roll. He doesn't seem able to do anything. What's wrong with him?

P'tit lets out a loud fart, which makes him cry. He blinks at the big windows, the excess of light, the yelps of the wheeling gulls.

Blanche casts around for something to put him in, because that's what you do with a baby. Her apartment seems changed, inhospitable. It doesn't have anything this terrible visitor needs.

The trunks she and Arthur brought from Paris! She hesitates, then starts to empty one of her own, because her lover will have a fit if she scatters his clothes. (And what'll he say about her bringing P'tit back here without a word of warning?) She piles her skirts and chemises on the nearest rush chair. P'tit wails on, the blank lament of someone who doesn't expect any remedy. Now she's down to the yellowed paper lining of the trunk—but that's too bare, the baby will bash his head on the hard staves. Blanche finds a blanket in a closet, then another, and does her best to pad the trunk with them before she puts a sheet down. It still looks too big, but that's better than too small, surely? On Folsom Street he had only a fraction of this space—no, Blanche is not going to think about the so-called farm of Doctress Hoffman's, because it makes her shake in a way she didn't while she was standing there quarreling with the nursemaid. She's going to bed P'tit down in this trunk if only he'll stop that mewing.

There. Ready. She picks P'tit up, swiveling him to face away from her. His crying wanes. She carries him over to the trunk—but what if putting him down in it prompts another outburst? Maybe better to wait till his mood has turned. Besides, he'll spread his terrible reek all over the sheet. It occurs to her that she shouldn't have put him on her bedspread, for that same reason.

Only when her own stomach lets out a loud rumble does Blanche stop to think that P'tit might be hungry. Infants eat often, don't they? She totes him over to look in the icebox. No milk, just scum in the jar. What the hell is she to feed the creature?

In the cupboard Blanche finds half a baguette. "*Voilà!* There you go." But P'tit doesn't seem to recognize it as food. She puts a chunk between his fingers. He puzzles over it for a long moment, then lets it drop to the floorboards.

She picks it up and presses it back into his small hand. Guides it to his lips—but he shrinks away.

Any normal child would gum the thing, surely? She looks into his mouth to check there's no blockage. Pulls up his puckered upper lip, though it makes him pant with fright. A year old and not a single tooth. Unless P'tit's worn them all away on his nasty doorknob? No, not even a stub. He's like a one-year-old newborn. A baby who'll never grow up—is that possible? A baby who'll stay this way, a perpetual living reproach to her?

Panic, beating Blanche's ribs like a drum. She needs a drink.

She ransacks the cupboard till she finds the wine they opened at lunch. Awkwardly, one-handed, she uncorks it with her teeth and pours herself a big glass.

Babies shouldn't drink wine, should they? It occurs to her to offer P'tit some water instead. She fills a cup from the jug. P'tit lets her move the slick doorknob away a few inches and press the cup to his mouth, but he seems to have no idea what to do; the liquid runs down his neck and pools in the little hollow at the base of his throat.

Surely Blanche can lay him down for a minute, just to change her clothes? She tries it, spreading yesterday's *San Francisco Examiner* across the middle of the sofa in the salon and putting him flat on it.

P'tit contracts as if in pain, face and feet drawing together, making the paper crinkle. It occurs to Blanche that he's trying to sit. She scoops him into an upright position, although his tiny limbs are oddly resistant. Props him, with a cushion, against the back of the sofa. There's something unconvincing about his pose, something out of plumb. He's a mismade rag doll. Every so often he shakes his head as if saying a querulous no to some unvoiced question.

"We've got to go out," Blanche tells him, speaking aloud to cut the silence. He needs diapers, clothes, a bottle, milk . . . but it's impossible, because she can't bear the thought of going back out into the scalding day lugging him with her. Not that such a tiny boy can weigh more than a cat, but he's awkward to handle because she's not used to it. She can't go out, can't have a bath, can't do anything but sit here staring at the ugliest, saddest baby in the world.

Self-pity brims behind her eyes. Blanche fills up her glass again and has a few bites of stale baguette so she won't get dizzy. Reaches down and cracks her silk bodice open, pulls it off. She can't imagine ever wearing the nasty thing again.

After wrenching her sweaty chemise over her head in the bedroom, Blanche pours out a little water and scrubs herself to get that unclean feeling off. No sound from the salon.

P'tit needs a wash too, needs it worse than she does. She makes herself walk into the next room. He hasn't stirred. He's giving the wall an accusing stare.

Blanche picks him up and brings him back to the bedroom, sits him awkwardly on the edge of her bed. She wipes him down, flinching whenever she touches one of the rough patches in the crooks of his arms or in his leg creases. P'tit doesn't flinch, or cry. She tugs the diaper's knots open with some difficulty and lets the cloth slip off. It seems almost heavier than the baby, caked with brown. How often did that crew on Folsom bother to wash the babies? Blanche finds she must place P'tit right in the basin to soak the hard stuff off his tiny wrinkled bag and to wash in between his shrunken buttocks. Has she got it all? A smear on the bedspread: *merde!* She scrubs at it with another rag, widening the faint brown circle.

Now Blanche feels at least a little cooler, and P'tit must too, though he still seems as hot as a baked potato to her touch.

He stares in the vague direction of her bare body. *Michetons* pay well for such a view, she'd like to tell him, petulant. Her swan-white flesh is no comfort to this child, no home. He doesn't know her from Eve.

"What shall we do now?" Blanche asks aloud.

No response except a shattering cough.

"Can you even hear me?" It strikes her that P'tit could be deaf and dumb, some kind of cretin for all she knows. Blank-eyed, barely alive. Why did she ever let her body make such a mistake? There are always ways—

Blanche shudders. That's a notion that shouldn't occur to a mother. Much too late to wish this small life undone. And yet she does wish it, every time her eyes approach him.

Not his fault. Her fault. For everything Blanche did before he was born, and everything she's failed to do since.

Damn Jenny Bonnet and her questions. And me for listening to them.

She tries to concentrate on practical matters. She rather regrets having thrown the foul little shirt in the stove, because she hasn't got anything else to put him in. It'll be all ash-caked now. Could she bear to poke the thing out and scrub it in what's left of the water? No, she'll leave P'tit nude for the moment, because the air might do his scabby skin a little good. But of course, he'll be pissing himself again soon if she doesn't find something . . .

Blanche looks through the mound of clothes on her chair until she finds an old petticoat. She rips it into three pieces. Forms one of them into a diaper, a crude loincloth, really; it gives P'tit the air of some small saint in his final sufferings. The cloth keeps coming loose on the left. He scratches at his hairline as if something invisible is biting him.

If she could just run out to get the things she needs—but she can't leave him here. Perhaps he does know how to roll, he's just too scared to do it while this strange woman's watching. Babies left alone wind up dead; Blanche has read about such cases. She'll have to haul him with her and manage somehow . . . but no, she can't carry a stark-naked infant around town. She's washed them both, Blanche reminds herself pathetically. She's done that much.

With nothing on but a chemise and a petticoat, she carries the baby from room to room to pass the time. She tries to keep her eyes off from the strangest parts of him: ankles, wrists, that sinister breastbone. At least he smells less disgusting now. "This is where Papa and I sleep," she says. "There's your *caca* on the bedspread that I'll have to wash before your father's very fine nose gets a whiff of it. And this room is where Ernest—your uncle Ernest," she improvises, though the phrase doesn't sound quite right, "he sleeps here when he's not at Madeleine's—that's his lady friend—and this is where we make our coffee and heat up dishes from restaurants . . ."

The knock at the door makes Blanche spin around so

fast she almost drops the baby. "Arthur!" She says it in relief but it comes out accusatory somehow.

P'tit bursts into tears. Coughs. Cries on.

"Chut," she says urgently, rocking him too hard. "Shush now for Papa." Crucial for him not to make a bad first impression.

It's not Arthur at all, it's some skinny *gamin*. Blanche wasn't thinking straight; why would Arthur need to knock? She realizes she's not even dressed, and she presses the baby to her chemise to cover herself up. The child gawks at her, handing over a note in familiar copperplate on pearly paper headed with the address of the House of Mirrors.

My dear,

I understand from Frau Hoffman that you've withdrawn your little one from her establishment. If I can be of service in helping you make new arrangements, do let me know. Otherwise I will expect you for your regular performance on Wednesday.

Blanche tears the note down the middle. New arrangements indeed. That treacherous *salope* can find herself another star dancer and see how her customers like it. "There's my answer," she says, handing the boy the scraps.

He's whistling as he trots down the stairs—not merrily, more as if he needs the rhythm to keep his feet moving.

A sense of anticlimax settles over her as soon as he's gone: a cloak of lead on Blanche's shoulders. P'tit has pissed right through his diaper and her fresh petticoat.

Twenty minutes later Arthur finally turns up. Without Ernest, for once, thank God. And it's all going to be fine, because he's utterly charming. He kisses Blanche as if he hasn't had the chance to do it in weeks and points his pencil-slim cane at the wizened new arrival like a magician flourishing his wand. "I didn't know we were to be honored with a visit, monsieur. How you've grown! *Viens ici, mon gars.*" Arthur blows on him and makes comical noises.

P'tit keeps up his frozen stare.

"What's this nasty thing?" Arthur tugs at the slick doorknob, but P'tit holds it tight.

Blanche cries out, "Don't."

He tilts those slim eyebrows that he gave his son.

It all spills out of her then, the whole sordid story of the Hoffman place, the weeklies, the paid-ups . . .

Arthur murmurs in outrage but interrupts before she's even finished. "You didn't know what it was like," he soothes her.

You, he says, not *we*. And certainly not *I*. As if it weren't Arthur who'd made the deal with Madame Johanna when Blanche was out of her mind with fever last September. Eight dollars a week: the price of three good blankets, say, or a best-quality corset. It sounds too little for proper care, now that Blanche is letting herself—making herself—think about it. No, probably not even eight dollars, it occurs to her; Madame, she knows, would skim off a percentage.

"Whatever made the Bonnet girl start asking about the baby in the first place?" mutters Arthur. P'tit, slumped in his lap, is gnawing on the doorknob.

Blanche hesitates. "It was—she happened to see his picture on my bedside table." That's not an answer. The irritation just below the surface of Arthur's voice is exactly what she's been feeling herself, but now she's compelled to justify their new acquaintance. "They were just the sort of questions that anyone would have . . ." She trails off. Questions that Blanche and Arthur should have been asking all year instead of busying themselves with their own pleasures.

His tenderest smile. "You're looking utterly exhausted, *chérie.*"

Blanche appreciates the sympathy, but it stings too. He and Ernest were eager enough to fuck her this morning; how can she be so transformed already?

"Gulli gulli!" Arthur tickles P'tit under the chin but gets no response. Takes both the tiny hands in one of his, lifts the limp arms. "Blanche. What's this?"

His tone makes her hurry over and peer at the rash of red spots in both the tiny armpits. *"Putain de merde!"* she curses. It couldn't be. Could it?

"Probably just a rash. Don't you think?"

Blanche can't speak, she's so scared.

"A summer rash, where the sweat's built up," says Arthur more firmly, lowering P'tit's hands. "If it was—"

"Face, hands, and feet," interrupts Blanche. She's read in the papers, that's how it starts. She's read other things too, such as the fact that it kills every third person who catches it.

"His face is fine," says Arthur.

She examines P'tit close up: scaly red patches, especially under his chin where the drool collects, but there's no rash, strictly speaking, either there or on his minute palms and soles.

"Well," says Arthur, rising to his feet and handing P'tit back to her, "I should start looking for a new place for him. Something much more wholesome, farther out of the City . . ."

Blanche shakes her head.

Arthur's adjusting his waistcoat in front of the mirror, smoothing the curve of his fob and its dangling trinkets: the lucky crystal pig Blanche got him back in Paris, a coral hand holding a tiny dagger . . .

How to explain that the location isn't what makes a hell? "You didn't see it."

"So we'll choose the next place carefully, together. A real farm—"

"No." Blanche almost shouts it. "We—I was an idiot," she says carefully, "to think eight bucks a week could buy the kind of looking-after he needs."

"So we'll pay twelve." Grandly: "Fifteen if we have to."

"These places . . ." She swallows her sob as if it's a hard crust. "The whole trade's a swindle." She tightens her grip on P'tit, and he starts to squirm. "We're keeping our baby right here."

A gentlemanly sigh. "We'll get someone in, then."

"Yes," says Blanche, letting out her breath. Someone to help, that's all she needs. It was on the tip of her tongue to suggest, out of long habit, that he ask Madame; she almost laughs. "The sooner the better."

"Perhaps, for now, Gudrun?"

"Nowhere to be found," laments Blanche.

"Oh, but I passed her on the stairs," says Arthur, making for the door.

A couple of minutes later he's back with the young seamstress.

Under her gleaming straw-colored braids, Gudrun's

wearing a wary look. "I know nothing," she says, hands up like a shield. "I was youngest in my family."

"So was I. We just need a little assistance," says Blanche soothingly. She looks around for Arthur, but he's disappeared into their bedroom. "Only until we find a nurse."

The Swede shakes her head, eyes on P'tit as if he might explode. "What he got?"

Blanche is at a loss.

"Is it disease?"

She clears her throat, outraged to hear her own fears stated so bluntly. "He's perfectly well, thank you!"

Both women watch the baby, who slobbers on his doorknob and lets out a low wail.

"He's hungry, that's all," Blanche insists. "Will you run down to the store for some milk and a bottle with a teat to put it in? Or hold him while I—"

"I run down," says Gudrun, fast.

The girl clearly doesn't want to touch him.

Clamping her teeth together, Blanche fetches some coins from her pocketbook.

Arthur emerges and pours himself some wine to sip while changing his dusty boots.

"Well, she's not going to be much use," Blanche tells him, listening to the ugly sound of Gudrun's low heels clumping down the stairs.

"I'll pop out this minute and start asking around."

Blanche hunches her shoulders to ease them. "*Mon amour*—what if she's right about the baby, though?"

He hoists his eyebrows as he adjusts the line of his striped pantaloons. "As she was the first to admit, she doesn't know anything."

Blanche glances down at P'tit in her lap. "His forehead—his chest—he bulges where he shouldn't. Look at his wrists and ankles." She whispers it, as if no one but the two responsible parties must hear. "He won't meet my eye. He doesn't even know how to smile—"

As if wounded by this list of his flaws, P'tit starts to cry, which makes him cough again. Blanche joggles him, clicking her tongue the way she would to calm a horse, which he doesn't enjoy at all.

"*Pauv' bébé*. Should I get the poor lad something while I'm out?" murmurs Arthur, fishing in the green chamber pot for banknotes.

"What kind of something?" asks Blanche.

A shrug as he straightens his cuff links. "A syrup or such. You know. For quieting."

Fury behind the hard plate of her forehead. "He's been quieted enough. I bet that *doctress* had them dosed to the gills."

"Still, of course," muses Arthur, "it's what he'll be used to. Seems cruel to cut him off all at once, especially if he's not quite well, with that nasty rash under his arms."

Blanche's eyes narrow, because all at once she can see right through this man. Arthur doesn't want his son here, making noise, making demands. He doesn't want to be put to the least trouble in the world.

*

On the fifteenth of September, Blanche is groggy from panic and lack of sleep. Bolted into the tiny lavatory of the train from San Miguel Station, she drags her hair into an approximation of a high chignon. She arranges a few ringlets over her forehead, then repins the flat straw hat as far forward as it'll go. She paints with speed and something near accuracy, bracing herself against the mirror as she applies a steady line of red to her upper lip. It's melting already, so she scours it off with a handkerchief and starts again, ignoring the knocking at the lavatory door. She rubs at the little scab on her cheek where the glass grazed her last night—Jenny! Christ, those skewed limbs, the puddle of blood—and it starts to run red again. Blanche presses on layers of powder till the mark is fainter, at least.

She finally returns to her seat, leans back on the knot of her bustle, and tries to take a full breath.

Someone at the end of the carriage is warbling what Blanche recognizes as a Stephen Foster tune; there's nowhere you can go to get out of earshot of his jingles. What an incongruously pretty day: the low peachy hills, the pale green sea in the distance. Sparse farms, and their owners heading with heavy carts toward the markets downtown because the train must be too expensive for them. Here comes the Industrial School on its arid plateau. A U.S. flag hanging limp above three long floors of cells. It's not a school at all, but a reformatory. A scattering of boys outside, pecking desultorily at the dust with hoes. A few straighten up to watch the train rocket by, as if it's their day's sole entertainment. Whenever Jenny came this way, she filled her pockets with candy to toss over the fence for the inmates, Blanche remembers. What a child that woman was still, at twenty-seven.

"Weren't that a female I saw over by the washing line?"

a passenger remarks loudly behind Blanche as he gets up to use the spittoon.

"No, they send the girls to the Sisters now," the wife informs him. "Ever since the supervisor got fired—for *taking liberties,* don't you know." The euphemism in a carrying whisper.

The Industrial School boys have been swallowed up in the dust already. Blanche stares out the other window, at a field of lettuce.

Chimneys growing in the distance. The train speeds up as they head down the long grade toward the passenger depot at Third and Townsend. The City's coming at Blanche like a bullet to the head.

At the terminus, it suddenly strikes her that Arthur could be waiting on the platform, scanning the crowds for her familiar face. Blanche reckons the chances that Detective Bohen has arrested him already are slim to none. But where else can she go today? Should she pick a random town to hide in? If she doesn't show up at tomorrow's inquest here in the City, the detectives might put a warrant out for her.

When Blanche gets to her feet, everything goes black for a moment. Now that she thinks about it, she realizes she's had only a sip of water today.

Her step slows as she moves down the platform toward the gate. Men are stacking a whole freight car full of ice, as neat as masonry, with chaff and sawdust for mortar. She scans the milling crowd for men with bird's-wing mustaches. She dreads the sight of that lovely sallow face she's woken up beside every morning since she was fifteen.

And yet . . . she's almost disappointed that Arthur's not here. It feels like a long time since they had their last battle, at the gaming saloon, just a week ago. Blanche shouldn't have allowed herself the satisfaction of sparring with him that night, she sees that now. Should have fallen to her knees in the pose of some penitent Magdalene and begged him to tell her what he'd done with their son.

So many ways to dispose of a baby. Hand over mouth and nose. A cushion, a blanket. A cord; a ribbon, even. A quick shake or a blow. A fall. A drain, a culvert . . . Or don't give him his bottle; that would do it, after a day or two, in this thirsty weather. Just go out, shut the door, and leave him to cry his way to silence. So many quick and simple means to finish off a small life that should probably never have started.

Blanche won't let the tears come, not in front of this pair of patrolmen displaying their seven-pointed stars for authority as they peer suspiciously into every face for pustules. The smallpox has been spreading through San Francisco since May, so what good do they think it'll do to examine arriving passengers now?

Outside on Third Street, the sun is dizzying. The push and clamor of the crowds overwhelm Blanche after three days of the silence of San Miguel Station. She finds a pump and bends to drink from it. Only a dribble; the pressure's low. She thinks of that reservoir she and Jenny saw being gouged out of the hill, up at the back of Sweeney Ridge. It won't be ready for a while yet. What'll happen if the City runs dry?

Her throat floods with acid, and she swallows it down. Her arm aches already from keeping the delicate green parasol between her face and the hammering sun. There's a Mexican slumped against a wall, wrapped in his serape. Funny to think his lot once owned this whole part of the world. A Prussian-looking busker pumping an accordion tiredly.

Blanche wishes she could afford a cab. She has to get hold of some cash today. Instead, she squeezes onto a horsecar going north.

"Terrible hot, ain't it?" a fellow remarks. "Ninety-five in the shade, they're saying."

Blanche tugs down her short lace veil and pretends she hasn't heard. A little conversation, a little flirtation . . . so many men think they can get a bit of her for free.

On Market, a Chinese man with a huge bundle of clean laundry tries to get on. But several passengers protest that the linens might be riddled with invisible germs, so the driver moves off without him. This is what plague has brought San Franciscans to, Blanche thinks: flinching from every smell, scrutinizing every face for danger, balking at sharing the same air.

At Morton Street, a couple of worn crib girls squeeze in. Blanche wonders if there's any truth to the rumor that each one, in her narrow stall, services up to a hundred customers a night. With a small shudder, she looks away.

All along Kearny, folks are cringing away from the glare, crowding to the shady side of the street. Every dive and barrelhouse is spilling over. *Temperance Lemon Cocktails,* offers one awning, but the drinkers loitering under it look half soused to Blanche.

The coupled hacks slow as they haul the horsecar up the slope on its smooth tracks, and the passengers brace themselves. Of all the unworkable spots to build a city, thinks Blanche with exasperation. *If you get tired in San Francisco, you can always lean on it,* she remembers Jenny quipping.

Chinatown smells like a urinal, which Blanche notices only because she's been out of town. The health inspectors have nailed disinfectant sheets over many more doors, and yellow flags hang like bunting for some canceled New Year. A Nordic-looking man plods up and down with a sign in the form of a gigantic arrow—FREE VACCINATION NO MONEY FREE TODAY—but he's not getting many takers, because the Chinese bachelors with braided pigtails down to their hips are lined up outside the herbal shops instead.

Recognizing the square tower of St. Mary's, Blanche jolts upright. She was heading home without thinking, but 815 Sacramento Street is the last building in the world she should approach today. Her brain's all rusted up this morning.

As the horsecar creaks past Sacramento, she catches a glimpse of the blue-and-white mansion: the House of Mirrors. Yes, that's where Blanche needs to go, she decides—for proof of her hunch that Madame Johanna told Arthur where the two women had fled to on Tuesday. How else can Blanche convince the detectives that it's Arthur who shot Jenny—by mistake, because he was aiming at Blanche, but that's still murder, no? "Driver," she shouts, pushing her way down the car, her orange carpetbag snagging on hips and bustles.

She stands at the corner, her head aching and her mouth so dry that she's not sure she's capable of speech.

A constant stream of Chinese bachelors parts around her, not an empty hand among them. Every man seems to be hauling a bale of shoes, a laundry bag, or a wet basket of sea life writhing on a bed of kelp; Blanche recognizes shrimp, squid, and those snails that always remind her of severed ears. Some of the men are toting their baskets on long sticks over their shoulders—in defiance of the City's new bylaw criminalizing that tradition, or has nobody told them it's a crime yet?

Gray's Undertakers is just a block away, at Dupont. Perhaps Blanche should head straight there, to make sure the—what are they called?—dieners aren't prettifying Jenny with their little pots of paint. But she finds she can't bear to, not yet. Her stomach is a tangled knot. She hasn't eaten anything at all since dinner yesterday evening. (*Splendid stew, if I may say, Mrs. Mac,* Jenny assured Ellen McNamara, though it wasn't.)

So Blanche turns north, going past a runny-nosed Irish fiddler who can't be more than ten. Chez Durand, just for half an hour, to gather her strength? It can't be safe to go where the French go—where a Frenchman might guess he'd find a particular Frenchwoman—but then, Arthur's hardly going to gun her down in a public place, is he? Even in his current crazed state, the man's intelligent, and he can't mean to end up on a gibbet in the yard of the Broadway Jail.

Under the striped awning, the brasserie's crammed with drinkers. Safety in numbers, Blanche reassures herself, stepping inside. The print of the Champs-Elysées is back up by the door, minus its glass. That's the only sign that Jenny was ever there.

"If we don't keep our liquids up," a female voice is remarking, "we'll like to expire by lunchtime."

Blanche hovers at the bar, trying to catch the eye of the owner. It occurs to her that Durand won't know the news, because it can't have hit the papers yet; Cartwright must be still working up his story for the *Chronicle*'s afternoon edition.

"Mademoiselle," says Durand with a nod of acknowledgment, shoving a young man off a stool so Blanche can sit down. "*Qu'est-ce que ce sera?*" His mustache so thickly lank it hides his mouth.

Blanche shouldn't have come here, not today. She can't be the one to tell him. She orders a plate of vinegary *choucroute*—the first thing she can think of—and a beer.

At the piano in the corner, a ginger-haired man is thumping an accompaniment for a plump blonde with a Languedoc accent who giggles when she fails to hit the aria's top notes. Blanche wants to slap her. She wants to slap everyone today, to pick up the whole sweat-slick City and punch its lights out.

When Durand comes over with her order, she looks at it queasily and takes a sip of her beer.

"If you see Jenny, tell her *j'en ai marre*. Enough!" he barks. "Since Wednesday I've been waiting. The season's nearly over, I tell them, it's halfway through September, time to eat leeks and apples, but they're still craving their *cuisses de grenouille . . .*"

Blanche's mind fixes on the frogs she released by the pond this morning. The small McNamaras licking their singed fingers by the bonfire.

"I'll get my supply from someone else next spring, if I can't count on—"

She makes herself break in. "Jenny's dead. Last night," she gasps, "down at San Miguel Station. We were—somebody shot her through the window."

"Bordel de merde!"

Blanche slides off the stool, needing to get out of this place.

Durand shouts in the direction of the kitchen. "Portal!"

A muffled roar comes back.

"Get out here!" he roars. "He won't believe it from me," Durand tells Blanche, taking her elbow and pushing her down on the stool again.

The smell of her pickled cabbage turns her stomach.

The long-faced cook comes out, his apron spattered red and brown.

"Tell him," the *patron* insists.

Blanche repeats her news, leaden.

Portal doesn't curse or interrogate her about how it happened. Instead, he caves in like a man made of paper. He staggers, he writhes in his employer's arms, tears flooding down his scarlet face.

Durand keeps kissing the side of his head.

Blanche's cheeks burn. She pushes her way toward the door, almost reaching it before she remembers her carpetbag and has to turn back to grab it, her eyes low. Portal is still weeping on the bar. These *foutu* Frenchmen!

In Madame Johanna's parlor at the House of Mirrors a quarter of an hour later, Blanche smooths her blue plaid flounces and tries not to count the minutes. Keeping

Blanche waiting is just the widow's little game, nothing worth losing one's temper over.

Her stomach growls. She should have eaten that *choucroute*. There's a fly buzzing intermittently against the window. Blanche arches a little, to ease the strain in her back. Funny how it never ached when she was performing on horseback twice a day or, more recently, doing leg shows in the Grand Salon upstairs.

What was the last one? Almost a month ago now; the Saturday night Jenny rode into her on Kearny Street. After Blanche went to Folsom Street and realized what kind of place Madame had consigned Blanche's baby to—after she sent back Madame's note, ripped up—she would have liked to maintain a stony silence and never lay eyes on Madame again, even if it meant forfeiting her pay for her last two performances. But three days ago, when Blanche had to flee town for fear of the *macs* and was desperate for cash, she swallowed her pride and came here for her hundred dollars—and the Prussian had the almighty gall to claim that the debt was the other way around. So Blanche wouldn't be back here today for any reason less serious than this: she must find evidence that Arthur knew she was going to San Miguel Station. Only when he and Ernest are in jail will she be able to take a breath without terror.

How much longer is the woman going to make her wait?

You came within an inch of death last night, Blanche scolds herself. Surely she can manage to sit for a quarter of an hour in a quiet room where the thick drapes keep out the worst of the heat and where she knows that she's not going to be shot at.

The door opens noiselessly. Blanche's head jerks up.

Madame Johanna, in pearl-gray silk. "Ah, my dear."

Blanche steels herself.

"You are not looking your best, if you'll pardon my saying so. Do take some water." Pouring two small glasses from the carafe. "I trust you've come with glad tidings about your little one?"

Blanche is rigid, eyes on the carpet. On Tuesday, why did she let herself complain to Madame about Arthur taking P'tit away? She's not going to say a word about it today. She can't trust herself not to burst into tears.

"Well," sighs Madame. "If the baby's lost for good, I do hope you feel the whole drama of snatching him away from Folsom Street was worth the candle."

"I trusted you," Blanche roars before she can stop herself.

"Indeed you did, to relieve you of a burden so that you could continue to work, more and more profitably, may I add, and live as freely as before."

"I didn't know what kind of rat hole you'd stashed—"

"Please don't waste your time and mine by playing the innocent," Madame cuts in.

Blanche clears her throat but still her voice comes out as a caw. "I only came here today because of my friend Jenny."

Madame puts her head to one side. "Jenny. Do I know a Jenny?"

Blanche bets she does: Madame knows everybody, from gentlemen high up in the state government to the least shivering nine-year-old smuggled into the House of Mirrors. "Jenny Bonnet."

"Ah, the girl with a taste for making a spook of herself in pants?"

Blanche forces herself to ignore that. "She got blown to pieces beside me last night. It was—it has to have been Arthur."

The pale mouth forms a little O of shock.

As fake as some old diva at the opera, Blanche thinks. How could she have borne this woman for more than a year of her life?

"Did a bullet do this?" asks Madame Johanna, leaning over to explore Blanche's cheek with one cool fingertip.

She pulls away and raps the accusation out. "What I find curious is that you're the only person who knew I was going to San Miguel Station."

"Did I know that?"

"Do you have the gall to deny it?"

"You may very well have mentioned it last time we met." The Prussian turns the gold ring on her finger. "Goods, clients, petty bureaucrats . . . you can't imagine how much business I have to attend to in a single day."

"But who else—how else could Arthur have found out where I was?"

Madame half smiles. "I've had no dealings with your *bel ami* in some months."

"What about his friend Ernest?"

"If I haven't seen one Siamese twin, I could hardly have seen the other."

Madame's a liar par excellence, but why would she need to lie in this case? Why would she even bother? It strikes Blanche with an awful clarity that Arthur wouldn't have gone to the House of Mirrors for news of Blanche, since—much to his fury—she'd broken with Madame more than three weeks before, the moment she reclaimed P'tit from Folsom Street.

She ransacks her memories of last Tuesday, when she set off for San Miguel Station in that buggy she hired from Marshall's. Blanche could swear she didn't tell anyone but Madame her destination. But of course—her stomach sinks—Jenny could have mentioned it to any number of people. Those unknown friends whose sofas she used to nap on. Jenny knew the strangest assortment of folks.

But Blanche presses on: "The detectives won't believe Arthur's involved, not unless I can show he knew where Jenny and I were last night."

"Ah," says Madame, letting the syllable out with a soft hiss. "Now I understand the purpose of this unexpected visit. You're asking me to swear that your discarded *mac* burst in here yesterday waving a gun, mustache dripping with foam, and that I, out of pique because you'd disrupted my schedule of performances, sent him off hotfoot to shoot up San Miguel Station?"

Blanche chews her lip. Put that way, it sounds like a third-rate melodrama.

"It's not that I have any objection in principle to misleading the authorities—especially these days," adds Madame, "since the board of supervisors seems to have embarked on the doomed venture of trying to whitewash a city that's been a byword for liberty. No, the problem is that my involving myself would draw the attention of the police to my business. And incidentally, the fable you propose would leave me open to an accusation of abetting—even inciting—a murder." She winds up with a little nunnish smile.

Salope: the word is salty as blood in Blanche's mouth, and it would be some relief to say it.

"As it happens," says Madame, "the only man who's been here inquiring after you is Signor Lamantia. He's sent to me twice in recent weeks, offering considerable sums just to know where you might be."

Blanche rolls her eyes. L'amant de Blanche; her Sicilian regular is just a buzzing fly.

"You really mustn't hide away," murmurs Madame. "The City's memory is so short. Unless you're planning to live on your rents, without dancing or *michetons*?"

It's living through the next few days that worries Blanche. "Just pay me my hundred dollars and I won't trouble you any further."

"Ah, still you misunderstand. Let me show you the figures, to make the matter crystal clear." Madame opens her ledger and slides it over. "Two show fees of fifty dollars each in the left-hand column. And on the right, your outstanding debits: costumes, musical accompaniment, refreshments, dressing, rehearsal and stage facilities furnished, advertisements circulated . . ."

"Hogwash," Blanche cries. "You can't work these madam's cheats on me. You take your finder's fee whenever you arrange a rendezvous, and it's never been part of our bargain that I pay for costumes or music. I ain't one of your stable. I'm an independent artiste, and the most popular ever seen at your house."

"Nor has it ever been part of our bargain that you can

quit on me with no notice, leaving me with no explanation to offer your many admirers," says Madame coolly.

"What *refreshments,*" Blanche demands, "the odd glass of brandy?"

"Everything costs, my dear. Since you decided to forgo my protection so abruptly last month—"

Protection? A muscle in Blanche's cheek twitches as she reckons the fortune this woman must have made off her hide.

"—well, I must recoup some of my losses by charging for what it's cost me to turn you into Blanche la Danseuse."

"To turn me into—" says Blanche, bewildered.

"You were a pregnant bareback rider," says Madame, "with very little to make you stand out from the tide of female flesh that washes into this City. You were raw material, from which, I congratulate myself, I constructed a figure of considerable mystique."

Blanche is speechless.

"Three hundred seventeen dollars, all told," Madame adds more briskly, pointing to the figure on the right, "which, reduced by your earnings of one hundred, comes to two seventeen. Will you be paying in notes or coin?"

Blanche grabs the ledger and pokes the column on the left. "What about adding this: 'Payment to Blanche Beunon in consideration of her not telling the police about the goddamn dying babies'?"

Madame looks as if Blanche has soiled her chair. And then her face changes—lights up. "Despite all the abuse you're heaping on my head in your pardonable state of distress after the shock of your friend's death, I would like to help you, for old times' sake. May I suggest you let me announce one final Saturday appearance of the Lively Flea, tomorrow night?"

Blanche almost laughs. This woman is made of India rubber. "You must be joking."

"For an unprecedented fee—say, five, no, ten times your usual. Five hundred dollars," Madame almost sings, marveling at her own kindness. "Which would clear what you owe me and leave you with almost three hundred to be getting on with."

Blanche swallows hard.

The Prussian's fiddling with her wedding ring, not just waiting for an answer but enjoying seeing Blanche squirm. Letting them both hear the silence that implies consent. "Until tomorrow, then?"

Almost three hundred dollars. Blanche doesn't open her mouth in case what comes out is *You cold bitch, I'll never work for you again.* She has so little cash in hand, she can't afford to give an unequivocal no. So she says nothing at all, just grabs her bag and makes for the door.

Almost cantering away from the House of Mirrors in her little mules, sweat breaking out on her forehead and under her arms. Forget the money for now. Blanche has to get off Sacramento Street before she walks right into Arthur or Ernest or one of their set. She ducks down the next passage, skirts a spill of cabbage leaves, and almost trips over an elderly man in the shadows. Only one sleeve on his shirt. An *R* burned on his dark gray cheek. He's singing nasally:

Here in this country so dark and dreary,
I long have wandered forlorn and weary.

His cap's on the ground in front of him, but there's nothing in it. His eyes are squeezed tight shut. Perhaps there were coins but some *gamin* snatched them already? There's someone like this every five paces in the City, metropolis of bums of all shades. Blanche supposes San Francisco is where they wind up because of the mild winters; they figure at least they won't freeze solid overnight. Jenny would have stopped and given him fifty cents for a bunk. Jenny would have learned the rest of his song, his story. *I just like stories,* she said, that first night at Durand's. Blanche can't afford to throw anything in his cap, she decides, and it'd only get stolen anyway.

" 'Do not detain me,' " he drones on sorrowfully,

For I am going
To where the fountains are ever flowing.
There's the city to which I journey,
My redeemer, my redeemer is its light!

There's the city. Oh; heaven is what he means, not San Francisco. Blanche speeds past the busker, away down the alley.

IV

SOMEBODY'S WATCHING

That August morning, the day after she's brought P'tit back from Folsom Street—*rescued* him, as Blanche thinks of it, so she'll feel valiant rather than simply miserable—her face in the great mantelpiece mirror looks a whole year older. Shoulders hard as boards. She used to do handstands on horseback, she reminds herself; carrying a baby around shouldn't be too much for her. She's feeling feeble only because she's barely slept. P'tit's seal bark got worse in the night, or perhaps it just seemed to because the tin sides of the trunk made it echo. (Arthur gave up at two o'clock and decamped to the sofa.) Clearly this is going to be as much work for Blanche as giving birth to the creature all over again.

"Light housework," Gudrun repeats like a protective incantation, tying on her apron.

"But this would be *instead* of housework—as I said, never mind the dishes if you'll just take him out for an hour or two so I can have a nap," pleads Blanche.

The Swede's golden head shakes firmly. "I told yesterday, no experience."

"You'll soon get the hang of it."

"I don't want," says Gudrun.

"What about wages on top of your board?" offers Blanche. "What do you make for sewing shirts?"

Still shaking her head. "I prefer factory."

"Whatever you're earning, we can pay you more," says Blanche, too shrill.

"I never be a live-in."

"No, no, you'll still sleep in your attic. It's only day nursing I'm talking—"

"I prefer factory."

Blanche gnaws her lip and carries P'tit into the bedroom without another word. She examines his puny armpits. At least all the patient sponging with ice water has cleared up the rash. She's going to stay in here until the young woman's finished the dishes and tidied up, because if Blanche starts a fight and Gudrun walks out, there'll be no one even to carry the chamber pots down to the drain in the hall.

The long Monday drags by. All P'tit seems fond of is his wretched doorknob. But he'll accept other things if Blanche puts them to his rash-rimmed mouth: bottles of milk, meat broth, bread pap out of a duck-shaped feeding boat. And of course his sugar tit, the little cloth bag of honeycomb (recommended by an American grocer) that she's tied to his sheet. P'tit lies there in his padded trunk, mouthing the sweetness. His spatulate limbs swim in a spasmodic way that Blanche finds not at all human.

He sicks half his meals up, but Blanche grits her teeth and reminds herself that that must be because his stomach isn't used to ample feeding or because something's gone down the wrong way, making him cough till he convulses.

His diapers overflow with brown liquid, and the stinking pile is rising. No one's hauled it to the laundry above Hop Yik's because Blanche forgot to ask Gudrun before the girl marched off to the shirt factory.

Arthur knows that Blanche has answered a note from Madame—but not that she did so by sending it back torn to pieces. He's of the view that Madame Johanna's so busy running the House of Mirrors, she's probably never been to see how Doctress Hoffman looks after all those babies, and besides, it's pointless to bear a grudge when there's no real harm done, *hein*?

Blanche stares at P'tit. Harm has been done. She's convinced that Madame knew exactly what she was doing when she sent P'tit to Folsom Street at barely a month old. What was the plan, for him to snuff it, natural-like, and be no further trouble to the Lively Flea? It's astonishing that P'tit has survived his first year on earth. No wonder he's . . . well, damaged goods. "Though doing well, considering," Blanche says out loud, with hollow cheer.

For answer, P'tit farts, sailor-style, and braces his swollen stomach with a look that—she's already learned to recognize—signals a violent squirting. "Don't leak on the sofa," she pleads, rushing to pick him up in time.

He can see her, at least. Blanche is sure of that much now. His hearing, she's not so certain about. The tiny hollows of his ears seem gummed up with wax, but when she tried to dig it out with the tiny spoon from the salt dish this morning, he started wheezing with distress. Her guess is that he can hear but he's doing his best to ignore her. When Blanche roars at him, he startles and cries, and she feels awful. He's come to tolerate her carrying him about the apartment—in fact, seems to rather prefer it to being left in his trunk—but can't bear anything in the nature of a caress. The few times his father's picked him up, P'tit's puked on his cravat or all over the ring—black onyx set in gold, with a scarab motif—that Blanche bought Arthur the first time she earned a hundred dollars in a single night.

She passes the hours yawning and wondering what—if anything—is going on behind that bulging forehead. P'tit's face remains closed, except when it pinches up in agitation. He hasn't had much to smile about, she supposes. But the bad times are over, doesn't he realize that? Or at least the worst times. He's home now, with Maman, in the best apartment in the building. He could make some effort . . .

She does know how absurd that sounds.

By evening, the heat of the day has thickened like a smell. P'tit finally falls into a snuffling doze in her locked arms.

A tap at the door. Has Arthur gotten so cockeyed he's dropped his keys somewhere? Blanche hoists the sleeping child and walks over to open it.

Jenny Bonnet, the pool of purple around her eye faded to greenish yellow, the swelling gone down. It was only two days ago when the thug walloped her chez Durand, Blanche calculates. That was in Blanche's old life, before she brought P'tit home.

Jenny's loose suit is flecked with mud, and there's a sack over her shoulder. "Hi," she says, with a grin. "Hungry?"

Blanche's first impulse is to slam the door in the woman's face.

But she's desperate for some lively company. Someone

who sees her as something other than a vehicle or a bottle filler; someone who doesn't wail at the sight of her face. And the fact is, if Jenny hadn't asked Blanche those nosy questions then P'tit would still be in that dark room at Doctress Hoffman's. And Blanche, for all her crabbed mood, can't wish that. So she steps back.

Jenny strolls into the salon. "That your little fellow visiting?"

"We've . . ." *Taken him back*? No, that sounds as if Blanche and Arthur gave him away almost a year ago. "He's staying here. That eye's on the mend," she remarks, to change the subject.

"I heal like all get-out," boasts Jenny. "How's the leg?"

Blanche half laughs. Her thigh, bruised from the collision with Jenny's high-wheeler. "I haven't had time to notice."

Jenny's taking off her jacket and waistcoat, quite at home.

"Bet you're glad to shed a few of those stifling layers," says Blanche.

"Says you, trudging around in a bustle even when there's no one but a baby to see you!"

Blanche grins, granting the point. "Any news of the world?"

"I had to get a fresh scab just to be let on the streetcar," offers Jenny, patting her upper arm. "Saw one unfortunate with tight sleeves obliged to peel her dress halfway down to prove she'd had hers," she adds with a dirty chuckle.

Blanche laughs too, picturing it; how awful for the girl.

"You know next door's boarded up?" says Jenny, jerking her head that way.

Her face stiffens with alarm. "Number eight thirteen? The boardinghouse?"

"Must be scores of poor saps in there. Six weeks of risking fines or lockup if they so much as step outside. And when it's Chinatown, the health inspectors rush to conclusions. I heard of one boy on Bush Street they dragged off to the hospital with a bad case of pimples."

A laugh escapes Blanche, startlingly deep. It makes P'tit leap as if he's been touched by Madame Electra at a fair. *"Chut,"* she whispers, rocking him back to sleep.

"This epidemic's given the authorities an excuse for playing the heavy with undesirables," remarks Jenny, setting her Colt on her folded jacket. "Cursing's banned now, did you hear? So's having the DTs, flying kites . . ."

"Kites? Surely not."

"Hey. Trust a jailbird to know the law to the letter." She holds out her hands. "Give us a look, then."

A look at what? Then Blanche realizes she means P'tit. "Bring that lamp," she says, leading the way into the bedroom.

Blanche lays him down on his back in his trunk, an inch at a time.

He sleeps on, spread-eagled on his grubby sheet in the pool of light. Nothing innocent about his severe little face.

"Pretty homely," Blanche whispers so the visitor won't think she's blinded by maternal feeling.

Jenny doesn't contradict her.

Which Blanche resents, perversely. She realizes she was hoping for someone to persuade her that this lumpenheaded goblin is a prince among infants.

"A year old, you said? Looks half that," murmurs Jenny.

P'tit's bowed legs curve inward; his feet have found each other.

"Well, he can move all his limbs, anyhow."

"He's deformed." Blanche says it out loud to hear how it sounds.

Again, Jenny doesn't say no. "Rickets."

Blanche doesn't know this English word. "What's—"

A shrug. "That's what it's called when they look like that."

A jolt of relief, powerful as whiskey in her veins. "Then there are other babies who look like this?"

"The ones who don't get enough," Jenny clarifies.

"Enough what?"

"Whatever they need. Don't know what it is, just how it looks when they go without it."

And what makes Jenny an expert on babies? Blanche wonders with sudden fury. "His stomach was always round, on visits," she protests.

Jenny grimaces. "That's just wind." She's bending over P'tit now, fingering his broad ankles and wrists.

"Don't disturb him," snaps Blanche.

"Just checking for lines."

Lines? Doesn't everyone have lines at wrist and ankle, creases at every point where the limbs need to bend?

"Weals, you know, if they've tied them to the beds."

"He can barely sit up, they wouldn't have—" Tears, with no warning; Blanche clamps her hand over her eyes to stop them. Why now? Why hasn't she been crying for her sickly, unsmiling baby all these past months?

This is the moment an ordinary woman might put her

arms around Blanche; rub her shoulder, at least. A kiss on the cheek or the hair. Some human comfort. But Jenny gives no sign of noticing her state. "No marks," she concludes, looking down at P'tit, head on one side. "I've seen worse."

That's such cold comfort, Blanche almost laughs. Her son's bones are misshapen, his muscles wasted away to nothing from lying jammed in a corner in that stifling chamber on Folsom Street. He's stunted. And though Blanche can think of several people to blame, her own name is at the top of the list.

"He'll mend," says Jenny. "Corkscrew?"

"What?"

"I need your corkscrew," she says, pulling a bottle out of her satchel.

"You said he'll mend," cries Blanche, grabbing her by the sleeve. "How do you—"

"I'm only guessing," says Jenny.

Blanche wants to punch her in the eye.

"Most things do."

"Do what?" demands Blanche.

"Mend."

She stares at Jenny.

"Sooner or later. One way or another. Now can I open this sherry?"

Blanche takes a long breath.

At the deal table, they sip from their glasses.

She should eat something while the baby's asleep, she tells herself. Is there any of that cassoulet that Arthur brought back last night? She wonders whether she can stomach it cold and save herself the bother of heating it up over the spirit lamp.

"You mean to keep him here for good now, your P'tit?" Jenny asks.

Blanche nods. "We'll hire a nursemaid. We'll be a proper family at last," she says, to convince herself.

"A proper family. Oh, that's a guarantee of happiness right there," says Jenny, sardonic.

"Where are your people these days?" Blanche wants to know.

"Gone to the devil, mostly! Are yours still in Paris?"

"They don't even know about the baby," admits Blanche. "But yours, are—"

A wail goes up from the bedroom. Jaw tight, Blanche trudges in. P'tit's scraping at where his hair meets his neck. He freezes at the sight of her. Stares as if he's never seen anything stranger. Then his eyes slide off to a corner of the room, chasing shadows.

Like it or not, I'm all you've got. The accidental rhyme jangles in Blanche's head. She scoops him up efficiently, turning his face from hers as she walks back to the salon. His diaper's still dry, at least. "Hold him a minute?" Without waiting for an answer, she dumps him in Jenny's arms and goes to the lavatory.

Just to splash her eyes with water from the jug. Just to rest her head against the door. The truth is, Blanche would like to stay shut in here for a week. If someone would take P'tit off her hands for only an hour, even, carry him out of hearing range so she could get some sleep . . . but Jenny's not that kind of woman.

When Blanche finally comes out, however, Jenny's lit the stove and is sautéing garlic in a casserole dish. The smell is glorious. She's got P'tit propped against the wall with cushions and she's trilling what sounds like a Creole song in his direction, accompanied by loud finger clicks and exaggerated faces. " '*Chapeau sur côté, Musieu Bainjo—*' " She mimes the dandy's rakishly tilted hat. " '*La canne à la main, Musieu Bainjo—*' " The twirling cane. "'*Botte qui fait crin crin, Musieu Bainjo—*' " The squeaky new boots. Her voice surprises Blanche again with its lightness. "Enjoys his music, don't he?" Jenny remarks, breaking off the song.

Does he? Blanche nods, as if of course she's noticed that. But P'tit's gaze still seems blank to her. The fact is, it hasn't occurred to her to sing to the baby in the day and a half she's had him here.

"Looks like he's waiting," says Jenny, watching P'tit as she might a hawk or an otter. "That makes sense, I suppose, if he's been used to lying in a crib all day."

Blanche tries not to think about the other weeklies in their dark room, the ones it wasn't her business to rescue. The ones whose parents no doubt have their reasons, reasons that seem good enough to them. And, oh Christ, the paid-ups . . . the ones she never actually saw but whose images torment her anyway. Now Blanche remembers what she dreamed last night in one of the little stretches of sleep P'tit let her have: that she was back in that house on Folsom holding a pillow and running from crib to crib, pressing it down on each face, leaning hard, snuffing out these abominable half-lives.

Her stomach rumbles, bringing her back to the present. She breathes in the warm aroma of the garlic. "What's going into that?"

"Frog legs, of course, fricasseed with sherry." Jenny

stirs with a sure hand. She pulls a blotchy creature—five inches long—out of her sack. It strokes the air convulsively. "Ever met a California red-leg?"

"Not close up and moving," says Blanche, making a face. "Why aren't its legs red?"

"Reddish, wouldn't you say?" Jenny holds the frog closer to Blanche, who squirms away. "Redder than other frogs', anyhow."

With its dark mask, the red-leg has the look of a bandit. Prominent ridges rise from hips to eyes. "They're horribly like us," Blanche remarks. "Fingers, toes . . ."

"Ten toes, but only eight fingers," Jenny points out. "He's a handsome fellow, don't you think?"

Blanche giggles. "How do you know it's a he?"

"Slightly thicker arms and thumbs . . ."

Without a word of warning, Jenny kills him with a quick jab of the knife to the neck. She turns the creature over, baring a surprisingly bright pink belly, and makes a slash across what Blanche can't help thinking of as his waist, then flips him again and scores the small of his back. With the steel tip of her knife, she yanks down the flecked skin as neatly as a pair of pants. Or, no, stockings, dangling in a tired tangle. She chops off the top half of the frog with a crunch and flicks it into the scrap bucket. The lower half, all firm buttocks and muscular calves, reminds Blanche of nothing so much as a boy out of the corps de ballet. Only the blunt feet betray the fact that this is not half of a tiny person.

Jenny works on, skinning and bisecting, throwing each pale pair of legs into the bubbling pot. "They can jump twenty times their length, did you know that? But their best trick is turning from tadpole to frog. Last summer I lay by a pond all day and watched one." Her eyes are alight. "In the morning she was a little algae-sucking wriggler. I saw her grow legs, bulging eyes, a long sticky tongue to catch prey and a big jaw to swallow it, a pair of throat sacs she could inflate like rubber balloons . . ."

Jagged sobs from P'tit, who's slumped sideways, off his cushions; his face is now pressed to the skirting board. Blanche sighs and picks him up. Too much to ask for, to have a bite to eat in peace, or a conversation.

"By sunset," says Jenny, "she was unrecognizable. A brand-new creature."

Blanche hums an old circus tune, swaying from side to side. P'tit does seem to enjoy that, or at least not object to it.

Jenny echoes the melody. "What's that?"

"Just the waltz they always played for the trapeze act." She swings P'tit, exaggerating her knee dips like some cracked old diva.

Jenny shakes the pan of frogs. "Do you miss your old life?"

Blanche looks up, forcing her eyes away from that nasty rash on P'tit's hairline. Need Jenny ask? How could Blanche not miss the liberty she's had all these months while P'tit's been on Folsom Street? She's paying for that freedom now, like a debt to some backstreet money-lender.

"Your Cirque d'Hiver, I mean."

"Oh." A long moment, while Blanche considers this different question. "I rather miss the horses."

Jenny nods. "What was your favorite act?"

"Ah, that would have to be the Courier of Saint Petersburg." Blanche smiles, reminiscing. "I rode in straddling two cantering horses—one wearing the flag of Russia, one the Union Jack. Then another horse came up behind with the Prussian flag and ran between the two I was standing on . . ."

"As you spread your legs a little further for the edification of the house?" sniggers Jenny.

"I gathered up the reins off its back," says Blanche, miming it, "and next came one representing Holland, then Belgium . . . then finally—to patriotic cheers—France!"

"What did you wear to compete with your six dandified horses?"

"A jockey costume. Till takings were down," Blanche remembers, "and our Monsieur Loyal put me in fleshings and a tiny skirt."

"So . . . from bareback dancing to the brand of legwork you do at the House of Mirrors," Jenny comments, "that doesn't sound like very much of a leap. You're still working with animals."

It takes Blanche a moment to get it: the red-faced men in their velvet chairs, hunched over their swelling *cigares* . . . She hoots, and P'tit starts to cry. Doesn't the little *con* mean to let her enjoy herself ever again? "On the whole, I prefer the stage to the ring," she tells Jenny.

"I would have thought horses a sight more likable than, uh, other beasts."

"Granted. But I don't have a Monsieur Loyal telling me what to do anymore," explains Blanche, "what to wear, when to practice . . ."

"What about your Madame Johanna, isn't she some

class of Monsieur Loyal? Any truth to the one about her dipping a girl's hands in boiling water?"

"That old tale? I don't know, but I wouldn't put anything past her," says Blanche darkly. "Anyhow, I'm done with that bitch. It was she who arranged—" Her throat locks, and she finds she can't finish the sentence. She bounces P'tit a little in her lap.

Jenny nods.

She's quick, this one, thinks Blanche; she doesn't need everything spelled out.

"What'll you do now?" Jenny wants to know.

Blanche wipes her sweaty lip. She really hasn't had time to make any plans yet. She musters a show of confidence. "The less I'm seen around town, the more the *michetons* will be willing to stump up when I do make myself available."

"What the newspapers call the scarcity effect."

"You're quite a reader, ain't you?"

"Ah, you figured me for an illiterate swamp-dweller?"

"No, I—" Blanche doesn't know this woman well enough yet to be sure when she's joking.

Jenny grins, tipping their meal onto two plates.

Blanche takes a chair, perches P'tit awkwardly on her lap.

Jenny blows hard on a pair of legs and leans over to offer it to the baby.

Who surprises Blanche by closing his hand over it, as if it's some kind of toy.

"You mean to choke him?"

"He's a Frenchman," says Jenny. "Got to start eating real chow sometime."

P'tit has touched the legs to his mouth, and he's nuzzling them with wary enthusiasm.

"Was it at your circus that you learned to dance?" asks Jenny.

Blanche nods, her mouth full of rich, winey meat. "If our Monsieur Loyal ever caught us sitting around between performances, he'd coach us in schottisches and mazurkas. And Arthur used to take me to the Bal Bullier. We saw Rigolette dance the cancan there, with nothing under her skirt." Happy days. Long nights, when Blanche could sleep whenever she wanted to, so she didn't go to bed till dawn.

But Jenny's eyes have slid to P'tit. He's dropped his bone, and a huge piece of glistening flesh protrudes from his mouth.

"Putain!" Blanche makes a grab for it, wrenches the slippery thigh from between his gums.

He lets out a cough of protest.

Jenny's helpless with laughter.

Blanche is not qualified to be left in charge of this child. He might be safer back on Folsom Street, she thinks with a shudder.

They're sampling a bottle of honey-yellow Sauternes now. "So if you're not going back to Madame Johanna, is your fancy man going to rustle up *michetons* for you?" Jenny asks.

"Never," says Blanche sharply. "Arthur's my lover."

"*Loafer,* isn't that how it's spelled?" asks Jenny with a lopsided grin. "I guess that's how French *macs* differ from Yankee pimps: they prefer not to lift a finger for their pay. And what about the young ape?"

"Ernest? What about him?"

"Well, is he your man too, or just your man's man?"

Blanche doesn't like either phrase or the bluntness of the question. "He has his own *petite amie,* Madeleine."

"*Macs* always seem to trot around town in matched pairs," observes Jenny. She mimes a preening horse in harness so precisely that Blanche giggles. "Guess they need pals to talk to, for whiling away the idle hours."

"Though Arthur and Ernest do have business affairs," Blanche puts in.

A tilt of Jenny's eyebrows. "You mean laying out your cash on one kind of bet or another?"

Blanche can only smile for an answer. Jenny's like a good strong drink when you didn't even realize you needed one. Maybe the reason Blanche has never been one for making friends is that the women she's encountered till now have bored her. Jenny's an odd kind of woman: part boy, part clown, part animal. An original, accountable to no one, bound by no ties, who cocks her hat as she pleases. Their closeness has sprung up as rapidly and cheekily as a weed. Blanche was meant to cross Jenny's path on Kearny Street on Saturday night, she realizes with a surge of conviction—even if the encounter left her with a few bruises. This is the friend Blanche has been waiting a quarter of a century for without even knowing it.

The scrabble of a key in the door. "Speak of the devils," says Blanche as she gets up.

The men reek of sweet, pungent smoke. "Ah, hello again, Frog Girl," says Arthur to Jenny. "Very cozy," he sums up, sweeping his cane around the room as a conductor might his baton.

Blanche stiffens. If he hasn't got the wit to realize the kind of day she's been having, left alone with the baby—

He crosses to plant a kiss on Blanche's cheekbone and another on P'tit's fist. "What do you make of my son and heir these days?" he asks Ernest. As if daring him to point out the obvious.

Ernest, taking P'tit in from sparse scalp to stubby toes, keeps his own counsel. He addresses Jenny instead. "Still in pants, I see. You wouldn't look half bad in a dress."

Is he flirting with her? Blanche wonders.

"Oh, I used to have a whole trunkful," Jenny assures him with a grin, "but they just didn't seem to fit."

"Any dinner left, *chérie*?" Arthur asks Blanche.

"Désolée," she apologizes, "nothing but bones."

"We'll go down to the chophouse at the corner in a while," he tells Ernest, filling two glasses with the Sauternes.

Arthur's back's been bad, so the men have spent half the day in a den off Pacific to see what a pipe might do for it. "I used to sprinkle the stuff on my food, but I found it burned my stomach," he's telling Jenny.

"Any luck tonight, *mon amour*?" Blanche asks him in an undertone, bouncing P'tit on her lap.

He pulls a few coins out of his jacket and tosses them in the air. "Ernest reckons the dealer's box was gaffed."

"I mean, any luck finding a nursemaid!"

"Ah, yes. No." He sighs. "Girls in this city, it turns out they'd rather grind away at any degrading shop work so long as they can boast of keeping their *independence*. Every one of them too good to go into service!"

Blanche would have appreciated knowing how many

Arthur asked before coming to this conclusion; where he looked, how hard he tried before lying down on a couch to smoke opium. But she can feel her voice screwed tighter in her throat already, and Arthur won't stand for her getting shrill, particularly when they have company.

Arthur opens another bottle of wine but spits out the first mouthful.

"Corked?" asks Blanche.

"No, just Californian," he says, squinting at the label. "*La vie est trop courte pour boire du mauvais vin.*" He quotes the proverb grandly as he shoves the window up to empty the wine into the street.

From the darkness below comes a shout that could be protest or jubilation, it's hard to tell.

"You could have left it for Gudrun," Blanche rebukes him mildly.

"Why isn't *her* life too short to drink bad wine?" wonders Jenny.

"Swedes don't know any better," says Ernest, pulling the cork from a dusty bottle of whiskey he's found at the back of a cupboard.

They talk gambling for a while. "The Chinese are the most loco for it," Jenny asserts. "Cockroach fights, grass-hoppers, frog races . . ."

"Frog races?" Arthur lets out a cough of laughter.

"It's the San Franciscan way," says Ernest through a yawn.

"It's nature's way," Arthur corrects him. "What's life but one big gamble? Born with good cards or bad, you still go bust in the end."

"No, but this place in particular—when miners throw

up a town pretty much overnight," Ernest argues, "every clod of dirt's a lottery to them."

"The *foutu* miners may have got here first, in '49," Arthur growls, "but it was we who really made something of the place."

"Here we go," murmurs Blanche to Jenny.

"So they squeezed us out of their filthy camps with their Foreign Miners' Tax," he goes on, pronouncing it scathingly. "Did we give a rat's ass?"

"I thought you folks arrived only last year?" asks Jenny in an undertone.

"He's speaking for all Frenchmen," Blanche tells her, mouth twisting with amusement at the image of her lover hoisting a pickax.

Arthur's declaiming as loudly as some street-corner agitator now. "We turned a stinking town into a real city of bachelors. Quick as the Anglos scrabbled gold out of the streams, we raked it into our restaurants, casinos, *bordels* . . ." He squeezes Ernest's shoulder. "To our glorious race, masters of the arts of pleasure!" They lift their glasses. "And to San Francisco, La Ville Sans Honte," Arthur roars, "beautifully shameless, best spot in the world to fuck money out of nothing!"

When the toasts are done, Arthur offers cigarillos all around, but only Ernest takes one. " 'Genuine Californian, Untouched by Oriental Labor,' " he reads off the label.

"No wonder they cost so much," jokes Arthur. "You know your little cigarettes are only the sweepings off the floor?" he asks Blanche.

"I do, *chéri,* because you tell me every time."

Jenny's filling a little clay pipe. "Now, this is the real deal."

P'tit, in Blanche's lap, starts to cough, so Blanche waves the smoke away. "Speaking of Oriental labor, aren't Chinese men said to make first-rate nursemaids?"

"There I draw the line. Me no likee coolie curling up in one of our cupboards." Arthur yawns as he stretches out on the sofa.

Blanche gives him a hard look. After they've lived in this neighborhood for a year and a half, how can he come out with that nonsense?

P'tit splutters and starts to cry. Blanche stubs her cigarette out in a saucer and stands, swaying him a little.

"It's not good to fuss over them at the first peep," remarks Ernest.

"Mm. You should always wait five minutes, my mother used to say," says Arthur.

She waltzes P'tit from side to side, trying to keep her temper. "*'Mais il est bien court,'*" she croons, " *'le temps des cerises . . .'* " It's very short, cherry time.

Arthur groans. "Something jollier, would you mind?"

"It's all code for the Commune, you know," Ernest remarks to Jenny, from the floor.

Blanche bites her lip. She shouldn't have sung that one and got him started.

"You reckon?" asks Jenny.

"Well, the cherries stand for bullet holes . . . *'Cerises d'amour au robes pareilles,'*" Ernest belts out in a passable baritone, " *'tombant sous la feuille en gouttes de sang . . .'* Drops of blood!—what else could it mean?"

It's hard to hear him above the baby's shrieks. Could

P'tit be tired again? Hungry? Must Blanche scrub another bottle and hope the milk in the icebox hasn't gone off?

Jenny's voice has turned excited. "Five years ago, in Paris—you must all have been there!"

Blanche, remembering the Commune—the piles of splayed bodies in the Luxembourg Gardens—says nothing.

"We were in it up to our necks," says Arthur.

"What, did you serve in the Guard?" Jenny, sitting up now, lets out a whistle.

"That wasn't the only way to be a revolutionary," snaps Ernest.

"Ernest was only a boy then," says Arthur, patting his friend's knee.

"We couldn't abandon the circus," Ernest puts in gruffly, "but we played our part . . ."

"We workers pushed the cannon all the way up Montmartre," Arthur reminisces.

Blanche holds in her snort. *We workers!*

"Now, that must have been some class of excitement," marvels Jenny.

"Liberty or death! Those were the days. We turned Paris into a little republic under the red flag—for two months, anyhow," says Arthur.

Blanche marches P'tit into the bedroom, trying to shut out the sound of Arthur going on as if he'd manned the barricades during those last battles instead of just getting into his tights and spangles as usual.

Her eyes catch on the lithograph on the wall, so familiar to her that she rarely notices it anymore. The naked girl sitting at ease on the grass beside her man, her lovely foot extended so casually between the legs of his friend in the tasseled hat, who doesn't seem to notice . . . That used to be Blanche, she thinks, startled. The one everyone wanted. And now look at her, lugging a baby like some ground-down servant out of an old Dutch painting.

"Did Gudrun bring the laundry back?" asks Arthur, putting his head around the door.

"I—" Best not to say that Blanche forgot to ask Gudrun to do it. "She never took it down in the first place," she says instead, wrinkling her nose at the basket.

"*Bordel!* I haven't a single presentable shirt to go out in."

"I can run down to fetch you some noodles—" Blanche's spirits lift at the thought of even five minutes away from the baby.

Arthur shakes his head. "I need to see an Australian at the docks about a rather splendid opportunity."

Blanche purses her lips. *Rather splendid:* that's the chamber pot emptied of money again. "Your shirt looks fine."

He lets out a little grunt of impatience, searching his trunk.

Blanche recalls a minstrel number a Belgian blonde does in top hat, tails, and blackface at the House of Mirrors. " 'When I go out to promenade,' " she croons with only a touch of satire, bouncing P'tit in time with the verse,

I look so fine an' gay,
I hab to take de dog along
To keep de gals away . . .

Not so much as a smile from Arthur. "A new collar, at least." He brandishes one. "This is clean but the points need crisping up . . ."

She walks past him, arms full of his thrashing son, into the salon, where Ernest is teaching Jenny the last verse of the tragic ballad about the Commune.

Jenny watches as Arthur lays out the fresh collar on the table and uses tongs to set the iron into the stove's embers. "Don't those things poke you in the throat?" she asks.

"That's the whole idea," he murmurs, eyes on his work.

"The whole *point,*" puns Ernest from the sofa. "Two stilettos to the jugular saying, *Head high, monsieur.*"

"That never occurred to me," admits Jenny.

"Because you, Mademoiselle Bonnet, are a slob who borrows the garb of our sex only for the purpose of wallowing in muck."

She laughs at that. Then addresses the baby in Blanche's lap, intoning with mock gravity:

There's too much of worriment goes to a bonnet—
There's too much of ironing goes to a shirt;
There's nothing that pays for the time you waste on it,
There's nothing that lasts us but trouble and dirt.

"I like that one," says Blanche. " 'Trouble and dirt.' "

"Hits the nail on the head, don't it?" says Jenny.

"We should hire a proper live-in help," says Blanche to Arthur, suddenly decisive. "Some really capable woman to keep house and mind the baby too. She could sleep in the second bedroom with P'tit—if you were to stay at Madeleine's," she adds, turning to Ernest.

"Is that how you speak to our oldest friend?" asks Arthur, his tone chilly as he makes the iron hiss along the linen.

Blanche's pulse thumps. "I didn't mean—"

"No, no," says Ernest with a tight chuckle, "I see which way the wind's blowing."

"I misspoke," she hurries to tell them both, "I—"

"Haven't you been listening to a word I've said?" demands Arthur, setting down the iron with a clink. "Nobody wants to live in with a blasted infant, especially not in Chinatown in the middle of an epidemic."

Blanche can't keep her lips pressed together. "Perhaps if you spent more of your time actually looking for someone to take care of your *blasted infant* and less of it lolling around in a pipe dream—"

His jaw hardens. "Well, perhaps if you'd given the matter a moment's thought before you galloped back here with him yesterday—"

"If the little fellow's only an encumbrance to you," Jenny breaks in pleasantly, "why don't you find someone to take him off your hands?"

Blanche turns on her. But it's Arthur Jenny's addressing.

"What do you mean?" he snaps.

"Just curious. I'd imagine there's folks who'd want a baby, no questions asked. White, male, more or less in working order . . ."

"Are you suggesting I sell my son?" asks Arthur in a tone of steel.

Blanche's hands are gripping each other so hard her long nails are digging into her skin.

Jenny shrugs. "Keep him or don't, is what I say. Fish or cut bait, but don't gripe."

Blanche is trying to remember the glow she felt earlier in the evening, the conviction that she and Jenny were destined to be friends. Now she's thinking: *Why did I let this provocateur in the door again?*

They're all staring at Jenny, who remarks, "A Chinese fellow once told me that back in his village, there's always a bucket ready."

"What kind of bucket?" demands Arthur.

"Filled with water, you know? For inconvenient babies."

The picture catches Blanche off guard, fills her with horror: P'tit, seen through water. The wavering image of that small face. "Stop," she pleads with Jenny.

The woman's eyes rest on her coolly. Then float back to Arthur. "You think you can't do it, he told me, but you'd be surprised."

No, Blanche insists to herself, *no. I'd never—*

"Listen, you stunted mule," Arthur roars, "try having a child before you open your *foutu* mouth on the subject."

"Time you left, Frog Girl," growls Ernest, very much the gorilla as he lurches to his feet.

But Jenny's already pulling on her waistcoat and jacket and then sliding her revolver into her trouser pocket. *"Bonne nuit, mes amis,"* she says, with a cordial bow.

Blanche puts her head around the bedroom door, silently, in case Arthur's sleeping. He's been laid low for the last three days. When he complained his back was bad again, and his head too, Blanche thought at first he was just suffering the effects of too much liquor or brooding over what Jenny'd said about P'tit—but then it turned into a scorching flu.

Blanche has been camped on the sofa beside the baby's trunk so P'tit won't disturb his father. Frankly, she's sick of waiting hand and foot on this tiny, unsmiling stranger. She wouldn't drown him in a bucket, but she can't say much more than that. Guilt hangs on her like a lead apron. There are moments, tying a diaper or transferring P'tit from one arm to the other, when Blanche begins to feel competent at this kind of drudgery, but that doesn't help; it only sharpens the feeling of estrangement from herself.

Ernest is at Madeleine's, ostensibly taking refuge from the baby's *caterwauling,* but really demonstrating how wounded his feelings were by Blanche's suggestion that P'tit and a nursemaid should have the second bedroom. (She might just as well have held her tongue, because she hasn't been able to hire anyone, despite hauling P'tit up and down all the grubbier streets of the Mission in search of hungry Irish girls, lying—with her best poker face—that there've been no smallpox cases within blocks of their apartment.)

Jenny hasn't shown up again, which is a mercy. Was she trying to shame Arthur into taking some fatherly responsibility the other night? Blanche wonders. Or can Jenny just not resist the pleasure of picking a fight?

"How are you this afternoon, *chéri*?" she murmurs, seeing Arthur's lashes flicker.

He leans up on one elbow and feels his forehead experimentally. "Quite restored."

His smile loosens all the strings in Blanche's body.

The apartment is as silent as some forest pool now P'tit's finally dropped off. "Today I really must go out for a shave," Arthur mentions, scratching the dark stubble that furs his cheeks.

So odd to catch him less than chic, unready for the world. "Some coffee first?"

His tongue explores his gums. "My mouth's a little tender."

"Breakfast?" offers Blanche.

Arthur's eyes crinkle at the corners as they rest on her. "I can think of one or two things that might tempt me . . ."

Blanche comes closer. He takes hold of the edge of her nightgown and slides it up her legs. The touch of his thumbnail is all it takes to liquefy her.

A whimper goes up from the salon. She stiffens.

"Oh, give him a chance to settle," murmurs Arthur, hands circling her thighs.

She lets him go on because it's been days and days; the two of them haven't had a chance to lay hands on each other since Sunday. This is more like it. The old Blanche, the ever-new Blanche, Blanche la Danseuse, seen and desired, stroked and seized and parted. Arthur pulls her onto his lap so fast that she loses her balance.

The wail repeats, still weak but penetrating, like a gull wheeling outside the window.

Blanche does her best to ignore it. She's squirming, writhing, in a frenzied tarantella. "*Chérie,*" Arthur murmurs, and she thinks it's an endearment but then realizes his hands are pivoting her, so it must be a request. He wants her facing away, so he can squeeze her breasts while she rides him, his hands conducting her movement. Allegro! His plump cock spearing her like a fish in a stream. Presto! Blanche gasps but Arthur won't relent, and every movement feels so damnably good it makes her cry out, but not as loud as P'tit's crying behind that closed door, keening in his battered tin box, sobbing his heart out for the *salope* who's failed him one more time, choking on his own tongue by the sound of it while his mother gets her dirty bliss—

A crash in the salon. Blanche is off the bed with a single shove.

An exasperated groan from Arthur.

Blanche finds P'tit skewed on the floorboards between his trunk and the sofa. She wipes his wet purple face, shushes him, checks his head for new bumps.

Arthur calls from the bedroom. "What the hell—"

"*Ça va,*" she calls back quickly. Well, she hopes P'tit's all right. He's as sweaty as a pig, and she prays he hasn't picked up his father's fever. "Well done," she whispers in one small ear. Climbing out of his trunk, that's something new he's learned: a sign of progress, surely? "A clever trick," she murmurs, "but we won't show Papa yet."

P'tit's calmer now, slobbering on his doorknob. The other hand creeps back to his hairline to scratch. A tuft of hair comes out in his fingers.

"Stop that," says Blanche, too sharply.

He lets out another sob.

She wipes the hair out of his hand and soothes him with a little waltz.

By the time she returns to the bedroom, holding P'tit, Arthur's pulling on his long silk socks and tucking his drawers into them. "Don't bother with coffee, I'll stop at a café," he says, not looking up.

"Very well," she replies, equally crisp, jiggling P'tit in her arms. It seems she's always to blame. Because she impulsively rushed P'tit away from Folsom Street four days ago? Or because she gave birth to him in the first place?

Arthur scratches his face, and then one sole. "It's tonight you dance, yeah?"

"Oh, will you be minding the baby?" she asks sarcastically instead of answering. Arthur's lost track, because it was last night, Wednesday, that the Lively Flea should have been displaying her charms at the House of Mirrors. Blanche very much doubts Madame Johanna was able to rustle up another headline act half as appealing. Sal, in the hat shaped like a horse's head? Scheherazade (born Mabel), gauzy veil over her nose, doing the hootchi-kootchi? Pleasurably, Blanche wonders whether anyone in the regular crowd demanded his money back.

Arthur's eyes have narrowed. "Watch your mouth." He's tightening his waistband, adjusting the buckle at the small of his back.

Is some of Jenny's cockiness rubbing off on her? Blanche wonders. Or is it just high time Blanche started standing up for herself?

The man's still hard for her; she can see that through the fine cloth of his narrow trousers. Despite her irritation, she throbs to finish what they started. If it weren't for P'tit on her hip, she'd push Arthur backward onto the bed and pull those trousers open again. *Teach me to mind my manners,* she'd tell him. *Cram yourself into me, ram me, split me in two.*

He pulls one sock off, rubs the bottom of his foot violently. "Come over here, would you?"

"Oh, Arthur, it's not a convenient time," she begins, cross at the thought of starting all over again and getting interrupted before she comes off. "Once he's asleep—"

"Just tell me what I'm looking at, if it's not too *inconvenient.*"

She steps closer. Stares at the red marks clustering on

Arthur's yellowish sole. Almost laughs, because it's incongruous: pimples on the flat of a foot. Or perhaps just a heat rash, like the one P'tit had when she brought him home. Her mind is circling, considering possibilities. All the things this spray of red on Arthur's foot—and his face, she can see it there too, now she's looking, the angry pattern rising through the stubble—all the things this kind of marking could mean . . .

"No." Arthur says it with authority. Draws himself up, the magnificent artiste Blanche fell in love with almost a decade ago.

"No," she chimes in. But instead of reassuring her man, reaching out to touch him, she finds her arms tightening around P'tit as she edges backward.

"Come to Chinatown? Are you mad, woman?" asks the doctor.

Blanche swallows a sob. She's left Arthur alone at the apartment, speechless, swigging brandy to ease his panic. Her lungs hurt from hurrying up and down hills with P'tit in her sweaty arms like some badly folded blanket. The first three doctors she approached shied away from her as soon as she mentioned her man had a rash on soles and face. The third charged her a whole dollar for a bottle of something labeled *Anti-Smallpox Specific,* though she suspects it's just sugared whiskey. This fourth fellow, an Irishman in a tiny room above an outfitter's halfway up Nob Hill, is buttoned up to the throat, a rubber handkerchief pinned over his face, so all she can see are the wary, rabbity eyes. "Please," she tries again. "Just to take a look—"

"I've seen what it looks like," he says gruffly. "And it won't get any prettier."

"But can't you—"

"He'll need opium for the pain. Are you vaccinated?"

"We both got the scratch, years and years ago," she protests.

"I'm sick to the back teeth of telling folks that the effect wears off." The eyes above the creamy rubber tighten with irritation.

Blanche stares at him. So ever since the smallpox came to town, she and Arthur and Ernest have been swanning round believing they were protected when they were only ignorant?

"I'll do you and the baby now, at least," says the doctor with a sigh.

She's too abashed to say no, though she flinches at the lancet he pulls out of his case.

He rubs the stuff into the cut on her arm with more force than seems required; Blanche chews her lip so as not to sob. He's gentler with P'tit, though he still makes him cry. "You aren't to be thinking this is a surefire thing," the doctor warns her.

"You mean it won't keep us safe?"

"Nobody's safe, woman. Especially not a mite of a thing like this," he comments, tying a bandage around P'tit's spindly arm, "so keep the pair of you away from bad cases."

This is the first genuine doctor's office she's been in on this side of the Atlantic; he's got a certificate on the wall. She should ask, while she's here. "Rickets." Blanche makes herself pronounce the memorized word. "Is that what it would be called, Doctor, when a baby looks like this?"

The eyes above the mask flick between P'tit and Blanche's peach silk skirt with what she recognizes as contempt. "That's one word for it."

Sunday morning, a tap at the door. Blanche lays P'tit down on the rug with his doorknob and rushes to intercept Gudrun. Measles, that's what Blanche told all her lodgers yesterday when she went round to collect their rents. That seemed better than saying nothing. "Best not come in today either," she tells the Swede now, as lightly as she can manage. "Arthur's still rather unwell and can't bear noise."

A faint but ragged cry from the bedroom. Blanche wipes sweat out of her eyes. With all those sores in his mouth, Arthur can barely form a word. Ernest is with him, she reminds herself.

"Not measles," says Gudrun, taking a step back on the landing.

The sore on Blanche's upper arm is throbbing, and P'tit's is swollen too. Their new vaccinations must have been from a bad batch. But does that mean they were fake, from some tube of slime a swindler sold the Irish doctor, or the opposite, that they were too virulent, in which case they should at least keep the disease at bay? That's what's distracting Blanche as she stares down Gudrun. "If you could boil up these sheets for me in your room," she presses on.

"I don't believe is measles."

Their eyes lock hard.

"It's not allowed to hide," mumbles the Swede.

Is Gudrun threatening to report them to the board of health? Blanche sways closer and speaks softly. "Do you want this whole building quarantined, really? I suppose you imagine they'll let the rest of you flee before they board us up? Huh! Have you enough food on your shelf for six weeks?"

Tears of terror in the seamstress's milky-blue eyes. "Monsieur should go hospital."

"Don't you read the papers? Nobody's coming out of hospitals alive." Blanche loses control of her voice. "They're slipping in each other's *merde* or lashed to beds and left screaming for water in the dark."

Gudrun shakes.

"All I'm asking is for you to keep your mouth shut. And boil laundry for us upstairs, morning and evening," Blanche adds, pressing her advantage. "I'll pay you good money. You'll be perfectly safe if the water's nearly scalding," she improvises. A sting of conscience—but Blanche can't manage without the girl's help, she reminds herself, and nobody's safe, anyhow. "Just add a cup of this—" She runs to fetch the enormous bottle of carbolic on the table, and pours a jugful for Gudrun. Then goes to fetch the basket full of stained sheets.

When Gudrun's gone, Blanche stands frozen, straining to hear voices from the sickroom. P'tit's fallen into a crumpled doze right on the floor. For a moment there's nothing for Blanche to do: what an unnerving sensation. Nothing, meaning everything. So much she wants to do for Arthur but she mustn't. Blanche remembers having him inside her on Thursday before he noticed the marks on his foot, and she shakes with dread. She mustn't go within arm's length of him now, because of that ache above her elbow, which means she may not be protected at all, and the same goes for P'tit. *Keep the pair of you away from bad cases,* the doctor said, looking at her as if she were the worst mother in the world, and this much is clear: Arthur's case is about as bad as it can be.

Food. That's something to do. What'll she get? A stew, a hash, a pie? It doesn't matter. Milk! Milk for P'tit, how could she have forgotten? But she can't go out till P'tit wakes up, because then she can take him with her so he doesn't bother the men.

This might be P'tit's only nap today, so Blanche mustn't waste this time. What can she do with it?

A creak of the bedroom door. Ernest, emerging with the covered dish he's using as a bedpan. The hot smell clouds the air. Blanche doesn't want him to catch her idle, so she busies herself over by the icebox filling another bottle of cold broth to have ready for P'tit. She glances at Ernest sideways to check his color: no sign of fever in the unshaven, concave cheeks. (She made him rush off to get a fresh scratch as soon as she told him the news about Arthur on Thursday.)

When he's emptied the dish into the covered bucket, he adds carbolic to the water in the basin and rinses the dish, then scours his reddened hands. All this without looking in Blanche's direction.

"Does Arthur want me?" she asks. Too high, like some vain girl.

"His blisters are swelling up," he says, not dignifying her question with an answer.

Christ. After a minute, Blanche asks, "Do you need—shall I get more ice? More laudanum?"

"He can't keep it down," says Ernest, as if she should have known that. "I'm trying morphine."

Has this man slept at all? The words burst from Blanche. "You know I'd be helping you nurse him if it weren't for the baby—"

Like a snake, he turns on her, practically spitting. "The same *foutu* baby you were content to stash out of sight, out of mind, for the past year?"

Blanche bites down on her lip so hard that her eyes water. That's exactly why she must keep P'tit out of harm's way now, why she has to go to such cruel lengths to stay out of range of Arthur's infectious touch and breath. She owes the tiny boy that much, surely. "If I were to catch it, so would P'tit," she wails.

A snort. "For all we know, it's him who brought it."

Blanche's hands contract into fists. "What bull is this?"

"Do you deny he's had a fever?"

"Only since his scratch!"

"The creature's been all coughs, vomits, and itches since you carried him in the door," snarls Ernest. "Too much of a goddamn coincidence, I say, that Arthur took to his bed not two days later . . ."

A vast rage fills Blanche. The City's one great hotbed of contagion, and this *connard* blames P'tit?

Ernest grabs a bottle of wine and some folded cloths from the drawer. Pulls a thin, dripping slab of ice out of the insulated box and wraps it in cheesecloth. "Arthur knows why you won't go near him. You want to save your own *satané* skin."

For a second she doesn't understand.

"Terrified of getting scarred, jeopardizing the porcelain perfection that is Blanche la Danseuse!"

"It's not about my skin, you son of a bitch."

Ernest puts his prominent jaw very close to her, now, and she smells his sweat. "Answer me this. Are you his woman or aren't you?"

I am, Blanche wants to say. *Always.*

He steps back. "If it's really the baby you're so scared for, why not send him away?" he asks with a sneer. "He'd be safer anywhere else."

"Send him where, back to Folsom Street?"

"Send him to the Dakotas, for all I care."

"If he—if I dump my son in one of those places again, he won't make it."

Hissed through his teeth: "And what makes you so sure his father's going to make it?"

Arthur's moaning something in the bedroom. *And*? Could that be what he's saying? *And* what?

Ernest claps his hands by her ear, making her jump. "He's calling your name, *putain.*"

Blanche, that's the sound. *Blanche,* through lips too lesioned to articulate.

She throws a glance at P'tit, still snuffling in shallow sleep on the floor of the salon. Then hurries as far as the door. If she goes into the bedroom but holds her breath—if she doesn't touch anything—

Ernest pushes in past her.

Blanche pulls out a handkerchief and presses it over her nose as she follows him, foot by foot, into the stinking room. *"Chéri?"* Muffled by the cloth that she hopes will somehow shield her.

The bare windows let in a merciless light. The man on the bed, wearing nothing but sweat-darkened drawers, is unrecognizable. Hair pushes through the scarlet pustules on his face and neck: a mask of burning wood. Dimpled red pearls, densest on his feet and hands and all across what used to be his lovely face. No, they're a swarm of bloated ants up his legs and arms, converging on the plains of his chest and belly.

Ernest, his face blank as any stoic's, starts to cover Arthur with cloths dipped in ice water. He lifts one of his friend's feet—so the swollen sole won't chafe against the sheet, she supposes. The muscular legs are bowed froggishly now. Ernest wets a rag with carbolic solution and very slowly wipes the seeping pustules on the foot. Even from the doorway, she can see the opalescent slime. He bunches the rag up, tosses it into a bucket, and begins again.

Blanche is trying not to gag. "I'm here, *mon amour,*" she says. The line sounds stagy. "Right here." Technically true: about six feet from where Arthur lies.

A strange droning comes from his throat for an answer. It goes higher. Descant variations on a tune of pain.

"Time for another morphine suppository," Ernest mutters under his breath.

It's clear to Blanche now that this is not just the camaraderie of two members of an old double act who keep each other company on the streets of San Francisco. Nothing could make someone do what Ernest is doing except love.

"What can I—"

"See to the brat," barks Ernest.

Only then does she realize that P'tit's wailing in the other room.

Side to side, forward and back, Blanche shuffles across the apartment on the first day of September, humming in P'tit's minute ear.

For a week and a half Arthur's seemed on the verge of death, yet the days stumble on. Blanche still eats, moves, even sleeps on and off, and babies always need looking after, especially this one, whose unfathomable eyes gaze on the world expecting the worst. *You're here now,* she wants to tell P'tit with a little shake. Here's Blanche, a woman who's willing to pick him up when he cries in the middle of the night. His mother. (The word still doesn't trip off her tongue.) A woman who's been neglecting her beloved as he lies ill, all for this disconsolate baby's sake. So why does P'tit still have the air of a parcel forgotten at a train station? She hums on. Scraps of opera, gutter choruses, sea chanteys, rhymes from the crowded little schoolroom on the Ile Saint-Louis that Blanche didn't know she remembered, any old piety or filth that might distract him: the whole repertoire of her quarter century.

Even hotter today. How can that be? Has the whole climate of the Bay been knocked off balance somehow?

Toward evening, Blanche thinks she hears a roll of thunder, but her ears might be tricking her. Her arm muscles are getting hard from nearly two weeks of carrying P'tit around. At this point she'd hire Satan himself as a nursemaid, but nobody will come near a yellow-flagged building, let alone move into it.

Her lodgers mutter together on the landings. They won't forgive Blanche for the measles story. She'd better not knock on their doors for their rents tomorrow. Blanche has no idea whether it was Gudrun or someone else who reported Arthur's case to the board of health; all she knows is that last time she went downstairs to the faucet and stepped out onto Sacramento to take a breath, there was a gaudy yellow flag hanging over the front door. But why haven't the inspectors turned up at the apartment door with all their fumigation apparatus demanding that Arthur be handed over? Perhaps the hospitals are all full. Blanche doesn't know because she hasn't bought a paper in days.

It doesn't matter. Nothing matters but Arthur and P'tit. Arthur because he's so ill; P'tit because she mustn't let him get ill. Her man and her child. How can Blanche weigh them against each other, and why should she have to?

P'tit's had enough of his bottle now, and he's slobbering over his doorknob. (She washes it when his grip loosens, in sleep, but she still hates the sight of the thing.) He must be teething, Blanche supposes. But then again, maybe teething's just what you call it when a child is cantankerous.

Ernest comes out with another bucket of rags to soak. He's a walking corpse. She tries to remember the last time she saw the young man eat more than a bite of anything. Oddly enough, they've never spent such a stretch of time together; they go about their different duties like an old married couple, with Arthur the child they dread to lose. But no, Ernest's more like the mother who sees to all the dreadful, intimate requirements of the sick. Blanche just goes out to buy whatever he asks or hauls water from the faucet downstairs, afraid to say a word to him.

The silence in the salon jars her nerves. Perhaps she'll go in and say a word, at least, to Arthur, while Ernest's busy.

Blanche plants P'tit beside the sofa. He can sit up these days. That's something, she thinks glumly.

She turns the door handle. Every day she thinks Arthur can't get any worse. She never knew the body could endure such changes. Today his hands are embroidered with huge rubies each half an inch across, globes so thick on his right lid that he can't open his eye. Blanche presses her handkerchief over her mouth and nose not because she thinks it'll keep out the invisible germs but to shut out the sweet, rotten stench. She gags, and it's not just the smell, it's the thought of the unbearable pressure Arthur must be suffering as each globe bloats and leaks. Is her lover going to burst apart in the end, dynamited from inside his own skin?

"It's Blanche," she says, though it comes out so husky she's not sure Arthur can hear her. Her eyes prickle with tears. Perhaps he's past hearing, so far away in his opiate nightmare that nothing reaches him from this shore. Besides, is there any truth left in that claim, *It's Blanche*? Is this still her, or is it some shoddy copy of the lively *petite amie* who followed him all the way to America? She is different these days, she knows that. Was it meeting Jenny Bonnet that began the metamorphosis? Or taking P'tit away from Folsom Street? Or has this different, older, somehow harder Blanche been hidden inside her all along?

She stands very still, watching for the slight rise and fall of Arthur's breath.

A hard rat-a-tat: the front door. She bolts out to the salon.

Ernest, tugging an obstinate shard out of the icebox, is ignoring it.

After a moment, Blanche decides he's right. Too risky to answer the door, especially at this time of the evening.

P'tit has slid to an uncomfortable angle. He's patting the carved leg of the sofa as if it's a pet. Blanche plucks him off the floor and walks him up and down, just for something to do, so Ernest can't accuse her of doing nothing.

"Hou-hou!" A muffled call through the door.

Blanche unlocks it one-handed to find Jenny, her smile a little softened with drink. Blanche hasn't seen her for the best part of two weeks. The tanned face looks as if it's never been battered, and her suit's even been laundered. She steps in jauntily, not waiting to be asked.

Blanche is suddenly aware of the danger for the visitor. "Didn't you notice the yellow flag?"

"I tore that down," mutters Ernest, still wrestling with the icebox.

She expects him to tell Jenny to get the hell out, but he reverts to silence.

"City's so carpeted with the things, it might be Carnival," remarks Jenny. "Who's sick? Not the baby?"

"Arthur," says Blanche, the name a stone in her throat.

Jenny grimaces and holds up a half-empty bottle. "Anyone fancy some rye?"

Blanche realizes that she does, very much.

Ernest comes over with two glasses to be filled. Then he

carries them into the sickroom, shutting the door behind him.

"Wouldn't have credited that dandy man for a nurse," Jenny remarks under her breath.

"I can't do it—I've got to—" Blanche's voice fractures, and she gestures down at the baby.

Jenny nods, and drains her glass in one. "Phew, it stinks in here. Let's get out for some air."

There's nothing Blanche would like more, but she has P'tit to look after.

"High time he saw something of his hometown," says Jenny, reading her mind.

She's right, Blanche decides. They need some air. "Keep an eye on him, then, while I make myself presentable," she says, parking P'tit on the floor, where he immediately starts to cry.

"Presentable for whom, pray tell?"

Jenny's mocking line follows Blanche into the little lavatory, where she scrabbles in her bag for her rouge. She's not going out without a bit of paint and a freshly pinned chignon, at least. The half-melted kohl keeps getting in her eye, so she blinks the flecks of black away.

When she emerges to choose a fluted wrapper from the trunk of clothes behind the sofa, she finds Jenny clapping for the baby. P'tit's expression is grave, as if he's listening for the melodic line in some almost inaudible symphony. But he is clapping along: slow, silent pats, palm to palm.

Blanche, dressed now, scoops P'tit up and follows Jenny toward the door. The strains of a melancholy violin rise from the bedroom.

"Ernest?" murmurs Jenny, eyebrows up.

"It soothes Arthur," Blanche whispers.

"Wouldn't soothe me, I'll tell you that much."

"*Chut,*" she shushes her, with an appalled grin.

Jenny leaves her bicycle where it's resting in the stairwell, and they step out onto Sacramento Street. The air's as baking hot as ever, but more breathable than in the apartment—or maybe it just seems that way because Blanche hasn't been out in days. The gaslit sidewalks are as crowded as if it's broad daylight.

"How long's Arthur had it?" asks Jenny.

"Tomorrow's the twelfth day," says Blanche.

"The fever hasn't come back?"

"No."

"Still breathing easily?"

"I suppose." Breathing's about all Arthur can manage.

"The Chinese call them beautiful flowers."

"What?"

"The blisters," says Jenny. "To flatter the goddess, don't you know—so she'll spare them and move on."

"Which goddess?"

"The smallpox goddess."

"They've got a goddess of goddamn smallpox?" asks Blanche.

Suddenly they're both giggling like children.

Blanche sobers fast. "The thing is, I heard from an iceman—and Ernest read it, somewhere too," she adds, "that if a smallpox case is going to make it, you'll know on the twelfth day, because the blisters start scabbing over."

"*When,*" says Jenny.

"What?" asks Blanche, confused.

"No need for ifs. *When* they scab over."

Blanche gnaws her lip and tastes blood. "You haven't seen Arthur."

"Still, I say your fancy man's going to come through." Jenny spins a stick and catches it on the back of her hand. "He's getting good care."

"Not from me." Guilt webbing in her throat.

"You're keeping his son safe. He'll understand."

Blanche wishes she believed that.

"How about his eyes, are they white?"

"Brown," answers Blanche, startled.

"The whites of them," Jenny clarifies.

Blanche is too ashamed to admit that she hasn't been close enough to Arthur to check his eyeballs.

"Most folks are surviving this, I heard, eyesight and all," says Jenny. "Sometimes barely a mark on them."

"I don't care if Arthur ends up with a few *marks*," Blanche snaps.

P'tit's getting heavy; she should have thought to bring a shawl to tie him on her back or hip, the way country women do. Though, now that Blanche pictures it, she realizes she can't bear the notion of looking like one of them. She'd rather shift him from shoulder to aching shoulder. It doesn't seem to occur to Jenny to offer to carry him awhile. Sometimes it strikes Blanche that she might be better off with an ordinary friend.

A pungent reek makes her glance sideways down the next alley. After a stall where two men in long aprons are gutting fish, there's a run of narrow buildings with those sliding door panels that display the blank faces of *mui jai,* Chinese girls standing ready for hire. "I wonder what they charge," says Blanche with professional curiosity.

"Don't you know the rhyme? Two bittee lookee, four bittee feelee, six bittee doee."

"Really?" Six bits; that's only seventy-five cents. "You wouldn't get a white girl or a Mexican for less than a dollar," says Blanche a little disapprovingly.

"Of course, the *mui jai* don't see a cent of that. So much for the abolition of slavery," adds Jenny, sardonic.

They're heading east, without discussion, as if a glimpse of the Bay promises an evening breeze, though they should know better, thinks Blanche. A Chilean in a poncho walks right into her as if he doesn't see her, almost knocking P'tit out of her arms. The baby doesn't make a sound. He seems stunned by the colors and cries of the passing multitude. This is said to be the foreignest city in America; almost none of these people were born here. Back in Paris, Blanche remembers, there are so many protocols, so many ways to behave *comme il faut,* "as things are done," because that's how things have always been done. But San Francisco's a roulette wheel, spinning its citizens and depositing them at random. Blanche has been driven around by cabbies who've claimed to be gentlemen temporarily down on their luck, and she's spent well-paid nights with *michetons* who've boasted that they began as coal miners.

Jenny lifts her hat at a one-man band in faded stripes, who nods at her. He's got pipes on a wire bracket around his neck, a fiddle in his hand, a large bass drum on his back. His elderly whine barely mounts over the skirmish of his instruments.

I'll scrape the mountains clean, my boys,
I'll drain the rivers dry,
A pocketful of rocks bring home—
So brothers don't you cry!

No ears, curiously, just little nubs; it must be that you need only the holes to hear with. "I never saw anyone earless in Paris. I wonder why so many Americans are born that way," remarks Blanche, jerking her thumb at him. "Something in the diet here?"

Jenny cackles.

"What?"

"That's how they dealt with thieves back in the Rush. Miners hadn't got time to spare for jurifying. Just lopped the guilty party's ears off"—with a nod in the direction of the old musician—"and went back to panning."

A year and a half here, Blanche thinks, disconcerted, and there's so much she still doesn't know about this country. The chorus fades behind them:

Oh, California,
That's the land for me!
I'm bound for San Francisco
With my washbowl on my knee.

"This way," says Jenny, suddenly ducking down Battery Street.

"Why?" asks Blanche, but she follows.

"Specials." Jenny glances over her shoulder to check that the pair of private guards is going the other way.

It amuses Blanche to see Jenny even slightly rattled.

"I thought it was only the cops who bother you—actual patrolmen."

"Well, as a point of law, they're the only ones with the power to arrest me," mutters Jenny, "but Specials like to impress their employers and earn tips by rounding up riff-raff and handing them over to the patrol."

Her gray coat, waistcoat, pants, soft hat—they seem so ordinary to Blanche now, it's hard to remember that Jenny's wearing them constitutes a crime. "And it's all worth the candle?"

"Come on," Jenny groans, "don't tell me you wouldn't put up a fight if someone tried to make you swap your tight frills for a grain sack . . ." She tugs at Blanche's mauve wrapper.

They pass an enormous organ on a cart: hundreds of pipes, and sinister-looking automata dancing on top to "The Ride of the Valkyries." The grinder cranks on with his right arm, which Blanche notices is nearly twice the size of his left, and with barely a pause the tune changes jarringly to the Habanera from *Carmen.*

Then they're going up a hill so steep she can't talk and carry P'tit at the same time. She should be turning back soon. What if Arthur needs something? "I'm bushed," she says at the top, panting, as she transfers P'tit to her other arm.

"Already? I like to stroll from Fisherman's Wharf to the Mission and right over to the Panhandle, just to see what's new," says Jenny. "The City's always growing like blazes, doubling every decade."

Blanche finds the thought unsettling. "Sounds like some ugly fungus."

"That's the fun of it. Take the loveliest spot on earth," says Jenny, arms out to encompass hill after hill, the Bay, the Pacific, "and scatter a litter of sooty old shacks all over it . . . It's a striking contrast for the eye, wouldn't you say? Then, for novelty, give the whole place the DTs."

Blanche laughs, nodding. "There was a bad tremor back in January that woke me up."

"You thought that little shimmy was bad?" Jenny crows. "Should have been here for the big one eight years back, when the City fell down around our ears. I'd been out on a bender, so I was half convinced I was seeing things. Cracks in walls opening and shutting like mouths . . . a four-story frontage dropped right off while I was watching."

Blanche winces.

"Fires, too, every couple years. When our ship came in, in '51, the whole place was up in flames. Streets charring, fir planks curling up like snakes . . ."

"You make it sound like the time of your life," Blanche objects.

Jenny dances from foot to foot. "Don't everyone crave a little zest to make one day different from the last?"

"Not that much zest," says Blanche. Thinking: *I liked my days the way they were, before everything changed.* After a minute, she asks, "Have you ever roamed farther afield?"

"Not too far yet," admits Jenny with a touch of sheepishness. "Been to Sacramento once, though it was knee-deep in water at the time."

"That would suit a swamp-wader like you," jokes Blanche, letting P'tit slide down to her hip.

"'Course, now that it's the terminus of the Transcontinental Railroad, I hear Sacramento's getting aspirations. They're bringing Chinese in to build up the levees, filling in the old streets, moving everybody up to the second floor."

"You're pulling my leg."

Jenny shakes her head. "Or if a building's got only one story, they use screw jacks and winch the whole shebang fifteen feet into the air." She's distracted by something in a store window. An odd-looking shotgun lies right-angled, as if snapped in two, on a satin pillow with an engraved card: *The Long-Awaited Anson and Deeley Boxlock.* Tapping on the next window, Jenny remarks, "You could think of having him sit for a new photograph."

Sometimes Jenny's non sequiturs make Blanche's head spin. Is this some kind of cruel joke about Arthur's face?

"The kid, I mean."

"Oh." When she looks closer, she sees the display is headed *Infant Carte de Visites and Cabinet Cards.* Discomfited, Blanche looks down at P'tit.

"The picture beside your bed's not much of a likeness anymore."

"Maybe when he's . . . grown a little," says Blanche. The photographs behind the glass show fat, bland babies in embroidered gowns. Maybe once P'tit's got some more hair to cover that protruding forehead, and a tooth or two, when he's no longer so red and scaly . . .

"He's bigger and stronger already," says Jenny as they walk on. "You're just too close up to notice."

"He can't do much more than flap around like a fish on dry land," Blanche complains. "Sometimes I think he'll never learn to crawl, even. I'll be hauling him around like some millstone for the rest of my days."

"Why'd you name him P'tit? Because he's undersized?"

She shakes her head. "For his father—he's really P'tit Arthur." Saying Arthur's name hurts her throat. Those bloodred blisters. "I was christened Adèle myself," she adds. Only the small sensation—a coin dropping—alerts her to the fact that this is the first time she's mentioned it to anyone in America. "Blanche was my circus name."

"When did you switch?"

"On the ship."

"Because America's one big circus?"

That makes Blanche laugh.

"He smiled," cries Jenny, pointing.

She examines P'tit's pained face. "Probably just wind."

Up ahead, the busy thoroughfare of Market Street slashes diagonally toward the docks. Blanche turns back west on Bush Street.

Jenny follows her, asking, "Why didn't Arthur and Ernest change to their circus names too?"

"Maybe because it might be hard to get much respect down at the Exchange," says Blanche, "going by Castor and Pollux."

Jenny sniggers at that.

"They took the names from the pair of elephants at the Paris Zoo. Who got butchered when we were under siege by the Prussians," Blanche adds regretfully.

Ernest insisted they should at least taste the original Castor and Pollux, as what he called a mark of respect, so he stood in line for hours and paid an appalling price for a slice. He and Arthur agreed that it was tough and oily, but Blanche wasn't able to bring herself even to taste it, despite her hunger. Dog, cat, rat. That winter, Paris restaurants vied with one another to see who could serve them up in the most delectable sauces, defying the invaders.

"If you were all such toasts of the town back at your Cirque d'Hiver, what made you give it up and come over here?"

Machine-Kneaded Bread, Blanche reads on a card in a storefront, *Guaranteed Free of Dangerous Perspiration.* "It was time for a change."

"Meaning, none of my business?"

"Arthur fell," says Blanche with difficulty. "His back—"

"Ah," says Jenny.

It was only a month after Blanche told Arthur she was pregnant. She was lacing herself tight to hide it from Monsieur Loyal and praying he'd take her back on after the confinement. "The crowd usually swoon for the flier because they think it's all his doing," says Blanche, "that he's somersaulting through the air, and the lanky fellow dangling upside down like a bat is just there for the flier to grab on to, see?"

Jenny's nodding.

"But the truth is, it's the catcher who times it all and makes the catch. His flier just has to trust him and fly."

"So what went wrong?"

"Arthur . . ." Blanche sighs. "Maybe he lost his nerve, I don't know. But it looked to me as if he snatched at Ernest's wrists and then slipped through his fingers." The plummet to the ground, the terrible sound.

"So it wasn't Ernest's fault that his old pal cracked his spine."

"Try convincing Ernest of that," says Blanche with a snort. Is that why Ernest is risking his own life to nurse Arthur now? she wonders. In Ernest's mind, does he owe Arthur a lifetime of protection—by some kind of unwritten contract—for having once let him fall?

They're going past the open door of a fan-tan joint where copper coins are heaped high and Chinese men shout their bets through the thick fog of smoke.

Jenny brushes a bill-papered wall with her fingertips. "Saw this astounding dog act one time," she remarks. "There was a rope hanging from the top of the tent, and the little fellow jumped higher than his head and grabbed it between his teeth—"

"A terrier?" Blanche wants to know.

A nod. "He bit down and wouldn't let go, swung all over the place, better than any of the acrobats. Holding on with his teeth!"

"Dogs, horses, they're born to please," Blanche tells her. "Now, house cats—I don't know why folks keep trying to come up with cat acts. You can bribe or beat a cat all day, and it's still going to sneak off through a slit in the curtain as soon as your back is turned."

Jenny's not listening, because she's studying a broadside pasted to a telegraph pole.

> Professor of Dancing, Newly Arrived from Philadelphia, Offers Instructions on the Latest Dances à la Mode as Seen in the Ballrooms of London and Paris. Expert on the Quadrille, German, Valse, Schottische, Zulma, Varsouvienne, Boston Dip, Redowa, Gorlitza, Galop, and Polka Mazurka.

" 'Private Lessons for Young Ladies,' " Jenny reads aloud from the bottom of the page. "I'll bet," she adds with a snigger.

" 'Send Them to Dancing School and Save Many a Doctor's Bill,' " Blanche reads over her shoulder. "Health is a smart angle. But the quack's not as à la mode as he thinks. I wouldn't be caught dead dancing the redowa anymore."

"You know all these fiddly steps?" Jenny asks.

Blanche smiles. "As well as you know your fiddly frogs."

P'tit starts to wail for no reason, as if an invisible assailant has punched him. *Bordel!* There's brown trickling down his leg. Blanche holds him at arm's length.

"He's crying for you," Jenny comments.

"I'm right here," Blanche snaps.

"No, I mean, for *you*—putting on a show for your benefit. I suppose crying's all the music a baby knows."

"Some music." She groans.

Jenny holds out her hands.

"He's all shitty."

"That don't bother me. I've seen it all before."

She deposits P'tit in Jenny's arms, expecting him to shriek, but he only stares at Jenny.

Blanche pulls out a handkerchief and scrubs her hands. "Where have you seen it all before?" This comes out too accusatory. "Have you younger sisters or brothers?"

"I was a shepherd for a while," says Jenny.

Blanche laughs under her breath. A female shepherd. Of course.

By the time she's rubbed the worst off her sleeve and skirt, Jenny and the baby are way ahead. Blanche catches up to them and finds Jenny halfway through the old tale about the Frog Prince, addressing P'tit with utmost seriousness.

He's rapt.

"Is that the one where she's obliged to kiss him in the end?" Blanche breaks in.

Jenny shakes her head. "Not this princess. Froggie asks for a kiss, yeah, but she says he must be kidding," she tells P'tit. "She picks him up and flings him against the wall."

Like the way Blanche has seen Chinese fishermen whack squid against walls to soften them, down at the docks? "Does that kill him?"

"No sirree. Froggie falls down, and up jumps a prince."

But Blanche is still brooding over the version her grandmother told her. The clammy embrace, the moist tickle on the lip. "How could being kissed and being smacked against a wall work the same?"

"Shock, I guess," says Jenny. "Shakes off his sham skin, leaves him wearing his real one."

And Blanche—just for a moment—has a vision as if from high overhead: Herself at the height of rage throwing P'tit against a wall. His scaly, misshapen body cracking in two when it hits, and her son standing up in a smooth and princely form.

She knows these are terrible thoughts, but they're not really hers, she tells herself, they're just the hallucinations of fatigue. She feels Jenny's eyes on her and looks away in case the frog-catcher can catch thoughts too.

Somebody's watching and waiting for him,
Yearning to hold him again to her breast.

It's an old soldier on the ground, bursting into song. No, not on the ground. He's legless, Blanche sees, and what's left of him is wedged into a child's pushcart.

Matted and damp are his tresses of gold,
Kissing the snow of that fair young brow.

The fellow's not so old either, Blanche sees when she looks closer. The War between the States is only a decade back, after all. His voice is richer than some she's heard on the stage; this fellow was wasted on soldiering. He keeps up the maudlin lament that shouldn't move her the way it does.

Pale are the lips of most delicate mold,
Somebody's darling is dying now.

She takes P'tit back from Jenny without a word, presses him against her collarbone.

Jenny sketches a salute and drops a coin into the soldier's tin cup.

Somebody's watching over Arthur, *somebody's waiting* to see if he'll make it, but it's not Blanche. What if she goes back to the apartment tonight and Arthur's lying utterly still in the bed that used to be theirs? She can't bear for his pain to go on but she can't wish it all to be over. He's not even thirty-two. And what would become of Blanche then? She can't imagine her life in San Francisco without Arthur. It drifts apart, in her mind, like shreds of fog.

They turn north up Dupont. Jenny flourishes her hand

at a restaurant, the Poodle Dog. "Famous for its *cuisses de grenouille à la poulette,* courtesy of yours truly."

Also famous for its third-floor assignation rooms, Blanche remembers, in one of which she spent a tiring night with a miner with black-rimmed nails who left her a bag of gold dust the weight of a plum.

Chinatown, lacking gaslights, marks its territory with red paper lamps, and the glowing globes remind Blanche that this stroll is nearly over. She dreads the thought of home.

She suddenly steps sideways. For explanation, she holds up her left boot.

"Sure is the biggest turd I've seen in some time," says Jenny. "Dog?"

"Let's hope so. That's a week of luck." Blanche scrapes it off her shoe using the frayed edge of the sidewalk, thinking of Arthur.

Jenny whoops with laughter. "I thought the whole point of luck is that it just happens."

Blanche purses her lips. "Maybe you can grab it sometimes, if you see it passing."

The hot sky's black by the time they reach 815 Sacramento. "I'm off," remarks Jenny in the stairwell, collecting her machine.

"Where to?"

"High-wheeling around."

"But where'll you sleep?"

"Ain't tired," Jenny assures her. "I already snoozed half the day away in Portsmouth Square."

"*À bientôt,* then," says Blanche shortly and heads up the stairs, P'tit heavy with sleep against her chest.

"Very soon. *Bonne chance,* and all that."

But it's not luck Blanche needs, it's knowledge. Someone who understands the obscure miseries of babies. Someone who's stumbled on a cure for smallpox. Someone who'd stay and make everything better instead of zipping off down the street whistling a tune Blanche doesn't know.

Upstairs, the apartment is silent. She manages to change P'tit's diaper without waking him, which is a minor miracle. Once she's put him in his trunk, she's weary enough to drop right down on the sofa in her street clothes. But first she makes herself go to the slightly open door of the sickroom.

That awful, sweet odor. Mercifully dim in here now, so she can't see anything but the silhouette of Ernest bent over the bed. Arthur moans, deep in his dream. Blanche's eyes adjust. Ernest seems to be bandaging—no, he's tying Arthur to the bedstead with long strips of cotton.

"What the hell—" Her whisper comes out louder than it's meant to.

Ernest turns on her. "Oh, *now* you come home?"

"What are you doing to him?"

"Stopping him from scratching." Ernest turns back to his meticulous work of looping the cotton around Arthur's slack wrists and attaching the strips to the metal frame. "Three scabs on his eyelid this evening, and they're itching like the devil. If he scratches them, he could blind himself."

Scabs?

The twelfth day.

It hits her: they're not going to lose Arthur after all.

*

It's the fifteenth of September, one day since Blanche should have died at San Miguel Station. Paying for her ham sandwich on Clay Street, for the first time since she's come to America she doesn't leave a tip on the counter. She stares into her pocketbook, adding up the coins. That icy Madame, with her invented *expenses,* has reduced Blanche to this, a fretful miser. Maybe Blanche should have gone to one of those free lunch places where all you have to pay for is your drink. Maybe she should have invited a stranger to buy her a proper meal.

Arthur could be watching her this very moment. She knows she's an easy target, standing a couple of blocks from her own building in broad daylight, as bright as some maypole in her blue plaid and yellow stockings. She shrinks behind her parasol and chews the sandwich so fast she almost chokes.

Her eyes are resting on a newsboy at the corner of Kearny. His cap and the impression he gives of only half filling his shabby blue jacket remind her of Jenny. "*Chronicle,* latest *Chronicle,* afternoon edition," he's bawling, pale behind his inky smears. Only now does Blanche's brain register what's printed on his big sign: FOUL MURDER; TROUSERED PUZZLE.

She shouldn't read it. What possible good will it do her to—

She gallops down to him and holds out a coin, unable to speak. Somehow afraid that this *gamin* will guess Blanche is part of the story behind his shrill headlines.

She finds a wall to lean against. Angles her parasol to hide her face as she fingers the front page. An engraving of a glum-looking woman in a sack suit; is that supposed to be Jenny? *Unknown Assassin,* says the headline. Blanche skips over the details she already knows. How bizarre to see what she lived through last night turned into an item tucked between stock prices and Crazy Horse whupping the army at Little Bighorn. Cartwright sounds as if he's still down there in San Miguel Station. He must have composed the piece in a terrible rush for it to be printed and sold all through the City already. Could he have telegraphed his report in? Blanche glances up at the nearest pole, picturing words hissing like lightning along the thin skein of wire.

He calls Jenny the Little Frog-Catcher. Why "little," when she was pretty tall for a woman? That has the ring of some sentimental novel. And "masquerading in men's clothing"—that sets Blanche's teeth on edge; was it Jenny's fault if her pants made unobservant people jump to the wrong conclusions?

> . . . had a strong distaste for domestic drudgery. She could hardly chase amphibians in trailing skirts and, besides, regarded the prohibition on the wearing of trousers as arbitrary and oppressive.

The journalist sounds as if he likes what he knows of Jenny but thinks it was somehow her own doing—or at least, to be expected—that she got herself blown to pieces. Blanche is reading too fast now, and she loses the thread. She doubles back.

> A real strong-minded, unconventional "character," who got into scrapes with the law from a tender age

> and whose arrests were prompted as much by drunken belligerence, truth be told, as by her eccentric costume and—

Arrested for "drunken belligerence"? Does Cartwright have a source among the patrolmen for that? "Truth be told." He's probably making up this moonshine himself.

Blanche leafs through the pages to track down the second half of the story, eyes flicking over hundreds of other items in tiny print. The heat wave's killing children in record numbers. Vandals who open hydrants will be liable to prosecution. A sketch of a rather lovely striped bonnet. "City health officer calls Orientals who refuse to report smallpox cases 'tens of thousands of treacherous snakes in our very bosom.' "

"Possibly Jenny was frail." That word trips Blanche up; she reads it again, and anger pulses behind her eyes. *Frail:* a namby-pamby euphemism for selling it. Oh, so now the pallid newsman is claiming Jenny was on the town? That's rich.

> . . . a social outlaw, then, but not deserving of persecution, especially in these United States to which so many are drawn by the promise of tolerance. It is to be hoped that the cowardly assassin who cut short the thread of her life will be brought to the gallows he rightly deserves.

Now Blanche's gaze snags on her own name, the first time she's ever seen it in print, except on a broadside outside the House of Mirrors. "A Frenchwoman of no character who performs at one of Chinatown's most notorious white establishments." That stings, although it's absurd for her to care. "Here follows the murdered girl's companion's story." Which sounds comical, something from a children's rhyme about the miller's wife's cousin's shoe . . .

The bed, the flying glass, a diagram of the McNamaras' four-room house with dotted lines to show the bullets angling in the front left window, going over the bent form of the "murdered girl's companion," right through the body of the Little Frog-Catcher, some of them even punching through the partition wall and flying past Ellen McNamara's head.

Nothing at all about Arthur Deneve. Did Cartwright listen to a word Blanche told him this morning? The man gives Jenny's dying words as "Adieu, I follow my sister." What sister? Sappy hogwash!

She reads on anyhow, hungry for any details, reliable or not. "Long before she took to the batrachian trade, Jenny dazzled in juvenile parts alongside her thespian progenitors." Blanche rereads that, puzzling over a couple of the words. Jenny, a child star following her parents—or letting them bully her—onto the stage? Blanche tries to picture her in frills and face paint, warbling and pirouetting. Actually, the image is not so incongruous. Jenny was a swaggering braggart; Blanche can easily imagine her putting on a great show of girlishness, if that was the role assigned. "On losing a third child, Madame Bonnet took to the demon drink, neglecting her first two," she reads. That's pretty specific; this can't all be invented, surely? "On her consequent demise the family was quite broken up."

Gone to the devil, wasn't that what Jenny quipped when Blanche asked about the Bonnets?

"The younger sister, Blanche, subsequently died at the state asylum at Stockton." Blanche blinks. The sister again. Could Cartwright have muddled up the names? Wouldn't Jenny have mentioned it if she had a sister called the same thing as her new friend Blanche—even if she didn't want to volunteer the information that the girl was a lunatic?

But no, of course; Jenny would rather dig up other people's histories than reveal the most basic information about her own. She liked to give the impression that she'd shrugged off her past with other cumbersome gear. As if she were entirely made up of transient stuff: stories, songs, and jokes. Blanche should have asked more questions and insisted on a few answers.

Altercation. Mayhem. Alibi. They turn Blanche's stomach, all these eagerly crowding words. She squints at the smeary print, trying to find the facts. The stableman, Charles St. Clair, who came out to San Miguel Station the day before the murder and had an argument with Jenny and Blanche about the rented buggy—Cartwright describes him as being "in the clear," because the other stablemen at Marshall's swear he was hard at work till after nine on Thursday night. "Deneve." Here's Arthur's name at last; Blanche goes back.

> Beunon is quick to point the finger of suspicion at her cast-off *maquereau,* Arthur Deneve, and his intimate Ernest Girard who she attests made threats of violence against both herself and Bonnet. But after the couple's sudden and acrimonious separation more than a week

ago, the said Deneve is known to have left the City for either the eastern states or his native France.

Blanche blinks at the words but they still don't sink in. "Known to have left the City." Known; who knows it? Who told Cartwright? How long *after* the separation? Arthur wouldn't have just upped and left town, surely. He did threaten to when he and Blanche argued at the faro table the other night, but surely that was bluster. Would he really abandon his life here?

When she and Jenny ran into Ernest four days ago on Waverly Place, he was alone, Blanche remembers. Could the Siamese twins have had a falling-out? Or has Ernest left town too, by now, and joined his comrade in France or the eastern states?

If it's true that Arthur's gone—

She drops the newspaper on the dusty sidewalk. Is it possible that Blanche has spent a week hiding from Arthur and a night and a day thinking him a murderer when he hasn't even been in California?

Don't be an idiot, she scolds herself. She knows he killed Jenny. It's weakness in her to let herself hope otherwise. Why believe Cartwright on this point when his whole article is riddled with inventions? No, Blanche knows in her bones that Arthur shot Jenny by mistake, aiming for Blanche. She knows, because she's aware she's done some things to half deserve it. (*Are you his woman or aren't you?* Ernest demanded when Arthur was on the verge of death.) She can feel Arthur's wrath even now, its long steel muzzle aimed at her across the City.

And P'tit. That's the real reason she'd rather not

believe Arthur fired the gun. Because if the father of her child doesn't have blood on his hands, if he's just a furious man like other men, then perhaps P'tit is safe and sound. Slumped against the wall, Blanche presses her eyeballs so hard, she sees spots. Dead, her child is probably dead, but probably isn't definitely, is it? Arthur could have rid himself of the nuisance of P'tit in some more temporary way, by sending him somewhere, some awful place like Doctress Hoffman's. P'tit could well be alive. Retrievable, salvageable. Blanche might as well hold on to that, since she has nothing else.

She looks down Kearny toward the corner of Sacramento. Because she's realized something. If there is any seed of truth in Cartwright's fabrications—if someone from the *Chronicle* went to number 815, asked around, and was told that Deneve had left town—then it may be the case that the *macs* have scuttled away from the apartment, at least. Blanche's apartment, and the whole building she owns from foundation to roof tiles: the one thing she hasn't lost. A roof over her head, to shield her. Somewhere she won't need anyone's permission or help; somewhere she'll be safe from threats real and imagined. Somewhere to hole up until she's able to get a grip on things again.

If it's true that they're gone . . . It doesn't matter that Blanche is broke, because she can go round to her lodgers' doors and drum up their overdue rents as soon as she's settled in. She won't need to dance for that Prussian bitch tomorrow night or throw herself on the mercy of one of her *michetons*. All she needs is a door that locks. Despite the sweltering air, despite the tightness and weight of her costume, Blanche starts to hurry down the street.

She's at her building in a matter of minutes. She stands craning her neck up at the blank windows, fiddling with the keys that hang from her waist, losing her nerve. A piper at one corner and a kid clacking a pair of spoons on his leg at the other. She tries to shut out the cacophony. Cartwright's line was curiously vague: "the eastern states or his native France." What if the *macs* are still occupying the apartment like scorpions in a crevice? Safer, on the whole, to turn away . . . except that Blanche has nowhere else to go.

In the dim stairwell, she takes a long breath. Her plan is to climb very quietly all the way to the attic and find out from Gudrun if it's true that Arthur's left.

On the second-floor landing, Blanche tiptoes past her own door as fast as she can, not letting the heels of her mules touch the floorboards. The whole building's oddly quiet. Of course, it's a Friday morning; people who weren't shot at last night are getting on with their ordinary lives. Not a sound from the Scottish photographers' rooms on the third. The Corfu men on the fourth must be at their pickle factory, and the fifth floor's silent too. At Gudrun's peeling door, Blanche hovers and then taps. Waits. Knocks again. No, the girl must be out at her sewing job.

Down Blanche goes, her steps slower now. The walls are slick with humidity. Number 815 Sacramento is no palace, but it's a pretty fine structure, for San Francisco. It should stand till the next big quake, at least. It's certainly better than the narrow rooms Blanche grew up in, back on the Ile Saint-Louis. Infinitely better than the Cirque d'Hiver quarters, all paint tubes and used rags, with a whiff of lion piss. Why did Blanche let Arthur mock her for being a little bourgeoise the day she produced the deed to the building like a magic trick? It was no small thing, making fifteen hundred dollars from dances and *michetons*. What's Arthur ever done since being invalided out of the circus but swan around town looking lovelier than Blanche does?

On the landing outside her own door, she freezes, cutting off the squabble in her head. She thinks of a shotgun, freshly loaded, and she suddenly can't remember how she convinced herself that coming home was a good idea. Just because of something she read—when everyone knows newspapers fill up with lies the way a gutter does with cabbage leaves. Didn't Cartwright make up Jenny's last words from scratch—simply inventing a poignant line, in his hurry—and smear her as "frail" for good measure? So why should Blanche give any credence to the rest of his verbiage?

Perhaps Ernest was here when someone from the paper came around asking questions, and it was he who claimed that Arthur—his blameless friend—left a week ago. Or perhaps the two of them told the lodgers to spread that rumor. They might have gone and come back already. Perhaps Arthur did take a train out of the City, to give himself an alibi for Thursday night, then made his way back as far as San Miguel Station. (Though how could he have known where Blanche and Jenny were? And what about the dogs, the dogs that didn't bark until after the gunshots? Oh, Blanche's brain is worn out from running on these crazily looped tracks.)

She puts her ear to the smooth grain of the door and listens hard. Not a sound. The *macs* could be fast asleep, of course; they often turn day to night.

She taps first, then scuttles backward and goes down five steps. If Arthur—or Ernest—opens the door, then she can start clattering downstairs before he's caught more than a glimpse of her. Blanche still moves as deftly as a circus rider, even in heels. It's a risk, of course, it's a terrible risk, but—

Nobody's answering.

Her skin is tight. She wants to flee. But she makes herself approach the door and slide her key in. Delicately, soundlessly, tickling the lock.

The door swings open slowly.

Nothing. Not a stick of furniture, even. Blanche blinks.

She walks from room to room, her feet echoing strangely. Gone, everything but the little stove, the walls, and the panes in the windows. No sign of P'tit's things, the trunk he slept in. All her clothes, vanished. Even the table and the bed. How on earth did they get the bed out?

Struck by a thought, Blanche runs back to the salon. Only a little circle in the fireplace where the green chamber pot used to stand so pertly. How much was in there the night she left, ten dollars or so in banknotes and coin? But another few hundred, her whole goddamn nest egg, in the old boot under the bed; they must have discovered that when they were emptying the place. Blanche bets that gave them a jolly moment.

Gone, everything vaporized as if she only imagined it, all the evidence of more than a year of her life. Is this Arthur's final, stylish joke? Suddenly drained, Blanche leans against the wall. The bare bones of the building: that's all she has left in the world.

A tiny scratching, familiar somehow. The sound of a key in the door.

She straightens up. Ready for flight, but where to, where can she hide in this echoing mausoleum? It occurs to her that neither Arthur nor Ernest ever fumbled with the key this way; even when pickled, they always entered with élan. So who—

Her ground-floor lodger stands in the doorway, his face a mask of shock. "Miss Blanche—"

"Low Long." She breathes out, so relieved she's almost laughing. "What are you doing up here?" He's always downstairs, overseeing the rows of cross-legged bachelors who sew his shoes.

He blinks rapidly. "Why you not New York?"

"New York?" Blanche repeats.

"With Mr. Arthur."

Her eyes narrow. "Why should either of us be—"

"Mr. Arthur—he say you go New York and he follow."

Why would Arthur have bothered spinning such a yarn to one of their tenants? "I don't know anything about Mr.—him," snaps Blanche. Then, her voice shaking despite her best efforts to control it: "I don't suppose you've seen my baby?"

"I know nothing about baby." There's a new quality to the man's voice that she doesn't recognize; irritation? "You get out quick, Miss Blanche, men coming soon for bunk up."

"Bunk up?" Bewildered.

"Here, here, here." Her lodger is pointing all around the apartment. "Ten men sleep every room tonight."

Pride, that's the new tone she's hearing. "Low Long,"

Blanche says as steadily as she can, "have you lost your mind?"

He doesn't seem to know that idiom.

"Gone loco?" She makes circles around her ear. "Was it you who took away all my furniture?"

Low Long stands a little straighter. "This mine now."

"What is? What's yours?"

"My building, eight fifteen Sacramento."

She gives him a cold stare. "All you rent from me is your little shoe shop."

He shakes his head so vehemently his braid leaps like a lizard behind him. "Legal own building all way up, five floor, plus attic make six. I pay your husband eighteen hundred dollar Saturday."

"You what?"

"Good American dollar, eighteen hundred."

Last Saturday? The very day after their battle at the gambling saloon, Arthur woke up alone in their bed and decided to sell the place out from under Blanche? She presses her lips together hard. "There's been a mistake."

"Many year I spend no cent, eat rice, little vegetable." Low Long's voice has taken on the timbre of a storyteller's. "Now top-quality rooming house on famous Sacramento Street, heart of Little China, space for many many, one man, one bunk."

She speaks through her teeth. "Get out of my building."

"Not your now, Miss Blanche, sorry. Old lodgers gone, new lodgers coming. Top-quality Chinese rooming house," he repeats confidently, like some huckster winding up his patter in the street. "You go New York, Mr. Arthur explain," he assures her, nodding.

"Mr. Arthur tried to shoot me last night. Mr. Arthur's gone Christ-knows-where," she roars, "with your eighteen hundred dollars and everything I had in the world."

For a moment, Low Long hesitates.

Blanche presses her advantage. "I'm sorry to tell you that you've been bilked out of your savings—swindled, you understand? He's not my husband, and he never owned this building, so how could he sell it? It's my name on the deed."

Instead of frightening him, that last word makes his forehead clear. "Deed, I have deed."

Isn't it behind the lithograph in the—

The bedroom walls are bare, Blanche remembers. Arthur took down the print of the picnic, the black-jacketed dandies and the beautiful naked girl, and found the goddamn deed.

"He sold it to you under false pretenses, then. Hand it over," she adds, holding out her palm in a queenly pose.

Low Long's eyes bulge.

"Never mind about the furniture. Give me back my deed and I won't fetch a patrolman." Blanche watches him to see if the word shakes him. Are there police in the City who'd defend a Chinaman's claim—defend it against a white woman's, even if that woman was a female Frog "of no character"?

"I have deed," Low Long repeats, dogged.

She examines the silk folds of his costume for any telltale bulge indicating where he might have put the document.

"Pay eighteen hundred dollar, all done official correct. My name, Low Long, on deed now."

And suddenly the fight goes out of Blanche. All she's

lived through since last night catches up with her, and blackness swims across her eyes. She leans back, presses her hands to the wall so she won't pass out.

"You go, Miss Blanche," says Low Long, not ungently. "Men coming make bunk."

She blinks to clear away the dark.

"Five minute, no more." Low Long makes an absurd bow. She hears his steps move out of the apartment, down the stairs.

Then she lets herself slide down the wall until she's on the floor. Her heels glide out in front of her. Limp as old cabbage. Her ankles are swollen. And her wrists. Thickened like P'tit's, except that in her case, it's due to the heat.

Whether Arthur's really fled the country or is just hiding out somewhere in this teeming City where Detective Bohen will never find him . . . it's over. It must be finished now, surely; their accounts settled. Eighteen hundred dollars he took for her building, together with whatever was in the pot and the boot, and what the bits of furniture would fetch, and her clothes. That hypocrite of a so-called bohemian who always claimed money wasn't worth a rat's ass!

Your husband, Low Long called him; Arthur must have passed himself off as that. He could have had the title for real if he'd wanted it, Blanche realizes that now. She chose her man when she was fifteen and that was all there was to it, so of course she'd have signed some register if he'd asked her to.

But no, Arthur preached free love—meaning that he could do what he liked, and it was never him who paid. It occurs to Blanche that English doesn't have French's useful distinction between *libre,* meaning that something's unconstrained, and *gratuit,* meaning that it costs nothing. *Free* thought, *free* speech, *free* love: the English word that Arthur was so fond of obscures the price of things. The man liked to come at life sideways, by a playful sleight of hand. *A certain grace to speculation,* wasn't that his boast? And it strikes Blanche that she's been just one of his more long-term speculations.

She stares from wall to empty wall. It's not a spiteful message, this denuded apartment; she sees that now. Simpler than that: Arthur assumed Blanche wouldn't be coming back from San Miguel Station. Wouldn't need her clothes anymore once she was in the ground. Blanche is surer than ever that he was the killer, whether he pulled the trigger himself or handed the dirty job off to Ernest. This was his grand vengeance on Blanche, because she had the gall to walk away in the end—away from him, Arthur Pierre Louis Deneve, aerialist extraordinaire turned daring speculator and man-about-town, debonair beau of the sporting set. He'd loved her for almost a decade—as much as a man of his monstrous egotism could love—or seemed to, at least, but he decided on her death as simply as he might order another bottle of wine, with a snap of his fingers.

The door squeaks slightly.

"That wasn't five minutes," she barks.

But the face that comes around the door is not Low Long's.

Blanche leaps to her feet so fast her heels slam like a flamenco dancer's.

"I've been in the café across the street watching for you," remarks Ernest.

Blanche's mind chatters to keep the terror at bay. He's twenty-one, but with the face of a skeleton. If this man is Arthur's shadow, it's the distorted, serpentine shadow of the end of the day.

Ernest takes a step closer.

"Low Long!" Blanche screeches like a parakeet. *Perfect,* she groans internally; first she threatens to set the cops on the man, and then she calls on his gallantry for protection.

"Stop that racket," says Ernest.

"Low Long!" No furniture to put between her and this elongated ape.

"Have you no shame, *salope*?"

"Shame?" She repeats the word in confusion, keeping her eyes on the impeccable curves of Ernest's dark jacket. Could he be hiding a pistol? A stiletto, more likely. *Won't spoil the line of a suit.* Why didn't Blanche pay attention over the years when the two friends made jokes like that? What stopped her from glimpsing what they've always been capable of?

"Telling the papers such *conneries,*" he growls. "As if Arthur knows or cares what happened in some dive at the end of the railroad track!"

Blanche blinks at him. Is this really a declaration of his friend's innocence? The last thing she was expecting. Her eyes keep searching for any hint of that stiletto. Of course, all Ernest really needs are his steely fingers around her throat.

"Probably one of those boozy hicks set off his varmint gun by tripping over it."

She nods, to pacify him.

"It could have been anyone," Ernest barks at her. "With

a history like Bonnet's—the fool made enemies wherever she went. She couldn't go a block without running into a fight."

Blanche considers sprinting to the door, reckons her chances of reaching it before Ernest can grab her skirts.

He takes a step closer.

"Don't hurt me," Blanche says, softly. Despising herself, even as she knows there's no other way to play it. Ernest is hardly going to throttle her here and now, with the building full of carpenters, she tells herself. If he meant to, he'd have done it right away, because killers don't waste time lecturing. Which means it's worth lowering herself to beg. "I'll leave town, tonight," she murmurs. "I'll go so far away, you'll never have to—"

"You won't go anywhere till you've cleared my friend's name, *putain!*"

She's nodding automatically, head bobbing like a toy on a spring.

"You had Arthur Deneve," Ernest marvels, leaning in very close to her. "You cold piece of veal, to turn your back on such a man at his lowest hour! To make him so sick of this city that he abandoned it—"

So that much of what the paper said is true, it occurs to her. Arthur's really gone. Absurdly, she feels the faintest pang of loss.

"—whereupon you defamed him in print, for sheer spite, as a murderer!"

Blanche is lost for words. What can she say, what can she do, to buy herself out of this? She'd get on her hands and knees and bare herself for this raging man if she had anything to offer that he hasn't had a dozen times before.

"So tomorrow," he growls, "you're going to walk into that inquest and tell the jury how wrong you were."

"Yes," Blanche breathes.

Ernest turns on his polished heel.

Relief floods her. She can't believe that's all it took: one magic word.

The young man spins around as if he's heard Blanche's thoughts. "And if you shilly-shally or equivocate—" Ernest is almost on top of her now, his breath heating her cheeks, the rope of tendons in his neck standing out. But he doesn't touch her. Strange, when you think how familiar he is with every inch of Blanche, that he can't seem to bring himself to so much as lay a hand on her now. "If you mess this up, goddamn it—"

Here it comes. Blanche waits for the threat as for a blade parting her skin.

"—I swear you'll never see the kid again."

Her mouth falls open.

Ernest doesn't notice her shock because he's spun away. Out the door already, shoes thundering on the stairs. He's gone.

She breathes in, so sweet it hurts her chest. Terrible hope hooks her.

P'tit!

He must be alive. How could Ernest threaten never to let Blanche see her baby again if her seeing him again is not at least a possibility? The man wasn't being crafty and calculating, just now; she's known Ernest long enough to read his tone, and she's convinced that he spoke from the heart. A malevolent, jealous, septic heart, but still. This much she'd bet: P'tit's alive, and Ernest knows where he is.

V

VIVE LA ROSE

Arthur gets stronger fast once his scabs form. On the fourth of September, he hobbles out of the bedroom on his friend's arm, looking like some mummy from a pyramid. Patches of scalp show through his hair. His nose wasn't this big before, was it? Two weeks of dark beard obscures some of the lesions, making him even less recognizable to Blanche.

She runs over to him, to hide her reaction. The almost sugary stench of his scabs.

"Watch out, it might still be catching," Arthur says, deep in his throat.

She falls back.

He seems to have lost all the lashes on his right eye. Blanche tries to smile. Arthur's dark pupils see right through her.

"Are you hungry?" she asks, to fill the silence. She tries to remember what there is: butter but no bread . . . "I could go out for something." She rakes through the detritus on the sideboard for that strip of twenty meal tickets for the corner noodle house.

"He won't be able to eat anything solid," Ernest rebukes her. "Is there soup?"

"I'll get some." Durand's horse-meat soup, perhaps: that delicious broth would restore any Frenchman to health.

"And more ice. Lake ice," he orders. "That factory-made stuff leaves a nasty residue."

Blanche watches Arthur letting himself down onto a cane chair by the window, as if everything hurts him.

P'tit sobs from the skirting board. He's just figured out how to roll, but only one way, so he always ends up with his face mashed against the wall. Every day, some inconvenient new skill, as if he's catching up on a whole year's worth of tricks.

Blanche snatches him up and hovers, looking at his pallid scalp through the wisps of hair. She can't carry him and a tureen of soup at the same time.

"This place reeks," Arthur remarks.

She's strangely embarrassed; she thought they were all going to pretend that they couldn't smell his illness.

"It's the baby," says Ernest.

Oh, *that*. "This morning's diapers," Blanche corrects him.

Arthur lets out a bearish roar.

She thinks it's about the diapers. Then she registers that he's rubbing his jaw savagely. A scab flakes off, leaving a puckered white hollow, as if some ghostly assailant has gouged him with a fingernail.

Ernest leans over and locks Arthur's hand in his own as if they're sailors arm-wrestling in a bar, but very gently, putting no pressure on the lumpy palm.

Arthur hisses. "I have to just—"

"You were a handsome man," his friend cuts in, "and you will be again, but only if you don't scratch."

Blanche looks at the place on the floor where the flake fell. Her own skin itches.

Arthur breathes out, his wasted muscles shifting under his shirt. Closes his eyes and moves his teeth as if he's biting an invisible rope.

P'tit starts to keen again, industriously.

" 'There's a good time coming, boys,' " Blanche carols in his ear, swaying him from side to side,

A good time coming,
A good time coming.

How does the rest of it go? What's so good about the good time, and when exactly is it going to come? she wonders. Blanche doesn't even know where she picked this song up. She repeats what she remembers, hoping to recall the next line:

A good time coming,
A good time coming . . .

"You're making my head ache as much as he is," remarks Arthur, eyes still shut.

"Your son likes music," she tells him. But switches to a waltz.

Arthur groans.

"Pick another *satané* tune," snaps Ernest.

Blanche breaks off, realizing what she's humming: *He'd fly thro' the air with the greatest of ease, / A daring young man on the flying trapeze . . .* She wishes she had the courage to carry on. To persuade Arthur that P'tit should know that his father once flew, that Papa was a god among men. She longs for Arthur to look up and nod, let her sing the song as proudly as Léotard's young acolytes always used to sing it. Past times, long gone, but does that mean they have to be forgotten? *You've survived,* Blanche wants to tell him. *Let's celebrate that much.*

But Arthur's altered face remains locked like a safe.

Blanche is swinging P'tit from side to side now, fast enough to make him dizzy, and it's hushed the child; she suspects she's happened on a sensation he really enjoys. Doesn't it make sense that the son of circus folk should have a taste for whirling? Even if he's inherited none of his parents' grace.

"Soup," Ernest reminds her, jerking his head toward the street.

It's the tone that pushes Blanche over the edge. She stares at Ernest. "Whose apartment—whose damn building do you think you're living in?" she demands.

His eyes flare, then slide to Arthur.

Who's looking up now, with eyebrows that cut arcs in the knobbled mask of his face. "My friend here," he says quietly, "has saved my life by risking his own while you've been playing at motherhood."

"Playing?" She screeches the word.

He winces, holds up one misshapen hand. "But what's past is past. What worries me is that you're so besotted with this baby, you seem to have forgotten the need to earn a living."

Ernest is nodding like a puppet. "It must be more than

three weeks since she's danced at the House of Mirrors," he points out.

"You know why I won't go back to that bitch," says Blanche, addressing Arthur only. "Besides, I don't need Madame to peddle my *cul* for me."

He shrugs, a movement that she can tell pains him. "That's the spirit. So why don't you go ahead and peddle it yourself?"

"The chamber pot's not empty yet, is it?" she demands.

"It's certainly not full."

"I thought you preferred to live for the day," Blanche mocks.

"Arthur prefers to live in style," Ernest tells her.

"Oh, *he* does? You mean you both do, and at my expense."

Arthur clears his throat exhaustedly. "Let's stick to practicalities. Why haven't you looked up some of the silver men? Or that railroad fellow, or that big Sicilian—what's his name, Lament? Lemon?"

He knows Lamantia's name perfectly well. "I've been busy looking after your son," says Blanche.

"Ticktock, ticktock," murmurs Arthur. "Let's not forget"—with a rueful, spasmodic gesture at himself—"how fast looks can be lost."

Get out of the room, Blanche tells herself. Ernest can fetch their *satané* soup.

She stamps her way into the bedroom, baby on her hip. Her room, or it used to be, before it had the reek of death. She pushes the window ajar and takes some long breaths. Arthur's inching back from the very brink, she reminds herself. He has a right to be bitter. No wonder he doubts her love, considering. She does love him, of course she loves him; Blanche has loved Arthur since she was old enough to know what the word meant. Their fondness has just gone temporarily astray. These are not ordinary times.

"Look," she says, staring down at a passing cart, "horsies."

But P'tit's turning his head away from the window, sniveling again. "*Chut, chut,*" Blanche hushes him, trying to make her voice sound more fond than weary. *Besotted?* What a joke, when Blanche is often as maddened by this baby as by a sliver under the skin.

Mothers in the street who caress their children—they may all be faking it, it occurs to her now. Like the girl in the story who was forced to open the door to the frog, let him feed off her plate, even allow him into her bed. The horror of it: the slime trail across the sheets.

All week, heat continues to fill the apartment like an invisible gas. Blanche's clothes seem to soak through the minute she puts them on. Ernest comes and goes, reeking of strange smoke; he's burning all the sheets and cloths in an oil drum in the street outside. Arthur shuffles around or lies in the bedroom in more or less speechless convalescence, fingers locked in his armpits to prevent them from scratching the remaining scabs.

Blanche is always yawning. Always on the verge of sleep, but P'tit won't let her have more than an hour at a time; it's the heaven she can never quite reach.

Soon all Arthur's scabs have fallen off. Ernest's steamed the bedroom so thoroughly that it reeks of sulfur, and the bedding's all new, but Blanche is still afraid to sleep in there somehow. She tells herself that she might disturb the convalescent if she brushes against him in the night, and she stays on the sofa, beside P'tit's trunk.

One evening, the seventh of September, Arthur asks if there's any wine, and Blanche fills his glass, as courteous as a stranger. If they're very careful, she believes, they should be able to edge their way back to where they were. Before the smallpox, before Blanche went to Folsom Street, before Jenny Bonnet and her questions. (Jenny hasn't turned up in a week, not since that walk they took, that sticky evening when Blanche didn't know if Arthur was going to live or die. That's the sort of friend Jenny is, Blanche reminds herself; no more to be counted on than a leaf on the breeze.)

Arthur dresses to the nines tonight—shakily, with Ernest tying his cravat for him, and doing his pearl waistcoat buttons, and hanging his gold watch just so. When Arthur practices a smile, the effect is grotesque. Still blackly forested all over his leprous face, because Ernest won't let him shave yet.

Blanche is not invited. She doesn't even know where the *macs* are going. She wonders whether Madeleine will be with them tonight. The woman has to be pushing thirty, but she's still angel-faced, Blanche thinks with a twinge of envy. Being saddled with a baby, Blanche feels as if she doesn't quite count as a woman anymore.

A sudden loud crack: another blasted lamp! Blanche spots the one with the shattered chimney and hurries over to blow the flame out. Cleaning the burners, that's one of those tasks that don't get done now. Blanche has assured all the lodgers that Arthur's no longer contagious, but they look askance at her if they pass her on the stairs, and Gudrun still refuses to step across the threshold.

Instead of falling asleep as he should this evening, P'tit gets more and more frantic. Returning from the lavatory, Blanche finds him on his feet—he's hauled himself up by one of the sofa buttons, of all things. She supposes a proper mother would be proud of him, and for a moment she tries to be. But one of the many things about babies that nobody told her is that every incremental advance makes them harder to handle. And the next moment he falls hard, of course, walloping his shoulder on the floorboards and then honking like some clubbed seal.

Blanche picks him up and props him, sitting, against some cushions. But before she can get away, P'tit is clawing himself to his feet again, heaving himself up on her brown polka-dot skirt like a sailor climbing rigging. Or, no, like Quasimodo straining at the ropes of the great bells . . .

She disengages his fingers. "Hold that," she says, standing him up against a table and pressing his small hands around the leg.

P'tit stares at her suspiciously. Blanche steps away, smiling.

He wails even before he topples like a felled tree.

Every time she tries to bed him down in his trunk for the night, P'tit leans over the tin rim as if plotting a jailbreak. Blanche can't leave him because he might fall right out. She crouches there in the dark room, on the edge of the sofa. "Go to sleep," she chants softly. "Go the hell to sleep."

P'tit's cry goes up a jagged notch, and suddenly Blanche

can't bear the injustice of it. She crouches, putting his goblin face up against hers, and shouts, *"Ta gueule!"*

The obscenity makes him freeze for a moment. Massive dark eyes fixed on hers. Then he shrieks even harder, and his hands shoot out. Such an unfamiliar gesture that at first she flinches away from the thickened wrists, thinking he's trying to throttle her. And then she understands. This is what breaks Blanche's heart, that even as P'tit's sobbing with fright, he's reaching out for her in a way he's never done before, a way she didn't know he could. How could the tiny boy want a hug from her right now with the tears she's caused still dancing on his red cheeks? Who begs for comfort from a tyrant? But P'tit is wrapping his arms around Blanche's head the way a drowning man might embrace a log.

And if she can't look after him properly, do this one thing right, then Blanche has no business making a hash of it. She should carry P'tit to Portsmouth Square and set him down on the grass. Walk away, leaving him to the mercies of whoever will take him. Never say she had a baby, never dare to call herself a mother . . .

The thought makes her squeeze P'tit so tight that he howls even louder. She couldn't walk away. Not now, not ever.

Pressed against her, belly to belly, P'tit clamps his bowed legs around her, and his head takes refuge on her collarbone.

" 'There's a good time coming,' " Blanche croons under her breath, " 'a good time coming,' " and she swings him from side to side. Things must get better, simply because they can't get any worse.

A shuffling dance, the smallness of him so heavy in her worn-out arms. Like a bareback act, its perfectly timed, smooth sway. She sings, P'tit calms; she sways, he breathes. It seems Blanche's muscles have already said yes. And this boy is made of her, after all, his bones formed from hers. Unbeautiful, but her own.

Much later, the sharp sound of a key in the door wakes her with a jolt, and she realizes that she and P'tit have been in the deepest, most peaceful sleep, face to wet face, sprawled on the sofa.

"Chérie?"

What's Arthur been drinking that's made him sound fond of her again? She extricates herself from P'tit's small limbs, sits up, and dresses her face with a smile, blinking, because Arthur's turning up the lamps.

"We've got company," he remarks, slurring only a little. He straightens his jade tiepin in the over-mantel mirror.

With pocks still clustered around one of his eyes like milk bubbling in a pan, Arthur's in the mood for company?

"Ernest's right on my heels, with a friend."

"Someone I know?" Automatically, Blanche scoops up the baby and carries him into the dark bedroom, pressing his face against her so the light and bustle won't wake him. As she lays P'tit in the middle of the bed, irritation ticks behind her eyes. She roots out a clean bodice, not able to tell the color, and not caring, because the last thing she feels like doing is primping to charm some *business associate* at this time of night. But she does want to be helpful, to match Arthur's civility with her own. She'll be—or at least give a decent impersonation of—the old Blanche.

She squeezes her heat-swollen feet into a pair of mules.

Arthur's opening a bottle of brandy. In the glare of the salon, Blanche sees that her bodice is light blue. She finds a stain on her skirt and picks at it, but it's too late to change, and the polka dots will obscure the mark. Well, at least she's made a visible effort. "So who's this—"

But she doesn't get to finish her question because the front door's opening. Ernest leads the way with the grandiose gestures of a butler; he always hams it up when he's drunk. The American behind him is short and scruffy, but then most men look so beside Ernest. This one must be important somehow, or surely Arthur, barely out of his sickbed, wouldn't have brought him home?

"*Enchantée,*" cries Blanche, gliding over.

The man is in the Alaskan ice trade, so they run though all the possible jokes about how much he's making these days. Mind blank, Blanche brings out Ernest's line about the *nasty residue* left by the manufactured stuff, and the American howls with mirth as if it's a dazzling bon mot.

Nobody alludes to Arthur's scarified face.

Blanche swallows a yawn and smiles even harder. When are the men going to get on to the meat of their tedious business and let their hostess slip away?

She excuses herself for a moment. In the dim bedroom, she checks to make sure P'tit is still asleep in the middle of the mattress. His small jaw works as if he's chewing on gristle.

Then she peeks out; if they seem to have forgotten about her, she won't go back . . .

But Ernest's eyes are watching for Blanche, hawkish. He jerks his head, beckoning.

Arthur throws his arm around her waist and kisses her on the neck as if they've been parted for years.

Blanche flinches, and tries to hide it. She reminds herself that he's cured. No reason to shrink away.

"Be nice to him, *hein*?" Arthur breathes spirituously in her ear. "Give him a dance."

The euphemism sticks in her craw. "Not now," she whispers, "not here." Still smiling in the American's direction.

"Our room," murmurs Arthur, with a tiny jerk of his head.

"That's not what I meant," she hisses.

"You need a stage?"

"This is where I live."

"What's the difference, exactly?"

Blanche doesn't know how to explain, but there is one.

Ernest refills their glasses, muttering in her ear: "Don't be a bore."

The chatter's died away. The American is grinning at her almost bashfully.

And then Arthur reaches out and finds her left nipple through her bodice. Presses it hard. It works, of course it works, as always, as if he's a lamplighter opening the valve and igniting the flame. But just because Blanche is getting wet doesn't mean she's not getting angry. She slaps his hand away.

"Let's not stand on ceremony," he remarks, no longer bothering to lower his voice. "It seems a late hour to play the prude."

"Especially," adds Ernest, "when we've gone to some trouble to—"

"Trouble?" Blanche interrupts, looking from one to

the other. "You bring home some trash off the street and expect me to put on a show for him?"

The American's going slightly purple.

"I'm sorry, sir, but you've been misinformed," she tells him, with an imperious gesture that starts him backing toward the door.

Arthur snatches at her elbow. "A quarter of an hour, that's all I'm asking. Now you've thrown off Madame Johanna, we need to bring in the trade. My investments require—"

"We?" she exclaims. "There's no *we*. I carry you—the pair of you—like monkeys on my back."

Now the American's looking mortified. "I don't mean to cause a quarrel." He'd be out the door by now if Ernest weren't gripping him around the shoulder with all the conviviality of a guard dog.

Arthur's asymmetrical eyes narrow at Blanche. "I'll have you know that I bring in sums, sometimes considerable—"

"A fraction of your keep."

"What are you, some penny-reckoning housewife?"

She lets out a sharp laugh. "I whore myself out to buy you suits and gems, to fund all your speculations—"

"Whore yourself out?" Arthur repeats, puzzled, disfigured head to one side. "But you were born a whore, Blanche. It comes naturally to you."

She stares. He's never called her that before.

Ernest spits the words. "You want to make a liar of Arthur, shame him in his own home, after all he's suffered these past weeks?"

"I'm going to bed," Blanche snarls.

"Not till you've spread yourself for our guest," says Ernest.

The American blinks, appalled.

She turns to Arthur. Is he really going to let his friend talk to her this way?

"How would you prefer her?" Arthur's speaking over her head to the American, with incongruous cheer. "Blanche is really not fussy. Bent over the table? Or on all fours like a bitch in heat? She enjoys it any way at all."

Blanche doesn't recognize him. The nasty residue of the man she used to love.

She marches toward the bedroom. But Ernest's put his long limbs between her and the door. "Don't relish hearing it said out loud?" he asks. "But you love getting banged every which way, up, down, and sideways. Why, when you were pregnant, Arthur complained you were constantly frantic for it, dripping like a melon."

She shuts her eyes, swallowing the shame.

"You'd fuck a nigger in a haystack," says Ernest. "You'd fuck a broom handle."

Is it me he hates, Blanche wonders, *or all women?*

"So get off your high horse and fuck this Yank."

Red spots before her eyes.

"Or kneel down and give him a below-job, at least."

Blanche Beunon of the Cirque d'Hiver. By what circuitous descent through stages of humiliation has she come to this?

"Cock, cock, cock," Ernest tells the American, pronouncing the word with a guttural relish. "The lady lives and breathes it. She's never met a *cigare* she doesn't fancy."

The visitor is edging backward.

"Stay!" cries Arthur. "I tell you what it is, she's angling to be forced a little. What say my friend and I hold her down for you?"

"Get away from me." Blanche's eyes shift between these crazy men.

"We can all join in," says Arthur, "make a sporting party of it."

It hits her with a cold certainty that this isn't about the *macs'* urgent need for money at all. It's a punishment. Why has it taken her so long to notice what Arthur really thinks of her? Perhaps he's been this all along: a beast in an urbane and elegant coat. Like bedrock revealed as the ground cracks open.

"I better get going," whimpers the American.

Blanche sidles up to him as if to whisper in his ear.

He blinks at her, almost hopeful.

Then she dives past, smooth as in the days when she could skip on a horse's rosined back as easily as on solid ground.

Arthur lunges at her and grabs her wrist but she wrenches herself out of his grasp, and the American shoves between them, protesting . . .

In the confusion Blanche is gone. She rattles down the dark stairs, her pulse thumping with exhilaration. Out into the steaming night, but she can breathe, at least, as she races down Sacramento, lanterns glimmering in windows, folks carousing on stoops. A beggar playing on—could that be a stovepipe? Blanche doesn't know where she's going. *Qu'importe;* in any case, she's out of there.

Halfway along the next block, a gull cuts past her with a yawp, and only then does she remember P'tit.

"Question: Who put you on the town in the first place?"

Eastern light slants in the window, stabbing Blanche in the eye. It's been a long night since she fled from the apartment. That medicinal cognac she let Jenny buy her when they bumped into each other in a dive off Clay Street, and then some cocktails, and more recently a bottle or two of Durand's inimitable wine. "Nobody put me on the town."

"Oh, come," says Jenny, thumping the long table at the back of the brasserie, "are you telling me you took to it spontaneous-like, for pure fun, when you stepped off the steamer?"

They're the last customers breakfasting; the others have all gone about their business or crawled off to bed. A lone waiter tosses sawdust on the floor behind the women. Blanche is past needing sleep. She just wants another glass of wine. "It wasn't like that either."

"So how was it?"

"I don't quite remember now," admits Blanche, the words tripping over one another.

"You sound bored of the game, that's all I mean," says Jenny.

"Do you think it was ever interesting?" snaps Blanche, contemplating the stain on her polka-dot skirt. "Seen one swollen *cigare,* seen them all."

"Ever think of throwing the whole thing over, then?"

She struggles to focus her eyes on Jenny. "You have some objection to girls on the town?"

"Not to the girls, just to what the town does to them."

Blanche shrugs. "It's as good a trade as any."

"Maybe, for a while. Till it trades them in. All I say is"—Jenny points one brown finger at Blanche's forehead, right between her eyes—"there's more to you than *cul.*"

Blanche can't decide whether to feel irritated or flattered. "How can you be sure?"

Jenny grins, as if that's an answer.

"What, should I give it all up and take to the vagabond life, like you?" Blanche scoffs.

A shake of the crop-haired head. "Nah, you don't have the calling. I can't see you bedding down under a tree. I picture you as your own boss, or bossing other folks."

Blanche laughs at the word *boss.*

"What would you say to setting up your own dancing academy," proposes Jenny, "and knocking all those so-called Professors into a cocked hat?"

Blanche rolls her eyes at this ludicrous notion. "To steal their customers, I'd have to be the crème de la crème. And where should I set up this academy of mine—on a stretch of gravel in Union Square?"

"You could rent a hall."

"I can just imagine what Arthur would say to that."

Jenny sits up straighter at his name. "Question: Which—"

"Enough of your questions!"

"This is my last, then: Would you prefer to have one child on your hands, or three?"

Three? Ah, Blanche sees what she's getting at.

"Those *connards,*" Jenny marvels. "A pair of fat skeeters swollen up with your blood."

Blanche's mind zigzags with fatigue. "I keep wondering which of them's changing P'tit's diapers—Arthur or Ernest."

Jenny guffaws. "Maybe they've tossed a coin."

"Serve them right, to have to look after him for one night, at least. Puddles on their pants!" But despite her flippancy, Blanche is feeling sick. Will the *macs* be awake to let the iceman in? If not, P'tit's milk in the sweating icebox could turn. If he spits it out, will they think to sniff it, or will they jump to the conclusion that he's just being cranky? "I should be going back," she says, sobering.

"I'll come along. I could do with forty winks," Jenny remarks, yawning.

Beside them at the table, Blanche belatedly notices, is a Durand boy—the one who guarded Jenny's bicycle that first night, or is this a smaller one?—fiddling with a cap pistol. It's not real, she realizes, just a novelty. When he shoots it, there's no crack of gunpowder, just a little metal man popping out and kicking a cowering coolie in the rear end. Her nose wrinkles. Really, the things folks find funny . . .

The waiter's slapping at the wood with a wet cloth now. Taking the hint, Blanche looks for her pocketbook, but in her flight from the apartment she didn't think to grab her bag. She's got nothing with her except her keys on their little chain.

"That's all right," says Jenny. "Put it on my tab," she tells the man.

They head out. Blanche's feet are stiff from the long night roaming around Chinatown. She staggers a little, squinting against the morning light. Really, the last thing she feels like doing is going home. But she can't sleep until she knows someone's at least given P'tit his bottle.

She and Arthur need to sit down and talk, today, without Ernest's snaky interference. Other doves have these bust-ups with their *macs.* You hear of them (and actually hear them, loud in the street) every night of the year. Never Blanche and Arthur, not till now. Last night he acted like a demented boar. But nothing actually happened, Blanche reminds herself, and perhaps nothing would have happened after all that threatening and posturing to impress the *micheton.* Sticks and stones, that's all. Arthur's not himself, and who would be, after coming back from the brink of death? The same goes for Ernest. The young man almost lost the friend he treasures most in the world. Blanche must make allowances.

First I need to sleep, she'll say, very dignified, when she enters the apartment. Later she and Arthur will share a bottle and civilly discuss how they mean to go on.

Jenny falls in beside her, thrumming a branch along the metal fence the way a small boy might.

Blanche turns her head. "You don't have to stick by my side."

"No particular place else to be," says Jenny. "And you could do with a hand, maybe, if those fellows have still got their dander up."

Blanche half laughs. "You sniff out any prospect of a scrap, don't you—like a dog getting wind of a sausage. You're packing your revolver, I hope?"

She says it mockingly but Jenny pats the outline along her leg with assurance.

"Arthur's still my man," Blanche warns her.

"If you say so."

"Why, what do you say?"

"Why ask me?" counters Jenny.

"Don't you shrug at me. I need some goddamn advice," says Blanche.

"Advice? As in, some wise old saw?"

"If there's one that fits."

"Here's one for you, then," says Jenny. "Life's too short to drink bad wine."

Blanche stares at her.

Heading up the second flight of stairs at number 815, Blanche prepares her arguments. She'll tell Arthur she's back, but only on fair terms. No more bringing *michetons* home or speaking to her—or letting Ernest speak to her—as if she's dirt under their shiny heels . . .

When she opens the door of the apartment, it's the silence that hits her. Everyone asleep—could it be?

It's all just as Blanche left it last night, except there's nobody here. The empty bedroom still stinks of disinfectant. She rushes to look in the trunk beside the sofa. Empty except for the black doorknob with its tidemarks of spit. "Where the hell have they gone?" she says to Jenny.

Out for a drink, taking the baby with them?

That's absurd.

Are the men roaming the streets hunting for Blanche so she can change the baby's shitty diaper?

She flops down on the bed. "I don't know what kind of game Arthur's playing."

"Can I take the sofa?" asks Jenny with an enormous yawn.

Alone in the room, Blanche sinks onto the pillows and tries to ignore the lingering whiff of sulfur from the fumigation. A little sleep will freshen her mind, she tells herself. By the time she wakes up, the *macs* will have wandered back in with P'tit, surely.

So quiet.

Men are bending her backward across a table; any number of men, she can't count. Their movements are deliberate. The pleasure brutal. When she cranes her neck around to see who they are, Blanche can't make sense of the faces, because they're melting, features dripping like candle wax onto her arms and legs. She cries out, in her dream, but can't stop, can't do anything but feel this, take this, the unbearable perfect pressure of—what is it? What is this slippery thing rammed inside her?

A doorknob, she realizes, letting out an appalled sob so loud it wakes her up.

P'tit's not here, still.

The parched sky has turned black, as if there's a tornado on its way. Blanche stumbles around the apartment. Everything the same, but horribly darkened, as if the world's beginning to char, paper held too long to a flame. Jenny like a dead woman on the sofa . . . Then blinking up at her.

"It's gone dark," Blanche wails.

Jenny glances at the window. "It does that, come evening."

"But—" Can she and Jenny really have slept the whole day away, since after breakfast at Durand's? And where could the men be? They can't have been lugging P'tit around all these hours. Blanche thinks of Ernest's blandly smiling Madeleine and wonders if they've gone to her place—above a grocery on Dupont, is that right? Free love; it occurs to Blanche to wonder whether the boon companions are sharing the ripe blonde now. With P'tit sniveling in some box in a back room. "I have to find him."

"Arthur?" says Jenny.

"My son!" Blanche is halfway out the door when she stops, realizing that she should pack some things, just in case. She hauls out an old orange carpetbag from under the bed and throws in a few items: a spare corset, boots, a parasol, face paint, her pocketbook. Diapers for P'tit, for if—when—she finds him. An empty bottle with a cleanish teat. The doorknob (though the sight of it makes her face scorch). That's all she needs for now.

The hours of the evening go by in a blur of sweat. Hours of trailing from café to bar, tapping at the doors of opium shops to inquire about a Frenchman with a bad back and a freshly pocked face, enduring the nosy questions, the satire, asking if anyone has seen two men with a baby. Blanche finds she has to tip a quarter each time she puts her head in a door because of some nonsensical new bylaw banning women from bars in the evening.

It's nearly midnight when, after ponying up a full half-dollar to the jet-faced doorman of one of the better-class gaming saloons, she finally spots Ernest's long black-jacketed back tilted over an oval faro table. And Arthur beside him, his face still looking as if it's been splashed with acid.

On the little stage, a fat soprano is giving "Una Voce Poco Fa" her best shot. Blanche makes her way through the crowd, which is pretty mongrel: a few black players, Mexicans, women, even Chinese—who must be high rollers for the white men to have let them in. She wishes she were wearing a less motley outfit, because the grubby blue bodice does nothing for the brown skirt or the egg-yellow mules. Blanche knows faro—one deck only, and the rules are child's play: you just set your stake on or between the cards you fancy on the board with its pasted layout—but she finds it about as entertaining as picking her teeth. Like all banking games, it's technically illegal in this town. It's her private conviction that if it weren't, nobody would bother playing it.

Standing in the table's cutout, the Scottish dealer wears its green baize like a skirt. *"L'une pour l'autre,"* he calls out, "the game's drawn."

Blanche summons her nerve and touches Arthur on the shoulder. He doesn't turn his head from his shaky columns of checks, which tells her that he saw her coming through the room. He sucks on his cigar, though it's gone out. His olive cheeks are still rimed with white patches, the longing fingerprints of death. He's been shaved, but not well. Perhaps Ernest did it for him, because no barber would take the risk? Mustache greased but askew. All in all, like a papier-mâché head in some Mexican fiesta.

Blanche looks for Jenny—who's still stuck at the door, she sees, in some kind of altercation with the doorman. "Arthur," she tries again. He's wearing a fob charm she's never seen before, snakes coiling around a bloodstone. Who gave him that?

"Double paix-paroli," the winner of that round calls in the dealer's direction, bending his cards in half.

"Arthur!" Urgent, but still quiet. Her temper shakes off the reins. "Where have you left P'tit while you're out carousing?"

"Well, if that don't beat all," murmurs Arthur.

"Monsters, the pair of you," she hisses.

"Oh, that's rich. This slut abandons her child," he remarks to Ernest—Blanche blushes despite herself, because the other gamblers are overhearing all this, and one diamond-studded old widow in particular is smirking—"and when I take steps to ensure his—my child's—well-being, she calls me a monster?"

His child now?

"May we proceed, gentlemen?" inquires the dealer.

"Steps," repeats Blanche in his ear, "what steps?" The two of them got tired of the wailing and stinks in a matter of hours, that's what he must mean, so they've dumped P'tit with someone else like Doctress Hoffman.

"What do you care?" asks Arthur.

"Masque," says a Mexican.

"Sept-et-le-va," decides the fat man beside him.

"I didn't abandon him," Blanche insists. "Just one night I was gone, that's all, and only because you made it impossible for me to stay, you disgusting animals! So tell me, who the hell is looking after P'tit?"

Jenny pushes through the crowd to Blanche's side.

"Que ça pue!" Ernest sniffs the air. "Brought in something on your shoe, did you, Blanche? Something froggish?"

"Oh, you're hilarious," Blanche tells him.

"I treated her too well, I believe," Arthur remarks to his friend, straightening his stacks of checks. "Spoiled her."

"If we were to let her come back," says Ernest, nodding judiciously, "it would have to be on certain conditions."

"She'd have to make up with the Prussian, for one,"

proposes Arthur. "And two, she'd have to start earning again, pronto."

"Treat you with respect," adds Ernest, counting on his fingers.

"And my friend the same," says Arthur, nodding at Ernest.

"And any visitors of ours."

Blanche's eyes meet Jenny's.

"Joke's over. Where's the kid?" demands Jenny in a voice that suddenly expands to dominate the table.

"You're interrupting the game," warns the dealer.

"And she'd have to begin by shaking this mischief maker off her tail, of course," adds Arthur.

Blanche is a pot boiling over. *"Va te faire foutre,"* she spits; he can go fuck himself. "Jenny's my only friend in the world."

Jenny turns her face toward her with a curious expression that Blanche has no idea how to read. Blanche looks back at her, refusing to qualify or explain what she's said.

"It's entirely up to you, of course," says Arthur. "But if you want your precious P'tit . . ."

Until this moment, Blanche was sure she was going to come back to Arthur. She's always been his, ever since she was a girl who gaped up at Castor and Pollux flying across the vast painted ceiling. But now, hearing his implied threat, that conviction falls away from her like a bracelet with a broken catch. She leans in very close to his puckered temple. "You're a no-account son of a bitch," she says, "and I would beg on the streets before I'd live with you again."

There's a second, a single second, when she could swear it hits Arthur, the fact of losing Blanche. And then—

"As it happens," he says, eyebrows tilting in the old confident way, "I'm thinking of going home."

Ernest pulls out his watch by the thick gold chain. "The night's still young, *mon vieux* . . ."

"Funny he calls it home," Jenny remarks to Blanche, "when the whole building belongs to you."

The dealer raps dully on the baize. "Play or settle up, gentlemen."

"Home to France, I mean," says Arthur.

The world splinters. Blanche looks at Ernest to see if this is his doing and reads shock on his hollow cheeks. Clearly it's the first he's heard of it.

"This *foutu* town, it's turned you into one of these American harpies," Arthur remarks to Blanche. "Back in Paris, I'll get myself a real woman like that." Snapping his fingers.

This is a stage trick, she's sure of it. Arthur's always singing the praises of the City of Liberty, so why would he ship back to the old country with his mangled looks and no prospects there? It's an utterly implausible volte-face, improvised to startle Blanche into falling to her knees and groveling for forgiveness, unbuttoning his pants and kissing his stubby *cigare*.

"With that face? You reckon you'd get another woman?" inquires Jenny mildly. She comes up close to examine Arthur, grimacing. "Whew, what an eyesore! String yourself with sparkles, but that won't make a Christmas tree."

Arthur pushes her an arm's length away and growls, "Why don't you crawl back to your swamp?"

"*Bon voyage,* then, and good riddance," says Jenny, "but first give the lady back her goddamn son."

"My son, you mean," Arthur corrects her.

"What makes you so sure of that?" asks Blanche through her teeth.

His expression tightens as he understands her.

A lie, of course, but one she couldn't resist throwing in his face, just to see how he'd take it.

"*Salope,* are you daring to suggest—" Ernest begins.

But Arthur cuts him off with a gesture. "Don't think I haven't noticed who's behind Blanche's new caprices," he says, turning his glittering gaze on Jenny. "What kind of freak barges around breaking up happy ménages?"

Is that what it was, Blanche asks herself, a *happy ménage*? Their life, the one they shared until that bicycle hit Blanche one Saturday night in the middle of August, seems centuries ago, far out of reach.

The tight-lipped dealer's gesturing over their heads to the doorman.

"She's a whore too, you know," Arthur remarks to Ernest.

Blanche turns to tell him that the word holds no sting for her anymore.

But it's Jenny he's nodding at. "That's how she earned her crust, folks say, back when she wore skirts."

Oh, this is fatuous. Why do men assume that every female in the world who draws the least attention to herself is theirs for hire? "You credit everything folks say?" Blanche scoffs.

"You've got the wrong Jenny Bonnet there," Jenny remarks with a slight grin.

"*Jamais de fumée sans feu,*" intones Arthur. "No smoke without fire." He sniffs the air as if he smells it.

"Imagine paying cash for a chew of that leather." Ernest hoots.

They don't believe this ludicrous rumor, Blanche sees now, they just want to cut Jenny down to size.

"May the rest of us please get on with the game?" demands the fat man.

The dealer's eyes are on the bouncers, who are working their way through the crowd toward the table. Blanche takes hold of Jenny's elbow.

"Gelding," Arthur barks, loud enough for half the saloon to hear. "Swaggering around town in muddy pants . . . don't forget you still have to sit down to make water."

Jenny bursts out laughing. "That's your trump card, really? You believe I lie awake at night wishing I could piss standing up?"

Arthur breaks out in a falsetto.

You will be all the rage with the girls,
If you'll only get a mustache . . .

"You reckon I pine for what you fellows have?" asks Jenny. He sings on, getting shriller.

You will suit all the girls to a hair,
If you've only got a mustache.

"Oh, trust me, I could glue one on if I thought it was worth a dead rat," says Jenny, stepping up and bending one wing of his waxed mustache.

Arthur's fist comes up fast, but Jenny's already ducked.

She dances out of range, her eyes exuberant, and then the bouncers are herding the two women toward the door.

*

One week later, on the fifteenth of September. Blanche is scuttling away from the building that used to belong to her. *Slow down,* she tells herself. *It seems that no one's planning to shoot you today.* Arthur's gone, she doesn't know where, but he's abandoned the City, that's what Ernest said just now, in a tone too wounded for him to be lying.

She passes a whole gang of pigtailed workmen carrying planks and ropes. Low Long's bunks, she realizes, as she turns her head and sees the carpenters filing through the door of number 815. Their denim overalls remind her of Jenny.

Old lodgers gone, Low Long told her a quarter of an hour ago, *new lodgers coming.* She wonders where the old lodgers scattered to when Low Long evicted them without notice, the Corfu men and the Irish and Chinese, the two Scotswomen and Gudrun; have they somewhere to lay their heads tonight? And Blanche, their stylish, top-of-the-bill landlady, is no different from them.

P'tit. His the one face that she can hold on to. Jenny's dead but P'tit's only lost. Ernest spoke—in the apartment just now—as if P'tit was alive, as if that went without saying. Blanche has no reason to trust him, but her years of familiarity with his every tone tell her to believe him. So she might get her baby back if she can somehow fix what she so clumsily broke this morning by blabbing about Arthur's guilt. All Ernest seems to require of her is that she walk into that inquest tomorrow and untell her story—whitewash Arthur's name, persuade the jury that everything she told Detective Bohen about vengeful *macs* was just the improvisation of a hysterical female. Easy! Blanche la Danseuse has never been afraid of an audience.

The heat's taken on the solid quality of a sponge. Thunder faintly rolls, and she keeps thinking she feels a drop, but it's only sweat squeezing out of her skin. Surely the weather must break soon and grant San Francisco the mercy of a storm? The cool mists for which Fog City is nicknamed must be hovering out there in the Bay, waiting to reclaim their peaks. So close, so close, like ecstasy just out of reach when you're riding the wrong man . . .

Where is Blanche to go? This toast of the town lacks the cash even to rent a room. Jenny would laugh. (So many things made Jenny laugh.) Blanche is the vagabond now. No home, not a friend in the world except a corpse lying in Gray's deadhouse a few blocks away, where Blanche can't summon the nerve to go. Nothing left to her but the hope of seeing her child again.

A baby on a woman's shoulder babbles and sucks its fist. Younger than P'tit, but fatter, healthier, pink-faced in the heat. Blanche looks away. Somewhere, down one of these sloping streets, hidden in some apartment in a skinny alley: P'tit. Only eight days since Blanche raced out of the apartment to escape the *macs* and their rich American and forgot to take him with her. Be honest: she'd briefly forgotten, in her panic and rage, that she had a child at all. That was eight days ago, which is a blink for a woman but a long stretch of sleepings and wakings for a baby. Eight days since she's held P'tit—not that he's ever been entirely fond of her touch. Does he retain any memory of Maman who plucked him away from Folsom Street and minded him night and day for a grand total of, what, two and a half weeks? Her thoughts strain toward him.

Tonight. She drags herself back to practicalities. Where will she spend tonight?

Of course she has resources to draw on. It's just a matter of picking one of her *michetons* and tracking him down in a way that doesn't stink of desperation. The answer's obvious at once: Lamantia, L'amant de Blanche, as the Sicilian likes to call himself, her most devoted admirer, who's been offering Madame Johanna *considerable sums* just to discover her whereabouts. Blanche already knows his.

She runs along the tracks following the next horsecar and jumps onto the step, almost catching the heel of her grubby white mule in her hem. She readjusts her carpetbag on her arm with a surge of revulsion for the few pieces of clothing inside it. They're all she owns in the world now, so she mustn't chuck the whole bag in the gutter and ride off with light arms.

Blanche gets down on Market. Lamantia's office is right opposite the fountain a former child star donated for the City's horses last year. (She thinks of young Jenny, in ribbons and a crinoline, dancing for the miners. What else didn't Blanche know about Jenny? What kind of a friendship do you call it when one party omits to tell the other the simplest facts about her life?) Under the monstrous column in faux bronze, the basin's full of boys today, men too, shoving one another aside to duck their heads under the lion's-mouth spouts. San Franciscans used to take pride in pissing in this fountain, but these hot days they're crowding in to slurp the water as if it's the finest brandy.

Blanche tips back her green parasol and stares up at the long windows of the granite building where she knows the Sicilian must be sitting, sweating over imports and prices at his mahogany desk, as he does every day except Sunday, when he visits his *mamma*. Is Lamantia daydreaming of his *bella bianca,* his beautiful white flower? Has he already read about Blanche in the news reports about San Miguel Station?

Two Specials lean against the wall. Blanche thinks for an awful moment that they're the same ones she and Jenny had to bribe last Monday on Waverly Place. She grabs a passing boy, his head soaked from the fountain: "Take a message for me?"

He puts a dripping paw out right away.

"You'll be paid when you've earned it," she snaps. "Go in those big doors and ask for Signor Lamantia. Don't give the message to anyone but the boss, you hear?"

"What message?" He's wiping his hands on his shirt.

She doesn't have paper or pen, and besides, Lamantia prefers to put nothing in writing. "Tell him that . . . that there's a white flower outside his window."

The *gamin* sniggers.

Blanche clips him around the ear. "Say it."

"White flower outside his window."

"Nobody but the boss, mind, or you won't get a cent."

Blanche stands waiting where she can be seen from the window, her carpetbag tucked behind her skirt. She tries to twirl her parasol charmingly, as if she just happens to be in the neighborhood.

"Company, miss?" mutters a passerby in a bowler.

She ignores him. Pretends to be listening to a dipso who's yowling cheerfully in the fountain, some gospel song.

She jumps when she feels a touch. It's the boy, tugging at her sleeve; she shakes him off.

"I said, I said, 'Miss,' but you didn't hear."

"All right," says Blanche, steadying her breath. "What's the answer?" She steels herself in case it's humiliating: *pressure of business,* or *some more convenient occasion* . . . Perhaps Lamantia will be too horrified by this showgirl's entanglement in a sordid murder to risk being seen with her?

"Palace, quarter of an hour," says the boy, jerking his head toward the gigantic edifice that takes up the whole next block. His hand is out—as if Lamantia wouldn't have paid him handsomely already.

"Don't push your luck," says Blanche.

The City's money is trickling south these days; the newly built Palace is an open plug hole sucking it all down toward Market Street. The biggest hotel in the world, it rears up like a cliff with seven thousand windows. Blanche shakes out her skirts and tries to muster some poise as she approaches the great doors.

The lobby's full of vast landscape paintings, old millionaires in top hats, and suave black staff in swallowtail coats and white gloves. It's almost silent, because the Turkish carpets swallow up the sound. The air is actually cool, as if Blanche is walking into a gigantic icebox; how do they manage that?

She has a brief, low-voiced wrangle with a clerk behind

a shimmering desk. "Yes, Signor Lamantia will be covering all charges . . . . Of course I've been a guest here before." Though in fact, this is her first time; Madame usually arranges such rendezvous in other hotels farther north, nearer the House of Mirrors. "Oh, and Signor Lamantia would like a bottle of champagne sent up right away," she adds. Of course the clerk recognizes Blanche as what the mealymouthed call a *fille de joie,* a "joy girl." She holds her dusty carpetbag low enough for him not to see it, but she's horribly aware of the scab on her right cheek from last night's flying glass.

At last Blanche is riding up to the seventh floor in one of the famous elevators, her stomach sinking.

"It's water that do it," the porter mentions in an accent she can narrow down only as far as the eastern states.

She stares at him.

"Water push it up," he adds. "Hydraulics."

She still has no idea what the man's talking about.

"Also we got pneumatic tubes for carrying parcels . . ."

Blanche shuts her eyes, which quells him.

The corridor she steps out on looks down onto the internal courtyard of the Palace, where carriages sweep in and unload guests in a forest of potted plants. Dizzy, Blanche squints up at the dome of opaque glass that, on a day this bright, resembles an enormous sun.

When the porter lets her into the bedroom, Blanche glances around carelessly, as if she's seen bigger and better. When he hovers, waiting for his tip, she ignores him. Finally he leaves, thumping the door closed behind him.

Cool in here, secluded behind the thick velvet drapes that seal off the bay window. Everything's carved out of teak, rosewood, ebony . . . the ceiling must be fifteen feet high. Utter silence.

Blanche uses the gleaming flush lavatory and puts in a little carbolic plug, to be ready. Wishes she were sure she had enough time for a bath, but she'll make do with a sponge-down.

Naked, she gives herself a judgmental stare in one of the many mirrors, wondering how to work some magic before Lamantia arrives. She could change into the orange-striped skirt in her bag, but that's the last clean thing she owns. And what if he walks in on her when she's halfway through reapplying her paint? How embarrassing that'll be, if the busy merchant has to stand around waiting for her to ready herself to impress him. Like letting the audience into the dressing room before the show.

Ah, here's an idea: Blanche will make a virtue of having nothing to wear. Working fast now, she scrubs all her paint off with a wet fluffy towel, lets down her dark hair, and shakes the curls out with her fingers. Raw girl is the look, for a novelty; her costume is nakedness. All to the good if it's not what Lamantia's expecting. Sometimes what men pay highest for is surprise.

Blanche dives between the crisp sheets. The bed is the most comfortable surface she's ever lain on. Though she supposes, after the shocks she's endured since this time yesterday, she'd think a haystack just as soft. Mustn't sleep, though, she warns herself. Must be ready . . .

The voices wake her with a start—Lamantia dealing with the porter at the door—but Blanche pretends to be deep in innocent sleep.

She knows he must be tiptoeing to the bed and

watching her. He leans so close that she can smell his hot breath, the bologna he had for lunch. He slowly slides the edge of the sheet away from her back. Sometimes men want to be seen looking, but other times, they congratulate themselves that they're managing to watch while remaining unseen.

After a minute or two Blanche stretches and blinks. Confusion—then Sleeping Beauty smiles for her tall, dark, heavy-fleshed prince, who is even more massive than she remembered. Lamantia wears no facial hair, but the shadow breaks through on his cheek by midafternoon.

"Amoruccia mia!" he whispers, planting a kiss on her cheek. "All these weeks, my dearest! Where have you been?"

So he knows nothing about her entanglement in a murder case. But the last thing Blanche wants to do is explain or say why she's come looking for Lamantia today instead of letting Madame Johanna set up the encounter . . . so she silences his mouth with hers. She's got a job to do.

This is one of her specialties: giving *michetons* the impression that what's happening is happening not so much because they want it as because Blanche, in her lip-biting, helpless way, needs it. Right here, right now: her desire is so urgent that she might just scream the whole hotel down if he—this particular man, out of all the men in the world, who possesses the secret power—if this man doesn't part her pearl-sheened thighs and bang the living daylights out of her.

Lamantia hasn't had time to take any clothes off. Blanche twists herself around and lies back, slides with every thrust of his so his long *cigare* seems to be shoving her farther and farther off the enormous bed. "Oh!" It's a simple backbend, nothing compared to what she used to manage in her circus days. Upside down, she keeps herself from falling on her head by pressing her splayed fingers to the floorboards. (Well waxed, she notes, with a lemony polish.) The pose reminds her of a Sabine-captive act she used to do, hair trailing behind her, on the most asthmatic of the circus's ponies. Blanche keeps her eyes on the glossy molding around the door, the sparkling chandelier, and lets herself imagine that she's cantering farther and farther and farther away . . . "Ah! Ah!"

Won't be long now till she's brought Lamantia off; they're coasting. So Blanche switches off the tick-tick of her brain and tightens her *cul* as if resisting each thrust. Sometimes for a day or a week she forgets how much she needs this: to be used, abased, crushed into something else. The Sicilian's not Arthur Deneve, of course. He's got none of that ruthless precision. (She scolds herself for thinking about Arthur, for summoning up that particular thick cock, those intelligent fingers.) But Lamantia's a man giving her what men give women and that's all she requires, surely?

Now she lets out a gasp so unladylike, so dreadfully guttural, that the businessman sobs like a boy who's appalled at his own badness and pumps even harder. Blanche always puts on a good show, but performing doesn't mean shamming—she's never needed to fake it. From the day Arthur taught her to do it, behind the elephant stalls, she's relished nothing as much as a fuck: the stuffed-to-bursting sensation that erases thought, the steam train of its movement, the frantic mazurka for two.

And on that kernel of truth Blanche has built a legendary persona. She feels sensations and cries them out as arias, takes every urge and tears the roof down with it: not a dry hole in the house. How did Ernest put it? That Blanche was obsessed with cock, lived and breathed it? It's awful, but there's a grain of truth to it. Men are tools Blanche uses for her satisfaction. Dancing, dancing, over a cliff into merciful darkness—

The two of them catch their breath, finally.

Lamantia leans up on one elbow and pours the champagne. The man's such a bourgeois, thinks Blanche. He's smacking his lips with satisfaction at his own wickedness because he's taken an afternoon off from facts and figures to bed the Lively Flea.

She slips away to the bathroom to douche because she can't trust the little plug on its own. The carbolic stings hard enough to make her hiss. Blanche has always had to do this, whether at home or with *michetons,* because most men balk at the clammy grip of rubber safes. She's meticulous about it. P'tit is the only accident she's ever had.

Tomorrow. At the inquest. If she does exactly what Ernest requires of her—

She mustn't think about P'tit and her hope of getting him back. Not here, not now. One task at a time.

"Bella bianca," Lamantia murmurs when Blanche returns, "what have you done to your lovely face?"

She rearranges it into a smile—but it's the little cut he's fingering.

Blanche considers evasion and rejects it quickly. No doubt Lamantia will hear about the murder at some point, and he can't stand to be lied to. In the past, he's thrown the odd jealous fit on nights when she's claimed illness but he's suspected she's been with another *micheton*. So she lets her face crumple. "I was . . . it was a piece of broken glass. Someone shot my friend through a window. In front of me."

His bushy eyebrows soar.

Her misery is true, so why does it feel like she's putting it on? "The papers are full of it—it happened down at San Miguel Station."

"I'm too busy to read the papers," he scolds her gently. "What friend was this?"

"Jenny Bonnet," says Blanche, choking on the name. "She caught frogs for the restaurant trade."

"That crazy girl in pants?"

So he's heard of her.

He goes off on one of his tirades in Italian.

Blanche can't make out more than a word or two. "I thought you were too busy to read the papers," she says sourly.

"This so-called friend of yours"—he's back to English now, rubbing at the scab on Blanche's cheek as if to erase it—"dragging you into her criminal circles—"

"Jenny didn't fire the gun!" And then Blanche locks her lips because if she lets out her wrath, it's going to wreck everything. She's here to make some money, she reminds herself.

So she produces a few weak sobs, though her eyes are bone-dry, and rolls around on the creamy pillows until Lamantia strokes the small of her back. "I hate for you to be mixed up in such things," he complains. "Exposed in the press—"

Blanche almost laughs. As if she has some respectability to lose!

"My name won't need to come up, I presume?"

"How could it?" she murmurs. The egotism of the man!

She lets him pour her another glass, to comfort her. The iced champagne is bitter in her mouth. He's dressing already. Lamantia's never stayed a night with her; Blanche is not sure whether he's married or just nervous about what his clerks might say if he came to the office in the same shirt two days in a row. Just as well that he's going—she'll be able to get some real sleep—but she finds herself offended that he's gotten all he needs from her already. Most men tire too soon for Blanche. (Not Arthur; he can ride all night. *Stop it,* she snaps at herself. Does she not have enough pride to give up panting for a man who's tried to kill her?)

The Sicilian lays some banknotes on the glossy bedside table. Since he's such a devoted regular, Blanche leaves the amount up to him, because in her experience, graciousness pays off. But she'll be needing some substantial funds soon to set herself up in a new apartment with a whole new wardrobe. (Room for P'tit? A live-in nursemaid? *Don't you dare, Blanche!* Her hope's like some eager dog straining hard enough to break its leash.)

"I may be dancing at the House of Mirrors tomorrow," she mentions, realizing that it's true. The fact is, Blanche can't think of a faster way to raise a good lump sum—almost three hundred dollars' profit in a single evening—than to swallow her bile and do one last show, since Madame's offered her such a bonanza for it.

Blanche expects Lamantia to be glad to hear that. Her

michetons generally love to watch her dance in front of other men, lesser men who can't have her afterward. Sometimes she thinks what a man is really paying for is not actually a rendezvous in a hotel room but the right to interrupt the dance, to yank Blanche off her pedestal and treat her like any ordinary woman. And yet they remain nostalgic for the mystery, the spectacle . . .

But this time Lamantia's round, stubbled face doesn't light up. "I wish you could be done with all that, my darling."

"A girl has to live," she says uncertainly.

"Perhaps Madame and I could come to some arrangement. Yes." He's looking startled now, exhilarated at his own daring. "If you could be a very discreet companion—perhaps we could settle on something private, exclusive—"

As Blanche told Madame this morning, she never wanted a keeper. But that was when she thought she had other resources: legal title to a six-story building on Sacramento Street, for one thing. Now Blanche has nothing. The notion of not having to find herself lodgings, clients . . . The temptation of letting somebody take charge . . . If any man can keep her safe from now on, surely Lamantia can?

A pulse bounds in her throat. Should she trust him with the whole story at once? The fact of the baby, and of his having been spirited away by his father, and of Ernest blackmailing her to lie to the coroner tomorrow if she ever wants to see P'tit again?

No. A superstitious conviction seizes Blanche that if she pronounces P'tit's name, that'll be the last time she ever hears of her son.

Besides, Lamantia might well be put right off her by

these entanglements. Men never feel quite the same about a woman's body once they know it's done that thing: widened and torn to push out a baby's head.

So Blanche plays for time. "I'm afraid I ain't Madame's to dispose of," she murmurs. "She and I . . . we've come to a parting of the ways. In fact, tomorrow night will be my final appearance at the House of Mirrors."

"All the better," cries Lamantia. "You're too good for that mob. That settles it. Let me look after you as you deserve."

"I'm overwhelmed," she says, honestly enough. "I'll have to give the matter the most serious thought . . ."

"You could have been killed last night," he lectures her, gigantic finger wagging in her face.

And Blanche gets a glimpse of how tedious it might be to be this man's mistress.

"You should take it as a sign to give up your disreputable associates, all that scum that floats around town," he says. "I'm offering you a fresh start."

But he hasn't specified dollars per month. The two of them have never mentioned figures, in the elegant game they've played. If Blanche were to put herself entirely into the hands of this man, she'd need to know the numbers first.

She blinks, clouds her gaze, as if desire has distracted her again. "Will you be there in the audience tomorrow night?" she murmurs, reaching out to put her small hand in his hot grip.

*

Early morning on Monday, the eleventh of September, and Blanche is lying awake in a cheap, odorous hotel on Commercial Street where she's spent the last three nights. Well, not so much a hotel as a house of assignation; girls thump up the stairs with their customers at every hour, breaking up Blanche's sleep. She's brooding on P'tit, wondering whether anyone is picking him up when he cries. Has he been doped with something "quieting"?

She hasn't dared go back to 815 Sacramento Street since the terrible scene in the faro saloon. *You're a no-account son of a bitch, and I would beg on the streets before I'd live with you again,* she told Arthur, and how fine the words rang out. But Blanche should have made sure she held better cards before indulging herself in grand declarations. Should have gotten firm possession of her apartment, her clothes, and her money before provoking the *macs.* (Why didn't she think to grab at least the nest egg from her old boot, at least, before she rushed out with Jenny to look for the men last Friday?) Above all, Blanche should have kept her mind fixed on P'tit. Couldn't she have managed to stay polite, even humble, until Arthur revealed what *steps* he'd taken for the care of the baby? What the hell did she think she was doing throwing down the gauntlet when the men still had P'tit?

This is why women don't start wars, she thinks with a flash of contempt for her whole sex. It's the blasted babies.

Blanche tries to make impossible calculations. Knowing Arthur as she does . . . but does she really know him at all, this enraged, scar-faced man? What's the best—or the least stupid—way to proceed? At night he and Ernest will be drunk. In the morning they'll be asleep. In the afternoon, the worse for wear. How long should Blanche wait for their wrath to calm down? Approach too soon and they'll scorn her, just like they did in the faro saloon. Delay too long and—could there be any truth at all to Arthur's boast that he's going back to France to get himself a *real woman*? Every day she waits is full of gnawing uncertainty about P'tit, his whereabouts, and his welfare, and Blanche is not sure she can bear many more of these days.

If she tracks the men down in a bar or at the gaming table again, knowing they have an audience will harden their arrogance. But if she goes to the apartment—steps into a room with them once more—then all the power is theirs. The last time she was there, after all, Arthur proposed to the American that they hold her down and take her three ways. No, Blanche decides, she has to speak to Arthur one to one, but in a public place.

*

A few hours later she's standing on Sacramento Street, watching the second-floor windows. This is her own building, she reminds herself with a sense of dull resentment, so why is she skulking outside it like a burglar?

Because she needs to know who's there. She's waiting to glimpse Arthur on his own, without his malign companion at his side to egg him on. Surely if Blanche catches Arthur coming out of the front door of number 815 or approaching it from the street, she can run up and throw herself beautifully, pathetically on his mercy? Appeal to his vanity, his boredom with this elaborate bluff, his wish to be master. It doesn't matter what cruel things he says to her, so long as he tells her where in this whole sweltering city she can find their son. She'll take P'tit off his hands, gratefully, and the two of them will be no further trouble to Arthur, ever.

Beside her, Jenny tilts her cap and squints up. Does a little shuffle. Jenny can't stand still; Blanche registers that only now, because it's the first time they've ever had to wait in one spot.

The half-moon, up in broad day, looks like some cheap bit of stage scenery.

Blanche returns her gaze to the second floor of the building.

"Seen that?" Jenny asks.

"What?" she says, jumping.

Jenny's jerking her thumb not at the building but at a broadside pasted crooked on the wall behind them. *Evangeline: A Burlesque*. "I dozed off in the middle," she remarks, "but the spouting whale was first-rate."

Blanche tilts her parasol and blinks up at the glittering windows. P'tit. P'tit. His name a hiccupping heartbeat.

Jenny flicks her cap up into the air and catches it on her elbow. The second time, she spins it way above her and crooks her neck so it lands neatly on her coal-black hair.

On the corner of Dupont a thick knot of workmen has formed around a fellow talking himself hoarse on a box. Blanche catches only a few phrases: *evil empire* and—*noisome vermicelli,* could she have heard that right?

"Just the anti-coolies," says Jenny, following her gaze.

The man's voice rises to a rusty whoop. "Let the capitalists quake, because their reign is over."

A single clap from someone beside him.

"They have opened the gates of this city to Oriental labor, whose octopus of disease now extends its fell tentacles into every quarter. Soon workingmen will rise up and deluge it in blood and fire!"

The applause is limp. As if San Franciscans have the energy to so much as pick their noses in this heat, Blanche thinks, let alone set a fire!

Arthur, Arthur, she calls in her head, watching the second-story windows. Does he still love her, a little, in some poisoned way? Is he keeping P'tit as bait to lure her back? But he must realize that after the things they've said and done, the two of them can't take up their old dance again. And why would he even want Blanche back if she's the nasty piece of shoddy he thinks her?

" *'Mardi i' r'viendra m' voire.'* " Jenny sings the old ballad under her breath, as if reading Blanche's mind. " *'O gai! vive la rose.'* "

He'll come back to see me on Tuesday; hey, long live the rose. Of course Blanche knows the carefree lyrics of the old song, but she's not in the mood.

Mais je n'en voudrai pas,
Vive la rose et le lilas!

Jenny lilts as sweet as some bird on a branch relishing the sun on its feathers.

Can she be taken at her word, Blanche wonders, the girl in the song? Is it true she won't open her arms to her man if he does crawl back to her? Or is that just something girls insist when their men dump them? She turns to look at Jenny. "Ever had your heart broken?" she demands.

Jenny only grins and cracks her knuckles, a sound that Blanche hates.

"Well, aren't you a slippery fish."

"Hope so," says Jenny. "It's the other kind that end up in the pot."

Blanche lets out a long, blistering breath. It's clear they're only going to annoy each other today. If this is friendship, no wonder she's never had much truck with it. "Don't you have any place you need to be?" She waits. "No frogs that need catching?"

"Delivered a couple sackfuls yesterday," Jenny assures her.

"This is my business." Blanche eyes the windows, the door, waiting for the slightest glimpse of Arthur. She realizes that she doesn't want Jenny to witness her abasing herself, offering anything at all just so long as he'll give P'tit back. "You ain't obliged to get tangled up in it."

"That reminds me," says Jenny, ignoring Blanche's comment, "you ever hear about the frog who got acquainted with a mouse?"

"I have the feeling I'm about to."

" 'Hey,' says Froggie, 'what say we declare our friendship by tying one of your feet to one of mine?' "

Despite herself, Blanche half laughs.

"Mousie's persuadable," says Jenny. "So the two hop along together to the meadow for their dinner. Then Froggie goes, 'What say we stand at the edge of the pond and admire ourselves?' "

"Oh no."

Jenny mimes the yoked animals leaning out dangerously over the water. "Froggie falls in—or jumps, some say, but there's no proof, and afterward Froggie can't say, for obvious—"

"Get on with it!"

A slow smile. " 'Help, help,' cries Mousie, 'I can't swim.' And Froggie answers, 'How do you know until you try?' " Jenny's voice has a hectic cheer. "So Froggie swims around croaking merrily while Mousie's swallowing a bellyful of water. But then Hawk sees them and dives." She mimes the ruthless swoop of the bird. "Lifts Mousie into the sky for a snack, see, while Froggie's dangling below from one little toe. 'Help, help,' cries Froggie, 'I can't fly!' And Hawk says—"

" 'How do you know until you try?' " supplies Blanche. Then, after a moment: "That's a terrible story."

"The best ones generally are."

They lapse into silence.

Blanche returns her gaze to the apartment windows. In her imagining of it, Arthur's going to step out of the building any minute now with P'tit on his hip. The man will look hollow-eyed, harried; the child radiant with relief at the sight of his mother. In the daydream, Blanche runs up, as graceful as a prima ballerina, and Arthur lets out a single sigh of capitulation and puts P'tit in her arms . . .

"Now, in the song, they get married, if you prefer that," says Jenny.

"What?" she asks distractedly.

" 'Frog and Mouse.' 'A Frog he would a wooing go,' " she croons, grunting very low in her throat and keeping time with her boot on the sidewalk,

Heigh ho, said Rowly,
A Frog he would a wooing go,
Whether his mother would let him or no—

"Something tells me this is going to be a long courtship," Blanche mutters, her eyes still fixed on the bland panes.

"I'll skip to the wedding, if you like," offers Jenny. "It was some party, let me tell you." She starts singing and tapping her sole again.

Pray, Mr. Frog, will you give us a song,
Heigh ho, said Rowly,
Let the subject be something that's not very long . . .

"Jenny—" Blanche interrupts hoarsely.

But Jenny keeps on as if she's getting paid for it.

Blanche is chewing her lip raw. What possessed her, the other night at the faro saloon, to hint that P'tit wasn't Arthur's? Of all the lies she might have invented in a spirit of malice, none could have put the baby in more danger. Is Blanche some kind of idiot or just too addicted to the pleasure of the moment to think about anybody but herself?

Jenny sings on relentlessly:

As they were in glee and a merry making,
Heigh ho, said Rowly...

Now she slips her arm through Blanche's and tries to swing her.

Blanche shakes her off harder than she needs to. "Is it possible for you to shut your trap for one almighty minute?"

"Girard, right?"

Blanche doesn't know what to make of that till she follows Jenny's gaze across the street and flinches. Ernest, hovering on the curb, staring in her direction: Could he have emerged from the building while she was looking away for a second? A horsecar clanks between them, cutting off her view.

"Ready," announces Jenny, rubbing her hands.

This was a bad idea. Blanche hurries away down the street.

Jenny gallops after her. "What are you doing?"

"We shouldn't be here." Glancing over her shoulder, Blanche can't see Ernest in the crowd.

"Hey," Jenny objects, "we've been waiting half the day."

"Waiting for Arthur, not Ernest."

"Don't back down now."

"I've seen what happens when you won't back down. You're a born fight-picker," Blanche cries. Where's Ernest gone? Not on the opposite curb now. Is it possible he didn't catch sight of the women after all?

"Some fights are ripe for the picking," insists Jenny.

And he's there, all at once, in front of Blanche, moving with the gait of a long-legged bird, eyes red-rimmed and his face so drawn and clammy that she wonders if he's ill.

Ernest seizes her by her elbow and marches her down the nearest alley, holding her close—a parody of a suitor. These Chinatown lanes all close in overhead like pleats in stained cloth. Waverly Place, that's where they are: Blanche recognizes the barbershop with the Tin How Temple on its top floor. Fifteen-Cent Alley, some call this, for the price of the haircuts.

"How dare you show your face," he's demanding, "you infernal whore."

He's not sick, she realizes, except with rage.

Jenny's right behind her but not saying a word. (Small mercies.)

"Ernest." As softly as Blanche can. "I'm so sorry for everything that's happened." There's a face watching through a sliding panel in the nearest door: a *mui jai.* Then a small hand, beckoning. Is the girl offering Blanche a refuge from the furious man, or inviting him in? *Two bittee lookee.* She forces her eyes back to Ernest. "All I'm asking for is my P'tit."

"How do you have the gall to pretend you're a woman? If you wanted that baby," says Ernest in a wolfish snarl, "if you'd ever really wanted him, wouldn't you have held on tight to him when he first dropped out of your hole?"

She cringes away from the words more than from his spirituous breath.

"No answer to that one?" He grabs her jaw with one hard hand, squeezes her lips together. "Then why don't you shut your mouth?"

"Hey, hey," says Jenny, pleasantly, at their side.

He barks over his shoulder. "Stand down, Bonnet, or I'll see to you."

"No, you stand down. You're hurting the lady."

"What lady?" Ernest yelps with a sort of laughter.

Blanche feels his grip relax a moment, and she shoves with both arms and wrestles her jaw away from him, staggering backward. The pain brings tears to her eyes. The *mui jai*'s pale face is gone from the door; the panel slides shut.

Instead of seizing Blanche again, Ernest turns to Jenny. "Settle something for the record, would you? Arthur maintains you're just an interfering meddler. But my money's on your being a dirty *gouine* who wants this muff for herself."

He flicks one finger at Blanche, who goes rigid when she understands him.

"Fact or fiction, *chérie*?" he asks, stepping close enough to Blanche to make her leap out of range again. "I just hope you charge high, for the dignity of the trade. Don't tell me you're doing this piece of filth for free."

Jenny cuts in relaxedly before Blanche can answer. "I declare, you fellows are the limpest pair of leeches I've ever encountered. You sponge off Blanche for the full of a year, then sulk like cast-off mistresses the minute she decides to go solo. Castor and Pollux!" She lets out a snort of mirth. "I say it's high time you get out there"—she waves toward Sacramento Street—"and peddle your own handsome asses."

Blanche can't believe Jenny just said that.

For a moment Ernest only stares, and then he's clawing at Jenny's jacket.

"Oy," she shouts, "hands off."

"That's my friend's shirt," he snarls, "the one that he—gentleman that he is—was kind enough to lend you the night we found you stinking up the sofa, and you never gave it back, you goddamn thief."

Jenny's fighting back in a tangle of arms and kicking legs. The gray jacket's half open, the pale green shirt loose in the vee of the waistcoat, buttons popping off. "You've torn it, you son of a bitch!" She's half bare, eyes bulging. She wrests herself away, skips to beyond Ernest's reach, and suddenly the Colt's out and pointed at him.

Putain de merde. How did Blanche let it come to this, murder about to be done in a Chinatown alley on a Monday afternoon in September?

"I give you fair warning—" Jenny speaks levelly, even though she's out of breath. With the hand not holding the gun, she wraps the ripped shirt around her to cover up her pale ribs, shoves it into her pants.

"Warning of what?" sneers Ernest, standing tall the way Monsieur Loyal always taught them. "It's not your clothes I'm going to rip to pieces, Bonnet, it's you. Whale the tar out of you, fix you for good and all, so you can't ever lure a woman from her man again."

"That's not what happened," Blanche protests, "you crack-brained—"

But the click of Jenny cocking her Colt makes a little pool of silence in Waverly Place. "Fix me?" Jenny says, smiling at Ernest. "You ain't the only one to try that. But I'll dance on your grave first."

"Jenny!" Blanche shrieks.

Ernest's eyes slide to Blanche, then back to Jenny. He jerks his head over his shoulder toward Sacramento. "You really mean to gun me down in broad daylight with witnesses all around?"

The three of them are standing very still.

"He's not worth hanging for," Blanche roars at her. Blanche could end up in jail for this business, along with her so-called friend.

Jenny purses her dry lips.

"I didn't think so," says Ernest. "You've made your bed. Time to lie in it." He turns his back on them and starts walking up the alley.

He strikes a pose at the corner of Sacramento. Peers in both directions, then lets out a piercing whistle through his fingers. "Officers!"

Is he bluffing? Blanche wonders. Police almost never come into Chinatown.

"Come on," she says, dipping to pick up Jenny's scattered buttons from the dust, out of an obscure instinct to erase all traces of the encounter.

Jenny's pocketing her Colt, very cool, and straightening her clothes. Waverly Place opens onto Clay Street at the other end, so they can be out of sight in half a minute.

But here comes Ernest, marching down the alley with two Specials. How the hell did he rustle them up so fast?

"Run," Blanche whispers.

"Ah, that'd be called resisting arrest," Jenny murmurs, "and those two know my face." She sounds faintly proud of the fact. "Afternoon, Officers." She tips her cap as she strolls to meet them.

"Well, if it isn't our old friend the frog-catcher," says the taller, red-faced one. "Done your time in County already?"

"Don't time just fly," Jenny replies.

"Been hunting today, I assume, from your costume?"

"Always on the lookout," she assures them.

"Ribbit!" croaks the shorter man.

"What is this, a strawberry social?" demands Ernest hoarsely. "This female is clearly in male attire. Do your duty and arrest her."

"Did this pup just try to tell us our duty?" the taller asks the shorter.

"As it happens, I'm on my way home to change," Jenny puts in.

"Into bonnet and flounces?" asks the shorter one, deadpan.

"Got a bustle waiting for me the size of a wagon," Jenny tells him, sketching it comically with her hands. "Now, I wish you both a good day . . ."

The taller puts a hand on her torn sleeve as she slides by. "Thirsty weather, this."

"Isn't it, though. Could I wish you well to the tune of two bucks?"

"I told you, she pulled a gun on me," protests Ernest.

"Try ten," the Special tells Jenny.

"Fellows! That's as much as the judge would fine me."

He shrugs. "Less fuss for all concerned, though. This way your evening's your own." His gesture takes in the whole City, as if he's offering it to her on a plate.

"What would you say to five?" Jenny asks.

"I'd say come down handsome now, Jenny, or you'll be back in the cells for supper."

"Five's pretty handsome," she argues, still smiling.

Jenny hasn't got ten, Blanche realizes, and she starts digging in her carpetbag for her own pocketbook.

"Take my five and call it quits?" Jenny splays the notes like a hand of cards.

"She's a thief too," Ernest bursts out. "That shirt belongs to Mr. Arthur Deneve—"

"And another five for your trouble, Officers," says Blanche, holding out the coins she's finally added up.

Jenny throws her an irritated look, as if Blanche has spoiled the game.

But the faces of the Specials have relaxed. They collect their winnings from the two women.

"Come on," says Jenny in Blanche's ear. She hooks her by the elbow and hurries her up the alley toward Sacramento Street. "It's all hunky-dory now."

"This is . . . this is corruption of the law to pervert the course of justice," Ernest roars after the Specials. "What about my friend's shirt?"

"Do we look as if we give a rat's ass about a shirt?" the shorter inquires.

"Dandy Frogs and their goddamn clothes," says the taller, rolling his eyes as they turn away.

VI

I HARDLY KNEW YE

On Tuesday, the twelfth of September, Blanche's mouth still hurts. For a bewildered moment, waking up in the sour-smelling rented room on Commercial Street, she thinks she's been gnawing at her own lips in her sleep, but then she remembers Waverly Place yesterday, and Ernest's vicious grip on her face.

She lies still, feeling it settle on her: ennui. How can she be frightened and bored at the same time? Nothing to do today except wait, worry, wait some more.

If Arthur were here, at least he'd fuck me. Blanche can't quite believe she's thinking that. But it's true, she could count on him for that much; he was always ready to bend her over something if he had ten minutes free. The man spent most of his life in one of two states: half hard or willing to be hardened. There was a primitive comfort to it, the familiarity of being penetrated, somehow sharp and blunt at the same time. Occasionally Blanche's mind used to float up to the ceiling and she'd look down and think: *How curious, those two, it seems so important to them, that bit of him pushing into that bit of her, in and out again, how repetitious*. But it worked. Fucking wasn't always exquisite but it did make Blanche feel like a woman, like she knew what she was made for. Like something was happening. Five times a day, sometimes; she had to douche so much, her insides stung. So, yes, Arthur's a son of a bitch, but she misses him.

There's a scrap protruding under the door; Blanche thinks at first it's just a square of light, but no, it's the torn-off margin of a newspaper, and it bears an unfamiliar scrawl: *Heading to the Eight Mile House for a couple days (San Miguel Station)*. Blanche has heard the name before; a saloon of some kind, on the frayed southern edge of the City, where Jenny sometimes puts up if she's stayed out late frog-hunting. So the note must be Jenny's way of saying good-bye after the unsettling encounter with Ernest and the Specials on Waverly Place. Or, rather, her way of saying *Count me out. Nice knowing you. Places to be, frogs to catch* . . . Anger flares in Blanche like a match.

And then she reads it again and remembers that Jenny rarely volunteers information. Perhaps it's meant as an invitation of a most nonchalant kind. Why would it be any of Blanche's business where Jenny was heading unless Jenny was suggesting Blanche come along?

So here's Blanche in a rented buggy an hour later making for San Miguel Station, because she can't think of anything else to do, and her instincts tell her it's best to stay out of Ernest and Arthur's way as long as they're in such a crazy rage. Since setting a pair of Specials on Jenny led to nothing worse than a ten-dollar fine, next time the *macs* might come with their knives: *fix you for good and all*. Blanche shudders, feeling Ernest's thumbprint on her lip. Just talk, that's all it was, probably, the kind of bluster men resort to in a row. But still. Time to get out of town.

After settling her bill on Commercial Street, Blanche doesn't have much in the way of cash left, but there's no point fretting, she tells herself. She could have taken the train but she fancied a ride, for once, hence the buggy. The speed of her motion stirs the parched air, making a sort of breeze. It's been so long, Blanche has forgotten how good it feels to have wind moving over her, still hot but not half so stale. Why doesn't everyone flee from the City who can?

It seems like years since Blanche has held a pair of reins. In the hack's head-down, put-upon way, he's got something in common with the circus horses who used to bear her balancings and flips. Wonderful to be up above the crowd, rattling over the cobbles of Stockton Street, making people hustle out of the way. She's overshot Mission before she knows it, so she makes a sharp right on Howard to ensure she avoids Folsom, because the thought of the weeklies and the paid-ups is bad enough but that leads to P'tit, to what kind of room he might be shut in right now and what he might be gnawing on for lack of his doorknob, which rolls heavily from side to side in the bottom of Blanche's carpetbag . . . Abandoning the City feels like giving up hope of finding P'tit. *Not for long,* Blanche swears to herself. What's the old proverb about running away? *Live to fight another day.*

She cracks the reins to hurry the old horse on. Just as the stable boy at Marshall's told her to, she's following the single train track right across the Mission District. The horse slows as they climb the grade. From up here Blanche can glimpse the sea's glittering tongue.

Through the Bernal Cut into Glen Canyon, and soon the bleak silhouette of what must be the Industrial School rears up on her right, with its scores of little windows winking through their bars; the stable boy told her to watch out for it, so she'd know she was almost at San Miguel Station. Fellows locked up in that place as old as twenty and as young as three, he mentioned—which disgusted Blanche. "Whips and gags for the troublemakers," the stable boy added with relish. When Blanche mocked him for crediting every rumor he heard, he insisted that it had all come out before a grand jury.

"Gagged and whipped is what you'll end up if you tell such lies," Blanche said to him, but with a smile and a dime to tip him for the directions.

The hills are arid, pink. Out in the brunt of the sun, Italian-looking families haul water from their rickety windmills and spread horseshit.

Then even the farms come to an end. Nothing but the County Road and the train line beside it, the last two exhausted runners in a race. A sign that's off one hinge: VARIETY OF LOTS NOW AVAILABLE FROM THE RAILROAD HOMESTEAD ASSOCIATION. A low wooden depot, silvery lettering faded almost past the point of legibility—SAN MIGUEL STATION—with a scattering of shacks around it. It barely deserves to be called a village. But then again, Jenny knows this part of the Bay, and some little nowhere's probably the safest spot to hide in till the *macs* calm down.

The dogs of the settlement yip at the horse as Blanche reins it in. One of the buildings is standing on blocks like wobbling stilts. How did it ever get through the last quake? A sign tacked up unevenly near the roof proclaims, in large, childish lettering, that this is the San Miguel Saloon and Hotel. Is that the official name of what Jenny calls the Eight Mile House?

A whoop of greeting from the shady part of the unrailed porch, where—Blanche squints against the light—Jenny's lolling in a weather-beaten chair. "Ladies and gentlemen," cries Jenny, "for your delectation, we have the honor to present that queen of motion, that eminence of equestrian elegance—"

"Did you come by train?" interrupts Blanche.

"Shin power," Jenny informs her, nodding at the bicycle that leans against the building's gappy foundations.

The windows are stuffed with rags in places. "High-class locale," mutters Blanche, getting down from the buggy and looping the reins over a post where a little palomino pony already stands.

"Ah, it'll grow on you."

The scrawny mongrel's hackles rise as Blanche comes up the steps, but Jenny makes the introductions. "Friend! Friend!" She's done a ragamuffin darning job on Arthur's green shirt, Blanche notices.

The screen door squeals open and a mousy boy bursts out, wiping his mouth.

"Mr. John McNamara Jr.," Jenny says, addressing him, "may I present Miss Blanche Beunon?"

Blanche automatically puts a hip a little to one side, makes her smile dazzle.

The boy's eyes go big as he nods at her.

"Had a bash at *Tom Sawyer* yet?" Jenny's asking him.

He nods fervently. "Reckon it even beats *Roughing It.*" Jenny whistles.

Blanche notices that John Jr.'s eyes have strayed to the high-wheeler. "I shudder to think of Jenny bumping out here on that contraption," she remarks.

"Oh, she knows her way," he tells Blanche. "Got her educating out hereabouts and all."

"Really?" She turns to Jenny.

Who's already springing off the porch to show off her bicycle. "Fancy a go, John Jr.?"

"Me too," whines a small girl, emerging around the door with another screech of hinges, a tinier boy behind her.

"Yiz'll stay away from that yoke before it snaps your legs to bits," orders their mother, stepping out with arms crossed on her flat bust.

"I wouldn't get up on it if you paid me a dollar," remarks an older girl, smirking in the doorway.

Jenny introduces Blanche to Mrs. Ellen McNamara and Mary Jane, Kate, and Jeremiah. (Why, Blanche wonders, must Irish families always have a John and a Mary?)

Then Jenny offers to give a demonstration. "Let's start with the coward's option—lean it against a wall. See this mounting step?" She taps a piece of metal sticking out just above the little rear wheel.

"Out of the way," says Blanche, surprising herself. She's already got her mauve skirt halfway up and tucked into her sash in three places.

Jenny just smiles.

The Irishwoman looks disapproving but she's such a slattern herself, who's she to frown?

Blanche takes hold of the gigantic handlebars and leads the machine away from the wall. *Coward's option!* Its cruelly tapered saddle is so high, she can barely see over it. But skill trumps size.

The McNamaras scatter at her approach. Jenny does a drumroll on her thighs. Does she believe Blanche can do it or is she just enjoying the prospect of seeing her friend make a fool of herself? Blanche runs a little to get the machine moving, puts her right foot on the mounting step, and stands up. But she's losing momentum already. Hops down, tries it again, sweating like a beast. Ducking, she gives a couple of scoots with her left foot, then—can she make it to the saddle in one jump? No, too high for her. She claws at the passing pedal with her left foot till it's at the top of its arc, then straightens up on that for an instant and throws herself into the saddle.

Jenny yodels with glee.

Blanche flails, her legs barely long enough to press the pedals with the balls of her feet, her toes stretching fit to rip at the bottom of each orbit. Wild zigzags—but then she begins to get the hang of the steering. Cuts a wide circle across the sandy ground between the Eight Mile House, the store, and the pond (probably deeper than it looks, she warns herself). She risks a turn of the head toward what she can't help thinking of as the crowd, all six of them.

The McNamaras are open-mouthed. John Jr. claps as if his life depends on it.

"My oh my," crows Jenny. "Enjoying yourself up there, are you?"

"Vastly," calls Blanche, breathless.

"Now there's only the dismount, which is considerably harder than the mount. Want a tip about how to get down in one piece?"

"*Va te faire foutre,*" Blanche says rudely, trusting the McNamaras don't know French.

A little later, she's sponging her sweat and dust off in the guest chamber. Well, that's the title with which Ellen McNamara dignifies the front left of the shack's four rooms. The bedstead—imitation black walnut—faces the window, as if there were a view to look at, not just the dusty scrape of the County Road. Instead of a curtain, a square of green baize, nailed at the top, hangs down to block the sun.

A needlework sampler with slightly jagged letters reads:

Mid pleasures and palaces though we may roam,
Be it ever so humble, there's no place like home!

Blanche thinks she recognizes that from a song. *Humble* is an understatement. She fingers the sheets uneasily. "I wonder how many of the brats share this bed when the McNamaras don't have lodgers?"

"Packed sardine-style," says Jenny, nodding.

Blanche mustn't think about P'tit, cribbed tight with who knows how many others. She arranges her few possessions on the dilapidated bureau beside the washstand. "The elder boy—you give him books?"

"Pass them on," Jenny corrects her. "It's that or use the pages to wipe my ass."

"Doesn't he go to school?"

A shrug. "As the fellow says, never let schooling interfere with your education."

"He likes you."

"Don't everybody?" A flash of a grin.

"Except the ones who want to *fix you for good and all,*" Blanche says in her best manly growl, which makes them both giggle.

The older girl's hovering in the doorway. "Mary Jane," says Blanche with a civil nod. "I know we must be crowding you some . . ."

"That's all right. Mammy and Dadda'd put us to sleep in the pond to make a dime."

Jenny laughs at the image. "One of these days you'll be grown and gone, Mary Jane."

A toss of the head. "Gone where?"

"Take a job in the City, maybe. You'll have a fine time, and your pick of the fellows too."

"Oh, indeed!" Flushing, the girl disappears into the saloon.

In the evening, McNamara Senior comes back from a laboring job, soaked through with sweat. Blanche and Jenny sit down with the family for some salt cod. (Blanche has already steeled herself, knowing that the Irish can't cook.) Jenny talks mostly to the little girl, Kate, who's teaching her some nonsensical song. Jenny repeats after her: " 'You don't have an arm—' "

" 'Ye haven't an arm,' " Kate corrects her in her whispery voice, " 'ye haven't a leg, ahoo —' "

" 'Ye haven't a leg, ahoo—' " Jenny breaks off. "What's *ahoo*?"

The small girl shrugs and sings on.

You're a noseless eyeless chickenless egg
Ye'll have to be put in a bowl to beg
Och! Johnny, I hardly knew ye.

"What are you saying, child?" Her father breaks his silence. "It's 'Ye'll have to be put with a bowl out to beg.' He's lost all his limbs in the wars, and the bowl's for the money he's begging."

"Once you've passed on a song, it's out of your hands," Jenny tells McNamara. "I favor the kid's version."

"Her *version,* is it? She's making a dog's dinner of it."

"Well, this Johnny sounds like something of a dog's dinner himself, so— "

"He's like a chickenless egg," insists Kate softly, "that's why he needs a big bowl to sit in or he'll roll away."

P'tit, rolling across the floorboards of the apartment, panting with effort . . . Blanche shuts her mind like a door, locking him out.

Later on, she and Jenny go over to Phil Jordan's grogshop, because he's got a better range of spirits than McNamara. Jenny treats them all to a rendition of something with dozens of verses called "Rye Whiskey," or maybe "Jack o' Diamonds," she can't quite remember.

After three cocktails, Blanche is distinctly cheerfuller. She trips back to the Eight Mile House and finds that the waning moon lends the ramshackle silhouette of San Miguel Station a certain charm. Her throat is aglow with liquor, even if her lip still hurts where Ernest's hand crushed it yesterday, on Waverly Place. The hem of her mauve skirt is brown with dust, but what does it matter when no one's looking? No need to dress up here, or match the City's arduous rhythms. San Miguel Station's a two-bit place between real places, an anonymous dirt spot on the map where, for the first time in weeks, Blanche can fall into bed without a thought in her head.

*

The morning of Saturday, the sixteenth of September, Blanche stands outside Gray's Undertakers and Music Shop. She's passed this bland yellow brick building probably a thousand times but never noticed it before. It's only two blocks west of her own building. (Blanche still thinks of number 815 as that, despite Low Long's sticky-painted sign that she saw as she was passing just now: enormous Chinese letters above smaller English ones reading GOOD LUCK ROOMING HOUSE.) After a long night alone between the cool sheets of the Palace Hotel, she's as ready for this inquest as she can make herself. Presentable, at least, because she's spent some of Lamantia's money on a costume that's sober by her lights, a pale pink-and-white pattern from high neck to flounced hem.

She's gathering her nerve to step inside when out of the corner of her eye, she sees something move. A house. An actual two-story frame building going by, creaking down the middle of Sacramento Street. Blanche stares. It's on rollers, hauled by a team of eight gasping horses. Pedestrians dive to one side or another. Someone's moving without having to change houses, she supposes; what a Californian shortcut! Jenny would be so tickled to see that, Blanche thinks. Abruptly missing her friend so much her stomach cramps.

A pair of bony arms suddenly wraps Blanche up. She recoils from maroon ruffles. The death's-head, that old ravaged dove Jenny had a soft spot for. "Maria," says Blanche, as politely as she can.

"Ma pauvre," sobs the old woman, mopping at her single eye with a scrunched handkerchief. "You really stuck it to those goddamn *macs* in the paper yesterday!"

Blanche nods uneasily.

"Fleas living off our asses," Maria pronounces. "Though I did get my own back on my Thomas," she adds, reminiscent.

"You did?" says Blanche, because it seems expected of her.

"He was just like your Albert—a dog in the manger."

Arthur, Blanche wants to correct her, absurdly.

"Took half my face off with acid. I could hear my own skin sizzle," says Maria with ghastly exuberance.

Blanche feels her gorge rise.

"Some splashed on Thomas, I knew, because I could hear him cursing about holes in his pants." Maria grins. The woman still has all her teeth, Blanche notices, even if they are yellow. "It was the pants that did for him, though. Captain Lees found where Thomas had stashed them under the bar, you see?"

Blanche is oddly impressed by that piece of detective work.

"The *connard* escaped from the pen after a year, but still," says Maria, sighing, "I'd had the satisfaction. Poor Jenny, though . . . Maybe we'll see those sons of bitches hang for it after this inquest?"

Blanche nods, trying to smile, but her face is contorted

with guilt. Thinking, *Not if it's up to me.* She's committed herself to her devilish bargain with Ernest. She's going to walk in there and testify that he and Arthur could have had nothing to do with Jenny's mysterious death. Almost ten by the clock over the door of Gray's. *Get inside,* Blanche scolds herself, *before the detectives come looking for you.*

Maria walks beside her. "Not to speak ill and all that, but Jenny was such a hothead. Should have known to stay clear of fancy men," she laments. "Didn't the last time nearly finish her off?"

"The last time . . ." Blanche is confused.

Maria puts her head to one side. "When the girl had to be pumped out with asafetida and warm water, must be five years back— "

Blanche swallows as people push past them into Gray's. So the police files were right about that much: an overdose. Could it have been accidental? "What had she taken?"

The old woman shrugs. "Laudanum, probably—isn't that our usual poison? Topping ourselves, it's an epidemic these days—a teaspoon can do it if you ain't habituated. Adrien wasn't the worst, as they go, but not the best neither."

Who's this Adrien who drove Jenny to try to kill herself? She never mentioned any Adrien. *Ever had your heart broken?* Blanche asked, when they were waiting outside 815 Sacramento last week, but Jenny claimed to be a slippery fish. Not so uncatchable, it seems now. Her heart not unbreakable at all.

"He wasn't the type to ever lay a hand on her," Maria rattles on as they step into the building, "but he might as well have beaten her, since he gambled away every *satané* cent she had—"

Blanche almost collides with a man in uniform just inside the door. "This Adrien lost her money?" she asks, just to be clear. "He was Jenny's man?"

Maria stares. "Her *mac,* you mean."

No.

But yes.

Frail, isn't that what Cartwright called Jenny in his article? And Blanche thought he was plucking the accusation out of the air. *That's how she earned her crust, folks say, back when she wore skirts,* Arthur sneered that night at the faro saloon, and again Blanche assumed he was just throwing any kind of mud that might stick. She's been deaf to everything that hasn't matched her own idea of Jenny.

Maria's one awful eye peers at her. "My dear. Didn't you know her at all?"

Fury, like a knot of gristle in Blanche's throat. But what can she say in her own defense? Jenny was easy to enjoy but hard to know.

The lobby's thick with chattering people. Which part is the deadhouse, where they'll have laid out what used to be Jenny? Please let them not have prettified her . . . It must be in the cellars, surely; that'd be coolest. But the crowd is moving up the graciously curved staircase, and Blanche mustn't be late, so she lets the press of bodies take her that way, carrying her away from Maria.

Her head's whirling from the old dove's casual revelation. *You've got the wrong Jenny Bonnet there,* Jenny told Arthur at the faro table, so lightly that Blanche never thought not to take her word for it. But all these weeks, is it Blanche who's had the wrong Jenny Bonnet?

Is it a fact that just about every female ends up selling herself at some point? Blanche wonders grimly. Even Jenny turns out to have been a soiled dove whose *mac* broke her heart when he wasted all her money, driving her to try to end it all. What a hackneyed plot! Behind Blanche's irritation at being lied to and made a fool of, there's crushing disappointment. Every misstep Blanche has made in her own life, it seems, Jenny made before her. The hypocrite! How dare Jenny have posed as a great eccentric, a dazzling original, the exception to all the rules of womanhood?

The upper room's stifling. Chairs behind several long tables, for the important folks, but little furniture otherwise. The standing audience has sucked up all the air already.

". . . of Jeanne Bonnet, supposed to have died by violence," a man with long white sideburns is announcing with exaggerated articulation.

Supposed? thinks Blanche. What, is there some reason to suspect that Jenny may have burst apart spontaneously? She swallows down a terrible giggle. Jenny would understand. Jenny would have been the first to find the hilarity in all of this.

The man with sideburns seems to be in charge so he must be . . . Swan, Coroner Swan, she remembers with an effort. He's addressing a group of awkward-looking men behind the table on the left—this must be the jury. Blanche bobs from side to side, wishing she were taller. She considers what she can see of the jurors' jackets, their faces, though she has no idea how to decode their expressions.

Will they be able to understand the first thing about this case? They never knew Jenny, not even in the partial way Blanche did.

You've got the wrong Jenny Bonnet, her friend says lightly, obstinately in Blanche's head. The Jenny Bonnet who was frail was a girl in skirts, long hair, paint. A girl who took an overdose five years ago and never woke up. *That's not me.*

In the crowd, a luminous white head stands out: Cartwright of the *Chronicle*. Blanche also recognizes Durand's greasy mustache. His mournful cook stands beside him.

Blanche is already rehearsing her lines under her breath. She means to do exactly what Ernest ordered her to in the empty apartment yesterday: clear Arthur's name. She'll swear she has no idea who fired a shotgun through the McNamaras' window on Thursday night, knows only that it certainly wasn't the upstanding stockbroker Arthur Deneve, who's been out of town for the best part of a week—she's learned since—and whom she must now confess to having slandered out of petty malice while half out of her mind with shock.

The script is bunkum, but who cares? Blanche doesn't know what'll come of this performance, except that neither Arthur nor Ernest will spend a day in jail. That's all right, she tells herself. What does the truth matter in the middle of all this misery? What goddamn good would justice do Jenny now that she's dead as a herring? P'tit: he's all that matters. P'tit, and Blanche's slim chance of seeing him again. So all she can do is what Ernest told her to. Put one foot after another, stepping blindfolded across the abyss.

So many eyes on her, as if she's spotlit. Whispers. Blanche realizes she's the main attraction, the survivor. "The murdered woman's companion." How like, but also weirdly unlike, her leg shows at the House of Mirrors.

Her throat locks. Could Ernest be watching in the crowd, making sure she's going to obey his commands? Surely that would be too risky, because the patrolmen might recognize him as one of the *macs* Blanche urged Bohen to arrest. No, Ernest won't show his face anywhere until this afternoon's papers report that the murdered woman's companion has changed her story, cleared him and his absent friend of all suspicion.

Swan takes off his glasses and swabs them and the bridge of his nose with a white handkerchief. "While thanking Mr. Gray—a distinguished former coroner, may I add—for his continued hospitality on these premises," he says, sighing, "I wish to put on record my grave displeasure that the coroner's office has *still* not been provided with its own mortuary designed on modern scientific principles."

As Swan drones on about hygienic sprays, slabs, and asphaltum flooring, Blanche shuts him out. She focuses on the man sitting below the coroner, listens to the woodpecker tap of his little black machine. He must be setting down every word everyone says. Jenny would have been intrigued by that, would have gone up afterward to ask him how he could possibly keep up with the speed of human chatter.

A dry little doctor called Crook stands up on a platform now and solemnly swears that he'll tell the truth, the whole truth, and nothing but the truth, so help him God.

Blanche realizes that all witnesses will be obliged to

swear on the Bible. It gives her a slight tremble. What Jenny would call pure dumb superstition.

"The deceased was a female of normal physiology," he recites from his papers, "adequately nourished and developed, with no appearance of disease." Jargon swims by—*nullagravida, rigor mortis, pallor attributable to exsanguination*—and Blanche tries not to take in the words. "The brain was medium in size, and firm in substance," says Crook. "No serum in the ventricles. The lungs crepitant." Is the language of autopsies meant to be veiled, Blanche wonders, so that folks won't have to recognize what's being said about their loved ones? "The stomach greatly distended, containing about two ounces of grumous fluid with a strongly alcoholic odor . . ."

The delicious cognac they drank on the bed at the McNamaras', now soured to *grumous fluid.*

"Eight wounds on the left side." Crook shows the jury the little box of bullets he dug out of what he calls the *cadaver.* "Hemorrhage from the wound in the neck, which alone would in my opinion have been fatal, even in the absence of the others . . ."

Blanche blinks, trying to follow. Nothing she could have done, then, once that bullet went through Jenny's neck? No way Blanche could have stanched the flow even if she'd been quick enough or clever enough to try instead of lurching around the room in the darkest confusion?

Crook anchors his gaze to his notes with one fingertip. "Also swelling and discoloration around both eyes, consistent with a blow of some kind."

Blanche's cheeks scorch. Why is he talking about that? What can it matter compared with what killed her?

"This bruising was incurred when?" asks Swan.

"Less than twelve hours antemortem, I would say, Coroner. I also noted considerable scarring on the—"

Swan interrupts. "This scarring, too, of recent date?"

Scarring? Now Blanche is bewildered.

"No, sir."

"Let's confine our inquiry to matters relevant to the death, Doctor."

Flustered, Crook edges his fingers down the page. "I found recent abrasions of the feet and hands, with embedded mud—but would judge them to be irrelevant," he concedes.

Their tramp on Sweeney Ridge, on Wednesday. *Irrelevant,* how Jenny spent the day before she died. But not to Blanche. She finds it oddly consoling to think of Jenny always in motion, spinning along on her high-wheeler or striding up a hill or crouching over a pond, all her energies focused on the hunt.

Coroner Swan is thanking Crook now for putting himself in danger to do his job. "Not many years ago," he informs the court in a sepulchral voice, "an assistant almost lost his life as a consequence of sepsis in a laceration received during a postmortem examination . . ."

Blanche has stopped listening, because a fellow in uniform is leading John McNamara through the crowd, passing not five feet from her, using his elbows to make room for the Irishman—who looks smaller here, somehow. Unmoored. Like some vagrant in a stolen Sunday suit, with reddened cheeks but skin chalk-white inside his collar.

"Calling next witness, John McNamara Sr."

Blanche has no idea when she's going to be asked to recite her lies, she realizes. As the only one who was in the bedroom when the bullets flew in the window, shouldn't she be first after the autopsy report? She'd rather get it over with, frankly—paint herself a fool, a typically irrational female, and get out of this airless chamber.

Coroner Swan keeps his inquiries focused strictly on the events immediately before the death. There's nothing about Jenny's history or her character. "Who was in the settlement on Thursday night, to your knowledge?"

"The what?" McNamara's got the eyes of a stunned steer.

"The hamlet, the village, if you will, of San Miguel Station," explains the coroner, as if to a child.

"Right, s-sir, right you are." McNamara's stammering. "Mrs. Holt the station keeper, now, for one, but I doubt she'd know one end of a gun from—"

"Confine yourself to the facts," Swan interrupts. "Nobody is expecting you to solve the crime—if indeed a crime has been committed," he adds, scrupulous.

If? As if someone stalking partridge by moonlight might have accidentally fired at the Eight Mile House!

There's Ellen in the crowd, tight-lipped with nerves, and Mary Jane. John Jr. must be minding the small ones at home, Blanche deduces.

"Mrs. Holt, Jordan," says McNamara, counting on his thick fingers, "Mrs. Louis—but her husband's away to San Jose at the moment—"

"This would be the Canadian, Louis de Frammant?" asks Swan, peering at what must be a list of names. "Or is that Dufranaut? The detective's writing is far from clear."

McNamara shrugs. "We just know them as Mr. and Mrs. Louis."

"Carry on."

"Miss Blanche—Miss Beunon, I should say—she drove herself down in a buggy. Tuesday, it was."

"And Miss Bonnet?" asks Swan.

No answer from McNamara.

"How did Miss Bonnet arrive?"

Does the Irishman want to avoid mentioning the bicycle? Blanche wonders. She broods again over what she dismissed as a cracked theory yesterday, that the McNamaras planned the murder as an elaborate way of stealing the expensive machine.

"By—by a high-wheeler," says McNamara, with an odd formality, "is how the person came down."

"Was it your understanding that these women were in flight from some enemy? Some persons in the City, perhaps?"

Blanche groans inwardly and pulls her straw hat so the veil hangs a little farther over her face. Despite his air of neutrality, of course Coroner Swan has read the papers and talked to the detectives. He must be trying to lead McNamara's testimony in the direction of the violent *macs* Blanche spoke of.

"I—my understanding was that the two—the individuals in question were just after a spree."

"Their intention being to indulge in hard drinking in your saloon?"

Blanche's mouth tightens. What else is there to do at San Miguel Station?

"In my hotel," McNamara corrects him pompously. "And in the liquor shop next door."

"This would be . . ." Swan consults his papers. "Philip Jordan's grocery and general store?"

"That's what he calls it, I suppose."

"Returning to your *hotel,* Mr. McNamara. Would it be incorrect to say that you make the greatest part of your profits from the sale of alcoholic beverages?"

McNamara grimaces. "There wouldn't be much profit in any of it."

Blanche can believe that.

"Did the women drink at your bar during the three nights of their stay?"

McNamara is shifting from foot to foot. "Everyone took their fill, anyhow."

"Everyone, meaning the two women?"

The Irishman's shaking his head desperately.

"They didn't drink?"

McNamara takes a great rattling breath. "What you have to understand, Your Honor, is that I'd no notion they were women."

Every eye in the room locks on him.

"Not that the both of them were, I mean."

Coroner Swan is squinting down his nose at the Irishman. "You believed the deceased to be male, despite being on record as having furnished her with occasional lodging over the past half dozen years?"

Laughter wafting up now.

"We're simple people," McNamara says with a groan.

"How were we to know the class of carry-on we were dealing with?"

Hoots of mirth now.

McNamara's disowning Jenny, Blanche realizes. Irrationally afraid his grubby saloon will be tarred by the association, he's trying to deny any friendship with the cross-dressing hellion who got herself killed there.

"What was the name you knew this, ah, putative male by?"

McNamara licks his flaking lips. "Bonnet."

"No Christian name?"

"Nothing very Christian about the person."

That raises another laugh.

Blanche is stiff with rage. Jenny's not a harlot now but a heathen?

It's some slight relief to her that Swan clearly doesn't believe a word. "You never connected this beardless, light-voiced Bonnet working as a frog-catcher," he summarizes dryly, "with Jenny Bonnet the frog-catching girl, notorious as a pants-wearer in all the City papers?"

McNamara mumbles something about not reading the papers.

Swan moves on to the events of Wednesday, the thirteenth, the night before the murder.

Blanche remembers riding back from Sweeney Ridge as vividly as if she were there now: the scalding pink of the setting sun. When she and Jenny reached the Eight Mile House, tired out, the two of them had a fancy for cocktails, but McNamara had no bitters, so they settled on a Martinez of sweet red vermouth, gin, and a couple of cherries from a sticky old bottle. Jenny fizzed like soda pop, singing at the top of her voice and drumming on the bar.

Swan is leading McNamara through the sudden arrival of stableman Charles St. Clair to retrieve the buggy Blanche had forgotten to return to Marshall's.

That quarrel was Blanche's fault, she'd be the first to admit. She had just about enough left over from what Lamantia paid her, so she could have settled up with the stableman. But how dared St. Clair track them down in San Miguel Station that way, barge in on their jollification and address them as if they were lowlifes? All Blanche did was point out that his boss would make more money the longer Blanche kept the buggy, so why cause her aggravation over it? At that point, in her reckoning, the row became St. Clair's fault, because he was the one who grabbed Blanche by the sleeve and mentioned the revolver in his pocket . . .

Shifting of the crowd now; St. Clair is pushing through, scowling, his muttonchop side-whiskers even bushier than Blanche remembered them.

"Is that the man in question?" asks Swan.

McNamara looks sideways at St. Clair. "I wouldn't care to say that it is or it isn't." He's clearly so rattled by the male-or-female business that he's afraid to state anything for a fact.

St. Clair lets out a laugh. "Why, that mick was so top-heavy Wednesday night, I'd be surprised if he could tell me from the side of a house!"

"You'll get your chance to testify, sir," says Swan coldly, "unless your interruptions oblige me to bar you from this court of inquest."

St. Clair, subdued, folds his arms.

"Now." Coroner Swan reaches into a wooden cube labeled *Evidence*. "Do you recognize this, Mr. McNamara?"

He peers at it. "It's her—it's Bonnet's Colt, isn't it?"

Another disturbance: a youngish man with a long doublepointed beard stands up. "As a point of information," he says in a distinctly Prussian accent, "the revolver is mine."

"And who are you, may I ask?" Swan sighs.

"Julius Funkenstein, sir, a dealer in real estate and movables."

"By which you mean a pawnbroker?"

"I have a variety of business dealings throughout the City . . ."

Won that off a California infantryman, Jenny crows in Blanche's memory.

"Then you may make application to the City treasurer in due course for the retrieval of your property, if such it is." Swan puts the gun back in the box.

"Humbly, sir," says Funkenstein, "she still owed me some nineteen dollars on it . . ."

That strikes Blanche as the saddest thing, somehow, that Jenny hadn't even paid off her gun. How many of her grand claims were hogwash?

John McNamara is creeping crabwise into the crowd but the coroner calls him back. "You, sir, are still under oath. Now, the following night, Thursday, the fourteenth. Did anything of note happen before the shooting?"

"Only that they had a bit of a barney, the women—I mean—" McNamara stumbles to correct himself.

"Bonnet and Beunon, yes. What was the nature of the dispute?"

"Bonnet was heading back to the City but Beunon wouldn't stand for it. Said she—Bonnet—was so stewed she'd ride into the ditch. Then they retired to, ah, our guest chamber. Bonnet went out on the porch for a pipe," he adds.

And Blanche can see Jenny, as clear as day. *Don't smoke that thing in here,* Blanche told her, so Jenny strolled out onto the moonlit porch, glowing like a ghost.

"In your nightshirt, correct?"

"Ah, my best one, that my wife lent her, yes."

That's how Jenny operated: Wandered through the world without the things everyone else called necessities. Rustled them up as required.

"They called me in to fix the blind," McNamara hurries on, "and to give them a drop of cognac."

"What was wrong with the blind?" asks Coroner Swan.

"It was slipping down, you know, skew-ways."

Like everything else in the Eight Mile House, thinks Blanche.

"Have you brought a piece, as instructed?"

"I have, sir, a bit that a bullet went right through," says McNamara, rooting in his trouser pocket until he finds the green scrap and holds it up.

Coroner Swan hands it to the jurymen, who pass it around as if it's a treasure map and confabulate in mutters.

"In your view, Mr. McNamara, would a person standing outside the window have been able to see through this blind, into the room, given that there was a candle burning?"

The Irishman blinks warily. "He might or he might not, sir, depending on his eyes."

"Perhaps we can take it as a given that his sight was good, judging by his subsequent success in shooting a woman dead?" Swan's getting tired; you can hear it in the occasional flash of sarcasm.

But the killer didn't need to see through the blind, thinks Blanche, because right after their shiftless bum of a landlord stuck it back up on its nail and left, the nail fell right out of the plaster. The green cloth was left hanging sideways with a gap down the side the width of a sword. Was it Arthur who somehow managed to sneak into San Miguel Station, pacify the dogs, get onto the rickety porch without a sound, and look in at Blanche and Jenny getting ready for bed? Or had he left the country already, having asked his faithful ape to see to Blanche, fix her *for good and all?* Was it Ernest alone who climbed up for his final trick, shotgun on his shoulder, with Arthur's orders burning like a brand on his heart?

McNamara's describing the gunfire now: the havoc, the gore. Blanche refuses to listen.

Next to be called up is not Blanche nor McNamara's wife, but his daughter, even though she's only fifteen. Mary Jane's done her best, ironed her frock (though from where Blanche stands, about five people behind her, she can see a stain near the hem).

She begins by repeating, as if by rote, what her father said about none of them having any idea that Bonnet was female.

Blanche can't stop herself from letting out a snort, which makes heads turn.

Mary Jane blinks several times.

"On Wednesday, the thirteenth, were you in the saloon when the stableman turned up?"

The girl nods eagerly. "He—Mr. St. Clair—said he'd spill Miss Blanche's blood if she didn't pay up right away."

Blanche doesn't remember anything as colorful as that.

"But Jenny—the person," Mary Jane corrects herself, "the person said she'd spill every drop of his."

"Did St. Clair produce a firearm?"

"Well, he had a revolver in his pocket and he kept fooling with it."

"And Bonnet?"

Care to receive a bullet through your brains, Jenny quipped to St. Clair, *or have you got plans for this evening?*

"She told my brother to fetch—"

Swan interrupts. "This would be John McNamara Jr.? Is he in court today?"

"Sure he's only twelve," calls out Ellen McNamara, histrionic, from the crowd.

"She sent John to go get her Colt," Mary Jane says, struggling on.

Blanche remembers being irritated by that. All those times Jenny walked around with the thing in her pocket and now, just when it would be handy to brandish, she'd left it under the mattress! St. Clair called Jenny a *half-size boaster,* Blanche remembers, and Jenny quoted something back at him about it not being the size of the dog in the fight but the size of the fight in the dog.

"I believed St. Clair might pull his piece out and gun us all down," Mary Jane goes on in a rush, "so I stopped him."

"How did you manage that?"

The girl stands a little straighter, smiles hesitantly.

Making up her next lie, thinks Blanche.

"I caught hold of his arm and asked him to please leave off, for my sake, and he said he would."

The vain little shammer!

What Blanche is remembering about Wednesday evening now is John Jr. slipping through the saloon with Jenny's revolver in his hands like some ingenious toy and putting it into her lap. Jenny grinned down at him, and said, *That's a boy!*

It could have got serious then, Blanche knew, except that the stableman funked it, which was what Jenny had been counting on. St. Clair announced that he wouldn't stoop to fighting a woman—but that was just his bluster. Magnanimous, Blanche reassured him that she'd pay in full for two days of buggy hire as soon as she returned to the City. The stableman stood a round for the whole house, *no hard feelings,* and then headed off with his buggy, quite cowed.

"Afterward," asks Swan, "did the visitors make any comment on the incident?"

For the first time, the girl seems flustered.

"Well, Miss McNamara?"

"She boasted she'd made him . . . take water."

The phrase puzzles Blanche.

"This is Miss Beunon you're quoting?"

"Bonnet," says Mary Jane in a small voice.

"Bonnet said she'd make him—"

"I heard her say to Miss Blanche, 'Reckon we made that fellow take water.' "

"Take on water, the way a leaking boat might?" Swan wonders.

The girl shrugs unhappily.

And suddenly Blanche gets it: not *take* but *make. Reckon we made him piss his pants,* yes, that's what Jenny said. Blanche almost laughs aloud.

Swan sighs over his papers. Then taps a phrase on one page. "Dr. Crook observed a pair of black eyes on the deceased—an injury of very recent date. Did you see anyone hit Bonnet that night?"

Mary Jane hesitates, and her eyes slide to her parents.

Blanche stiffens. Have they coached her on this point?

"That night or the following day," Swan prods, "any blow which could have occasioned bruising?"

"No blow that I saw, sir," says Mary Jane scrupulously.

Blanche's pulse is hammering with relief. Though she guesses that the McNamaras are leaving out this particular incident to avoid giving the impression that their so-called hotel is the kind of dive where fistfights break out every five minutes.

"The next evening, Thursday, the fourteenth," Swan says, moving on. "When did you last see the deceased?"

"A few minutes before it—before the shooting. I'd been lying on their bed. It's my room when we don't have lodgers," adds Mary Jane awkwardly, "mine and my little sister's and brother's."

"Are you in the habit of such familiarities with a guest whom you believe to be of the opposite sex, Miss McNamara?"

The coroner's punishing the family for their lies, Blanche realizes.

The girl flushes to the eyes. "I was only being friendly."

"Let me put this delicately. Are you *friendly* with men who visit your father's saloon?"

"I am not!" A sob escapes her. "I don't know how you—"

"That's all at present. You may step down."

Such power men have, thinks Blanche, when one of them merely hinting that a girl's on the town sends her racing as if from a rattlesnake.

The funny thing is that nobody on the witness stand has mentioned Jenny's criminal past. From reading the papers, everybody's aware of the drunkenness and whoring and scrapes with the law; that knowing judgment lies behind every word they all say.

Blanche needs the lavatory. If she isn't called up to give her testimony soon, she doesn't know how she's going to last . . .

"Next witness, Charles St. Clair."

This is ridiculous. Don't they want to hear from Blanche, the one person who was there, right there in the room?

She pushes her way to the rear while St. Clair is answering a question about the correct address of Marshall's stables.

A knot of newsmen at the back, taking notes. She averts her face.

"Miss Blanche?"

Cartwright; she hurries through the double doors to get out of range. Blanche can't bear his sympathetic gaze now. Not when she's about to change her tune and contradict every honest word she told him yesterday. In what terms will he denounce her in the *Chronicle* tomorrow?

The toilets are rather grand: mahogany seats and marble basins. Blanche realizes why she's feeling so sick, and it's not just the lack of breakfast. All morning she's been expecting Detective Bohen to stand up and lay out the whole situation in his authoritative tone: the sinister Frenchmen who attacked Blanche and Jenny last week, and threatened worse . . . Then, even if Blanche denies everything, there'll still be a good chance that the jury will lay the blame where they should, at Arthur and Ernest's door. But instead, everything that's been said so far amounts to a dull recounting of Jenny's last few days. As if she brought the shower of bullets down on herself!

Which means that if Blanche doesn't point a finger at the *macs,* nobody will.

What does she mean, *if?* She won't point any finger. Blanche made up her mind in the apartment yesterday the moment Ernest mentioned P'tit.

She swigs a palmful of water from the tap. *I was out of my right mind yesterday*, she rehearses. *I was in such a state of hysteria when I spoke to Mr. Cartwright and Mr. Bohen, I'm afraid I plucked two names out of the air. There's been some bad blood between myself and my compatriots Messieurs Deneve and Girard* . . . Blanche shudders. Will she have to tell the court about her lost baby to explain the bad blood? But the story reflects poorly on Blanche, as if she's the kind of crib girl who, cockeyed with laudanum, squats in an alley to give birth and then staggers away, so addled that she doesn't know dream from real . . .

No, she must keep silent about P'tit, hold him in her mind like a candle on the verge of being snuffed out. His life—*if* he's alive, Blanche reminds herself, *if* she read Ernest's tone right, *if* this is not some elaborate trick—his life may be in her hands as much as it was when she snatched him out of the weeklies room on Folsom Street less than a month ago.

I admit I bore a grudge against Monsieur Deneve, she practices. *I realize now that he could have had no way of knowing that the deceased—that Jenny and I were in San Miguel Station. Unbeknownst to me, he had already gone abroad, besides. I wish to express my deepest regret for having accused him falsely.* The formal lines ring hollow. If Blanche is going to do this—betray Jenny for the merest possibility of seeing P'tit—then she should at least deliver a convincing performance.

Ernest ought to have told her exactly what to say when he barked out his orders in the empty apartment yesterday, should have set her lines to learn by heart. It occurs to Blanche now, bending over the sink, that perhaps he's expecting her to make up some brilliant new theory that'll send the detectives off in another direction. Should she mention the stolen bicycle and cast aspersions on the McNamaras? Or posit a madman roaming through the City's hinterlands? Blanche would be more than willing if only she could think of a halfway plausible story.

She needs the toilet again. Runs for it.

Elbows on her knees, Blanche feels a cold worm of doubt. *You'll never see the kid again,* Ernest threatened yesterday, and somehow she's puffed that up into a promise that if she does this right, she'll get P'tit back. What, does she really believe that Ernest, having tried to kill Blanche and ended up blowing Jenny to pieces, will read the report on the inquest in this evening's papers and decide that Blanche is a good girl after all? Will he wander Chinatown with P'tit on his fashionable hip, carrying a stack of clean diapers, until he finds her and hands her baby over?

It's flimflam, the notion that she's entered into some kind of unspoken contract with a murderer! Ernest has more than a few reasons to hate Blanche, and she has no basis for trusting him. What if she goes into that courtroom now, swears on the Good Book and clears Arthur's name, walks out onto Dupont Street—and never hears from either of the men again? Ernest will leave town tonight, she guesses. Blanche will have betrayed her friend's cause for nothing. And she'll never know what's become of her baby. Blanche was aware of all this already, but she's been trying not to think about it. Whatever she tells the coroner, whichever way she twists, one thing's pretty much sure: she's lost P'tit.

Weak-legged, Blanche emerges from the lavatory. She reels in the sunlight as she walks out of the undertaker's. *City Health Officer Orders Fumigation of Every Building in Chinatown,* a headline thunders.

Yeah, yeah, she remembers Jenny kidding, *when the next quake comes they'll probably blame that on the Chinese too.*

A busker with a sweat-soaked shirt and the staring eyes of the blind is chirping away merrily, accompanying himself on two pairs of bones:

Some folks get gray hairs,
Some folks do, some folks do;
Brooding o'er their cares—
But that's not me nor you.

Jenny would have stopped to listen to him, swapped a verse or two. Jenny would have told Ernest where he could shove his threats. Jenny was sometimes blue, maybe, but never scared.

And it's as if the ripples have cleared from Blanche's mind. She sees that she has nothing to gain by lying. No matter what she says in court today, no matter how eloquently she blames the McNamaras or some mysterious hoodlum, Ernest is not going to hand P'tit back to her. It's such an obvious bluff, a halfwit could have seen through it. In all likelihood, her baby's stashed someplace worse than Folsom Street, all paid up. Or floating in a sewage tank.

Blanche presses her hand over her mouth, hard.

What do you reckon, Jenny? Should I march in there and tell the truth, never mind the consequences?

Then her mind changes back again, with a sickening lurch of gears. If there's the slimmest chance . . . Whether this works or not, in years to come Blanche has to be able to tell herself that she tried, bet everything, for P'tit's sake. This is what mothers do for their babies: they bite their tongues and let the world ride them into the ground. So Blanche is going to walk back into that inquest and make a liar of herself for the merest hope in hell that P'tit will be spared—just as she was so strangely spared two nights ago, when the bullets whizzed over her head instead of through it.

"Miss Beunon!"

She spins around.

It's Cartwright, lifting his blue glasses to wipe his shiny nose. "Didn't you hear them call your name? Better hustle before Swan finds you in contempt."

She doesn't know what that means but it sounds bad.

Putain, all this fretting over what to say, and she may miss her chance to say anything!

Cartwright trots along beside her, into the building. “Did you hear Girard was arrested?”

Blanche wheels around, stares at him.

“Last night,” he adds.

She hurries on in confusion, heels clickety-clacking down the corridor.

This changes everything. If Ernest is in jail being interrogated right this minute, then surely the detectives will crack the truth out of him? They’ll find some fragment of evidence that he went out to San Miguel Station on Thursday and shot Jenny. In which case, this inquest is Blanche’s best—her only—chance to speak up loud and clear, with the world listening, and nail the sons of bitches.

“Miss Beunon, I presume?” asks Swan sourly as she scuttles up the aisle formed by the crowd.

Blanche is too breathless to speak, almost. And suddenly wonders if she’s committing a crime by not using her paper name. (That equestrienne, Adèle Beunon, whose idea of danger was slipping off a horse—how far away she seems to Blanche, how ignorant.)

She steps up on the little platform. From this position she can see the crowd so much better. She slaps her hand on the Bible and says “I do” almost before the clerk has finished the question. Like a wedding, she thinks. Then: *Concentrate.* No more faltering. Arthur’s left town and Ernest is locked up. The tide of power has turned.

“How long have you known the deceased?”

“A month. Not quite,” Blanche admits. That sounds bad, somehow, shallow.

"At what point did you become aware that she was a female like yourself?"

A female, but not like myself, Blanche corrects him in her head. "I was never under that misapprehension," she says coldly. "When the occasional fool read her wrong at twenty yards, that wasn't Jenny's lookout, was it? If somebody takes me for the queen of England, am I to be had up for impersonation?"

Gales of laughter—and Blanche wasn't even trying to be entertaining.

Swan casts a repressive look in all directions, like a circling whip. "Was it you or she who suggested meeting at San Miguel Station on Tuesday last?"

"No, but—" The story's racing too far ahead, and Blanche has to get a grip on it. "I'd left Arthur, you see, and he was eaten up with spite—"

"This would be Arthur Deneve?" Swan fingers his notes. "Your, your *mac,* I believe your compatriots say?"

"My lover," she says flatly. But why is she calling Arthur that, Arthur who's destroyed everything? *Lover?* Blanche could laugh, she could puke with the absurdity of it all. At the very moment when she stands up to testify against him and Ernest, she's invoking love?

"When did the connection end?"

She blinks at Swan. "Ah, a week—ten days ago, perhaps—" How to pick one moment and say that's when love ended, or when it was found to never have been there at all? "He formed a vicious grudge against Jenny." *Against me, really,* she wants to say. Because it was Blanche who shamed him by refusing to service the American he brought home, and before that, because she wouldn't go near him during his smallpox, and before that, because she carried the baby home from Folsom Street, and because, because—there's always another layer to the onion. But saying any of that will lead to Blanche having to explain her conviction that it was her, not Jenny, the gun was aimed at, and that strikes her as an unnecessary complication for a jury whose members are looking more than a little bewildered already.

"A grudge of what nature?"

"He—" Blanche fumbles for words. How to simplify enough that the jurors get the main point, which is that Arthur's the murderer? "He was furious with Jenny because—I was going about with her a bit this summer, and he thought it was she who put it into my head to break with him."

"Was it?"

"No! I left him because—I couldn't bring myself to—" No, Blanche mustn't tell the story of the *micheton* Arthur and Ernest brought back to the apartment, because that'll just fix her in every listener's mind as a harlot.

"Miss Beunon?" Wearily.

"He took my baby!" It comes out of her in a wail.

"There's no reference here to any baby," says Swan, flicking through his notes.

"Our little boy, one year old," Blanche adds. Does she sound sad enough? Her sorrow is real, Christ knows, but it's hard to display it on demand. "He—Arthur and Ernest, they stole him away from me."

"This would be . . ." The coroner scans the pages. "Ernest Girard. Where is this child now?"

"I don't—" Her voice is shaking too much for her to finish.

Swan asks no more. Makes a note.

Blanche closes her eyes. If P'tit is dead already, then she's doing the right thing by denouncing the bastards who did it. And if by any chance he isn't—

She sees herself visiting Ernest in jail tonight and crisply demanding to know her child's whereabouts. If P'tit's alive, why wouldn't Ernest give him back to her at this point? She might even be able to make him fork over some of her stolen money. Anything's possible, now Ernest's under lock and key.

So she spills out more and more, eager to make the jury understand before Swan can interrupt her. "The two men stayed in my apartment—the building I owned, the whole building, number eight fifteen Sacramento Street—and then, I learned just yesterday that they sold it out from under me for eighteen hundred dollars. Arthur stole two or three hundred more in cash from me besides that, and took it all away overseas. Left me with only the clothes I have on." Does all this sound too mercenary? "But my child," she cries, "all that matters is—"

Swan interrupts with a question. "Did this Deneve make actual threats against the deceased?"

Blanche hesitates. "Yes." Ernest did, on Waverly Place, and he must have had Arthur's approval, because Arthur was the master in that pair. "He and Girard . . . They tried to have Jenny arrested." That's a mistake; why bring up Jenny's criminal record? Hurry on. "They said they'd fix her, throw vitriol in her face." Blanche is embellishing, but only a little. "Oh, and another time, I forgot to say, Arthur begged me to return to him, he went down on his knees—" If she's going to beef this up she might as well make it a good full-blooded scene, and after all, she's not lying, exactly, just filling in the gaps, the times when she wasn't there. For all Arthur's bravado, there must have been moments when the scarred man wept for the loss of Blanche, mustn't there? "And Ernest cried out, 'Don't fret, Arthur, I'll avenge you, I'll blow out the brains of these two infernal whores!' "

That last expression raises a satisfied hiss from the crowd.

There. It's done. Blanche takes a long breath.

Swan's expression is dubious.

Blanche is barely paying attention as he takes her through the events at San Miguel Station (which sound so petty—rides and meals, as if she and Jenny were on a pleasure jaunt to a seaside resort). But when he asks about the black eyes, she blinks. "Yes, Jenny fell off a horse against a tree." Plausible? But if you fell off a horse, surely what you'd hit would be the ground. "I mean, she rode smack into a low-hanging branch, and then she fell down," Blanche adds. *Chut,* don't overcomplicate it.

"Was she drunk?" asks Swan.

Blanche doesn't want the jurymen to think of Jenny as a no-account dipso, because then they won't care who killed her, but she must make the accident credible. "She . . . had some taken."

"Mr. McNamara has testified that Bonnet drank all Thursday evening," says Swan, "and that you prevented her from going back to the City."

"I reasoned with her," Blanche corrects him, "for her own safety." *Safety?* Dead an hour later. Guilt turns Blanche's tongue to stone in her mouth.

"Now, the deceased got into bed before you, yes?"

Blanche nods. "I sat—I was sitting on the edge."

"What were her last words?"

She won't cry, not here in front of all these gaping strangers. As if a person's last words matter so much more than all the others. "She didn't say anything."

"Nothing?"

Qu'est-ce, that's all Blanche remembers hearing after the gunfire, which could have been the start of *Qu'est-ce que c'est que ça?* or *Qu'est-ce qui m'est arrivé?* But maybe it was an English word after all, it occurs to her now, that choking guttural, then a final hiss in the dark: *kiss,* is that what she heard? Could Jenny have been asking for a kiss before all the life spurted out of her? But Jenny had never asked Blanche for any favors—not a shirt, not a dollar, and certainly not a kiss.

"One final point that troubles me, Miss Beunon," says Coroner Swan. "You told Detective Bohen that you were crouched down, untying a gaiter, just when, outside the window, the murderer was aiming the gun?"

She bristles; *crouched down,* that sounds deliberate, surreptitious. Could he be implying that she was in on the plot? "I didn't know, did I?" As if Blanche's body could have been expected to feel the danger coming. People have no idea of the things that don't happen to them—the lives they're not living, the deaths stalking them—and thank Christ for that. Hard enough to get through each day without glimpsing all the hovering possibilities, like insects thickening the air.

"Does it not strike you as more than a little coincidental?"

Blanche shrugs rudely. Coincidences happen all the time. Fate touches one fingertip to the spinning top and knocks it over. What was it but fate, that hot night on Kearny Street, that made Jenny crash her high-wheeler into Blanche out of all the hundreds of thousands of people in San Francisco?

But Swan's still brooding. "Let's consider the statistical probability of your just so happening to bend over at the very moment the assassin pulled the trigger. You dipped out of the line of fire, with the consequence that the eight bullets went right over you, within inches of your body."

What does he want Blanche to say? That she's sorry she's alive?

"It strains credulity," mutters Swan. "That's all."

She waits. Oh, he means she can get down?

"No more witnesses," declares the clerk as Blanche steps into the crowd.

That's it? But nobody's jumped up with the missing pieces of the puzzle, Blanche thinks, bereft.

The waiting's hard to bear. The audience members shuffle, chat, eat nuts, sip from little flasks.

Then a surge as the jury files back into the airless room. Do these men's faces bear the righteous expression of Americans who've determined to send a pair of Frogs to the gallows? Blanche can't read them at all.

The foreman is hoarse with nerves but still seems to relish his moment in the limelight. "We find that the deceased came to her death by violence, by gunshot wounds specifically—" He clears his throat.

She wishes he'd get on with it.

"—at the hands of persons unknown to the jury."

Blanche almost groans. Is that old news all this rigmarole of an inquest has come up with?

"But we further find that, in the opinion of this jury, the evidence strongly points to Arthur Deneve and Ernest Girard as principals or accessories to the crime of murder."

Murmurs of excitement in court.

Ah, now, this is more like it, this might do the trick. *Principals or accessories:* that has a serious ring to it. Is that enough to drag Arthur back from wherever he's run to? France, even? And Ernest, locked up in a police cell. They'll hold him now till they've squeezed enough evidence out of him. Surely he'll pay in some measure for those eight bullets?

"Thank you, gentlemen," says Swan. If he's disappointed that the jury didn't reach any more definite conclusion, he clearly believes it would be improper to show it. "Funeral to follow at two p.m. sharp."

Blanche stumbles out with the crowd.

Her stomach growls, startling her. She hasn't eaten today. Strange, how the petty needs continue to clamor in the middle of serious ones.

Detective Bohen stands on the sidewalk outside Gray's, holding forth to newspapermen. "I wouldn't go so far as to say the rate of bloodshed has *doubled* during this unseasonable heat, although—"

He's interrupted. "What does it cost to hire a killer in this City, sir?"

"From two hundred up to a thousand dollars, according to our sources," says Bohen.

"Have you received offers of aid of a clairvoyant nature?"

"Unsolicited offers, yes, as usual, but—"

"Mr. Bohen?" Blanche calls.

He glances at her.

She needs to know. "*Principals or accessories:* Is that enough?"

He frowns.

The newsmen scribble in their notebooks and smirk at Blanche.

Bohen draws her aside, barely touching her elbow. "Miss Beunon—" The reporters float a little closer. "Gentlemen," he barks over his shoulder at them, then leads Blanche a few steps away.

"Is the verdict enough to hang Girard, at least?" she hisses.

"*Persons unknown* is the pertinent phrase."

"But the jury—"

"Only a coroner's jury, and all they have is a hunch. It may be a hunch on which I look with some sympathy, but it's no more than that."

"But the evidence says—it *points* to the two of them, that's what the foreman said," says Blanche, hearing herself whine.

"A criminal case requires more than *pointing,* Miss Beunon," he snaps. "I've heard no proof of either Deneve or Girard traveling to San Miguel Station on Thursday or inducing someone else to do so."

Her mind is spinning with frustration. "Well, can't you interrogate Ernest—tell him it'll be him or Arthur who'll pay for this, come down on him hard—"

"I can only imagine what kind of methods are used in Parisian police stations," says Bohen coldly, "and occasionally I do envy your *gendarmes* the free rein they're given. It is highly inconvenient that our citizens have the right to be considered innocent until proven guilty."

She grits her teeth. These smug Americans and their rights. "I just mean, shouldn't a prisoner be made to tell all he knows?"

"This morning, Girard told all he needed to tell, which was that he spent Thursday evening in the lodgings he shares with one Madeleine George. A fact that Miss George promptly confirmed, leaving us with no further justification to hold him."

Blanche blinks. Madeleine? That *salope!* "But a woman would always lie for her man."

"There were other witnesses, acquaintances who visited the pair that evening."

She almost snarls. "Well, even if that's true, Ernest could have hired some hoodlum—"

"So could anyone, Miss Beunon—so could you, for that matter—but there's no proof."

She might take offense at that, but something's stuck in her head, something the man said a minute ago. *No further justification to hold him.* "You ain't going to let Ernest go yet?"

"As a matter of fact, he was released some hours ago."

The cry that comes out of her mouth sounds like it's made by some small animal seized by a hawk.

The detective's face creases with annoyance. "These things take time. Slowly but surely, with a rigorous application of logic—"

Blanche stumbles away from him without another word.

"Miss Beunon?" Now it's Cartwright of the *Chronicle* at her elbow.

She shakes the reporter off. "You told me half an hour ago that Ernest was in jail, but they've already let him out!"

"Is that so?" He grimaces. "Look, miss, I'm doing my best."

"Doing your best to sell fish wrap."

"I hope boosting sales of the *Chronicle*'s not incompatible with striving for justice—"

"You're all bull," she cuts in. "Inventing Jenny's last words! 'Adieu, I follow my sister . . .' "

"If I leave anything out, the editor fills it in," says Cartwright, sheepish. "I'm afraid what we term *the news* is something of a crazy quilt of fact and fiction."

But Blanche has turned away, quickly leaving the newsman behind.

There's that monstrosity of an organ at the corner, the automata still ducking and waving to "The Ride of the Valkyries." Blanche goes the other way to escape its din.

What has she done?

P'tit's slipped through her fingers one last time.

She decided to be clever today, didn't she, to put on a dazzling turn, defy Ernest's warnings, laugh him to scorn while he was in the lockup. When all morning he's been walking the streets, a free man. Standing in the crowd at Gray's, perhaps, face obscured under a tilted hat, listening to every rash word escaping from Blanche's mouth? Whether Ernest heard her in person or whether he's going to read it in the papers later, he'll come to the same conclusion: that bitch has played her last card.

VII

BANG AWAY

Her first morning in San Miguel Station, Wednesday, the thirteenth of September, Blanche wakes to the sight of Jenny in a pair of blue overalls riveted together with what look like beads of brass. "What in the world have you got on?"

"Only cost me two bucks," says Jenny, grinning over her shoulder as she adjusts her belt, "and the fellow swore they'll outlive me."

"Just don't ever wear them into the City or you'll start a riot."

Jenny slides her Colt out from under her side of the mattress.

"I thought you were going frogging at the pond," says Blanche.

"It's gone green in the heat. Frogs turn up their noses at scum."

"I didn't know they had noses."

Jenny grins, pulling a box of cartridges out of her satchel.

"So what are you planning to hunt instead?" Blanche asks.

A guffaw. "Who goes hunting with a revolver?"

"I never claimed to know or care about guns," snaps Blanche.

"Thought I'd give the kids some target practice," Jenny explains.

When Blanche finally crawls out of bed, half an hour later, and emerges from the Eight Mile House in a wrapper, she finds the three younger McNamaras in a knot around Jenny.

"You're aiming high," Jenny's telling John Jr.

"Am not." The boy fires again and misses the bale of straw.

"You ain't flinching, at least."

Another bang; straw puffs at the very corner of the bale. "Dang it!"

Blanche is charmed by the childish euphemism that the twelve-year-old mumbles as if it's a serious cuss.

"Accuracy's a sight harder with a handgun," Jenny comforts him. "Care to show Miss Blanche what you can do with your old varmint gun instead? I once saw this boy hit a can at thirty yards," she tells Blanche.

Blanche widens her eyes. "I don't believe it."

John Jr. blushes as red as he might if Blanche rubbed up against him. She didn't mean to flirt, exactly; it's just her stock-in-trade.

"Go get it," Jenny tells the boy.

"Dadda sold the varmint gun, a month back," he mutters, squinting at the target as he lifts the revolver again. This time, the bale thuds and sends up a cough of dust.

"Now that's the ticket," murmurs Blanche.

John Jr. doesn't look at her, but he's flushed to the tips of his ears, and she can't help enjoying this little exercise of her powers.

Jeremiah's whining about it being his turn.

"I'll hold it with you," says his sister Kate.

"No."

"Otherwise you'll shoot your foot off, you know you will."

"All by self!"

Blanche thinks of P'tit. Of all the dangers he could be getting into wherever he may be.

The squabbling brings Ellen McNamara out and breaks up the lesson. With a few martyred sighs—"Breakfast's cleared away hours ago"—she agrees to toast a couple pieces of bread while Blanche is dressing.

Looking out through the dust-caked window of the saloon a quarter of an hour later, Blanche spots Jenny unhitching the horse from the buggy that has *Marshall's* stenciled on the side. She runs out, still chewing her toast. "Where are you off to?" It comes out more shrill than she meant it to.

"There's a creek up on Sweeney Ridge where I always catch a sackful," says Jenny, nodding toward the hills to the south. "Care to come along?"

Blanche hesitates, looks down at her polka-dot skirt. She doesn't want to be stuck at the Eight Mile House on her own all day, but . . .

"Don't let all your froufrou prevent you. John Jr. can lend you a pair of overalls."

"Not on your life."

But Blanche goes back to the bedroom and removes

her bustle, at least, and swaps her white mules for a pair of flattish boots. She borrows the boy's golden-brown pony. Offers to rent her, that is, but John Jr. stammers something about any friend of Jenny's being a friend of his. Blanche rewards him with her silkiest smile.

"Saddle slipping on you?" Jenny asks when they've been riding a few minutes.

"I feel as if I'm wallowing in a basket," complains Blanche.

"Ah, you must have ridden English-style at your circus."

"French-style," Blanche corrects her.

"Well, better learn to ride Western or this poor palomino's going to flick you off into the nearest gulch," says Jenny. "Leave her mouth alone, for starters."

"Then how's she going to know who's boss?"

"Let her have life, liberty, and the pursuit of happiness, I say, so long as she gets you up the hill."

Blanche rolls her eyes but transfers both reins to her left hand and leaves them slack, like Jenny does. And John's pony does seem to know what she's doing; she must have been up this way before.

They skirt around dairy farms, going past a mountain that Jenny says is named San Bruno. "So how about a few tricks, now the pony's used to you?"

Blanche glances sideways at her, incredulous.

"Go on, I've never known a genuine equestrienne."

"A genuine *putain,* these days."

Jenny gives her a look so fierce that Blanche yanks on the bridle without meaning to, making the palomino shake her creamy head furiously. "What?" Blanche demands. "Why be squeamish about the word?"

"You're more than that," Jenny insists. "Don't let those sons of bitches reduce you to that."

Blanche is startled.

"The way you dance, the goddamn artistry of it—there's not a one can touch you."

Blanche decides to be droll. "They can afterward, if they pay extra," she mutters.

Jenny ignores that.

They ride on for a minute. Something's puzzling Blanche. "You've never seen me dance."

"Ain't I, though?"

Blanche stares at her. "At the House of Mirrors?" It's never occurred to her to scan the faces under the top hats and bowlers or wonder if all the audience is male. And why would it matter, exactly? she asks herself in some confusion. Hard to explain the prickling feeling it gives her to know Jenny was among the watchers one time. Jenny, slouched on one of the Grand Saloon's red velvet chairs with her hat tipped over her eyes, unnoticed, because everyone was ogling the little festooned stage where Blanche la Danseuse was giving it her all. "What took you there?"

Jenny shrugs. "What takes me anywhere?"

A drink, Blanche supposes. For novelty, for fun. Blanche hasn't even done a leg show since she met Jenny, she realizes, calculating. So the Lively Flea must have been the first Jenny knew of her, long before the collision on Kearny Street. (And never breathed a word of it either. *Who are you and what's your story?* Jenny asked that first night; a question with a lie wrapped in it.) "The night you came. Was I good?" Blanche finds herself asking, though before the words are out of her mouth they embarrass her.

"Good?" Jenny shakes her head.

Blanche looks down, hot-cheeked.

Quoting Blanche's own phrase back at her, Jenny says, "You're the goddamn crème de la crème."

Blanche angles her face away to hide her smile.

They're moving up onto Sweeney Ridge now. Every blue curve turns to scrubby brown, seen up close.

Jenny's different on this ride, Blanche notices: peaceful as she sways in the saddle, quiet for long stretches. It's a side of her friend Blanche has never had the opportunity to glimpse before. As if Jenny has a prickly city self who gets into slanging matches in bars and a country self who's at rest, somehow. Blanche couldn't stomach living in the middle of nowhere, but she can see that something in the air here makes Jenny breathe easier.

It's getting steep. Jenny jumps down and hitches the rented hack to a lightning-cracked thorn tree. "Bring you back some water in a while, all right?" she murmurs in his pointed ear.

"Don't tell me we've got to walk now?"

"Just a little farther."

The heat's a rug hanging in Blanche's face, and with each loud breath, she pushes it away.

Jenny heads off along a humid stretch of fern-lined trail.

"Looks as if it's been raining up here," Blanche hazards.

Jenny shakes her head. "Fog drip. That's what the plants live on."

An orange-and-black butterfly goes right by Blanche's cheek, making her jump. Jenny points out figwort, poison oak's red leaves, and a sticky coyote brush that she claims can survive anything, even fire. The air's sickeningly heavy with lilac, like boiling honey. A couple of black-tailed deer go by, foraging in the tangled evergreen. "Seen porcupines up here," says Jenny, "snakes, miner's cats . . . I once almost stood on a coyote's paw, and it leaped ten feet in the air."

"And you?"

"Nearly as high," she admits with a chuckle.

Blanche has to stop talking as they close in on the summit. When they finally come to a halt, she heaves the scorching air out of her lungs. Her left calf's cramping. They stand looking down the parched slopes. Ocean on two sides, as if the women are balancing on the spine of some colossal whale with scarred flanks. "The land looks scraped bare."

Jenny nods. "When I had a flock down there in San Mateo, you could still stumble across the odd redwood, three hundred feet high. Not anymore."

"What made you leave off herding?"

She makes a face. "Got to feeling too shackled."

Blanche laughs breathlessly at that.

"You try sticking with fifteen hundred sheep for months on end," Jenny protests. "I'd rather be footloose." She turns, suddenly businesslike, and points to a little creek some distance away, edged with saplings. "Now, here we go, this is prime frog territory."

"Why don't I hear any croaking?" asks Blanche as they walk toward the water.

"They're probably tuckered out from the heat," says Jenny. "Besides, some kinds make more of a whistle or a chirp."

"The red-legs you're hunting, what do they say?"

"Depends what they mean."

"What do you mean, what they mean?" asks Blanche.

"Well, they don't make their music just to pass the time," says Jenny, grinning. "Got to want something to sing about it, no?"

Blanche supposes so.

"They might be shouting out, *Here comes the rain,* or *Predator nearby,* or *Help!* The females have a special low call for *Get off my back, I ain't in the mood.*"

Blanche laughs. "You speak frog!"

"Well, I've been known to try," says Jenny, rueful, "but they don't seem to understand my accent. I do like to come up here after a winter rainstorm to listen to the chorus. Like some crazy orchestra."

"What's the chorus?" asks Blanche.

"A bunch of frogs."

"A family, you mean?"

Jenny shakes her head. "Just the males. Frogs aren't what you'd call family-minded. When the males are keen to breed, they'd deafen you." She lets out a series of short grunts, then a final growl: "Uh-uh-uh-uh-uh-grrrr."

Blanche giggles, reminded of an expressionless banker who never thrusts more than a dozen times before he collapses across her body.

Jenny grins, reading her mind.

"So what do you call a bunch of female frogs?"

"No such thing." From her satchel, Jenny pulls out a burlap bag, and creeps up to the bank of the creek. "Now let's hush, or they'll hear us coming."

She dips to wet her bag. Then stands wide-legged in the rushes, keeping her eyes on the water.

"Ain't you got a net even?"

Jenny puts her finger to her lips, stern all of a sudden. "An old Frenchman taught me the knack," she murmurs under her breath. She stoops, graceful, fingering apart the dense cattails. Her brown cupped hands plunge—

A small splash. She shakes off a handful of slime.

"Did you just miss one?" whispers Blanche.

"Getting a touch late in the season now," mutters Jenny with a hint of melancholy.

"Excuses, excuses!"

Blanche is soon bored. The stink of water hanging on the humid air; frogs themselves might not smell, but their creeks sure do. She slaps her ear to dislodge a mosquito. Wonders about snakes. Her whole body's slick with sweat.

Jenny dips and comes up holding one lashing, squirming leg. "Good-size hopper, must be five inches." She tosses it into her burlap sack and folds the top over. "Care to hold the bag for me?"

"You must be kidding."

Jenny gets into the rhythm of it now, pincering frogs by the waist one by one. Sometimes she strokes their little stomachs.

"You cuddling them now?" Blanche scoffs under her breath.

"Stops them going loco in the bag." Jenny is almost unrecognizably calm, shin-deep in muck.

The day's softening to dusk by the time she packs up. "Well, I'm damned if I'm going to chop-chop all the way into town tonight," says Jenny with a great stretch.

It hadn't occurred to Blanche—but of course, Jenny

would have to go back into the City to sell what she's caught.

"Durand's customers are just going to have to wait a bit longer for their *cuisses de grenouille.*"

"But won't the creatures die if you keep them in that sack?"

"Nah, they'll mostly just sleep."

"What do they eat, anyhow?" Blanche wonders.

"Anything the greedy bastards can fit in their mouths. I threw in a few worms so they'll be less inclined to chew on each other tonight."

"Is this where you always hunt?" Blanche asks as they walk back in the direction of the horses.

Jenny shakes her head. "I go all over. Sometimes as far down as the Seventeen Mile House. There's a sag pond hereabouts I wouldn't mind trying before we turn back . . ."

"All right." Blanche follows her down a side trail. But when it rounds a corner, the slope before them is gouged away. Horses churn the earth up with huge machines. "Loggers?" she wonders.

Tight-lipped, Jenny shakes her head, pointing to one of the enormous bonfires in which trunks are turning to ash. "Hey"—she stops a man walking by with an ax on his shoulder—"what's going on here?"

"Spring Valley Water Company's damming the pond. Putting up an earthen wall a hundred feet high," he says with laconic pride.

"The hell you are!"

Blanche groans inwardly; Jenny can lose her temper in a heartbeat.

"Who gave you the blasted right to—"

"Whoever sold us the blasted pond, that's who," the workman interrupts, turning his ax in a faintly menacing way. "You want the City to choke of thirst?" He looks Blanche up and down, and it seems as if he's more disgusted by her mud-flecked polka-dot skirt than by her friend's denim overalls.

She finds herself blushing. "I'm beat," she says to Jenny in a pleading undertone. "Let's head back to San Miguel Station."

*

Jenny's two days' dead, and Blanche is in a basement noodle house on Dupont, a few doors away from the undertaker's, gulping down some kind of fishy stew the waiter brought her.

She can't remember all she just said at the inquest, or even how she said it. If Blanche had put things better, a little more eloquently, moved those jurymen to tears—if she'd given one of her legendary performances—might they have ended up finding Arthur and Ernest guilty of conspiracy to commit murder, instead of merely concluding that the evidence *points to* their involvement?

P'tit. P'tit. The tiny weight of him, a bullet lodged in Blanche's lung. By denouncing the *macs* in such vehement detail this morning, she's thrown away her last chance of persuading them to give her son back. All she can do is try to stay out of their way and wait for a miracle, for the City's famous detectives to solve the case and carry P'tit back to her, safe. Blanche does know how childish that dream sounds. But what else can she do? It's impossible to make plans for herself as if P'tit doesn't exist. She can't decide anything, go anywhere, without knowing what's happened to her baby. (That wretched, ugly, beloved baby.)

In the meantime, she needs some substantial funds. Having blown so much of the money Lamantia gave her yesterday on this pink costume, she can't live for long on the rest. Blanche is supposed to clear three hundred by dancing at the House of Mirrors on Saturday—that's tonight, she realizes with a jerk. But she can't quite imagine summoning it up, whatever knack Blanche la Danseuse once possessed for leaving hundreds of men roused and rapt.

She asked Lamantia to come and see the show, Blanche remembers now. She hasn't said no to his offer to take her into keeping; it seems she can't afford to say no. The question may be moot, though. By this evening the businessman might have found the time to read an afternoon paper, which will enlighten him about his little white flower. The child Blanche never mentioned; the French thugs she's been living with; the obvious conclusion (the most alarming thing to such a man as Lamantia) that she can't keep hold of her tongue. He might not think her a suitable candidate for a mistress anymore. This fills Blanche with a curious mixture of disappointment and relief.

Her head's full of the Detritus of the inquest: everyone's lies, half lies, evasions, pontifications. Claims that, when Blanche tries to grasp them and knot them into a narrative that holds together, prove as slippery as pondweed.

And Swan—whatever was the coroner getting at when he kept going on about how it *strained credulity* that Blanche bent down just as the killer fired?

Suddenly she can't swallow. Nausea grips her. She lets

the piece of miscellaneous shellfish in her mouth drop back discreetly into her wide ceramic spoon and pushes the dish away.

Blanche tries to remember how she became convinced as she sat on McNamara's barrel sticky with Jenny's blood—no, how she convinced herself—that she, Blanche, must have been the target. It seemed to make an awful sense at the time. She couldn't believe that it was only luck that saved her, the fluke of doubling over to struggle with that knotted lace just as the killer's finger squeezed the trigger. It was guilt, too, that made her decide she was the one those bullets were meant for; she was crushed by a feeling of responsibility for all this horror. And a strange sort of vanity, perhaps; Blanche can see that now. Everyone puts herself at the center of the story, imagines the world giddily spinning on her own axis. Blanche couldn't believe that she was just playing a walk-on part in Jenny's bloody drama.

But here in the noodle house it occurs to her that there's another explanation, much simpler than the one-in-a-million fluke of Blanche being spared by an accident of timing. Arthur or Ernest—she can't be sure which, and their dark faces have melted into a single monstrous mask in her mind's eye—perhaps they came to San Miguel Station to kill Jenny, not Blanche, and that's just what they did. Whichever of them held the shotgun and looked through the sight, he chose not to shoot Blanche. She doesn't know why, but she's pretty sure she knows what happened. He waited calmly until Blanche, struggling with her laces, bent out of his line of fire, and then he blew Jenny to pieces.

Her gaze snags on a clock on the restaurant's mantelpiece. Almost one already. The funeral's at two.

The fact is, it would be considerably safer for Blanche to skip the ceremony. What she said about the *macs* in that courtroom will have provoked such wrath in Ernest—he may have refrained from killing Blanche on Thursday night, for his own obscure reasons, but that doesn't mean he won't do it today. If Blanche is going to walk behind Jenny's coffin, she might as well have a bull's-eye painted on her forehead.

But she finds she simply can't do it, can't stay away from the funeral. And she has to see Jenny's face one more time, it occurs to her, before they nail the lid down.

The placard outside Gray's says *Memento Mori.* Blanche stares at the boy holding it up. "What's a—"

"Photograph of the victim, fresh took," he rattles off, "thirty cents for a cabinet card, gilt-ruled, carte de visite only a quarter or five for a dollar . . ."

He's lifting the top off his box with enthusiasm, but Blanche averts her eyes from the glossy images and makes for the front door of Gray's.

What if she's too late already? In the marble-floored lobby, a man's going by in some kind of white uniform. "Pardon me, sir, but where do you keep the . . . the bodies?"

"Mortuary," he answers, jerking his thumb downward.

That must be a fancy word for deadhouse. She speeds down the granite steps, her heels clacking.

Somehow she assumed the room would be empty, but it's crammed: doves, miscellaneous men, grubby street kids of both sexes . . . The mortuary has the air of a high-class fishmonger's, decorated for a festival. Flowers on stands all around, but there's a tang in the air, something faintly off underneath the perfume. Three coffins, each lying on a bed of chunked ice, but only one of them is open. It's ringed with gawkers, five-deep.

"Excuse me." Outrage flares up in Blanche when she can't get through. "Let me by."

"Don't push so," cries a woman.

"I was with her," snaps Blanche. "I was there, at San Miguel Station."

This wins her a little elbow room. People stare, mutter, even smirk at her as if she's some kind of star. "Blanche la Danseuse," she hears somebody say.

She ignores all that and shoves her way to the front.

Jenny's corpse looks infinitely strange. Partly because the short hair's been combed back neatly—more neatly than Blanche ever saw her wear it. The dieners have made her look like . . . a girl. A crop-haired, weather-beaten girl, head resting on a small white pillow. Somehow pale under her dark tan: *exsanguination,* wasn't that Crook's word? All the blood's been wiped away. Just a girl, swollen around the left eye with bruising showing through the paint, because somebody punched her in the face just a few hours before somebody else shot her dead.

Blanche stares, trying to fix the image in her mind like a photograph. A memento mori. The small brown hands are—not exactly joined as if praying, but clasped around a white flower. Incongruous, as if Jenny is personifying Virtuous Suffering in some tableau vivant. It's not the pristine charity nightshirt that's transformed her; that's a neutral garment, one a man might wear. It's more the fact that she's not strutting, not swaggering, not moving at all: still.

Blanche would be better off turning away and wiping this hoax from her memory. Surely at any moment her friend's going to let out a horse laugh and spring up, somersaulting out of the coffin, crowing, *Fooled you all!*

Blanche stands and watches and holds her position despite all the others jostling to get in. There's another burr stuck to her thoughts. Something else that was said at the inquest; what was it? The autopsy. Something about Jenny's body. *Considerable scarring,* that was it. But Blanche never saw any scars on Jenny. *Not recent,* according to Dr. Crook. Old scars from a fall, a crash? Lord knows Jenny was accident-prone. This Adrien, did he leave his mark before he blew all her money? But no, Maria insisted that the *mac* never hit Jenny. *Considerable,* that sounds to Blanche like more than one punch, one gash. If it wasn't this Adrien, then—

That very first night Jenny came back to number 815. Pulling Arthur's green shirt on over her head the way men do, snapping at Blanche when she went into the bedroom: *A little privacy!* Then, even down in San Miguel Station, in the room they shared for three days, Jenny kept her clothes on. Even on Wednesday night, Blanche remembers now, pulse thumping faster. Why didn't Blanche wonder then? Was Jenny a touch prudish, for all her blunt talk? Did she prefer to keep her femaleness out of sight, out of mind? It was just one of Jenny's many oddities.

Blanche worms her way around to the head of the coffin, possessed by a terrible curiosity. Standing behind Jenny's pomaded hair, she slips her hand under, where the nape is soft against the ironed pillow.

A gasp goes up from the watchers. "What do you think you're doing?" demands a man behind her.

Blanche ignores them all and slides her fingers underneath Jenny, right down the back of the starchy nightshirt. The flesh is so chilled. She can't feel it, what she's looking for, *considerable scarring*. She's going to have to see for herself.

"Hands off, miss!"

"How dare you disturb the dead?"

Somebody yanks at Blanche's arm but she fights him off, and before she can lose her nerve she reaches across the body and grips Jenny's shoulder, pulls hard enough to make her roll sideways. Blanche was prepared for the corpse to be stiff, but it's not. Jenny moves languidly, that's all, like a sleeper who's hard to rouse. An awful smell rises above the florals.

The crowd's in an uproar, shouting for the dieners. Hard hands on Blanche's shoulders. She growls, throws them off. Working fast, holding Jenny with her left arm and ripping at the nightshirt with her right; a tightness, then a popping as a button flies off, and now she can see Jenny's back, which has a strangely purple tinge to it. An awful jagged hole, and then another, but Blanche is steeled against the sight of them. There it is, *bordel!*—a ladder of pink lines from the tops of the shoulder blades all the way down as far as Blanche can see. The claw marks of some strange beast. Too many to count. Not one whipping, she reckons; long years of them. Hot pink, a whole page of angry, unfading lines.

Two dieners seize Blanche's arms and haul her away,

then hustle her up the stairs. "Could be had up for interfering with a cadaver!" scolds one of them.

Blanche sits on the curb outside the undertaker's, her head reeling. Puts up her parasol so that no one will see her face.

She knows she's touched what she shouldn't have; laid bare what should have stayed hidden. Jenny was most herself with her clothes on. Sorry, Blanche is so terribly sorry. For seeing what Jenny never wanted seen. For not understanding until she saw. For not looking till now.

She curses her own slow wits. "Got into scrapes with the law from a tender age"; it was right there in Cartwright's article. The McNamara boy even told her that Jenny had her *educating* near San Miguel Station, and what schools are there out that way? Only the brutal facade of the Industrial School, which isn't a school at all. *Whips and gags for the troublemakers,* the boy at Marshall's mentioned. But the inmates at the Industrial School must all be troublemakers of one sort or another, or else they wouldn't have been sent there. As *young as three*. Skinny boys pecking at the ground with their hoes as the trains rocket by; Blanche remembers the small faces disappearing into the distance. But there used to be girls at the Industrial School too, didn't there? Blanche should have guessed, should have heard what Jenny never said. *Some folks just like to hit kids*, Jenny remarked the evening they met, as if mentioning the weather. *I've seen worse,* she said another night about P'tit's bowed legs. *I've seen worse;* was Jenny trying to prompt Blanche to ask her where? To shake a straight answer out of her for once? *Weals, you know, if they've tied them to the beds.* Jenny almost spelled it out; came within an inch of saying "they tied *me*."

How many years did she spend in that nightmare of an institution grubbing at the earth behind the fence? The supervisor finally got fired for—what was it the woman said on the train yesterday?—*taking liberties*. Imagine how many *liberties* the man in charge can take with children before someone calls for a grand jury investigation. Blanche shudders, rocking backward and forward. What did he—what did they all—do to Jenny, to a girl who refused to be like other girls? The ladder of pink scars. And other things that don't show up so clearly. How hard did they try to break a spirit as playful and pugnacious as Jenny's?

The tears are spilling out of Blanche's sockets; her head has turned to hot liquid and she's moaning like some blinded calf. Crying not for Jenny's death, but for Jenny's life. For the short, lousy lives of all the children.

After some minutes Blanche wipes her face and tilts her green parasol back a little. She estimates the size of the gathering crowd; well, no fear of Jenny going lonely to the grave. Some must be gawkers, of course, but many have the swollen eyes of friends who are mourning. Real friends; old friends. For all her irksome qualities, Jenny had that gift—she could make you care about her without hardly trying. She had hundreds of friends, clearly, while Blanche had just one. For less than a month. And Blanche, reckless and ignorant, led that friend straight to the barrel of a shotgun.

She chews her lips, scanning the crowd. No tall, mustachioed Frenchman standing ready to gun her down. But it's not as if Ernest would do it in public, anyhow. He'll find a private moment.

Two mules stand hitched to a wagon draped in black cambric: the *corbillard. Hearse,* that's the English word, but it's not one Blanche has ever had reason to say. There's a stir behind her, in the door of Gray's, and she heaves herself upright and gets out of the way. Two men with crepe bows on their hats carry out the draped coffin as if it's very light and place it in the hearse. *Croque-morts,* they call them back in Paris, the death crunchers.

A pair of uniformed women emerge with baskets and wreaths of lilies and carnations and arrange them on the coffin. Trying to soften the unmistakable shape, Blanche supposes.

There's some *gamin* barely bigger than his sandwich board parading past as if he's at a fair: MYSTERIOUS MURDER OF FRENCH FROG GIRL. ADDITIONAL PARTICULARS FROM THE SCENE. "The father's twenty minutes late already," somebody comments behind her.

The old actor who lives in Oakland now; Blanche forgot all about him. She still can't quite imagine Jenny with anything as ordinary as a family. Where were they, what did they do to help her when the judge sent her to the Industrial School?

The sandwich-board boy turns and Blanche reads what's on the other side: WOMAN'S MANIA FOR WEARING MALE ATTIRE ENDS IN DEATH. Fury, acid in her throat.

There are three carriages lined up behind the hearse. Blanche realizes she's going to be left behind, and she doesn't even know where the funeral is taking place. She hurries alongside and tries to look in the open windows. The third carriage is empty. In the second she recognizes a ghastly face among a bright-costumed knot of *filles de joie*. "Maria," she makes herself cry out.

The one-eyed hag beckons Blanche in, though the carriage is a squeeze already. Maria makes the introductions, and Blanche can tell the others are titillated to meet her. She forgets their names at once and leans against the worn upholstery, shutting her eyes.

She's picturing Jenny back when she was one of this tribe—bustle and frills, painting and primping, bringing all her earnings home for her *mac* to throw away on the table of his choice. The image sickens her; shames her, almost. It's like a warped reflection of Blanche's own life. No, Jenny should always have strolled loose-limbed, up- and downhill, taking the whole City for her stage.

There's so much Blanche still doesn't know about Jenny's past. She opens her eyes and looks out at the milling crowd. She wonders exactly what kind of trouble with the law got Jenny locked up in the first place. Could she have been in one of those gangs of adolescent hoodlums for which San Francisco's notorious? What kind of crowd did she run with, before the Industrial School and after?

Jenny was on the town for a while, Blanche knows that much. Moving in the sporting set, with its quick enmities and long memories. And at one point things fell apart badly enough for Jenny—despite her ebullient spirits—to decide she was better off dead. How would this Adrien have felt about Jenny walking away from him after she woke up from her overdose? Blanche wonders whether he might have nursed his resentment over the years, the way Arthur nursed his. What old debts did Jenny carry, what old scores did others want to settle with her? She was enough of a thief to swipe a priceless bicycle, after all. What other laws did she break? Could frog-hunting really have been the sole source of her cash? And why has Blanche been assuming that Arthur and Ernest were Jenny's only enemies, that Jenny's getting tangled up in Blanche's complicated life was the only possible reason for her to have been killed?

These thoughts make her dizzy. It's unbearable, the not knowing. Most of the time Blanche is sure of what happened, because she can feel Arthur's hatred like a fire under her feet. But every now and then, the pieces fall apart in her mind and she can't fit them back together. Two days since the murder, the *nation's finest* detectives, newsmen *striving for justice,* a resolute coroner, and yet nobody seems any closer to the truth of how Jenny died.

"Le voilà enfin," exclaims Maria, "at last."

An old man limping up the street, the crowd parting for him: this must be Sosthenes Bonnet. Well, not that old. He still has a performer's uprightness about him, and a clever face. Not like Jenny's, though; nothing about him is like Jenny that Blanche can see. Only his stunned stare at the hearse gives him away as the chief mourner.

Someone opens the door of the third carriage and puts the step down to help him in. It's what's-his-name, Portal; Blanche belatedly recognizes the lachrymose cook from Durand's brasserie.

Now the hearse is pulling away, and all the carriages are following.

The small cortege heads down Dupont a few blocks, then turns west on Geary Boulevard. They've left most of the crowd behind at the undertaker's. "Where are we going?" Blanche asks the girl beside her.

She goggles. "The cemetery, where else?"

"But which one?"

"Odd Fellows," supplies Maria. "They've donated a plot."

"Very suitable," an older woman in bloodred rouge quips, "since Jenny was such an odd fellow!"

Maria shuts her up with a gesture.

"Oh, come," the woman complains, "she enjoyed a laugh at her own expense . . ."

Blanche doesn't want to hear any of it. Not their witticisms, nor rebuttals, nor sentimental musings on Jenny's character . . . Blanche can't bear to find out that everyone in the City knew Jenny better than she did.

"Did you get that scratch from a bullet?" the youngest-looking girl asks her.

Blanche shakes her head and shuts her eyes again.

Another one tries: "Is it true you went crazy in the deadhouse and dragged her corpse about?"

"Chut!" Maria shushes them loudly.

"Well, if we're obliged to squeeze so tight we might as well get some conversation out of her," the first mutters.

The carriages drag slowly through the hillside cemetery, a little city divided into neighborhoods. Carved signs mark out the sections belonging to the firemen, the typographers, the Protestant orphan asylum. The Chinese vault, where bodies are kept ready to be sent back to their homeland, is strewn with what looks to Blanche like the remains of a banquet: rice, joss sticks twisted black, singed squares of that curious pretend money they make out of paper stamped silver or gold. *Low Long,* she once asked her lodger, *why do your lot work so hard?*

The shoemaker told her that they had to save up enough to send themselves back, *either-either.*

Either what?

Pay for journey back, Miss Blanche, dead or live.

So their bones wouldn't lie restless in California, you see. Blanche considers the bleak question now: Where will her bones end up?

They pass a much bigger, tonier cortege; hear violins. She feels oddly nettled that Jenny's isn't the only funeral in town.

They come to a halt now. She cranes out the window and sees the black-suited *croque-morts* lifting the coffin down and placing it at the side of a pit with freshly spaded edges. (The soil is reddish, bone-dry.) The women spill from the carriage, shaking out their skirts. No priest, Blanche suddenly realizes, which means no eulogy, no requiem. Are they going to put Jenny in the ground without a word? No music, even? That doesn't seem right.

The sky is white-blue, steely hot. Rain on a funeral sends a soul to heaven, Blanche remembers, but no chance of a drop today. Now, there's a curious thought: Jenny in heaven. Angels, robes? Somehow Blanche can't imagine her anywhere but San Francisco, always wandering down some steep street, just out of sight.

The pallbearers are lifting off the wreaths and the fringed pall. Blanche pushes near enough to see the coffin. A glass plate set into the lid. She wriggles closer, not caring whose foot she steps on. But the light is bouncing sideways, so Blanche can't get a last glimpse of the face. It's as if Jenny is setting off in some futuristic machine toward the stars.

Gravediggers in dusty overalls lower the coffin on straps. Then pull the straps back up, loose now. They glance around for instruction. Nobody seems to be in charge. The staff from Gray's stand still, as if their duty is done. Sosthenes Bonnet has covered his face with his hands, Blanche notices.

In a shaky voice, an elderly woman strikes up what sounds like a hymn.

Through all the tumult and the strife
I hear the music ringing—

Most of the small crowd join in, some of them dissonantly. Sosthenes Bonnet's rich old voice comes in on the third line.

It finds an echo in my soul—
How can I keep from singing?

Blanche remembers Jenny singing. She did it like breathing. The child star could have stayed on the stage, warbling and strutting with her parents, pleasing the crowds. Could have done any number of things. To think of all the lives Jenny tossed aside so she could live this particular one. And who's to say she ever regretted it?

After a couple of verses, the hymn peters out. The diggers hoist their shovels.

A wave of anticlimax weakens Blanche's legs. What now?

The old actor is making his halting way from the grave back to the carriage, leaning on Durand's arm.

Blanche seizes her chance. "Monsieur Bonnet?" she calls, hurrying up.

"It should have been Paris," she hears him complaining to Portal, on his left.

"Monsieur Bonnet?"

He blinks at Blanche rheumily.

"Mademoiselle Beunon," supplies Durand. "She was with Jenny in San Miguel Station."

The expressive face contracts. "Mademoiselle." A sketched bow. "I was just remarking that my daughter should rest in Paris."

"Not at all," says Blanche too sharply, following his gaze to the pit that the gravediggers are starting to fill in. "Jenny loved this city ever since she saw it burning."

"Burning?"

"Saw it from the ship, the day you landed," Blanche prompts him.

He shakes his head.

"She told me—" Blanche starts.

"There'd been a fire some weeks before, I believe," says Sosthenes. "Blackened stumps everywhere. But nothing burning anymore, no. They were rebuilding already."

"But Jenny insisted—"

Portal scowls at Blanche and takes the old man by the elbow.

"Jeanne was barely two when we came to this place," says Sosthenes with a sorrowful smile. "How could she remember anything of the journey?"

Blanche is thrown. Is the man's memory gone, or was Jenny's deceiving her? (Even at twenty-seven, Jenny had had a long time to lick grit into a pearl.) Was she spinning a yarn, setting the stumps alight again to transform her ordinary arrival into a hero's landing? How many of her anecdotes were fictions, Blanche wonders, and did Jenny even know the difference anymore?

Sosthenes is walking away, and Blanche remembers what she really needs to find out. She raises her voice. "How many years was she in the Industrial School?"

He turns, gapes. But he's not denying it.

"Leave him be, mademoiselle," protests Durand.

Blanche presses on. "Couldn't you have saved her from that?"

"Saved our Jeanne?" Durand is trying to move Sosthenes toward the carriage, but the old man twists away and comes back to Blanche. "If we could have saved her from her own nature," he says with a trembling mouth, "we wouldn't have had to ask the judge to send her to that place at all."

Blanche blinks at him. "You *asked* him?"

A proper family, Jenny quips grimly in her head, *that's a guarantee of happiness.*

"I begged him on my knees," admits Sosthenes with a grandiloquent gesture. "It was said to be a sort of quarantine for the young—a house of refuge from the corruptions of the City, so that delinquents could be reformed before they fell into serious crime."

How could Jenny have paid regular visits to this poor excuse for a father? Brought him a share in her earnings? "Did you ever see the skin on her back?" Blanche demands.

His face crumples like a page. "We didn't know what it was like in that place," he says. "We had so little notion—"

"Scarred," she interrupts, "like the hull of a goddamn boat!"

Tears are scoring his cheeks now, which gives Blanche a certain satisfaction.

Durand and Portal, waiting for Sosthenes some yards away, are looking daggers at her.

How did Jenny mislay her rage? Blanche wonders. She had a talent for starting a row but none for holding a grudge, it seems. She kept her chin high, her scars covered up, her gun in her pocket. Bicycled past the Industrial School regularly, and instead of burning the place down, she just tossed gumdrops and lozenges over the fence.

The father takes Blanche by the hand; she flinches from his hot grip. "Jeanne was unmanageable, uncivilizable," he confides. "*Un enfant sauvage!* With my wife not well and our younger girl in tears all the time—I simply—how could I have been expected to—"

"How convenient," barks Blanche. "Pack one off to rot in the reformatory and the other to die in the asylum."

"Our Blanche didn't die, only the baby," Sosthenes says, confused. "They'd have sent word, wouldn't they?"

"What baby?" She's nearly shrieking.

"My daughter was *enceinte,* you see, though I never knew the exact, ah, circumstances. At the asylum—the poor creature, he didn't live a week."

Blanche is almost too angry to speak. Another baby? Jenny's nephew. Was this one nudged along toward his death? she wonders. Did anyone in the asylum feed him, even? Hold him? All the missing children. Washed into the world against their will, to do their time, a day or a year, before being sent out of it again. *P'tit,* she cries out silently, *P'tit.*

Durand's cook is at Sosthenes's elbow, leading the old

man away from Blanche. "Stop harassing a grieving old man," Portal throws over his shoulder.

Guilt paralyzes Blanche. What right has she, of all people, to accuse?

Jenny's father sobs something as he goes. "It's all true, Adrien."

Adrien.

No. The cook? Portal, the cook at Durand's?

Wait. It's a common enough name, Adrien.

But how common could it be among Frenchmen in San Francisco who were friends of Jenny's? A cook who might well have been a *mac* until he lost all his money. (Jenny's money, Blanche thinks with renewed fury.) Who knew Jenny long enough, well enough, to tease her and take her teasing; to persuade his boss to buy her frogs; to weep like a baby when he heard she was dead at twenty-seven.

The cemetery's almost deserted now. The carriage of doves has left without Blanche.

She starts walking east, toiling through the thick air. Her parasol wobbles overhead, weighing down her arm. She's busy trying to make sense of Jenny; she's flabbergasted. To try to kill yourself over a man because he's wrecked your life—and then, years later, to treat him as a friend? *Forgiveness,* is that the word for it? It seems too simple a term for whatever happened between Jenny and Adrien Portal. Some deeper alteration, then? When Jenny left off skirts and put on pants, did some old scars not bother her anymore—did they no longer feel like hers? *You've got the wrong Jenny Bonnet.* Had Jenny managed to convince herself that she'd metamorphosed into someone entirely new?

"Miss Beunon!"

Cartwright, trotting behind Blanche. Where did he come from? She shakes her head furiously.

"A single question."

She marches on.

"Please." He pants. "Help me make sure your friend's story doesn't fade away."

"It's on every front page," she snaps.

"It's been only a day and a half. By Monday she'll be lucky to get a paragraph at the back between stolen watches and run-over dogs."

Blanche halts. Purses her lips. "What's your single question?"

"Are you acquainted with a man called Lamantia?"

Her mouth falls open. The journalist couldn't possibly know she spent last night with Lamantia at the Palace Hotel, unless the *Chronicle*'s having her followed. "No," she says automatically, turning her eyes away from Cartwright's blue-glass-covered ones.

He persists. "I think you've heard the name, at least? He's an importer on Market Street."

She keeps shaking her head. It doesn't sound as if he knows about the Palace. Curiosity's like a pebble in her shoe. "Why does he matter, this Lamantia?"

"I don't know for sure that he does. But he was in San Miguel Station on Wednesday morning."

When she and Jenny were off frog-hunting on Sweeney Ridge? Blanche steps away from the newsman in confusion and panic.

"Yesterday Mrs. Holt told me about a stranger getting off the train on Wednesday," adds Cartwright, keeping up with her. "A big man, dark, citified. She hadn't thought to mention it to Detective Bohen, because it was on the day *before* the murder!"

But what could possibly have taken Lamantia to San Miguel Station? The Sicilian wasn't even aware of Blanche's connection to *that crazy girl in pants* till she told him about the murder yesterday. Unless—

Blanche stumbles, almost falls. On second thought, wasn't it rather overdone, his insistence that he'd heard nothing at all about the case? *Too busy to read the papers.* Perhaps he wasn't too busy to hire someone to track down his *bella bianca* after Blanche dropped out of view for a couple of weeks and left him pining. Didn't Madame volunteer the fact that he'd been making inquiries at the House of Mirrors? How much had he paid Madame for the information that Blanche was at San Miguel Station?

Her pulse drums in her throat. What if Lamantia came down and made further inquiries about the women visiting from town? What if he somehow got it into his head that this eccentric frog girl was responsible for his favorite's absence from the House of Mirrors? *This so-called friend,* that's how he'd described Jenny yesterday. What if Lamantia, wanting to bully Blanche into accepting his permanent protection, formed a wild plan to scare her away from her riffraff connections by . . .

By what, gunning her friend down in front of her? This is ludicrous. But what does Blanche know about the man, really, except how he fucks? *Let me look after you as you deserve,* Lamantia wheedled at the Palace. Him being the killer makes no sense, but since when have men's cravings to own women ever made sense?

"Miss Beunon?"

She waves Cartwright away. She has to think. Because if by any chance Lamantia is behind the murder, then that would mean Arthur and Ernest are . . . well, not *innocent,* that word will never fit. They're snakes in the grass, child-stealers, brutes at the very least. But if they didn't shoot Jenny, they're not quite demons. A notion that chokes Blanche like a pair of hands around her throat. Can Ernest possibly have been sincere yesterday at the apartment when he railed against her for defaming his friend as a murderer? When he gave her one last chance to make things right and get her baby back? A chance Blanche threw away today at the inquest like a used handkerchief.

"Mrs. Holt said the gentleman wandered around as if lost," Cartwright rattles on, "but then he struck up a conversation with the chicken farmer."

The change of tack bewilders her. "What chicken farmer?"

"This Louis fellow, the Canadian. I checked, and he really has been in San Jose since Thursday. But it seemed a touch too convenient that he'd happen to leave San Miguel Station on the very morning of the shooting. And aren't chicken farmers usually stone broke, and so perhaps ripe for tempting?" Cartwright speaks as if telling the plot of some thrilling dime novel.

"What are you talking about?" demands Blanche.

"The importer could have hired this Louis, you see? The wife—when I pressed her, she admitted that her husband did talk to an Italian on Wednesday, name of Lamantia."

"You're raving," Blanche tells Cartwright, putting one finger on his lapel. The newsman is chalk-white in a lake of sunlight. Now that she's taking the trouble to look at him, she can see that he probably hasn't had any sleep since yesterday. "If this Canadian left San Miguel Station on Thursday morning then he couldn't have shot Jenny, could he?"

"He might have contracted the job out to someone else," says Cartwright uncertainly, "so he could go to San Jose and provide himself with an alibi, you see."

A substitute for a substitute, like some corridor of mirrors? "It's a crossroads in the goddamn scrublands," Blanche retorts. "How many killers for hire do you imagine could be found there?"

"Phil Jordan?" he suggests with a shrug. "John McNamara?"

"It's too complicated. It's nonsense. My Arthur did it!" Blanche screams at him. (Why did she say *my*? Why, after all that's come between her and that man, does she still slip into thinking of him as hers?) "I've been telling you, all of you, but none of you seems to listen."

Cartwright's breath hisses tiredly. "The problem is, you see, the lack of evidence—"

"Evidence be damned. Who wanted me and Jenny dead? Arthur. Because I dared to walk away from him after all these years," says Blanche with a sob that's almost triumphant, "and it was Jenny who gave me the strength to do it, and she died for it."

She stalks away.

She's almost at the gates of the cemetery when Cartwright hails her again. "Just one more question—"

Blanche groans.

"Only for background," the journalist pleads, "to liven up the story. What was the appeal?"

Is that a legal term? she wonders.

"If I may ask, I mean—" His cheeks are rose red. "What was it that attached you so powerfully to this particular girl?"

Blanche stares at him. And growls, "You never met her."

On Dupont, when she finally gets back to Chinatown from the cemetery, the evening heat's streaking the burnt cork on a young song-seller's cheeks. On arrival in America, Blanche was disconcerted by blackface minstrels, but now she doesn't bat an eye even when they're wearing skirts. This one is pealing out his song in falsetto, holding up the freshly inked lyric sheets in one hand and his petticoats in the other:

The bullfrog married the tadpole's sister,
Old Aunt Jemima, Oh! Oh! Oh!
He smacked his lips and then he kissed her,
Old Aunt Jemima, Oh! Oh! Oh!

He doesn't look at all bad, actually; prettier than some real girls. The music gives Blanche a reason to stand still and catch her breath.

She says if you love me as I love you,
Old Aunt Jemima, Oh! Oh! Oh!
No knife can cut our love in two,
Old Aunt Jemima, Oh! Oh! Oh!

Her thoughts move turgidly. She has to do it, this one last show for Madame Johanna tonight. After clearing her spurious debt to the madam, Blanche should have almost three hundred dollars left. That should be enough to buy her some kind of future. Rent, food, clothes. It'll give her time to hide away from the *macs,* at least, and wait for P'tit—or for news that he's never coming back. Blanche presses her hand to her face for a moment.

She steps aside to avoid a knot of tourists following their guide out of a temple, all of them clutching overpriced incense sticks. Then she walks the other way, toward the House of Mirrors.

In a few minutes she's standing by the stately doors of the blue-and-white mansion. The sign is fresh painted and almost as tall as Blanche.

FOR ONE NIGHT ONLY!
THE LIVELY FLEA'S FAREWELL TO THE TOWN.
LAST DANCE OF MURDERED GIRL'S BOSOM PAL.

Well, Blanche might have known Madame would milk the tragedy. She's almost surprised there isn't a large drawing of Blanche wearing nothing but a bloodstained corset.

The expressionless doorman lets her in. She can hear waves of laughter from the Grand Saloon; she pauses and puts her eye to the crack between the doors as she's passing. Some burlesque about the epidemic? Lola and Paquita with what looks like—could it be?—fresh cranberries pasted all over their arms, chests, and faces. A month since Blanche has been here. The gaudy thick carpets, oil paintings, marbles, and, above all, the long mirrors are a shock to her senses.

She turns down the corridor that's just for performers. Her skin crawls. Just one last time.

The empty dressing room at the end has been freshly wallpapered. She fingers the familiar costumes. Hourglass-shaped ball gowns, orthodox enough until they end above the knee. Military: fringed trunks, frogging, and tassels. The Andalusian outfit has a calf-length split skirt and castanets. The alabaster statue costume, more or less transparent. Hamlet, complete with Yorick's skull, and boots that lace to the thigh. A bowl of wax fruit, a bow and arrow . . . Nothing looks appealing. It was always shoddy glamour, Blanche can see that now.

Suddenly decisive, she pulls on a peasant skirt from one costume, a shiny bodice from the Andalusian set, a little bolero jacket.

There's a faint tap at the door. "My dear, so glad," says Madame Johanna, putting her head around the door. Then her eyebrows soar. "All in mourning black tonight?"

"It seemed fitting." Blanche keeps her eyes on the tiny faux-pearl buttons she's doing up. "Ever so tasteful, the sign out front," she adds, scathing.

The Prussian spreads her cloud-gray sleeves. "My doors are open to all who seek sensation. I don't discriminate."

"Well, that's for sure," Blanche mutters, tugging an opera glove up past her elbow. She needs to ask about Lamantia, just to put to rest that strange theory of Cartwright's that she's been turning over and over in her mind. But she'll wait until after she's danced, because she can't afford to start another quarrel right now.

"The Professor wants to know what you mean to treat us to tonight."

" 'Flea' and 'Bang Away, Lulu,' " says Blanche.

A pause. "Just two numbers?"

"Oh, I think that'll provide enough *sensation.*"

Madame is clearly debating whether to press the point, to demand a lot more for the extraordinary fee of five hundred dollars. Instead she withdraws.

Blanche goes to stand outside the door to the stage, recognizing the final thumps of Fabienne's flamenco skipping-rope act. The piano's been tuned, which is some relief. She goes over her routines in her head, trying to block out the sound of Madame's hushed, thrilling voice as she warms up the crowd for the enigmatic Blanche la Danseuse.

Blanche opens the door a crack to check whether the lights have gone low. She waits for silence. The excited babble of the audience dies away in the near dark.

She walks onto the little stage, as formal as some courtier. A storm of applause when the lights flare up. Blanche averts her face until the cheering subsides. She makes a rapid scan of the whole room: not a single velvet chair is empty, and there's no sign of Lamantia, thank Christ. He can't have been involved in the murder; he just can't. But then what was he doing out at San Miguel Station on Wednesday?

The tune is a nervous tarantella, slow at first, then it starts to hurry, and Blanche twitches. It's a simple routine, no intricate steps to remember or feats of flexibility to perform. She simply pretends there's something in her clothes, flea, spider, skeeter, bee, wasp—it really doesn't matter so long as she imagines it vividly enough. The music's half the trick of it: stop and start, itchily agitated, then more and more maddened as the invisible parasite starts to bite. Madame's always advertised the Lively Flea as Blanche's specialty, "straight from gay Paree," and in June, when some girl on California Street started doing it, Madame sent a bouncer over to put paid to that. But the fact is, Blanche picked the gist of the act up from another showgirl who spent only a few weeks at the House of Mirrors before heading off to Chicago. The only difference is that Blanche plays it in earnest, not for laughs.

Tonight what she pictures is one of the vicious mosquitoes from San Miguel Station. She flinches, twists, spins around on herself. Her fingers pursue the invisible invader up her gloves, down her neck, under her sweeping black hem. Every *micheton* in the house must be able to imagine where the bug's got to, every tiny fold and crevice.

The tarantella's driving Blanche out of her mind now, and she's peeling her gloves off and flinging them away, her own hands molesting her, plunging up her skirt, raking her thighs, clawing at her skin as if she wants to shed it . . . No flesh-colored tights tonight because she's broken with protocol, and her pale, flawless legs are bare. Her eyes are terrified. She wrenches off the bolero jacket, hears a seam rip. She fights her hair in its chignon until it falls down. She tears the black satin bodice open down the middle and fake pearls explode onto the floorboards.

Some of the *michetons* in the audience look more alarmed than aroused, it occurs to Blanche, but does she give a good goddamn? She goes into one last fit of frenzy and collapses in the middle of the stage.

"Whoooooo!" Men are throwing up their hats and catching them, roaring "Blanche! Blanche! Blanche!"

She waits for the clamor to die away. Do they like her like this, laid low? Hair in her eyes, kohl halfway down her cheeks, kneeling in a plain corset and drawers like any destroyed woman?

The Professor's eyes are as neutral as ever. He gives Blanche that private nod that means *Ready?* Then launches into the simple, jolly chords of her last number.

Rage; Blanche recognizes the feeling at last. Deep down revulsion at the prospect of spending another night of her life turning this old crank.

She summons her forces and stands. Hand on one hip, like some slapdash streetwalker. " 'I wish I was a diamond,' " she begins sweetly,

Upon my Lulu's hand,
And every time I wiped my ass
I'd see the promised land,
Oh, Lordy—

Her gestures are broad, almost clownish, and the men love it. For the chorus she throws out her arms, conducting the audience like an orchestra.

Bang away, Lulu—
Bang away good and strong.
Oh, what'll we do for a damn good screw
When our Lulu's dead and gone?

Blanche used to find this song funny, used to relish its casual obscenity. Tonight for the first time, she's struck by how sad it is.

She capers blithely across the stage. " 'My Lulu had a baby—' " Her voice wobbles badly over the word; she didn't see that one coming. But she presses on, only a note or two behind the piano.

She named it Sunny Jim.
She dropped it in the pee-pot,
To see if it could swim.

P'tit in a culvert, a storm drain, a sewer? *Don't. Don't. Sing on.*

First it went to the bottom,
And then it came to the top.
Then my Lulu got excited
And grabbed it by the cock,
Oh, Lordy—

She won't falter, won't offer Madame any excuse to dock her pay tonight. She'll give all the sons of bitches their money's worth. She dances faster and faster. The verse about the candle, the verse about the railroad coupling pin. The *michetons* join in the chorus every time, thrilled by the filthy words. Blanche has the impression she could sing on forever and these men would stay here, hunched over their erections, roaring their part back at her.

Some girls work in offices,
Some girls work in stores.
But Lulu works in a hotel,
With forty other whores,
Oh, Lordy—

She trots out the verse about the sister with syphilis, the one about the minister, the one about the trucker. This song is never going to end. As in some dance of death, the characters parade in Blanche's mind's eye, all these grotesque humping revelers.

My Lulu got arrested,
Ten dollars was the fine.
She said to the judge,
"Take it out of this ass of mine."

That reminds her of Jenny, of course, Jenny with her flip appeals to the jury, her quips to newsmen, her crazy whims. So strange to think of Jenny coming to the House of Mirrors. This year, last year? Blanche wishes she'd known. Wishes she'd had the wit to notice Jenny with her hat down, in a chair at the back like any of the fellows, watching.

Bang away, Lulu,
Bang away good and strong—

Just another couple of verses. Blanche shuts her eyes and roars it out for Jenny. Dances for Jenny, who's in a hole in the ground tonight. Who for her own reasons thought Blanche the crème de la crème.

When Blanche looks out into the audience next, she sees the silhouette out of the corner of her eye: the long, broad outline of Lamantia, elbow propped on the far edge of the stage. His eyes moist, his smile appalling. And she flees.

Before she slams the stage door behind her, Blanche hears the protests of the crowd and the Professor improvising a jerky cadenza to wrap it up.

*

At the Eight Mile House in San Miguel Station, the night of Wednesday, September thirteenth, is sticky. Jenny and Blanche have had a long ride and a hike up Sweeney Ridge, then a quarrel in the bar with the stableman from Marshall's when he came for the buggy. There's been a lot of merriment and even more liquor. Jenny's in rare form. She insists on buying the hack from Marshall's and John Jr.'s pony each a bag of oats for a treat, because you never know, it might be one of their birthdays.

It's all quiet now. The saloon's empty and the McNamaras have settled down in their back room. Blanche and Jenny are sprawled on the bed drinking cognac by the light of a single candle. Jenny's shed her jacket and waistcoat, for once, and Blanche is down to chemise and petticoat but she's still too hot.

"You'll never give up, will you?" asks Jenny out of nowhere.

"Give up on what?"

"The kid."

Without warning, a tear slides from Blanche's left eye.

Jenny doesn't move to wipe it away as a regular friend might.

It runs sideways across Blanche's tilted cheek and drops to the wrinkled bedspread. She blinks back the others. "It's only been . . ." She counts in her head, the exhausting stretch of time since she fled from the apartment last Thursday night, fled from the threat of rough handling by three men, but still, how could she have forgotten P'tit? "Six days, that's all."

"Yeah, but I don't think you'd give up on getting him back even if it was six years. Even though—no offense," says Jenny, "but you didn't seem one hundred percent enamored of P'tit while he was with you."

Blanche gives Jenny a hard look. But can't deny it. *One hundred percent enamored.* Who can claim to be that? "It's the training," she says hoarsely. "Circus is all about persistence. In a play, if the actors fluff a line or a move, they just push on, don't they?"

Jenny nods. "Got to keep the story moving."

"Well, circus crowds don't want the story, they want the trick they saw on the bill, and they won't go home till they get their money's worth."

"So you're saying that circus folk, once they dig their teeth in—"

"Arthur's just the same, and so's Ernest," says Blanche, leaden. "No surrender."

The silence that falls between them has hurt in it, but a sort of fellow feeling too.

"Apropos," remarks Jenny, "you ever hear about the two frogs hopping through the woods?"

"Oh, just get on with it and tell me." The green blind Jenny fixed has come off its nail again already, Blanche notices.

"Hopping along, happy as Larry"—Jenny mimes the frogs with her hands along the folds of the bedspread—"till they tumble into a pit. They screech for their friends, of course. All the other frogs gather around and peer down. Well, those two unlucky fellows try their damnedest to get out."

Blanche fakes a yawn. "Is this going to be one of your longer stories?"

"They jump, jump, and they're bang-up jumpers too but the pit's just too high. They get tired. Then tireder."

Another yawn, even wider. "I know how they feel."

" 'Give over,' the other frogs start calling down to them. 'It's never going to happen. You're as good as dead. Hate to say it but we told you so. Always reckless, strayed where you shouldn't . . . ' So one of those two frogs finally croaks." Jenny acts his collapse and death, a final pathetic *uh*.

That gets a giggle from Blanche.

"But the other, he keeps right on jumping. 'Damnation,' the other frogs are shouting, 'what kind of a crack-brained creature are you? What's the point? You could be done with all your pain by now if you'd just lie down and let out your last breath.' But you know what? That frog won't leave off no matter what. Hops and gasps and hops and moans, worn out, blood on his feet . . ."

"Enough!"

"And now it's getting dark."

Blanche groans. "Is this poor fool going to suffer all night?"

"Poor fool, my ass. You know what? Finally leaps so high, he's out of the hole!"

"Great," says Blanche. "*Bonne nuit.*" She's just saying that for impudence; in fact, she's wide awake.

"His friends—so they call themselves," Jenny adds darkly, "they gather round. 'Why'd you keep on jumping when we told you it was impossible?' That frog grins at them, and says, 'It just so happens I'm stone-deaf.' "

Blanche puts up one hand like a child at school. "That makes no kind of sense. If he's deaf, how can—"

Jenny swats Blanche's hand down. "He's reading their lips, I suppose, close to. 'When I was down in the pit,' he says, 'I figured y'all were cheering me on.' " She lets out a huge whoop of laughter. " 'Cheering me on!' "

Blanche shushes her. "Everyone's asleep."

"We're not."

"I would have been, half an hour ago, if you hadn't insisted on talking my ear off."

"No, you wouldn't."

Blanche flips over onto her back. "I should be worn out after trekking all that way up a mountain and down again."

Jenny chuckles. "Sweeney Ridge is hardly a mountain."

"Ain't you one bit tired?"

"I don't get tired."

"You lying hound."

"Unless I've been up for a week," Jenny concedes.

"Everybody gets—"

"I ain't everybody."

"Oh, hold your bragging tongue for once." And Blanche flings out her hand to cover the woman's mouth.

Jenny catches her wrist this time, holds it hard.

All of a sudden Blanche knows why she's so awake. Knows what she's itching for, desperate for, what she hasn't had in what seems like weeks.

Jenny's not looking away, like you'd expect. She's on the verge of laughter.

Blanche tugs her wrist out of her grasp.

Jenny reaches for her cognac on the bedside table and finishes it with a swirl and a gulp, but without taking her eyes off Blanche.

Is the woman a cold-blooded thing, Blanche wonders, beyond ordinary human urges? "Stop watching me," she says, for something to say.

Jenny's eyebrows go up.

"Some like to watch more than they like to do. Is that why you came to the House of Mirrors that time?" Shaping the question into a dart. "Is that your particular poison?"

A ghost of a smile.

"I've had men pay through the nose to watch other men take me," remarks Blanche, turning away and rolling onto her belly. "Some like to peek through a knothole in the wall. Or loll in an armchair and know that I'm seeing them watching. Some prefer to give instructions: 'Pull her nipples, rub her bit . . . ' " She waits.

"And you?" asks Jenny after a few seconds, oddly courteous.

"What about me?" Too loud. "I'll rub anything. I lick, I swallow, I fuck." The words stir Blanche as reliably as touch. "I suppose you're expecting me to say that I hate it all? That I'm some downtrodden little angel yearning to rise above the muck of my trade?"

"Why would I be expecting you to say that?"

The tone, its calm neutrality, pushes Blanche over the brink. "I like it all, even the stuff I don't much like," she says, spelling it out. She needs Jenny to understand this. "Whatever's done to me, as a general rule, suits me fine."

A nod.

"You might as well know what you're dealing with."

Jenny says nothing, only nods again. Not smiling anymore.

The silence between them, like a heavy blanket, unbearable. "You just going to lie there like a bump on a log?" demands Blanche hoarsely.

"It's all right," says Jenny.

"What is? What's all right?"

"Whatever you do. Whatever you want."

"Don't you dare tell me what's all right," spits Blanche.

"It's all hunky-dory." Jenny rolls up one sleeve.

It's panic that's making Blanche so mean. "Don't do me any favors," she warns Jenny. "You've got nothing I need."

The woman takes her time. Starts rolling up the other sleeve.

"You know what you are, Jenny Bonnet?" snarls Blanche. "Not one thing nor the other, just some kind of *gelding*." Arthur's insult is the only weapon she can grab hold of this minute.

Jenny doesn't say anything to that.

What happens then—

What does it matter what the two of them get up to, exactly? It's just bodies doing what they must.

Same old notes, Blanche thinks at one point, but arranged into unfamiliar music. *How do you know until you try?* What Jenny does to Blanche, what Blanche finds herself surprised into doing, none of it's so very different from what she's done a thousand times before, and she reminds herself of that at certain moments, to keep from howling, because they're only a thin partition wall away from the sleeping McNamaras.

She's lost every stitch she was wearing but Jenny's clothes are still on. At one point Blanche reaches under the hem of that shirt and Jenny collects that hand, does something to it that makes Blanche's whole body double over and convulse. Jenny's trousered thighs are hard, much like a man's; her small hands are as dry as a man's; her mouth on Blanche's prickling skin is nothing like a man's. She's a slight woman who looms huge in the candle's yellow light. That contemplative expression, those burning eyes.

Held down, Blanche grinds her face into the mattress. Filled, crammed, crushed, taken, and strangely enough it turns out a fist can be just as much of a cock as a cock. More purposeful, even, because of the curiosity with which that fist moves, plotting Blanche's undoing. Blanche bites down on the pillow to stifle her cries. She's a breaching whale, a powder blast in a mine. Her nails score the sheet, and her spine cracks like a whip. Bullets of bliss go through Blanche, blowing her apart.

*

Saturday, the sixteenth, Blanche is undressing at the House of Mirrors. Three days since Jenny laid hands on her. Hands that lie boxed underground tonight, holding a white flower.

With shaking fingers Blanche yanks off her tights in the little dressing room, not caring when the gauze rips. She's climbing back into her own sweaty pink dress when Madame appears in the doorway with a glass of brandy. "A rather ungracious exit, *hein*? No encore for your devotees?"

"Lamantia, in the front row," says Blanche, rounding on her. "Did you see the way he was looking at me?"

"That's what they pay for."

"No, he was different tonight. Hungry." The words burst out of her. "He was seen in San Miguel Station on Wednesday."

Madame's eyes are wary, as if Blanche is gibbering.

"The day before Jenny was shot! You're the only one who could have told Lamantia I was there."

A sigh as the Prussian hands Blanche the glass, as if it's medicine. "Yesterday you insisted I gave Monsieur Deneve the same information. Is this to become a daily accusation?"

Blanche gulps the brandy. She doesn't know what to think. *Think* isn't the right word for the fog of suspicion that fills her head. It just can't have been Lamantia who shot Jenny, nor this Louis fellow. Arthur left town a week ago, and Ernest's friends claim they were with him and Madeleine all that evening. The case is goddamn unsolvable.

"Was that really your last dance?" says Madame.

"My last for you," mutters Blanche as she carries on dressing, fast.

A silence. She feels the madam's appraising eyes on every line of her body. "Of course, one can't help but wonder how many years longer these opportunities will be within your grasp."

Blanche presses her lips together, fumbling with buttons.

"You do have a head on your shoulders and a certain natural stamina," remarks Madame Johanna. "What I ask myself is, Are you entirely lacking in ambition?"

Blanche is going to ignore the baiting and get this cuff fastened if it kills her.

"This Californian dream is just that, for most folks who make it this far," observes Madame with a wintry note of pity. "There are still fortunes to be made, but only by the energetic, and that's how it must be, I suppose; ninety-nine in the gutter for every one in a mansion."

In a matter of minutes, Blanche promises herself, she'll walk out the door with her cash in hand and never come back.

"At thirty-three, with business so demanding . . ." A sigh.

Only thirty-three? Blanche is appalled. That creased skin, like a much-turned ledger . . .

"I sometimes find myself drawn to the idea of taking on a junior partner," Madame goes on, "a protégée to train up. Perhaps open a branch house."

Blanche doesn't understand for a second. And then: "You can't mean me. A madam?"

"You've never aimed so high?"

Blanche doesn't answer, but her face shows what she thinks of that.

"Ah," says Madame, "you prefer to carry on letting one man after another use you like a toilet?"

Blanche's eyes narrow.

"You've always lacked judgment when it comes to carnal matters, my dear," says Madame. "I really fear for you. If you follow your sentimental heart and take on another handsome parasite, the pair of you may starve by Christmas."

"I loved Arthur." The words explode from Blanche.

"Yes," says Madame. "It's the downfall of this profession. Really, *love*—one might as well put a blade in the other party's hands and guide it home." She mimes the cut along her throat.

"You talk like someone who's never been fucked," retorts Blanche.

"It's not an experience I've felt the need to try."

That startles Blanche. "But—Mr. Werner?" Staring at the gold ring on the bony finger. "Just a *mari de convenance*?"

"He only ever existed on paper," says Madame, "which I would call the most convenient kind of husband of all."

Blanche lets out a gulp of hilarity. To think that this emporium of all the vices, this auction block for maidenheads, has been run all these years by a virgin!

"I thought perhaps I glimpsed certain potentialities in you," says Madame regretfully. "That under my guidance, you might turn out to share my flair for substitution."

"Substitution?" Blanche puzzles over the word.

"Swapping other bodies for our own, I mean. Taking a managerial role. All business is a matter of trading one thing for another, isn't it?" The Prussian's warming to her theme. "Wouldn't you prefer to be a chess player, for once, my dear, rather than a pawn?"

Blanche shakes her head, marveling.

"I'd take a smaller cut than Deneve did, and do it more honestly. I wouldn't use you up and call it *love*."

The word makes Blanche's voice crack into a laugh. "You and I have never even liked each other."

A shrug. "A little pepper improves the omelet."

Blanche has heard enough. She crosses her arms and

leans in very close. "The barefaced gall of you. Offering a *partnership* when you sent my baby to a slow death at the hands of that so-called doctress!"

She expects outrage, denial, the same old bluster.

But Madame looks right back at her. "Frau Hoffman is one of this City's necessary evils. A sort of human machine to deal with pregnancies in whatever way those inconvenienced by them require: abortion, shelter, adoption . . . She is somewhat"—she hesitates over the word—"*hardened* by her work, of course. Babies die, and not just on Folsom Street. They come into the world weak, even the longed-for ones, and many of them continue to weaken. Each disease takes its percentage."

"It's you and Hoffman who take your percentage!" roars Blanche.

Madame goes on as if addressing an appreciative audience. "Death is the state toward which infants tend, just as it's in the nature of milk to turn and beef to spoil. Like clockwork toys, they're born with their end wound up tight inside them, all ready to spin itself out."

Blanche stares at her.

"Water, food, clothing, cleaning, that sort of thing improves their chances, of course. Touch, I suppose," adds Madame. "The doctress's baby farm is similar to any farm in that she encourages some crops and discourages others, depending on the market. You still may not get what you've paid for, due to uncontrollable variables, but you certainly won't get what you don't pay for," she points out with a touch of sanctimony. "Last September, when your man banged on my door, I asked him what you two would pay to have the child nursed out. I needed to know how much you wanted your P'tit to live. How much you'd stake, you see?"

"And Arthur offered eight dollars a week?"

"I suspect he picked the figure at random."

"The son of a bitch! Why didn't he ask me?"

"You were out of your mind with fever. Besides," says Madame Johanna, "what would you have proposed if he'd run home to consult you? Fifteen?"

Blanche wants to believe that she would have said fifteen.

"Twenty?"

"That's ludicrous." She goes on the attack. "What was your cut, I'd like to know?"

Madame considers her for a long moment. "Four."

"Four out of eight!" So just four dollars a week made its way to Folsom Street, to keep P'tit alive.

"Like my countrywoman, I'm running a business. Given what you were earning from me, you could have afforded twenty," Madame tells Blanche. "You could have told your fancy man to pay any amount of money—or you could always have kept your baby at home."

"Who offers to pay *any amount* for anything?" Blanche protests.

"Someone who sees her infant not getting any stronger month after month, I suppose."

"Shut your mouth."

Madame steps very close to her. "What you really can't bear is that I know your hard little heart as I do my own. You wanted to be rid of that baby."

"I did not!"

"Well, perhaps you weren't quite decided, so you hedged your bets and paid eight."

"Enough!" Blanche seizes her bag. "I want my five hundred dollars."

A tiny sigh. "Less the two hundred eighteen you owe me for expenses—I'm adding on the cost of the tights you just destroyed," explains Madame, "that's two hundred eighty-two."

"Plus"—P'tit was with the doctress about fifty weeks; Blanche multiplies that by four dollars—"the two hundred or so you made off P'tit."

"Don't push your luck," says Madame silkily.

Blanche opens her mouth to argue, but nothing comes out. She's suddenly wrung out like a rag.

Madame counts the notes and coins out of a long mesh purse. "You should stay here tonight," she remarks.

Blanche gives her an incredulous look. Does this spider never leave off weaving her web?

"My doorman tells me there's likely to be trouble."

"What kind of trouble?"

Madame shrugs. "A hullabaloo of some sort. Several buildings on Kearny have been torched already—"

"Enough of your swindles." Blanche holds out her hand for the cash.

"Why her?" Madame's ash-colored eyes have an oddly shiny quality.

"Who?"

"Jenny Bonnet. What could she give you but grief? What could she do for you that I couldn't?"

Blanche's stomach turns as she understands. For as

long as she can remember, ever since she was a creamy-skinned girl doing pirouettes on horseback, she's known herself to be desired. This is the first time it's ever made her shudder.

A wild surmise flickers in the back of her mind. "Was it you?" Blanche whispers.

"Was it I who—"

"Did you send Lamantia to San Miguel Station? Was he supposed to shoot Jenny or just fire over our heads? Were you trying to scare me so badly that I'd crawl back to you on my knees?"

Those gray eyes roll upward. "Heaven preserve my patience." Madame's voice is a businesswoman's again. "You have a lunatic imagination."

Blanche's cheeks are on fire. It's true, she's tilting at windmills. "I wouldn't put anything past you," she mutters, stuffing the money into her pocketbook and then dropping that into her carpetbag. "Didn't you once dip a girl's hands in boiling water?"

She's repeating this old rumor only for effect, but the Prussian shrugs. "Hands are inessential in this line of work. I knew she could wear gloves."

Blanche shrinks away from her.

"Your sort often overestimates your importance to this establishment," says Madame. "Everyone's replaceable."

On her way out the door, Blanche takes one last swig of the brandy.

"Also, hasn't it occurred to you that if I wanted someone dead, I would use some more discreet and reliable method than a gun?" inquires Madame. "For example, a soluble, delayed-action poison . . ."

Blanche spits brandy down herself.

And Madame, for the first time since Blanche has known her, laughs.

*

Sacramento Street seems no rougher than usual when Blanche puts her head out and looks both ways: drunks, quarrelers, the odd screeching woman. Madame was no doubt inventing the *trouble* on Kearny to keep her at the House of Mirrors a little longer, but Blanche turns in the other direction just in case. She hurries along the street, carpetbag under her arm.

On the next block, two whites have cornered a nervous Chinese man, are threatening to saw off his pigtail as spoils, but that's nothing out of the ordinary for a Saturday night; Blanche knows that her intervention would only make things worse. She's suddenly ravenous. Nothing but expensive brandy in her growling stomach, the same brandy her ruffled bodice reeks of. What Blanche needs is some dinner. She needs somewhere she can grab a bite to eat and distribute her money carefully among various parts of her costume, as she hadn't time to do before she rushed away from Madame's. And then a bed for the night, in a room with a lock strong enough to let her sleep without fear of being robbed.

The Oyster Grotto, that'll do. Blanche could just fancy a bucket of oysters with a half loaf . . .

But the door's shut and barred, and when she bangs on it—because she can see lights in the back—nobody answers. Standing there, thumping the knocker, Blanche realizes she's clutching her carpetbag tight enough to advertise to all and sundry that it contains hundreds of dollars. She forces herself to relax her grip and swing it by her side as she walks, as if all it holds is a change of clothes.

Not a single chow house seems to be open tonight. This is ridiculous.

Then Blanche smells scorching on the air, and when she reaches the corner of Dupont, she sees why. Oh Christ, Madame wasn't lying. It registers with Blanche for the first time that all that anti-coolie nonsense may be more than that. A Chinese laundry's in flames, and a gang of white workingmen won't let the firemen get near. Blanche watches, openmouthed. Somebody's going to get hurt in that building if those *cons* keep this up. The chief fireman aims the big hose squarely at the crowd of workingmen now, blasts their faces. Howls, screams, but suddenly the flow subsides, because some of the rioters have hatcheted through the hose . . .

Blanche rushes the other way, one block, two, scurrying along in her little mules. All she wants is some blasted dinner. She'd settle for a cab, if she can find one, or even a horsecar to take her out of Chinatown. Up ahead, the street's thick with foot traffic that, as she nears it, looks more and more like a mob. From the alley to her right, a raucous chorus. " 'Bang away, my Lulu . . .' "

The familiar song must be coming from some bistro or barrelhouse where Blanche can sit out the fuss, have some hot food, and tuck away this wad of banknotes that's bumping along in the bottom of her carpetbag. So she ducks down the alley—

And realizes her mistake. A score of men outside a

dark-windowed building (DOUBLE HAPPY WASHING, says the sign), staving in the glass with pickaxes and shovels. They're sweating, thrilled with themselves. " 'Bang away, my Lulu,' " they roar as they work,

Bang away good and strong.
Oh, what'll we do for a damn good screw
When our Lulu's dead and gone?

Blanche freezes, but one little fellow's spotted her already. "Hey, miss."

The man beside him is stuffing a rag into a bottle. He strikes a match and puts it to the rag, then tosses the burning bottle through a broken window. The laundry's empty, by the looks of it. The owners must have been wise enough to flee hours ago, Blanche tells herself.

Here's the thing about running: it makes people chase you. So instead of running, she gives the group her most confident, girl-on-the-town curtsy: "Gentlemen."

Half a dozen of the men swagger over to Blanche, keeping up their song.

I took her to the Poodle Dog,
Upon the seventh floor—

Blanche throws the next line back as gamely as she can manage, because if you can't lick them, it's safer to join them. " 'And there I gave her seventeen raps,' " she sings sweetly, " 'and still she called for more, oh, Lordy—' " She's eyeing the building. No sign of flames inside; maybe the fire went out when the bottle smashed onto the floor.

" 'Bang away, my Lulu' " they roar back, delighted with her, " 'bang away good and strong—' "

But Blanche isn't listening to the song anymore because she's heard something. A faint, high-pitched animal sound over the clamor of voices.

"That's a baby." Softly, to herself at first. Then she shouts at the man who threw the bottle and is standing watching the building intently. "Don't you hear the baby?"

He doesn't turn his head. Keeps watch as smoke begins to puff out the gap-toothed windows.

Again, that mewing. "Listen," pleads Blanche. If there are people in the laundry, huddled behind the sinks and wringers, why aren't they screaming?

"That's a cat, I reckon," says one of the gang, sliding his arm around Blanche. "Yum-yum chow kitty!"

She shakes him off. The sound, pitched almost inaudibly high over the crackling of timbers. "Put out the goddamn fire," she shrieks at the bottle man, "there's a baby!"

He looks at her, finally. "One coolie down, then," he crows, "just a few tens of thousands to go."

Blanche is rooted to the spot. Tiny flames flare in the man's small eyes.

"What's in this bag you're hugging so tight, miss?" the one slipping his hand around her waist wants to know.

"Oh, little enough," says Blanche. "Got anything that can fill it up?" she adds with automatic lewdness, holding on tight to her bag while straining to hear cries from the crackling house . . .

He wrenches the carpetbag out of her grip, this little man, and puts his arm in it up to his brawny elbow.

"Come now, would you rob a girl's frillies?" Blanche

asks, tugging on the bag, still trying to lay on the charm with a shaking voice. Behind her, the laundry roars with flame. If there were people in there, would they still be holding their tongues? A cat, that's all, Blanche tells herself, sobbing a little. It must have been a cat.

The fellow lets out a joyful whistle. Holds up her pocketbook, coins spilling, notes dancing on the air. He waves the first fistful like a flag.

Blanche will get no better chance to run, and she's off already, because her body thinks faster than her mind. She hares off up the alley, one shoe heel slamming on the cobbles, the other mule left behind along with her bag, her clothes, her money, every blasted thing she's got in the world.

The men aren't even following, she realizes at the corner; they've stayed laughing by their fire. "So long, Lulu," one of them roars after her.

She stumbles down Dupont in case they change their mind. Another fire patrol rattles past, men with hatchets and ladders hanging off the wagon. Patrolmen clattering by on wild-eyed horses. One shoe's worse than none, Blanche concludes after two blocks. When a half-grown boy brushes past her and tries to squeeze her breast, she pulls her mule off and hurls it at him.

She's not safe on these streets. The House of Mirrors? Never again. Her mind scrabbles for other addresses. Low Long? Blanche threatened to set the law on him yesterday. And besides, he and his new renters will be boarded up tightly, tonight of all nights. Durand? But the restaurant owner knows Blanche as the cracked *salope* who taunted a grieving old man at the graveside this afternoon. Maria?

How gratefully Blanche would throw herself on the one-eyed hag's mercy if only she knew where Maria lived. So it's come to this. Blanche has nowhere to go, no one in this whole city who'll take her in.

Panting with agitation, she picks the next alley and checks to make sure that it's quite dark before she ducks in. So small, it's more of a drain, and it smells like one too. Blanche edges behind a leaning pile of rotting planks and hunkers down. Arms tight around herself. She can smell brandy on her clothes, the slime of vegetables, ash from the fires.

At least she got away from the rioters before they could finish their celebrations by riding her until she was torn apart. At least she's not trapped in that burning laundry like those Chinese who refused to make a sound, if they were really there. If Blanche wasn't just imagining what she heard. *Count your blessings, Blanche. Count your goddamn blessings.*

Her ears attend to the distant pandemonium. She watches the bright end of the alley for the silhouettes of men. Something goes by in a flash. A high-wheeler? Her heart hammers. It wasn't Jenny. Blanche doesn't believe in ghosts. She shuts her eyes so she won't see it again. Squeezes them closed, wrapping the darkness around her.

VIII

WHEN THE TRAIN COMES ALONG

Blanche doesn't exactly wake when the pitiless sunrise pries her eyelids up on the seventeenth of September, because she hasn't exactly slept in this nameless alley, or so it seems to her—but there are gaps in her memory of the night. What's bothering her most, she finds, is hunger. Not her dead friend and the impossibility of proving who killed her, her lost baby and the men who stole him, the rioters who snatched almost three hundred dollars from her last night, her lack of a home and clothes, her having no earthly idea what to do next . . . No, it's breakfast that presses on her mind. How to rustle up breakfast.

Blanche pounds her numb thighs to rouse them. She wipes her face on the slightly cleaner inside of her wrecked pink dress and struggles to her feet.

Shoeless, filthy, and broke, she can't pass for anything other than a woman at the end of her rope. Blanche could probably find a stranger to buy her a drink—which comes with food—at one of the City's free-lunch places, except that they don't open till eleven on Sundays and Blanche is dizzy already. So she starts walking, picking her way carefully along the sidewalk to avoid putting her stockinged soles on a shard of glass. Men throng by, bent under bundles and baskets on the now-illegal poles. There's no day of rest in Chinatown.

Of course Blanche remembers some of the names of *michetons* who've paid high for a night with her. She could seek one out and send him a tear-smeared note saying that she was attacked by the mob last night and needs to throw herself on the mercy of the most honorable man she knows. That should drum up enough for a new outfit and a room, at least. That's how Blanche la Danseuse would get herself back on her feet this morning.

But this Blanche stumbles on, weighed down by self-pity, and self-contempt too, because it feels as if every bad thing that's happened to her in the last month has been her fault. The sky's turned a strange pale gray that doesn't make the air any cooler. Blanche wipes the humidity off her face with her sleeve. She's walking for the sake of keeping moving, the way Jenny used to do, but with feet already beginning to blister.

As she limps along, Blanche torments herself with plans of how she'd spend those two hundred and eighty-two dollars if she had them back. (If only she'd waited another minute at the House of Mirrors and hid the money in her corset instead of carrying it in her bag, like some naive girl, for the first muscled *con* to grab.) Clothes, a room—no, a whole apartment of her own, with one key to the door. If she had all that, if she looked like a woman of substance, she'd sweep into Detective Bohen's office every morning from now on, demanding to know what he'd discovered about the *macs* and their movements. She'd hire half a dozen sleuths of her own to comb the City for a baby boy with a turnip forehead and his father's slim eyebrows.

She's almost at Townsend, she notices; the South Pacific terminus.

Blanche goes in and hovers near the ticket desk, trying to give the impression that she's waiting for a friend. She knows—having once had plenty of cash—that when rich folks pay for things, they sometimes drop coins, and they don't look very hard for them if they're small ones. And after five minutes of shuffling and scrutinizing the dusty ground, she does find a quarter. Blanche lurches to the nearest Mexican stall and buys beans and coffee. Helps herself to half a bowl of mushroom ketchup too, while the owner's looking away, because who knows how long this breakfast's going to have to last her? She's on the bottom rung now.

Her stomach's full but Blanche still feels awful. Her head's in a pincer grip. No hat, no parasol, nothing to put between herself and the sun. Her nose is full of the reek of chlorine from the boxcar where they're fumigating the outgoing luggage and mail sacks. She stares at the black silhouettes of the trains. The last time she was here, two days ago, she was coming back from San Miguel Station with a fresh graze on her cheek.

"Whoa!" There's a busker singing, shuffling by the barrier. The same black man Blanche failed to give a coin to yesterday? No, younger, and no brand on his ashy cheek, just streaks of sweat.

When the train comes along,
When the train comes along,
I will meet you at the station
When the train comes along.

Every time Blanche hears a song now, she feels Jenny behind her shoulder, listening, commenting, memorizing.

If my mother ask for me,
Tell her death done summons me;
I will meet you at the station
When the train comes along.

"Passengers for the Espee, Espee, South Pacific to San Jose," a ticket-seller's calling tiredly.

A ragged line forms. A man in a top hat gives Blanche a curious glance.

She looks down at her grubby stockinged feet and feels herself flush. On an impulse, she flutters to the gentleman's side. "Sir? Pardon me for disturbing you . . ."

"Move away, miss, unless you got a ticket," the ticket-seller warns her.

But she clings to the passenger's smooth-sleeved arm. "I'm trying to get home to San Miguel Station." Why did Blanche say that? It just came out, as if it were true. "In all the commotion last night—my bag—"

"San Miguel Station?" the gent repeats with interest, hanging back as the other passengers push past. "The site of the murder?"

Blanche improvises. "It was . . . it took place in my father's saloon," she whispers.

His eyes bulge.

"I was called to the City to give evidence at the inquest, you see, and some awful fellows snatched my bag, and now . . ."

"First class for this young lady," he calls, clicking his fingers for the ticket-seller and pulling out his wallet.

She was hoping for cash, but a ticket's something, at least. She might as well sleep on a train as in a stinking alley.

"You must tell me all," he says in Blanche's ear.

Her gorge rises. She'd rather give him a below-job in the lavatory, frankly. But if it's sordid details he wants in return for his fifty cents, fine.

She shares a cushioned bench with the man and spins him a garbled version of Mary Jane McNamara's week; shows him the little scab on her right cheekbone and blames it on a bullet that came through two walls.

Dizzy, Blanche asks for a dipper of ice water from the refreshment cart, but the gentleman insists on pouring her a jot of whiskey from his own flask instead. Then he takes great pleasure in buying her a peach and a bag of nuts. "Sugar candy too?"

She thinks of the Industrial School, and the candy Jenny used to throw over the fence to those miserable boys. The varieties on this cart all look unappetizing to Blanche, but she supposes children's tastes are different, especially if they're living on a reformatory diet. So she chooses a sachet of clove-flavored wafers, brownish lozenges printed with women's faces, and pinkish objects called Conversation Candies with cryptic messages right on them: *Married in Satin, Love Will Not Be Lasting.*

When she can bear no more of the kind gentleman, Blanche excuses herself "to freshen up."

In the corridor, two of the black porters are chuckling together. They hush at Blanche's approach and move off down the train in different directions.

She stares at the window. Spots on the sooty glass: raindrops! It's been months. Oh, a good storm cracking this leaden sky, that would be something . . .

In the next carriage, an Italian's singing a snatch of "Voi Che Sapete," blithe and off-key. Blanche dozes for a minute, leaning against the window.

Then wakes from some muddled dream of a baby with no face. P'tit. How long will she dream of him? If Blanche just knew she'd never see him again . . . She almost wants it. No! It's just that the waiting, the not knowing—that's the worst of all.

She can't shake off the things Madame Johanna said last night. The image she showed Blanche, like a reflection in a tarnished, buckled mirror: the Lively Flea, a thoughtless pleasure-seeker who farmed her baby out to strangers and would have been relieved to hear he was dead. *No, that wasn't how it was,* Blanche wails in the privacy of her head, *that was never how it was—*

She can't prove it. There's no judge to whom she can justify her mistakes.

Here's the question: If Blanche is such an unnatural, rotten-to-the-core bitch of a mother, shouldn't she be able to forget P'tit now? *Everyone's replaceable,* according to Madame. Forget his unsmiling face, his translucent ears, that doorknob he—goddamn it! The knob's lost too. For nine days she's been carrying it around in the bottom of the carpetbag the rioters pulled out of her arms last night. Blistering tears blind her.

The silhouette of the Industrial School rears up on the far left. Blanche remembers her candies and roots in her pocket for the paper sack. Wrestles with the window. Humid air blasts her face. The fence, here comes the fence, but no boys. Where are the boys? Blanche needs to throw these candies to them but—

Sunday, *satané* Sunday. What, do they lock the kids in their cells right through the Sabbath?

Blanche flings the fat bag anyhow, for Jenny.

Instead of sailing over the fence, it hits the wire and rebounds into the dust. What a pathetic throw. Now the boys will only be taunted by the sight of the bag. Will one of them be able to reach through with a hoe or a stick and hook it, retrieve the chalky disks and lozenges before the insects swarm them? Will the second boy punch the first, snatch his hoe from him? Will Blanche's dumb gesture lead to nothing but fights, or will a single imprisoned boy get a taste of sweetness and know somebody cared just enough to throw him a blasted candy?

San Miguel Station coming up now. Blanche has no good reason to get down there, today or ever again. She could just stay on the train and try to nap before the conductor throws her off in some faraway town . . .

Instead, she hobbles down onto the tiny platform. A face in the window, the gent who bought her the ticket. His hand up in an excited gesture. Blanche doesn't wave back.

*

The morning of Thursday, the fourteenth, Blanche wakes late with a sore head in the front room at the Eight Mile House. The bed empty beside her, as smooth on that side as if the sheets have never been touched. As if what happened last night between her and Jenny was just a figment of her filthy imagination.

The day's sliding away from Blanche already.

Blanche tries to remember how drunk she was last night. About as drunk as usual. About as impulsive. About as whorish. *If you can remember any of it,* she's heard it said, *you weren't that drunk.*

McNamara's nightshirt, folded on the bureau. Could Jenny have gone back to the City already? Did she leave first thing this morning, or in the middle of the night, right after Blanche lost consciousness? Could Jenny not even look her in the eye today?

But when she slides her fingers under the mattress, she finds the Colt. And when she looks under the bed, she glimpses the sack of frogs Jenny caught yesterday on Sweeney Ridge.

Blanche puts on a fresh white bodice over her mauve skirt—as if what she wears even matters here in San Miguel Station. She manages to wheedle some coffee out of Ellen McNamara, but it tastes burned. She sits in an old rocking chair on the porch, holding her cup.

"It wasn't half this hot last summer," she mentions to Ellen when the woman steps out with a basket of wet sheets.

A look of contempt from the Irishwoman. "Sure a summer like this has never been known."

Still no sign of Jenny. Where could she be?

"Is—does Jenny come down here often?" she asks Mary Jane the next time the girl steps out on the porch.

Mary Jane wipes sweat out of her eyes with the back of her hand. "Often enough."

"On her own?" Blanche fans herself with a three-day-old copy of the *Examiner.*

"Or with friends from town."

Which friends? wonders Blanche with a surge of perverse resentment. She fans herself harder.

Friendship. Blanche has no talent for it, she decides. Less than a month she's known Jenny Bonnet, and what an almighty hash she's made of it.

John Jr. is over by the pond throwing stones in, one after the other, and watching the ripples. (Funny how universal that impulse to make your mark, even on water.) Now somebody's stopped to talk to him. The chicken farmer from the cabin to the east, is it?

A piercing pain in her leg; Blanche looks down to see what's biting her and slaps her leg, but she's missed it.

Nothing to do, nowhere to go. Blanche puts her head back and tries to doze.

A whirring sound. Jenny glides out of a dust cloud on her high-wheeler.

"Where did you disappear to?" calls Blanche, too accusatory.

Jenny jumps down, grinning. "Bicycling around."

"Around where?"

"*How,* more like. Had a go at riding backward."

"That would explain the blood trickling down your arm," says Blanche, aiming for witty rather than irritable.

"Doing it's the only way to learn," says Jenny. "Thought I'd give John Jr. a turn too, but the boy's in some class of sulk." She glances over at the pond, where John Jr. seems to be brooding over each pebble before he flicks it into the water.

Ah, thinks Blanche, perhaps the lad's feeling neglected by his old pal from the City. Jealous, even, that Jenny has someone else with her to talk to.

Jenny's stashing her high-wheeler between some desiccated shrubs and the porch.

"Afraid someone will pinch it, the way you did on Market Street?" mocks Blanche.

A chuckle. "Would be a shame to lose the thing before I've got the knack of riding backward." Jenny throws herself into a fraying cane chair. Drums something like a jig with her boots.

"You're restless today," Blanche comments.

Jenny shakes her head. "Born restless. Nothing special about today."

Blanche looks away. So they're pretending nothing happened in the night. Fine by her. Perhaps if she and Jenny play it this way, everything will stay more or less as it was. She squints past the lopsided VARIETY OF LOTS NOW AVAILABLE sign, the derelict patches between the dunes, all the way north to the nude hills of San Francisco. "These *foutu* flies keep chewing me," she complains, rubbing at three red marks on her right foot.

"Ankle-biters, not flies," says Jenny. "Need to get yourself a pair of gaiters."

"Oh, you reckon I should go shopping?" says Blanche wryly.

"Maybe Mary Jane'd lend you a pair . . ."

The dog's nosing around Blanche, so she pushes him away.

Jenny scratches him behind the ear. Then she looks out beyond the porch, and her gaze becomes unfocused, as if she's been smoking opium.

"What makes your eyes go like that?"

A blink. "Like what?"

"Hazy," Blanche specifies. "What were you thinking about?" Is that a safe question?

"Oh, you know. Volcanoes, quakes . . ."

"Volcanoes?" she repeats, startled.

"Doesn't have to be volcanoes," Jenny concedes. "Just some kind of excitement. No warning, the ground boils over like a casserole, the railroad flips, buildings tossed in the air . . . It's all going to end sometime, so why not hurry that up a touch and find out what's next?"

Blanche shakes her head at the craziness of this.

Jenny yawns. "Want a book?"

"What would I want with a book?"

"Suit yourself." Jenny pulls one out from under her chair and turns to a page she's marked with a stalk of wild grass. The binding's gilt on green, with a drawing of a traveler at the end of a jetty gazing out to sea.

"What's it about?" asks Blanche after a minute.

"What it says," murmurs Jenny.

Blanche reads the title, then reads it once more, to make sure she has it right: *Around the World in Eighty Days*. "Is that even possible?"

Jenny shrugs without looking up. "They're barely past San Francisco, and Indians are attacking, so I guess I'll have to read on to find out."

Blanche takes the hint.

It's the quiet that's unsettling her, she decides. Downtown, there's always some kind of hubbub, whether street music or just the babble of tongues. Here at San Miguel Station, the still air seems to press on her ears.

It must be a quarter of an hour later when Jenny yawns and looks up at the horizon. Blanche follows her eyes.

"That's Blue Mountain," Jenny remarks, "the highest of the City's hills."

Blanche examines the flat-topped cone. "Don't see anything blue about it."

"Ah, come down in the spring, you'll find it one big sea of baby blue eyes."

The spring? Blanche doesn't even know what she'll be doing tomorrow. She's tempted to point out the unlikelihood of her coming back here at any season, but that might sound sour. "You'd rather be up there," she counters.

"Blue Mountain?"

"Away in the bush, anyhow, not sitting on a porch. So what's stopping you?"

Jenny seems not to hear the provocation. "Got to bring yesterday's sack of wrigglers up to the City later," she says.

Blanche's lips tighten. "And leave me here bored out of my mind?"

"Come back up with me, if you like."

"It's not safe, not for either of us. Those things Ernest threatened us with on Waverly Place—do you think he was just running his mouth?"

Jenny puffs out a breath. "No lead in his pistol!"

But Jenny doesn't know Ernest, nor Arthur, not really. She can't see past the dandy affectations, the peacock gear. A few weeks' acquaintance hasn't taught her to be afraid of them.

"I reckon I can look after myself, anyhow," she concludes.

Blanche bristles at that. "Meaning I can't?"

A shrug. "All I say is, I'm riding back to town today."

"Suit yourself," says Blanche.

A pause. "It could be after dinner, if it makes any odds to you."

Blanche sniffs.

Jenny returns to her book.

This waiting around is more than Blanche can stand. She marches into the saloon, where she finds Mary Jane behind the counter, smearing glasses with a rag. She asks to borrow some gaiters to keep off the insects.

Mary Jane supplies them without a word.

Blanche swaps her little mules for her boots and laces the gaiters up over them, right to the knee. Then asks the girl for a bottle of rye, because why the hell not, and brings it out onto the porch with two glasses.

Jenny bursts into a lively verse at the sight.

I'll eat when I'm hungry
And drink when I'm dry;
If a tree don't fall on me,
I'll live till I die.

"*Santé.*" Blanche clinks their glasses before handing one to Jenny. "You know a lot of drinking songs."

"Easiest ones to remember, I guess—the alcohol helps them soak in."

McNamara comes home from his laboring a while later and accepts a glassful to get the dust out of his throat. "Would you be old enough to remember how pricey drink was in the war?" he asks Jenny.

"Would I! When the tax came down after, I went on such a spree . . ."

Ellen McNamara calls them in for platefuls of what Blanche reckons must be boot leather.

"Splendid stew, Mrs. Mac," says Jenny.

More drinking afterward, at the bar. The settlement's quiet tonight. Jordan comes in and remarks that the Canadian's away to San Jose.

Jenny asks for a sweet cocktail.

"We've no bitters," says McNamara.

"Angostura? Gentian? Orange, even? What class of a drinking establishment is this?" she teases him.

"There's all kinds of bottles in my shop," offers Jordan.

"Would you be poaching my feckin' customers now?" asks McNamara.

"Ah, come on, they're paying you rent," Jordan points out. "Let me sell them a cocktail."

So the women go over to Jordan's and have a few, even treat him—and McNamara, who follows them to see what all the fuss is about, though he finds the sweet stuff hurts his teeth. He brought his fiddle too. It makes a screechy racket but there is something festive, Blanche decides, about a song played at full volume in the middle of nowhere.

" 'Who gonna shoe yo' pretty little feet?' " they all chorus.

Who gonna comb yo' bangs?
Who gonna kiss yo' rose-red lips?
Who gonna be yo' man?

" 'Lawd,' " Jenny winds it up with a raucous whoop, " 'who gonna be yo' man?' "

But once McNamara goes back to his saloon, Jenny stands up and says, as if sober, "I'm off, folks."

"Now? Don't be absurd," says Blanche.

"Off where?" asks Jordan.

"To the City, with my frogs, otherwise they'll turn cannibal and my name will be mud with my customers."

"You should have gone hours ago, before dark," objects Blanche. 'You're so drunk now, you're likely to ride into a ditch."

But the young woman's already picking her way across the sandy ground between the two buildings.

Blanche races after her.

In the saloon, McNamara's leaning on his bar.

"Where did I hang up my coat?" Jenny wonders.

"Don't let her have it," Blanche tells him.

"None of my lookout," says the Irishman.

"Come on, man," she scolds him, "you know Jenny's too tight to pedal that machine."

"Give my coat here," says Jenny sternly, clicking her fingers at McNamara. "And where are my boots?"

"She can't even find her boots," Blanche points out, "let alone the road."

"Oh yes, I—"

"Let me," she tells Jenny, with a show of exasperated helpfulness. She nips into the front bedroom and finds Jenny's boots under the bed. She shoves them farther back, into the darkest corner. "No sign of them," she calls as convincingly as she can. While Blanche is at it, she fishes the heavy Colt from under the mattress and hides it behind her stockings in the top drawer of the bureau.

Jenny stamps into the room behind her. "Give me my blasted boots."

"Where could you have left them?"

"Stop playing about."

"You're a fine one to talk." She ducks behind Jenny to shut the door so the others won't hear them. "You really mean to cycle through Chinatown, with Ernest and Arthur out to tear you limb from limb?"

Jenny sighs. "I ain't about to hide away for the rest of my days, if that's what you mean. I never did a thing to those *connards.*"

"Didn't you?" It bursts out of Blanche.

Jenny stares at her.

"It all began the night I met you," says Blanche furiously, "with your harmless, just-curious sort of questions."

"Since when is there a law against questions?" says Jenny.

"You meddled in my affairs. You got me thinking, fretting, fired up—"

A shrug. "You must have had a few things that needed thinking about."

Rage behind Blanche's eyes. Her life's combusted, and this firebrand's warming her hands at the flames. "You broke us up, me and Arthur, whether you meant to or—"

"Lady," Jenny cuts in, "I couldn't give a dead rat whether or not you spend the rest of your life with that louse."

Blanche's face is scalding. "Then how did I end up here? Less than a month ago, I was happy as a clam, living with Arthur and dancing at the House of Mirrors . . ."

"Happy as a clam?" repeats Jenny, ironical.

"See? See? You're doing it again. I was happy *enough,*

and then you ran me down on Kearny Street," Blanche cries, "and everything started to topple. You, with your prying and probing—"

Jenny's lip curls. "What, you mean I asked questions like how come you didn't know where your own baby was living? If you could call that living?"

Blanche gasps. "Listen to yourself! Don't pretend you didn't have opinions from the start."

"What did my opinions matter? If some chitchat with some stranger *toppled* everything, then everything must have been resting on a single brick."

"You're a pernicious troublemaker," Blanche roars. "You zoom round picking fights, then play the innocent. *Who, me, Your Honor? No sirree, poor little frog girl who just wants to wear her little ol' pants in peace!*"

Jenny puts her head to one side as if examining a rare species of insect. "Why are you being such a contrary bitch?"

"Because you won't take the least goddamn responsibility for—"

"Responsibility?" She repeats the word as if it tastes sour in her mouth. "What, I fuck you once and we're married now?"

Blanche's fist moves before she knows it, plants itself right between Jenny's eyes with a crack of bone on bone.

*

It's Sunday morning now, Jenny's second day in the baked ground of the Odd Fellows Cemetery. San Miguel Station is so quiet, Blanche can hear her own breath.

"You haven't heard from him?" she asks Mrs. Louis, leaning on the jamb to stop the woman from shutting the door of her cabin.

The chicken keeper's wife has wary eyes. "I wouldn't usually," she says so softly Blanche has to lean into the smoky dimness to make it out.

Bare feet. Like Blanche's gaping-stockinged ones today. Two shabby females, Blanche thinks with a shiver, little difference between them. "Why wouldn't you hear from him usually?"

"Louis doesn't like to be answerable to anyone."

Blanche considers that. Not even to a wife? Especially not to a wife, perhaps. She thinks about marriage, all those girls longing for a ring. "He had a visitor last Wednesday?"

A nervous shake of the head.

"You told that reporter. You said Louis got talking to a stranger on Wednesday, a big, dark man called Lamantia."

The woman's mouth trembles. "No law against that, I hope."

"What did the fellow want?"

"He was inquiring as to buying property in the township."

Property? Blanche frowns in confusion. Perhaps that's just what Louis told his wife. "Did you talk to him yourself?"

"I don't talk to men behind my husband's back. Especially not Sicilians."

"Why especially not—"

Mrs. Louis angles herself closer to whisper, "Cosa Nostra."

"Oh, come." The pompous importer, one of them?

"You don't mess with those folks' business," she hisses.

So Lamantia's a genuine mafioso who, out of some warped longing for Blanche, came down to San Miguel Station and paid the first idle man he ran into, Louis the Canadian, to murder Jenny? Whereupon Louis immediately fled town? This theory of Cartwright's is so implausible, Blanche doesn't know why she's here badgering Mrs. Louis.

She turns away without another word to the woman. *Drop this nonsense,* she orders herself. *Get out of here.*

McNamara is emerging from his outhouse, pulling up his pants. He eyes Blanche, startled, and nods at her.

She knows what a sight she must be: bareheaded, in her filthy pink dress, one big toe sticking out of its stocking. She should cut straight across to the station and wait for the next train back to the City. (Though how she's going to talk her way onto it without the price of the fare this time, she doesn't know.) "Mr. McNamara," says Blanche with a nod when she gets close enough to be heard. Holds up her hand to shade her eyes, like some squinting beggar woman.

"You're back."

She shakes her head. "I'm departing for pastures new," she improvises drily.

"Well, now, I wish I could say the feckin' same. This benighted spot!" The Irishman's eyes trace the lines of the sandlots. "The fellow that foisted it on me swore blind San Miguel Station would be going great guns soon. I'm waiting and waiting, and still my best customer's my wife, and she never pays her tab."

Blanche manages a smile. "Well. I hope you manage to sell up one of these days." She turns toward the depot.

"I'd a sniff the other day," says McNamara under his breath.

She looks over her shoulder. "A sniff of . . ."

"A prospect, like."

"Somebody who wanted to buy the saloon?"

McNamara nods mournfully. "A City gent, this was. Though I doubt he'll be back, now the place is a byword for bloodshed."

Blanche stares at McNamara. "Was this . . . Wednesday?"

"Could have been."

"An Italian, was he?"

McNamara makes a face. "Don't know about that."

"His name—"

"Sounded more like your crowd to me."

"His name sounded French?" says Blanche, too sharp. "Lamant, something like that?"

The Irishman's forehead is creased. "You know this fellow?"

"I can't tell if I do, that's why I'm asking."

"I forgot to ask his bloody name," says McNamara, "but he sounded Frenchish himself."

Her head is spinning. French, not Italian? "This was a tall man, dark, yes? Smartly dressed?"

McNamara nods.

Lamantia, it must be. Clearly this dullard can't tell one European accent from another.

"Dropping off him," adds the Irishman.

"You mean—his fat?"

"His clothes, dropping off him," says McNamara irritably. "A living skeleton."

Blanche can't speak for a long moment. Then she manages to ask, "Had he . . . a mustache?"

"Longest I've ever seen. So he is a friend of yours."

She shakes her head in dread. "I don't suppose he was pockmarked at all?"

The Irishman shakes his head. "Face like a blank page."

Blanche turns away so McNamara won't see her expression. Ernest Girard. Posing as Lamantia!

Having somehow found out where the women were, Ernest must have rushed to San Miguel Station like a vindictive puppet acting for his absent master. And when he found Blanche and Jenny gone to the hills, he got into conversation with the first men he encountered, and soon chanced upon one desperate enough to kill a woman for cash in hand. Louis, familiar with the settlement and all its dogs. Louis, who must know how to use a gun to keep foxes away from his paltry flock. Blanche never bothered to exchange a word with the Canadian on Tuesday or Wednesday; he was just part of the scrubby landscape. Louis must have pretended to set off for San Jose that Thursday, then snuck back in the dark to do the shooting, and fled to San Jose for real afterward, to make his alibi. But for Ernest to give his name as Lamantia, ensuring that any suspicion would fall on another tall, dark man of Blanche's acquaintance—now, that was brilliant. If she didn't hate the bastard so much, she'd admire his style.

Headache worse than ever, Blanche thinks she might puke. Pulse beating its crazy drum. She must get back to the City and tell the detectives what she's figured out.

As she stumbles toward the railway track, she sees John Jr. riding his pony in a wide circle. Not a bad seat. The palomino's golden in this light. The boy's mousier than the beast, but still worth looking at simply because he's so young. That won't last.

He flinches at the sight of Blanche. Pauses, tightens the reins as if to gallop off. How he must be missing Jenny, the way she'd ride into San Miguel Station with her jokes and her pistol-toting toughness and greet him like a comrade. Did she spin her awful upbringing into funny stories for John Jr.? Entertain him with tales of how she spat in the bogeymen's eye in that prison for children just over the hill?

The pony remembers Blanche. Trots over, looking for a treat. Blanche reaches to pat her pale flank. Suddenly so dizzy she doesn't believe she can make it to the railroad depot. The world contracts to a burning ring. Skin feels dry enough to crackle and slough off.

Blanche is on the ground. Wet suffocating cloth over her face, a winding sheet—

She fights it off.

"Just trying to sponge you some, Miss Blanche," says the boy. "You keeled over. I reckon you took a turn from the heat."

Blanche struggles to sit up. Sick as a dog, she shudders. She sips the jar of lukewarm water John Jr.'s holding to her lips. He's fanning her ineffectively with his small hand. She takes the wet rag from him and presses it to her face, her throat, her chest.

"What can I—"

"Just stand between me and the sun," she tells him in the voice of a very old woman.

The pony noses Blanche, tickling her neck.

John Jr. has a twisted look about him. "Your arm still pains you?" she asks.

She expects him to deny it, in the way of males, but he nods.

He might grow crooked around this injury. Blanche reaches up to check for a dislocation, as they always did in the circus, but John Jr. ducks away as if her fingers burn him. Does nobody ever touch this boy? Is he lost in that strip of time between the cuddles of childhood and the greedier caresses of adulthood, with nobody so much as laying a finger on him except to punish? Blanche thinks of Jenny, the whip scars forming a grid of pain all up her back. Is Blanche going to see her friend in every gangly boy now? "You poor lad . . ."

"I'm almost thirteen and that's a man, or near as makes no difference."

What a curious tone: pride mixed with something darker. A boy who thinks he's a man. A boy who wanders at night, maybe, if it's too hot for sleep. Maybe even puts his hands on what's not his? Takes what's there for the taking?

"John," Blanche starts, gently, so as not to alarm him, "I don't suppose you'd happen to know where the high-wheeler's got to?"

He shakes his head. Not surprised by the question, though.

Maybe he couldn't bear to let anyone have it after Jenny? Did he keep it, not to sell, even, but just for the gleaming glamour of that monstrous front wheel? To stroke sometimes, to keep hidden away so that when all the fuss is over, he can go for midnight rides along the dirt track toward the City and remember his friend Jenny?

"Tell me where it is, John Jr." Stern, but also seductive, trying to bridge the gap between herself and this child, because Blanche must have the bicycle for the price it'll fetch—she realizes that now.

And his arm shoots out as if it's not part of him. One spatulate finger pointing at the pond.

Blanche stares across the sandlot at the flat water.

John Jr.'s taken off already, ahead of her, so fast she almost fears he means to throw himself in. Kids form such wild notions, it's a wonder any of them live to be full grown. "John Jr.," she bawls as she runs.

Blanche catches up with him at the edge, where he's standing, staring into the pond. Her pity's mixed with frustration at the thought of what he's done, because the precious machine will be half rusted by now. Wasn't it enough to burn Jenny's books? Did he have to leave no trace of her? "Whereabouts?" she demands. "Was it this side you threw it in?"

"Don't matter."

"You need to wade in for me and drag it out."

John Jr. shakes his head. "Best put all that behind you now."

She stares at him. *All that,* meaning Jenny?

The boy gnaws his lip. "It weren't none of your doing, Miss Blanche."

But whose fault was Jenny's death if not Blanche's? Who else brought Ernest on her trail like a bloodhound, all the way to San Miguel Station?

John Jr. shakes his head so hard a drop of sweat flies off. "She'd got a hold on you."

Blanche puzzles over the phrase.

"You can't take the blame. I saw, I saw it all." He's purple in the face now.

Blanche squints at him through the brutal sunlight. "Saw what, John?" Fumbling his way to the toilet in the night, could the boy have glimpsed Louis with the gun?

"Couldn't help it, could I, with the blind all askew?"

The porch. John Jr. must have been sleeping on the porch. Goddamn it, Blanche should have thought this through before. Even the McNamaras wouldn't be stupid enough to let a boy of his age share a bed with his sisters. Where else would John Jr. stretch out with his blanket on a summer night but on the porch? Was he there, curled up in a shadowy corner or behind a barrel, when the chicken farmer climbed up with his gun? "What did you see, exactly?" she demands.

"Bad enough to watch," he wails. "Don't make me say. Ain't you got no shame at all?"

Shame. Suddenly Blanche understands. Not the murder, that's not what John Jr. saw. He's not talking about Thursday at all, but the night before. He witnessed what she and Jenny did when they thought the McNamaras were all asleep. While the blind was hanging askew, leaving a space the width of a blade, just enough to let a child outside glimpse what he shouldn't.

She speaks with difficulty. "Whatever you think you might have—"

"Don't baby me! I know dirt when it's right in my face."

Blanche takes a ragged breath. "Listen to me."

"Always reckoned Jenny was just eccentric in her ways," the boy says with a sob, "something of a character. But she turned out to be some class of he-she-I-don't-know-what, making a whore of you!"

The awful ignorance of children. "John Jr." Blanche feels as if she's trying to be heard from the bottom of a pit. "I'm that already."

He shakes his head, fierce. "It turned my stomach so bad I don't think I'll ever be right."

"How it may have seemed—" She clears her throat. "That's not how it was."

"Try and whitewash her sins now she's gone," roars John, "but I watched her strip you bare as a twig. She held you down and hurt you bad, used you like a beast of the field!"

Blanche shuts her eyes briefly, remembering. "No," she whispers.

He shakes his head as if he's got a fly in his ear. "I should have done something then and there. Shouldn't have faltered. Dadda taught me how to see to a mule-footed calf."

A mule-footed calf? What the hell is he talking about? "You dumb boy," says Blanche. Sorrow in her bones now at the thought of them all getting older and no wiser. (All but Jenny.) Sorrow that makes her reach out to enfold this hurting creature . . .

John Jr. presses a kiss on her mouth so hard it hurts.

She pulls away, covering her bruised lip. "Jesus, child!"

"It was for you." He says it flatly, the way a man would, but with tears streaking down his face.

How was that kiss for Blanche—the kind of graceless,

hungry kiss any twelve-year-old grabs from any woman, years before he's allowed?

No.

Not the kiss; that's not what was for Blanche.

Should have done something then and there. It's in the boy's face, the besotted eyes that want to tell her everything. The truth punches her in the gut.

"No." Catches her breath. "You couldn't have."

"Oh, couldn't I just?" he answers with an awful attempt at cheek.

The boy's in some class of sulk, Jenny remarked on the last morning of her life. Had she figured out what John Jr. had seen the night before, how he felt about it? Had Jenny decided—as she decided about so many things—that it didn't matter?

Blanche can picture it so clearly. John Jr. outside that bedroom window on Thursday night, leaning on the sill to peer through the gap where the blind had slipped away from the glass, the stock of the shotgun set irrevocably against his small shoulder. How fearful he must have been, how raging, aiming to blast away all his mortification. To expunge his weak fondness for a friend who'd turned out to be an obscenity in disguise.

Blanche's hand clamps his shoulder so hard, he cries out. "You tell me everything," she says in a voice she doesn't recognize, "or I'll drown you like a puppy."

But the boy's face has sealed up.

She lets go and tries mocking him. "Where'd you have got hold of a shotgun, even?"

John Jr. jerks his head in the direction of the scattered cabins. "Louis bought our varmint gun off Dadda, didn't he?"

The old family weapon, the one the boy learned to kill pests with. Blanche didn't even know a varmint gun could be a shotgun. *Saw this boy hit a can at thirty yards,* Jenny told her, proud of her protégé. But this time John Jr. didn't hold it firmly enough, did he? This time his hands must have been shaking, though not enough to put off his aim, not when the young woman he meant to kill was sprawled against a headboard less than ten feet away. Just enough to let the weapon recoil and punch him in the shoulder.

"It's in the pond," says the boy, jerking his head toward the greenish water. "I threw it in, after, before I ran to . . . to the necessary."

He can kill a woman, Blanche marvels, but he can't say *toilet* without faltering.

The words are spurting out of the boy now. "Louis came around on Thursday morning, asked where Jenny was. I got to cussing her." He sobs. "He made me swear on Mammy's life not to tell, then he said he just so happened to have learned that the same individual was pure trouble, and there was a person from the City who'd be uncommon grateful if a stop could be put to her."

"What person?" She knows it was Ernest, acting on Arthur's orders, but she needs to fill in the whole appalling story, put it back together, like broken glass forming a pane.

John Jr. shrugs.

"You didn't care who wanted you to shoot your good friend Jenny? Who promised to be *grateful,* to the tune of what?"

The boy's lower lip protrudes. "I wouldn't have done it just for the money."

The priggish tone! As if by gunning down Jenny for

what he saw her do to Blanche, he was following some higher law. "How much?" Blanche shrieks.

"Two hundred in silver," mutters John Jr. He roots in the pocket of his baggy overalls and pulls out a drawstring bag.

She stares at the dangling, puckered mass of it. But why, she's still wondering, why did Ernest buy only one death with this much cash, not two?

"You can have every penny of it, for all I care," he assures her, his voice rusty. "I wish I never—"

And then Blanche is grabbing his wrist, shaking the bag like a rat whose neck she needs to break: "I don't want your blood money!"

The boy pulls away and makes to throw it in the water; he's got his busted arm bent back for a long pitch—

Blanche rips the bag out of his fingers.

Heavy in her palm. Repulsive.

"It weren't the way I thought." John Jr.'s wailing. "All the—" He makes a gesture in the air, and she can see the blood jetting out of Jenny all over again.

"What did you think spilled out when you shot someone?"

"I waited till you leaned right over, Miss Blanche. I only meant to save you."

"Save me?"

"From *her.* I didn't reckon the glass would fly so far." He reaches out to touch the tiny mark on her cheek.

"Get those hands off me!"

John Jr. looks at his thin fingers as if he's never seen them before.

"You're going to hell," Blanche tells him.

He nods.

She turns on her heel, clutching the moneybag tightly.

One man passed the buck to another man, who passed it to an almost-man. A *flair for substitution,* isn't that what Madame called it? Guilt jumping from one to the next like a flea, a germ, a distorted whisper. Are there no children in the world anymore?

Step after step, Blanche walks to the depot.

"You're here again," remarks Mrs. Holt at her little window.

"Here and gone." Blanche makes her hand go into the drawstring bag. The first coin she pulls out is a silver half-dollar, very shiny. She hands it over so fast it spins on the counter and asks for a first-class ticket to the City.

A train, puffing out its hot exhaust . . . but it's heading the wrong way, toward San Jose. Blanche watches it, dull-eyed. She should have thought to ask Mrs. Holt when the train to San Francisco was due, but she's not sure she could have summoned that many words.

She's not expecting anyone to get off the train, but several do. One of them is Detective Bohen.

The two of them stare at each other as he erects his black umbrella against the sun. "Miss Beu*non,*" he says, pronouncing the final nasal with mocking emphasis.

Now's her moment. What better chance to explain the whole bizarre story than right here and now at the scene of the crime, where Blanche can lead him straight to the wet-faced boy? But the soot catches in her throat. "What—what are you—"

"Our investigations are ongoing," he declares, surveying the hamlet as if he can see right through all these thin shack walls. A few paces away from him, the other City folks don't seem to know where they're going. They argue in low voices and consult the newspaper one of them is carrying under his arm, then they set off toward the Eight Mile House.

Proof. Bohen will insist she provide evidence. Blanche has the bag, at least: payment for murder, wrapped in a drawstring pouch. But what does it prove? Money bears no trace of what it's bought.

"We may not yet have been able to pin this crime on any one of those *macs,* but we mean to root out the whole nest of them." Bohen's tone is so expansive now, she wonders if he's had a few drinks on the train. "Back in the Rush," he goes on, "Captain Lees tells me San Francisco was packed with your kind, like a can with clams. The scum of the world, putting up their freak show again every time it burned down."

Blanche stares at him. Is the detective trying to provoke her?

"But the City's growing up. Almost thirty years old now," Bohen concludes with satisfaction. "And on behalf of her decent citizens, the captain and I mean to clean house." He's pulling out his notebook and a mechanical pencil.

Nobody can skim the scum off San Francisco for good, Blanche thinks. It'll only come back with the tide.

No, the detective's not waiting for an answer from her. It seems he's forgotten Blanche already as he adds details to what looks like a complicated diagram of San Miguel Station.

Her head turns the same way as his. John Jr. is still

standing by the pond, a lightning-stunted sapling. Should she tell Bohen this minute? Surely they could find the varmint gun if they dragged the pond. Fish sporting along the stock, laying their eggs in the trigger. Chasing through the spokes of the bicycle too. Wouldn't the weapon and the high-wheeler back up her claims, if not prove them?

Bohen whistles under his breath as he sketches in a line.

The visitors from the City are outside the Eight Mile House now, pointing excitedly at the shattered window. It occurs to Blanche that they're tourists, murder tourists. The first of many? Maybe McNamara's going to turn a profit, after all. He'll sell them overpriced rotgut and tall tales of the hoodlum or hatchet man who snuck into San Miguel Station one dark night and blew Jenny Bonnet apart. Having not the least idea of what his own child has done.

As Blanche's eyes rest on John Jr. again, she's winded by an awful sympathy. It doesn't feel like hers. More like some foreign body lodged in her throat.

Jenny, out of the corner of her eye.

The boy shot you in your bed, Blanche growls at her.

A shrug.

What's that supposed to mean? Surely this is one thing you can't shrug off.

A hint of a grin.

They don't hang juveniles anymore, Blanche adds furiously. *The worst they'll do is send him to a reformatory.*

The Industrial School, just over the brow of the hill. The awful coincidence of it. That's where a judge would send a murderer of twelve years old. John Jr. might end up lying down in the same cell where Jenny lay a decade ago.

Yes, then, since you're asking, Blanche roars in her head, *yes, I do want him arrested in front of his whole stupefied clan. Dragged away, whipped, gagged—good enough for young John. I want him damaged worse than you were. Locked away for the rest of his sorry goddamn life.*

"Still here, Miss Beunon? My advice for you would be to head thataway, out of my jurisdiction," says Bohen, jerking his thumb south toward San Jose.

It's at this moment that Blanche decides not to say a word. Let Bohen pontificate and waste his Sunday here, waste any number of days, while the truth slithers away from him like a snake in a woodpile. Blanche is going back to the City to get the evidence she needs, and then she'll hand it to Cartwright of the *Chronicle,* because he's the best of a bad lot, the only one who's paid attention. And in the end everyone who's hurt Blanche, everyone who's scared her or talked down to her, is going to pay.

"Her name's Madeleine George," she says to the pigtailed cigar maker sitting on his mat at the corner of Stockton and Clay.

"What you say?"

She shouts over the discordant wheeze of the twenty-note barrel organ parked beside them. "Madeleine George." The grim-looking parrot has dirtied the grinder's shoulder, and the tin cup on top of the organ is empty, but the Italian just keeps cranking out the same polka.

"Girl like you?" the cigar maker wants to know.

Do all white females look alike to a Chinaman? But Blanche is younger than Madeleine, she wants to tell him, absurdly. No, he must mean a girl dressed to advertise herself. (The first thing Blanche did after getting down at Third and Townsend was find herself a dress shop and spend a considerable amount of the silver from the little bag to get herself fitted out from head to toe in a serious black-and-white stripe. She's painted high, too, for going on the warpath.) "Yes," she roars over the organ's death rattle.

Suddenly, blessedly, it stops. The Italian, eyeing an approaching Special, scuttles away to avoid arrest.

"She lodges above a grocery, I believe," Blanche tells the cigar maker.

His expression is uncertain, but he points at a skinny four-story building: "Many Frenchie girl in there."

It turns out to be the wrong building, but someone there knows the right one.

A quarter of an hour later, Blanche has tracked her way to Madeleine's door. She takes a breath and wipes a stray hair out of her eyes. She's met Ernest's *petite amie* only a couple of times, but nothing in the blonde's wide eyes intimidated her then. Blanche is going to make the woman say where Ernest is if Blanche has to rip her earrings out to do it.

She taps, softly, so as not to sound like the cops or a rent collector. Waits. Then knocks again.

Ernest's talking over his shoulder to someone as he tugs the door open. Looking healthier than when she saw him last though a little less elegant, with some whitish stain on his lapel. He turns his head and sees Blanche.

Who's got her lies ready, as well as her truths. "They found the gun," she raps out.

Ernest slams the door between them.

"I'll go straight to Detective Bohen, then, is that what you'd prefer?" Blanche calls out.

Voices inside the apartment.

"Madeleine? Madeleine, are you in there? Enjoying home life with a murderer, are you? Feel quite safe sharing his bed?" Blanche is shouting it loud and clear enough to be heard all over the building. "Did he tell you he was too much of a coward to pull the trigger on Jenny himself—so he hired a chicken farmer, who hired a *twelve-year-old?*"

The door's flung open again. *"Ta gueule!"* growls Ernest.

But Blanche won't shut her trap. Never mind that all she's got is a child's story which that child is unlikely ever to repeat. She can bluff as well as any cardsharp. "Louis and John Jr. are both in the lockup," she announces.

His rangy body twitches. "I don't know what you're talking about."

"Where's—" To her mortification, her voice breaks. She tries again. "What have you done to P'tit?"

"He's perfectly well, no thanks to you." Ernest's eyes bulge in outrage. "As if I'd ever hurt Arthur's son."

And for a moment Blanche can't see, can't hear. Relief shoots through her veins like sugar, and she realizes that she never did quite give up in the ten days since she's seen P'tit. Hope was a cut that wouldn't close over. "Prove it. Why should I believe a word you say? Where is he?"

A slight hesitation. "I'm afraid I have no—"

"Yes, you do, you false son of a bitch."

"The arrangements are a matter for his father. I expect Arthur will be coming back one of these days, with his bride," says Ernest, landing the word like a knife.

And it does stab Blanche, of course it does, for a

moment. A long moment. But she's too much of a veteran performer to show it on her face.

"I just received a telegraph, you see," says Ernest, goading her. "Arthur's in New York, and he's married a French girl."

"I don't give a damn if he's married a skunk," Blanche manages to say, almost lightly. "But how disappointing for you, Ernest."

The long face darkens.

"The minute he's out of your reach, he gets hitched? Trades in *la vie de bohème* for bourgeois comforts? It sounds to me like your double act has had its last hurrah."

"You understand nothing," he says gruffly. "Arthur won't stay away forever. He entrusted his child to me, didn't he?"

"Entrusted?" mocks Blanche. "He *dumped* P'tit on you, you mean. I can't believe you're still willing to stand by the fellow who's made you play second fiddle all these years. Don't you see? He's left you behind, his bootlicking lackey, to hang for what he told you to do."

"Arthur's a prince among men." The words break out of Ernest like sweat.

She rolls her eyes.

"Willing to let you get away scot-free," he marvels. " 'Let her go,' he told me as he packed his trunk. 'Women are like trains, there'll be another along in five minutes.' "

Blanche stares. Could that really be what Arthur said about losing her?

"And when I saw you rattling that buggy down the street last Tuesday, all frills and flounces, not a care in the world—" snarls Ernest.

Oh, how horribly simple: the name of the stables was painted on the buggy. All Ernest had to do was call in at Marshall's. The boy, the blasted stable boy; of course Blanche had to tell him where she was going, so he could give her directions. When Ernest came inquiring about a Frenchwoman who'd just hired a buggy, the boy would have had no reason not to tell him that she'd been heading for San Miguel Station. "But why only Jenny?" Blanche breaks in. "Why did you tell Louis to spare me? Was it because you knew Arthur would never forgive you?"

Ernest lets out one scornful cough of laughter.

A small sound from an inner room. What is it?

He says it so low that Blanche strains to hear: "It was because you're the goddamn mother."

It comes again, that muffled little sound. Ernest's head whips around and he's moving to shut the door but Blanche has got him by the sleeve.

The door bangs on her arm, forcing a long scream out of her. But she doesn't let go, she won't let go, she'll never let go because she knows whose small wordless voice she's hearing. "P'tit! P'tit!"

"Crazy *salope*—"

When Ernest opens the door enough to kick her away, Blanche thrusts her whole self through. He grabs her by the skirt and she pulls away hard enough that it rips at the waist. She's in the apartment and here's P'tit, wearing only a diaper—

And walking. Can this really be P'tit?

Still stubby at wrist and ankle, thick-foreheaded, but less so, somehow. His skin clearer. His eyebrows almost elegant. Up on his own two feet. P'tit, her P'tit, though he shows no sign of recognizing Blanche. He pats the wall-paper, sways like a drunk.

The blonde is behind him, in only a limp chemise and petticoat, her hair tangled. Looking her age, for the first time. "Blanche," says Madeleine, her mouth trembling so she can hardly form the syllable. She reaches down for P'tit's little shoulders.

"Hands off," howls Blanche.

"I only—"

"Hands off my baby!"

And then Ernest does the strangest thing. Drops to his knees, puts his lips to the child's round skull. "Turning into the spit of your father, aren't you, P'tit Arthur?" he says, very gently.

"Just P'tit," Blanche corrects him under her breath.

She should have recognized that milky stain on Ernest's lapel. The man has a knack with the boy, she realizes. Now, there's a joke. A natural father. When was it, over the past two weeks of harboring Arthur's child, that Ernest began to fall in love with him? For his absent friend's sake, at first, but it's well beyond that now, Blanche can see. His arm hovers in a half circle behind the boy, just in case he wobbles. The tenderness.

P'tit Arthur Girard, not Deneve, that's who P'tit could grow up to be if Blanche left him here. Because a killer might make a good parent, after all, a much better parent than the woman who pushed the baby into the world in the first place. Blanche briefly considers the gracious mothering Madeleine would give P'tit. How Ernest would shield him in a way Arthur never managed. And P'tit, well, she supposes he wouldn't remember anything else.

No.

"He's the price," she growls at Ernest. "I take him now, this minute. Or I'm going straight to Bohen with what I know, and they'll keep after you till they prove the rest, and you'll be on a gallows by Christmas."

At first Blanche has no idea if her improvisation's going to work. Ernest's face is a wooden mask.

Madeleine's tired, delicate features contort as she looks from the man to the child. The woman will do anything to save one of them, thinks Blanche, if she can only decide which one.

Blanche runs to scoop P'tit up. He wails and flails, but she's ready for that. She's out on the landing and thundering down the stairs, pressing her boy to her. She feels that surge of warmth, and this time she remembers what it means: not love but piss. Or the love that's mixed with piss and can't be separated from it.

*

Thursday evening, the fourteenth of September, Blanche goes back out to the saloon.

John Jr., who's been reading a book by bad light at the bar, stares up at her.

In an undertone, she asks his mother for some ice.

"What for?" says Ellen.

The whole family must have heard the women's quarrel just now, and Blanche punching Jenny in the face. The Irishwoman's just trying to humiliate her by asking. "Jenny got a black eye earlier, riding," Blanche lies blankly.

A sniff. "Dangerous business, riding."

"So do you have a bit of ice?"

"I do not, so. The last cold thing in San Miguel melted a month ago."

"A fresh steak, then?"

"Would you be having *pommes frites* with that, miss?" A dry laugh. "Where do you think you are?"

This isn't a cathouse, that might be what Ellen's hinting. *Take your filthiness elsewhere.*

Blanche keeps her mouth shut. She returns to the bedroom and shuts the door behind her.

Jenny's flat on her back on the bed.

"You more than half deserved it," says Blanche, but all the fight's gone out of her.

"Take that as an apology, shall I?"

"I thought apologies weren't worth the candle," she says, risking quoting Jenny's line back at her.

"Yours aren't, that's for sure."

The flesh all around Jenny's eyes is puffy when she sits up. It'll be black and blue by morning, Blanche reckons.

Sorry. Blanche is so sorry, for the blow and for everything else, for all she's dragged Jenny into this summer—but she can't say the word.

"Guess the frogs will have to play Scheherazade," Jenny remarks.

Blanche stares at her. "This is one of those moments when I don't know what the hell you're talking about."

"They're reprieved for one more night," explains Jenny.

"Ah."

"Though, does it count, I ask myself, if they're living in a dark sack?"

"Beggars can't be choosers," says Blanche.

"Well, as the fellow says, never put off till tomorrow what can be put off till the day after . . ."

Blanche is not sure which of them lets out the first yawn, but there seems no reason to stay up any later.

Jenny sheds her layers and shakes the dust out of them. In McNamara's long nightshirt, she wrestles with the window shade, then calls their host in to take a look at it, and bring them a drop of cognac while he's at it.

Mary Jane comes in with the glasses while her father's tinkering with the blind and stays lolling on the bed after he's gone.

"What do you mean to make of yourself, Mary Jane?" Blanche wants to know.

Her eyes narrow. "When I get out of here?"

"Yeah."

"I don't know. All I think about is the getting out."

The distant whistle of a passing train.

Jenny opens her tobacco pouch. "Twenty-minute ride," she says, nodding north, "you could be a whole different person."

"What happened to your face?" Mary Jane asks in a way that shows she knows already.

"*Qu'importe,*" says Jenny with a grin.

"Is that French for something?"

"Yeah, French for 'mind your own damn business,' " says Blanche.

The girl flounces out to the saloon.

Jenny watches Blanche over the pipe she's filling.

"Take that stinky thing outside, would you?"

"It keeps off the skeeters," says Jenny, but she steps out on the porch with her pipe and matchbox.

Blanche can hear Mary Jane in the back room talking to her mother. Jenny, just outside the window, gives the dog a good scratch and talks to him in a pretend-fierce voice. The candle flame's straight and steady; there's not a hint of breeze to stir the heavy air. Blanche remembers the night they met. How she sang a snatch of "Au Clair de la Lune" as they climbed up the dark stairwell. " *'Ma chandelle est morte,'* " she croons now, " *'Je n'ai plus de feu.'* " My candle's dead and I've no more fire.

From just outside the window, the familiar refrain, in Jenny's lighter, melodic voice:

Ouvre-moi ta porte,
Pour l'amour de Dieu.

Open up to me, for God's sake.

Blanche would prefer to leave the window up an inch or two but the bugs are starting to whine their way in, drawn to the candle. She struggles with the frame and lowers it with a thud. Her hand brushes against the green baize and it droops on one side, goddamn it. Nails come out of these chalky walls as easily as teeth out of an old skull. Blanche peers out through the narrow gap and sees Jenny wrestling with the dog in the moonlight, everything weirdly silver.

Nearly a month since Jenny crashed into Blanche's life and—it could be said—Blanche crashed into hers. *If you meet an obstacle you can jump free,* Jenny boasted. But not always. You have to allow for some damage.

Jenny comes in then, sets her empty pipe on the bureau, and jumps into bed.

"Moon's up," says Blanche, yawning.

"Everyone's a moon, as the fellow says."

"Huh?"

"With a side nobody sees," adds Jenny. She's leaning back on her elbows, her swollen face turned toward Blanche. Who, undoing her chemise, feels the familiar sensation of eyes on her. Something could happen or not, it could go either way, and who's to say it much matters? Maybe the two of them came closest to each other yesterday evening. Or even tonight, at the moment when Blanche punched Jenny in the face. Maybe they've started to diverge again, drifting apart, two twigs in a stream.

On the edge of the bed, Blanche stoops to unlace her borrowed gaiters. A train hurtles north, close enough to shake the Eight Mile House. She bends to undo her second gaiter, ripping at the laces. Tries an old Picard air under her breath, though why is she singing a lullaby when there's no baby to hear it?

Dors, min p'tit quinquin,
Min p'tit pouchin,
Min gros rojin . . .

Sleep, my little child, my little chick, my fat grape. The laces are snagged. Blanche hauls up her mauve skirt and sets her right ankle on her left knee, the canvas printing her skin with grit. The gaiter clings to her round calf like some old skin that won't be sloughed. Mud flecking the floorboards, the dingy sheets . . . this whole four-room shack is probably crawling with fleas and lice, but somehow Blanche doesn't care. Happiness as un-pin-downable as a louse: you feel the tickle of its passage but your fingers close on nothing.

Blanche plucks at the gaiter with her longest nail. One second and she'll have it undone.

Dors, min p'tit quinquin,
Min p'tit pouchin—

That's Jenny joining in, her voice clean as a bird's, her eyes wide open. "And the rest, how does it go?"

"Like this." Blanche bends right over to wrestle with the lace, her lungs filling, stretching rib cage, muscles, seal-plump skin, corset, dress, as she sings a mother's warning to a baby who just won't sleep:

Te m'fras du chagrin
Si te n'dors—

The cracks come so hard Blanche thinks they're thunder. The candle's out.

A sulfurous tang in the dark, less like a thunderstorm than fireworks, but who could be setting off fireworks? What is there to celebrate on the fourteenth of September? Outside, the dogs of San Miguel Station bark in furious chorus.

"*Qu'est-ce—*" Is that what Jenny says, or just a gasp, a hiss?

And Blanche says, "Wait."

*

"Let's count our silver," she says to P'tit now in the quietest private compartment, the one at the swaying end of the slow Sunday train heading inland to Sacramento. "There's a dollar. See Lady Liberty? And this one's an Indian head." Never too early for a child to learn his coinage. "Here's a half eagle. Have a chew on that, but don't swallow it . . ."

Blanche has the impression P'tit appreciates hearing her talk, or hearing talk of any kind. One of these days, she supposes, the child will begin to figure out what she's saying. He sits stiffly, looking absurdly small against the adult-size seat. His movements aren't random spasms anymore. It's as if he's conducting an unseen orchestra. His gaze seems more ambitious as he mouths the dollar. She wonders if P'tit even remembers his doorknob, the one Blanche lost to the drunken rioters. What does it mean to miss something you can't hold in your memory? Children learn to do without the things they used to weep for. They move on, as everyone has to.

What a fraud Blanche has felt, ever since she picked him up and ran down Madeleine's stairs this afternoon. Like a woman who's stolen a baby.

But no looking back. No giving a rat's ass about bygones. Blanche doesn't intend to pronounce the name of Arthur Deneve ever again. She suited him very well for his salad days—his years in the circus, and even after the fall that ended them. She was a witty, tipsy companion who earned her own money, asked little of him, and never said no. Who made just one mistake—called P'tit—but then kept that mistake out of his sight for the best part of a year. Yes, Blanche can see now that she was never the girl Arthur would end up marrying. And though she has regrets, that's not one of them. Good luck to this French bride of his, who can have no idea what she's taking on. "It turns out he didn't care enough about me to order my murder," she remarks to P'tit.

The child glances her way.

"At least you don't have killer's blood in you, that's something." Blanche gives him her biggest grin.

His mouth twitches.

A smile. A goddamn smile! Gone as quick as a mouse, but still.

She feels the glow for a long minute before she remembers that it was probably Madeleine who taught P'tit to smile, a week ago. Madeleine who saw him take a first step, with fawn-shaky legs. Blanche missed it. One way or another, she's missed most things. Well, too bad. P'tit will just have to forget Madeleine, and Ernest, and number 815, and the farm on Folsom Street; everything that came before. Blanche will make him believe he's always lived in the city of Sacramento. She means to lock the past up in her heart and never let this boy guess he was ever anything other than treasured.

Blanche rubs her bruised arm and stares out the window at the baked land. They'll see something of America at last. Ninety miles of it, at least. Why Sacramento, of all destinations? Perhaps simply because Jenny told her about it: booming, growing upward as well as out, almost literally pulling itself out of the mud. There should be room for enterprising newcomers there. Room for Blanche and P'tit. Or perhaps it's simply because Blanche has spent a year and a half living on Sacramento Street, which gestures toward—and is named for—that upstart city. It seems like some kind of sign, and she doesn't have any other to follow.

The hot air's half water this evening; it's as if they're breathing in steam. P'tit's cheeks trickle with sweat, and Blanche wipes them with a new handkerchief. Less than a hundred dollars of the silver left, because she had to buy so many things this afternoon, with no time for bargaining before the train left. A valise for each of them, bottles and clothes and diapers for him, new dresses for herself—sober by her standards, but chic, and her new bustle's the *dernier cri* in fashion: high, with ramrod-flat front and sides.

Also, of course, a two-dollar gold ring as evidence of Blanche's loss in the epidemic. (She's got her story ready, with its sniffs and sobs. *My late husband was such a good provider.*) By the time she steps down in Sacramento, she means to be every inch the lovely widow. One whose dancing academy will be known from the start for its emphasis on ballroom etiquette. (Well, Blanche might as well make a feature of being a lady, if she's to steal customers away from all those so-called Professors.) Jenny would approve of this plan, even if she was more grasshopper than ant herself. Would approve of the blood money getting spent this way.

Blanche makes a stack of the coins now and shows P'tit how to knock it over. Here's where a normal child would laugh, surely? Blanche laughs, to show him how it's done.

P'tit gives her a look that strikes her as wry.

And it occurs to her that he may be smarter than he's willing to show, too smart to laugh on cue.

Arthur stole this money and more from her in the first place and shared it with Ernest, who hired Louis with some of it, and Louis took his cut and passed two hundred of it on to John Jr. The look in that boy's eyes when he held out the bag to her. Think what such a sum could do for the McNamaras, and yet the boy couldn't bear to keep it.

Is that why Blanche didn't seek out Cartwright at the *Chronicle* before she left? She told herself that she was too busy getting ready so she could leave San Francisco by nightfall. That the newsman wouldn't be at his office on a Sunday evening. That Blanche can write to him as soon as she's settled in Sacramento. But it occurs to her now that she never will.

Because Jenny wouldn't give two bits for justice. Not that kind of justice. Not a blundering boy, whom she cared for, packed off to that grim so-called school for having let himself be bribed and pushed to the point of doing something so terrible that he's never going to forgive himself, anyhow. Instead Blanche has paid John Jr. back with the crushing weight of his own future.

Some crimes are better not solved, maybe. Some scars better kept covered up. Blanche lets herself pretend that blurry reflection in the spattered glass is Jenny, pedaling along beside the train. *I don't forgive him, though,* Blanche tells her.

A shrug.

Don't expect me to forgive, not one single bullet.

A grin.

To let John Jr. get away with murder means doing the same for the other two, Ernest and Louis. That's not fair, but what is? Life brings all manner of punishment and Blanche just hopes those men will get their share. Ernest's already lost everything he loves best: Arthur and Arthur's son.

Blanche's face is turned away from the past, toward the

city of Sacramento, where it sounds like citizens rise above grim realities, winching their whole lives into the sky. She's not going to drift into things anymore, because her life is no longer only her own. She'll be a boss, but not a tyrant. She'll rent rooms above her dancing parlor and hire a girl to mind P'tit during classes. He's light on his feet, so maybe Blanche can teach him to dance. *How do you know until you try?*

She drops the coins back into the bag one by one. P'tit makes a thrusting motion that she decides to take as an attempt at doing the same. "That's right, in the bag," she says, putting his fist over the opening. "Now let it go. Go on, drop it."

But P'tit keeps a hard grip on the coin. It must be easier to grab than to let go. She watches him gnaw on it. "Very good," she says. "Cut some more teeth. You're going to need them."

He's got three already, three sharp little wedges Blanche managed to count on the railroad platform in the City before he had enough and bit her finger. To think that they must have been lying in wait all these months, ready to spring up. Ten days with a murderer and his harlot have done P'tit nothing but good, Blanche has to admit. His features are still melancholic—the heavy forehead, the huge sunken eyes—but at moments he strikes her as somehow beautiful. It's all in the eye of the beholder, of course. That's Blanche: his beholder.

The bag's as heavy as a heart. Before this was blood money, it was fuck money. Cash Blanche earned from her dancing or *michetons* and tossed into the green chamber pot in the fireplace or stuffed in her old boot or bought her building with—and then Arthur liquidated that money again when he sold the place to Low Long. (Blanche won't sneer, anymore, at the folks who keep their heads down and toil, because they're earning themselves a kind of liberty, a dollar at a time.) Like water, money springs up, trickles down, picks up soil, and sheds it again. Still, the coins shine when she rubs them on her black-and-white skirt. This is hers and P'tit's, earned over and over, and she'll spend it on what they need, and what they fancy: train tickets, meals, rent, a bird-shaped musical rattle that P'tit's going to love more than he ever did that old knob.

She bobs to kiss his humid forehead, one of those automatic gestures to ward off evil. That's what Blanche is going to do whenever she gets an impulse to shake her son or smack him: kiss him instead. She means to pay P'tit back for all her past crimes, one moment at a time. Her best strength is a terrier one: bite the rope and don't let go. She's going to bind P'tit to her with indefatigable love. *One hundred percent enamored,* and more. Each day a cliff she'll climb again from the base.

Never mind how she and her son got to this point, speeding along toward the city of Sacramento. *Keep him or don't,* isn't that what Jenny advised Arthur that night in the apartment? *Fish or cut bait, but don't gripe.* Blanche has lost this child twice, but she's damned if there'll be a third time. She and P'tit have wreaked such havoc in each other's lives, come through so much blood and shit, paid so high for each other—this bargain's got to hold.

Your Maman's a flawed jewel, she could tell him, *and there's no fixing that.* There'll be no overnight metamorphosis—but certain things about her are changing already. Perhaps, at twenty-four, she's growing out of being so stupid. Blanche will always like her drink, but she'll try to make big decisions in the sober light of day. She'll probably always require a good deal of fucking, but from now on she's going to hold on to her independence. She will be fierce in P'tit's defense. Ambitious for his happiness, and hers.

P'tit's feet curl in their little boots. He doesn't like them, but Blanche is going to make sure he's always got good leather between him and the splinterish world. " 'Who gonna shoe yo' pretty little feet?' " she croons, clapping her hands softly.

A flash on the horizon. Blanche looks out the window. Could that have been lightning? She listens for a rumble, but all she can hear is the thunder of the wheels. Rain spits at the glass. She almost laughs to think how Maman back in Paris would scold: *Stop singing, you'll bring on a storm!*

P'tit lets out a wail and kicks as if to shake off his stiff boots. He'll be sturdy on his feet in another few weeks. Running away from Blanche, no doubt. She'll have to race to keep up.

Water is striping the glass now, turning its glaze of dust to rich mud. "A proper rainstorm," she marvels to P'tit.

The transparency of his small ear makes her feel like a she-wolf. But it strikes her now that it's P'tit who's been protecting Blanche, all this time, sketching a magic circle around her, not the other way around. It was because she was this boy's mother that Ernest didn't let himself instruct Louis to kill her too. What a joke! She's alive today only because hers is the body from which this odd, unwanted, fought-over child sprang.

Rain's whipping down hard now, hard enough to cut the autumn's long fever and wash this foul old world clean.

Things ricochet. You can turn the weather with a song. *The knack of riding backward:* now, there'd be a trick to learn. Jenny wouldn't be dead if she'd never crashed into Blanche on Kearny Street. P'tit wouldn't exist if Blanche had never met Arthur. Facts as hard as rocks, and Blanche has to pick her way among them, find her balance, with an acrobat's cocky smile.

She rubs at her cheek, and the tiny scab falls away.

Up ahead of them the engine sends out its long moan. The rain slams sideways against the window. *It's cheering us on,* she tells herself, like that stone-deaf frog in the story. P'tit's leaning back, on the verge of sleep. His moist eyelids flicker, fighting it. Nobody wants to give in, be snuffed out, surrender. Nobody wants the day to be over. Blanche holds her son like a sack of gold dust. *It's all going to be hunky-dory.* Sings in time with the juddering train: " *'Dors, min p'tit quinquin, dors.'* "

AFTERWORD

Almost all the characters in *Frog Music* come from the historical record, and I worked with and around the known facts of their lives:

Jenny (or Jennie/Jeanne/Jeannie) Bonnet (or Bonnett) (ca.1849–1876); her father, Sosthenes (or Sosthène) Bonnet (1825–?); mother probably named Désirée Leau Bonnet (1818–ca.1873); and sister, Blanche Bonnet (1856–?);

Adèle Louise "Blanche" Beunon (or Buneau) (1852–1877) and her son, name unknown (1875–?);

Arthur Pierre Louis Deneve (or DeNeve/De Neve) (ca.1844–?) and his wife from December 1876, Emilie (or Emily) Baugnon (or Baugnan) Deneve (ca.1858–?);

Ernest (or Earnest) Girard (or Gerard) (1856–?) and his wife from 1880, Madeleine (or Madeline/Madelein/Madaline) George Girard (1845–1908);

Adrien (or Jean Pierre-Adrien) Portal (1824 or 1839 or 1843–1904), Charles St. Clair, Coroner Benjamin Swan, Dr. Crook, Julius Funkenstein (1845–?), Doctress Amelia Hoffman (1829–1889), Detective Benjamin F. Bohen (?–1903), and Maria Lafourge (*floruit* 1856);

At San Miguel Station, John McNamara Sr. (1830 or

1835–?), Ellen McNamara (1830 or 1835 or 1839–?), and their children Mary Jane McNamara (1860–?), John McNamara Jr. (1863 or 1864–1881?), Kate McNamara (1867 or 1869 or 1870–?), and Jeremiah McNamara (1870–?); their neighbors Philip Jordan, Mrs. Holt, Pierre Louis (or Pierre Logis, or Louis Deframmant/de Frammant/ Dufrannon/Dufrannant/Dufranaut/DeFramond) and his wife, Caroline.

Two characters inhabit a gray area. Madame Johanna Werner and her brothel on Sacramento Street are described only in Herbert Asbury's footnote-free *The Barbary Coast* (1933), and the businessman known to police as L'amant de Blanche, whom I have called Lamantia, is mentioned only in two newspaper articles, years after the murder.

The only characters I have invented are Cartwright the journalist, Durand the restaurateur, Low Long the shoemaker, Mei the grocer, and Gudrun the help.

Although many records were destroyed in San Francisco's earthquake and fire in 1906, much remains. *Frog Music* draws on roughly sixty newspaper articles (from 1872 to 1902) about Jenny Bonnet, as well as on the annually published *San Francisco Municipal Records,* the U.S. Federal Census (1870, 1880, 1900, and 1910—the 1890 records were badly damaged in a 1921 fire, and almost all of what remained was later destroyed by government order), ships' passenger lists, and French, Irish, U.S., and Canadian birth/baptism/marriage/death records.

Not that using such invaluable sources is ever simple. Nineteenth-century reporters often made up details to fill in the blanks in their research. Like newspaper articles, legal documents are full of variant spellings and dates. In addition, century-and-a-half-old type or (even worse) handwriting scanned into databases can end up as gibberish. So I had to make many educated guesses, especially when it came to the clashing and at times ludicrous testimonies given at Jenny's inquest. I have also changed a few facts for the sake of the story, simplifying the sequence of events leading up to the murder and presenting Blanche as just as fluent in English as Arthur when in fact she spoke through an interpreter at the inquest.

There is one myth I would like to put to rest. Jenny Bonnet shows up all over the Internet these days as a proto-trans outlaw: presenting as male, persuading women to give up the sex trade and forming them into a thieves' gang. Attractive though this image is, it seems to derive from one highly colorful article that was not published until three years after the murder ("Jeanne Bonnett," *Morning Call*, October 19, 1879) and an equally unsubstantiated popular history from 1933 (Asbury's *The Barbary Coast*), and I have found no evidence to substantiate it.

Despite the renown of the San Francisco detective force, the investigation of Jenny's murder was dogged by confusion and delay. Several years on, Detective Bohen and his colleagues would come to the conclusion that Arthur Deneve paid Pierre Louis two thousand dollars to kill Blanche (rather than Jenny) and that Louis bought a farm back in Canada with the money. Louis was arrested there in July 1880, after his battered wife, Caroline, accused him of having shot Jenny (by mistake, instead of Blanche), but he killed himself before the San Francisco detectives could gather enough evidence to extradite him. This police theory—conveniently pinning the blame on a dead foreigner who was said to have earned an extraordinary figure (even by California hired-killer standards) for having shot the wrong woman—seems riddled with holes to me.

Then again, the explanation *Frog Music* offers of this still unsolved murder is only an educated hunch, which is to say, a fiction.

Getting back to the facts: You may wonder what really did become of Blanche and her nameless son after she told Coroner Swan that Arthur and Ernest "stole away my child, a little boy one year old, and at the present time I do not know where he is." While writing the novel, I had no idea whether she ever saw her son again. I knew of one article published three years after the murder (the aforementioned "Jeanne Bonnett," *Morning Call,* October 19, 1879) that claimed that Blanche died of throat cancer within the year, but the piece had the ring of French naturalist fiction, and the illness in particular sounded like a heavy-handed symbol for Blanche's unspoken secrets—so I didn't believe a word of it. It was only during the final copyediting of *Frog Music,* when I was trawling through online archives one last time for any sources I might have missed, that I came across a much more credible report—a laconic paragraph in the *Sacramento Daily Union* of April 26, 1877, noting that Blanche Beunon had died of throat cancer in San Francisco's French Hospital on April 24, leaving her son (said to be two years old) in the care of a family in Oakland. The reporter got Blanche's age wrong—thirty-five instead of twenty-five—so I suppose it's within the realm of possibility that he got her identity wrong too, but I doubt it. This is the only time I have ever found myself actually grieving for someone dead a century and a half. The one crumb of comfort I can find is that the lost boy was found and was reunited with his mother, if only for a matter of months.

As for the other characters: On immigrating to America with Blanche in 1875, Arthur Deneve described himself to a ship's clerk as an acrobat, and on another voyage in November 1876, he called himself an artiste. When he was briefly detained in New York after the murder, he spun reporters a yarn about being an analytical chemist trained in his father's Paris firm (a fictional one, as far as I can tell) who'd given it all up to take the lowborn, pregnant Blanche to America; he also claimed that Blanche gave birth to four children (in two and a half years!), only one of which he believed to be his. What we know for sure is that Deneve married Emilie Baugnon in New York and the couple declared to a ship's clerk their intention of returning to France for good.

Probably in the same spirit of self-aggrandizement, according to an 1874 passenger list, Ernest Girard claimed that he had been an official back in France. He and Madeleine George married in 1880, and the census of 1900 shows them still in San Francisco, without children.

As for Jenny's surviving family, two years after the murder, Jenny's sister, Blanche Bonnet, was released from Stockton State Hospital into the care of a friend at whose house she stayed on as a servant. In 1884, Sosthenes Bonnet, "paralyzed," was still living on the charity of his friend Leo Samson at a saloon in Oakland.

I did not have to invent or even exaggerate the twin plagues—the heat wave and the smallpox—that hit San Francisco in 1876. By the time the epidemic petered out in

July of 1877, leaving four hundred and eighty-two dead, it was clear that Chinatown could not have been the epicenter of infection, since only sixty of the some sixteen hundred reported cases lived there. But of course the new city health officer, John Meares, explained that away by claiming that the Chinese must have hidden several hundred more cases.

My novel's Sinophobic riot, set in September 1876, is a fictional foretaste of a far worse real one that took place in July 1877, when the economic crisis now known as the Long Depression finally reached San Francisco. On that occasion, over the course of two days, a crowd of roughly five hundred white rioters burned down twenty laundries and killed four Chinese people before the police, aided by about a thousand volunteers (dubbed the Pick-Handle Brigade), managed to stop the violence.

Blanche's building, 815 Sacramento, is said to have become a "rookery" for thieves and then (possibly by the mid-1890s, and definitely by 1905) the headquarters of the Chinese Salvation Army, whose mission was to help indentured Chinese women get out of prostitution. A few minutes' walk north, at 1314 Stockton Street, Jenny's destitute ex-lover (or ex-husband, according to one source) Adrien Portal gassed himself in his rented room in 1904. Chinatown was devastated in the 1906 earthquake and fire, so the streetscape in which my characters lived exists only in photographs today.

The shabby settlement of San Miguel Station was often called simply San Miguel, but I have used its full name to avoid confusion with either California's inland town of San Miguel or the offshore San Miguel Island. The McNamaras outstayed all their neighbors, and John Jr.

died there in 1881, at sixteen and ten months—no cause given. His elder sister, Mary Jane, is likely to be the woman of that name who got a job at the Golden Gate Woolen Manufacturing Company in San Francisco. Jeremiah probably grew up to be the Jeremiah McNamara recorded on a 1900 California voter-registration list as living just a couple of blocks away from what had been San Miguel Station—by then rebranded Ocean View—and seven years later he (if he is the fireman Jeremiah McNamara) was the first of the family to vote. Ellen was still alive in 1910, living with her younger daughter, Kate, Kate's husband, and their four children. The suburb was finally swallowed up by the OMI District (Ocean View, Merced Heights, and Ingleside), and my best guess as to where the McNamaras' saloon stood is the intersection of San Jose Avenue and Alamany Boulevard under the shadow of Highway 280 today.

According to Herbert Asbury's *The Barbary Coast*, Madame Johanna Werner's brothel on Sacramento Street—which I have dubbed the House of Mirrors—was known for virgin auctions, and it began to decline in the late 1870s when her supplier Johnny Lawless was jailed for selling a fourteen-year-old girl to a crib (bottom-level brothel) in Oregon.

Baby farms were a paradoxical institution. You could describe their function as infanticide by neglect or as child care, without which many parents (working, single and unsupported, poor) could not have managed to keep custody of their children at all. (And the death rates in municipal institutions such as foundling hospitals were so astonishingly high, you could call them de facto infanticidal too.) In Britain in 1868, the public was alerted to the dark side of baby farming by a series of articles in the *British Medical Journal,* but in the United States—despite the occasional case, such as the trial of Madame Parselle that year—suspicion was slow to spread. It took the founding of a network of child-protection organizations to shine a spotlight on this issue. The year of Bonnet's murder, 1876, saw the launch of the San Francisco Society for the Prevention of Cruelty to Children, and among its first targets was Doctress Amelia Hoffman. (Learning that Blanche and Arthur had their baby nursed out from shortly after birth, I chose Hoffman's notorious premises, which seems to have moved between different buildings on Folsom Street but according to several of her advertisements was on Folsom between Tenth and Eleventh Streets.) Convicted several times, she used various stratagems to avoid jail, and in 1887 she had the gall to offer the City of San Francisco both her baby farm and her ten-acre suburban home (right beside the Industrial School, at San Jose Avenue and Ocean Avenue) for the founding of an orphanage on the condition that she and then her son Frank would be its superintendents for life. Hoffman's offer does not seem to have been accepted, and she died leaving a fortune in 1889.

Despite the child-abuse scandals that plagued the San Francisco Industrial School (where Jenny Bonnet was incarcerated in her teens), it survived its grand jury investigation and stayed open till 1891, when the building was converted into the city jail for women. The site is now covered by the campus of City College of San Francisco, a piece of Highway 280, and Balboa Park.

When San Francisco's Odd Fellows Cemetery was closed, in the 1920s, all the remains—which would have included Jenny's—were moved to mass graves in the Greenlawn Memorial Park in Colma, California.

The California red-legged frog was eaten to the brink of extinction in the late nineteenth century, and it remains a threatened species, mostly due to ongoing habitat loss. The frog-leg trade (which includes both wild-catching and farming) wreaks great damage on ecosystems today, particularly in developing countries.

Everything Jenny quotes with the words "as the fellow said" comes from Mark Twain, famous resident of San Francisco during part of her adolescence (from 1864 to 1869), who I'm sure would have been her favorite author. She may not have read Walt Whitman, but some of her thoughts coincide with his. Blanche paraphrases Whitman's "I cock my hat as I please," and Arthur borrows several bon mots from Charles Baudelaire.

I'd like to take this opportunity to thank:

Autumn Stephens, whose *Wild Women: Crusaders, Curmudgeons, and Completely Corsetless Ladies in the Otherwise Virtuous Victorian Era* (1992) first drew my attention to Bonnet, as well as to Annie Hindle (the protagonist of my second play, *Ladies and Gentlemen*) and Annie Taylor and Madame Restell (the subjects of two of my short stories), which makes Stephens's witty, illustrated guide the single most inspiring book on my shelves;

The late great Kevin Mullen, former police chief and popular historian, for his account of Bonnet, drawn from the department's files, "The Little Frog Catcher," in his

The Toughest Gang in Town: Police Stories from Old San Francisco (2005);

William B. Secrest for *Dark and Tangled Threads of Crime: San Francisco's Famous Police Detective, Isaiah B. Lees* (2004), the sole source I know on the indomitable, scar-faced Maria Lafourge;

Nayan Shah, whose *Contagious Divides: Epidemics and Race in San Francisco's Chinatown* (2001) I found most helpful, particularly on the smallpox outbreak of 1876;

Daniel Macallair for his invaluable "The San Francisco Industrial School and the Origins of Juvenile Justice in California: A Glance at the Great Reformation," *Journal of Juvenile Law & Policy* 2 (Winter 2003);

Jurgen Kloss for his insights into the history of "Rye Whiskey" (http://justanothertune.com/html/tarwathie.html) and all the song hunters at www.mudcat.org for their zealous tracing of the muddy, ever-proliferating roots of folk music, especially Professor Jonathan Lighter, whose recent book about "Johnny, I Hardly Knew Ye," entitled, ironically, *"The Best Antiwar Song Ever Written,"* saved me from parroting the old myths about this famous song;

Librarians who went out of their way to help me over the past decade or so on my flying visits to the San Francisco Public Library, the California Historical Society, the Bancroft Library (University of California, Berkeley), the New York Public Library, and the Weldon Library (University of Western Ontario), especially Ms. Hamashin of the California State Archives for graciously looking up the medical records of Blanche Bonnet (Jenny's sister) at the Stockton State Hospital and discovering that it was not she, but a baby born to her, who died there;

Naomi Edel for taking me to San Bruno and Coyote Point to get a sense of Jenny's landscape, and fellow novelist Ellis Avery for thoughts on writing Frenchness in English;

And Professor Clare Sears, whose fascinating work on public space in nineteenth-century San Francisco includes the only scholarly investigation of Bonnet I know of, a probing chapter entitled " 'A Tremendous Sensation': Cross-Dressing in the 19th-Century San Francisco Press," in *News and Sexuality: Media Portraits of Diversity* (eds. Laura Castañeda and Shannon B. Campbell, 2006). Professor Sears, author of *Arresting Dress: Cross-Dressing, Law and Fascination in Nineteenth-Century San Francisco* (2014), went to the considerable trouble of making me up a parcel of otherwise unobtainable newspaper reports about Bonnet. It's a kind of intellectual generosity I've found to be very common among academics, but still, shown to an extreme by Clare Sears.

Gratitude as always to everyone at my loyal and zealous agencies (Caroline Davidson Literary Agency in London and Anderson Literary Management in New York) and to the energetic and brilliant teams at my publishers (Little, Brown; HarperCollins Canada; and Picador).

I want to thank some great friends: Alison Lee for convincing me that I could write a crime novel, Wendy Pearson for critiquing a late draft, and both Daniel Vaillancourt and my beloved mother-in-law (luckily for me, a translator), Claude Gillard, for improving the book's 1870s French.

Finally, *bisous* to my three bilingual loved ones for

bearing with me as I stammered in the *boulangerie* during our extended stays in the South of France.

For anyone curious to learn more about the murder that was generally known as the San Miguel Mystery, I will be posting an annotated list of sources on my website: http://www.emmadonoghue.com/images/pdf/the-san-miguel-mystery-the-documents.pdf.

And if you'd care to hear twentieth- and twenty-first-century recordings of the songs quoted in *Frog Music*, please go to http://8tracks.com/emmadonoghue/frog-music/.

SONG NOTES

CHAPTER I: DARLIN'

"L'Canchon Dormoire" ("Song for Sleep"), aka "P'tit Quinquin" ("Little Child")

Written by Alexandre Desrousseaux (1820–1892) in 1853 and published in the second volume of his *Chansons et Pasquilles Lilloises* (*Songs and Satires of Lille*) in 1869, "L'Canchon Dormoire" is the most famous of his over four hundred songs. The lyrics are in Picard—also known as Chtimi, Rouchi, or Patois, a language closely related to French, spoken in several northern French regions and parts of Belgium—and this lullaby has become the unofficial anthem of the city of Lille.

"Darlin'," aka "Darling," "Honey Babe," "You Can't Love (But) One," "Darlin', You Can't Have One," and "New River Train"

This is the only piece for which I have invented my own variation on a traditional song. "Darlin' " seems to have been widespread from the end of the nineteenth century; Alan Lomax in *The Penguin Book of American Folk Songs*

(1964) describes it as "the national chant of a rebellious American libido." Its counting-song form (technically a progressive chain) is strict, but the lyrics vary, and from the 1920s on they have often included a chorus about riding a train. Some versions are not suggestive at all, and others only mildly so. I have pushed mine in the direction it seemed likely a burlesque performer would take them.

"Au Clair de la Lune" ("By the Light of the Moon")
This French song seems to have begun in the late 1770s as a *contredanse* tune (a Gallic variant of English country dancing) known as "La Rémouleuse" ("The Grinder Girl"), "Air du Gagne-Petit" ("The Low-Earner's Tune"), or "En Roulant Ma Brouette" ("Rolling My Barrow"). It is often attributed to the composer Jean-Baptiste Lully, apparently for no better reason than his preeminence in French baroque music. The tune acquired these lyrics about a pair of lovers by the time of its first publication as "Au Clair de la Lune" in 1843 in *Chants et Chansons Populaires de la France* (*Popular Songs and Ballads of France*) and finally ended up as a nursery rhyme.

On April 9, 1860, Edouard-Léon Scott de Martinville made a phonautograph recording (a transcription of sound waves as a line on paper) of a ten-second snippet of "Au Clair de la Lune," which seems to be the earliest recognizable record of the human voice and of instrumental music. In 2000, U.S. researchers converted the graph back to sound. The result was so high-pitched that they thought it was the voice of a girl, perhaps Martinville's daughter, but when they played it at the correct, slower speed, it turned out to be a man singing, probably the inventor himself. You can listen to it at http://en.wikipedia.org/wiki/Edouard-Léon_Scott_de_Martinville.

"Little Brown Jug"

This American ode to committed drinking was published in 1869 by "Eastburn," the pseudonym, and middle name, of Joseph Winner (1837–1918), and it was the one real hit among his more than twenty known songs. Like many composer's works, this song was then absorbed into the folk canon, going through many variations over the next century and a half.

CHAPTER II: I HAVE GOT THE BLUES

"For Work I'm Too Lazy"

The quatrain Jenny sings here is a maverick or floating stanza—meaning one of those pieces of debris that pop up over and over in the river of folk music. This is the earliest published version of the lines I have found, in a variant of "Rye Whiskey" collected by Newton Gaines from a cowboy friend in Texas in 1926. The quatrain often turns up in songs of the "Rye Whiskey" family (including "Jack o' Diamonds," "The Cuckoo," and "The Sporting Cowboy"), which have British origins but are most popular in the United States. It also appears as a stand-alone fragment entitled "For (the) Work I'm Too Lazy."

Sometimes *tie-hacking* (cutting lumber into railroad ties) replaces the generic *work* as the task that's too demanding, while (amusingly) *investment* can substitute for *begging,* but the third term is usually *train-robbing,* and *gambling* is the life the singer always seems to choose in the last line.

"The Flying Trapeze," aka "The (Daring Young) Man on the Flying Trapeze"

This most famous of circus songs is an English tribute to Jules Léotard, the French acrobat who pioneered the art of the flying trapeze at the Cirque d'Hiver in Paris in 1859 and whose name would later be immortalized as the term for a one-piece costume. Published in 1867, it had words by "George Leybourne" (the stage name of music-hall performer Joe Saunders, 1842–1884) with music by Gaston Lyle, arranged by Alfred Lee (1839–1906).

Interestingly, the song is as much about daring young cross-dressing women as daring young men, since it's a complaint by a man that his beloved has been seduced away from him by a circus man who makes her pass as a boy and perform on the trapeze to support him financially.

"I Have Got the Blues"

This playful lament about a hangover, published in 1850, seems to have been the first song with *the blues* in the title. (It's given as "I Have Got the Blues To Day!: A Comic Ballad" on the cover of the sheet music, but more simply as "I Have Got the Blues" inside.) The words are by Miss Sarah M. Graham with music by Gustave Blessner (1808–1888), a well-known composer of waltzes and mazurkas who taught school in New York State and collaborated with Graham on at least one other comic song, "Nanny's Mammy."

"Près des Remparts de Séville" ("By the Ramparts of Seville," aka "Seguidilla")
After getting arrested for a knife fight, the heroine of *Carmen* (1875) sings this glorious aria in order to seduce the hero into untying her bound hands. The music is by Georges Bizet (1838–1875), a French composer now famous for this, his final opera, but who died of a heart attack at thirty-six, convinced that *Carmen* was a total failure. The words are by Henri Meilhac (1831–1897) and Ludovic Halévy (1834–1908), collaborators for two decades; they based the libretto on the 1845 novella of the same name by Prosper Mérimée, and he in turn was probably influenced by Aleksandr Pushkin's narrative poem *The Gypsies* (1824).

CHAPTER III: THERE'S THE CITY

"I'm a Pilgrim"
This hymn, an allegory about a journey through "this country so dark and dreary," was popular in white Southern worship. The words were published anonymously as "I'm a Pilgrim" in *The Southern Zion's Songster* (1864) but were actually adapted from Mary Stanley Bunch Dana Schindler's "A Pilgrim and a Stranger" (in her *The Northern Harp,* 1841), set to the Italian tune "Buona Notte." (After publishing two volumes of Calvinist hymns, the poet—best known as "Mrs. Dana"—shocked her followers by converting to Unitarianism, and ended up as an Episcopalian.)

By the 1880s, "I'm a Pilgrim" had been adopted and adapted by black churches, contributing greatly to the famous spiritual known from the 1920s variously as "A City Called Heaven," "Poor Pilgrim," "Pilgrim of Sorrow," "Tossed and Driven," and "Trying to Make Heaven My Home." "I'm a Pilgrim" is an ancestor to a whole family of songs on the wayfaring-stranger theme in the gospel/folk/bluegrass/country repertoire.

CHAPTER IV: SOMEBODY'S WATCHING

"Musieu Bainjo," aka "M'sieu/Misieu/Monsieu/Miché/Michi Bainjo," and "Voyez Ce Mulet Là" ("Mister Banjo," aka "Look at This Buck Here")

This was described by its editors (in *Slave Songs of the United States,* 1867) as a slave song heard before the Civil War by a lady correspondent of theirs at the Good Hope Plantation, St. Charles Parish, Louisiana. They gave it in more or less standard French, but an 1887 editor claimed that it was usually sung in Creole patois, as follows: "*Gardé piti milate, ti banjo! / Badine dan lamain, ti banjo! / Chapo en ho côté, ti banjo.*" Others have suggested a minstrel-show origin for this song.

Mulet here is usually translated as "dandy," but in fact it has several related meanings: buck (as in a male deer, but often used of male slaves in English), mule, and mulatto (a term that derives from the Spanish word for mule). The type of dandy the song is satirizing is an urban free man of color nicknamed for the banjo, the most popular instrument among black musicians. The tune echoes several famous dances: the bamboula, the habanera, and the cakewalk.

"Le Temps des Cerises" ("Cherry-Time")

This tear-jerking ballad was written by the French revolutionary Jean-Baptiste Clément (1836–1903) during his exile in Belgium and set to music and published in 1871 by his friend the tenor Antoine Renard (1825–1872). An unsubstantiated story claims that Clément traded Renard the rights to the lyrics in exchange for a fur coat. When Clément joined the cause of the working-class Communards in Paris in 1870, they took up this song as their anthem.

"Commence Ye Darkies All!," aka "Commence Ye Darkies" and "Commence, You Niggers All"

"When I go out to promenade" is a fourth verse added (by 1854) to a song first published in 1849 as "Commence Ye Darkies All!" by W. D. Corrister. A white guitarist/songwriter who was based in New York in the 1840s and in San Francisco in the 1850s, Corrister played with many early blackface-minstrel groups. Interestingly, the extra "promenade" verse was remembered the longest, turning up without attribution in journalism and fiction of the late nineteenth and early twentieth centuries.

"The Housekeeper's Tragedy," aka "The Housekeeper's Woes/Complaint/Lament," "Life Is a Toil," and "Trouble and Dirt"

"There's too much of worriment goes to a bonnet" is the third of nine verses of a poem published as "The Housekeeper's Tragedy" in *Arthur's Lady's Home Magazine,* volume 37 (1871), by Eliza Sproat Turner (1826–1903), who included it in her 1872 collection *Out-of-Door Rhymes*. Turner was a widely published writer and activist in women's, antislavery, and anti-animal-cruelty causes. The piece appeared as a five-stanza song called "The Housekeeper's Woes" (attributed to an H. A. Fletcher) in 1871's *It's Naughty But It's Nice Songster,* and then with the four additional stanzas, attributed to H. A. Fechter, in an 1887 folio edited by Richard A. Saalfield, *Comical, Topical and Mottoe Songs*. The melody published in 1887 is quite different from the usual tune taken down with these lyrics in various parts of America from the 1880s on, and nothing is known about the composer of either.

Scholars disagree about whether the song is a feminist protest or a piece of music-hall mockery. I incline to the former, because I find it more credible that jokers would have borrowed Turner's text for their own satirical purposes than that she would have taken a satire and offered it as sincere.

"Oh, California," aka "The California Song," "I Came from Salem City," "The Gold-Digger's Song," and "Oh, Ann Eliza"

This was known all over the world as the theme song of the 1849 California Gold Rush. It is sung to the melody of—and in some ways is a parody of—the minstrel song "Oh! Susanna" (1848) by Stephen Foster (1826–1864), known as "the father of American music." The original lyrics were attributed to an immigrant called Jonathan Nichols, and subsequent variants range widely in setting and detail; the version Jenny and Blanche hear was published in *Out West* in 1904.

"Somebody's Darlin' "

This began as a widely loved American Civil War poem for a dead soldier, generally attributed to French immigrant Marie Ravenal de la Coste. At least seven different people set it to music during the 1860s, but the only version that has lasted is the one published in 1864 by John Hill Hewitt (1801–1890), the New York–born "Bard of the Confederacy."

CHAPTER V: *VIVE LA ROSE*

"There's a Good Time Coming"

These words are from a utopian vision poem (1846) by Scottish writer Charles Mackay (1812–1889), now remembered for his *Extraordinary Popular Delusions and the Madness of Crowds.* The poem was set to music by an English composer Henry Russell and—independently—by an American one, Stephen Foster (1826–1864). Foster wrote 156 songs, including a long string of hits, but made little from them due to the weakness of copyright law in his day, and he died at thirty-seven with thirty-eight cents in his pocket.

"If You've Only Got a Mustache"

This 1864 song has a tune by Stephen Foster and lyrics by his friend George Cooper (1840–1927), who often wrote comic songs for Foster and other composers.

"Vive la Rose" ("Long Live the Rose"), aka "La Méchante" ("The Wicked One") and "Mon Amant Me Delaisse" ("My Lover Is Leaving Me")
This folk song about betrayal has been collected in different regions of France; the lyrics vary, and the refrain is shared with several other songs. "Vive la Rose" is often described as eighteenth century in origin but does not seem to have been published before its inclusion in *Chants et Chansons Populaires des Provinces de l'Ouest (Songs and Popular Ballads of the Western Provinces,* 1866), which is the version Jenny sings here.

"The Love Sick Frog," aka "The Bull Frog," "The Bullfrog Song," "Frog Went a-Courtin'," "A Frog He Would a-Wooin' Go," "A Frog Went a-Walkin'," "Frog in the Well," "The Frog's Wooing," "King Kong Kitchie Kitchie Ki-Me-O," "There Lived/Was a Puddie/Puggie in the Well," and "Crambone"
This perennially popular ballad began in Scots in the mid-sixteenth century, with English versions published as early as 1611. The variant Jenny sings was published as "The Love Sick Frog" in Dublin around 1807, with music for piano or harp by Irish singer/instrumentalist/composer Thomas Simpson Cooke (1782–1848). David Hyland has created a magnificent compilation of over 170 verses of this song from twenty-nine sources at http://home.earthlink.net/~highying/froggy/froggy.html.

CHAPTER VI: I HARDLY KNEW YE

"Home! Sweet Home!," aka "Home, Sweet Home"

This song is adapted from the 1823 opera *Clari, Maid of Milan,* with libretto by expat American actor/dramatist John Howard Payne (1791–1852) and music—based on a Sicilian tune—by the English composer Sir Henry Bishop (1786–1855). It became popular with troops on both sides of the American Civil War and was said to have been banned in Union army camps for its tendency to incite nostalgia and therefore desertion.

"Johnny, I Hardly Knew Ye"

In a short, impeccable study with the tongue-in-cheek title of *"The Best Antiwar Song Ever Written"* (2012), Jonathan Lighter demolishes the legend of this song as a tragic, antiwar eighteenth-century Irish folk ballad that was distorted into the pro-war "When Johnny Comes Marching Home" by Patrick Gilmore in 1863. Lighter establishes that "Johnny, I Hardly Knew Ye" was composed and published in 1867 by the English music-hall writer/manager Joseph Bryan Geoghegan (1815–1889)—who, incidentally, had a total of twenty-one children by his wife and mistress. Geoghegan may have borrowed the wild interjection "ahoo" from a blackface-minstrel song.

"Johnny, I Hardly Knew Ye" became a huge hit for the star comic singer Harry Liston and was received by generations of audiences in England, Ireland, the United States, and Australia as pure stage-Irish hilarity. Only around 1915, Lighter shows, did a war-sickened audience begin to hear it as anything but fun. The Irish Republican movement adopted it as anti-British propaganda, and protest singers from the 1950s on tinkered with the lyrics to bring out what they saw as its nascent, pacifist rage. The original tune fell by the wayside, and these days it is usually sung to the tune of its 1863 predecessor "When Johnny Comes Marching Home."

"Some Folks"
Published in 1855, this insouciant ode to individualism and "the merry, merry heart" is yet another bestselling song by Stephen Foster (1826–1864).

CHAPTER VII: BANG AWAY

"How Can I Keep from Singing," aka "My Life Flows On in Endless Song"
This famous hymn seems to have begun as a poem entitled "Always Rejoicing," published in the *New York Observer* on August 7, 1868, by "Pauline T." Others attribute the words to Anna Bartlett Warner (1827–1915). All that's clear is that the tune is by American Baptist minister (and composer of some five hundred hymns) Robert Lowry (1826–1899), who included both music and words—claiming credit for only the music—in the 1869 songbook he helped edit, *Bright Jewels for the Sunday School.*

"Old Aunt Jemima," aka "Aunt Jemima Ho Hei Ho"
This minstrel-show song, drawing on slave work chants, is usually said to have been written in 1875 by a man who performed it often, Billy Kersands (ca.1842–1915). An extraordinary African American acrobat, Kersands was

a graceful two-hundred-pounder who could fit several billiard balls in his enormous mouth and whose trademark dance, Essence of Old Virginia, was a forerunner of the soft-shoe shuffle.

But the facts are more complicated. James (Jim) Grace, Kersands's fellow performer from the Callender's Georgia Minstrels (the most successful African American troupe), published "Old Aunt Jemima" in 1876, claiming authorship of the words and music. In 1876 the variant Blanche hears—with lyrics hinting at a violent threat to an interracial relationship—was included in Sol Smith Russell's *Jeremy Jollyboy: Songster,* "as sung by Joe Lang," a white blackface performer and theater manager. There is an 1873 publication with the title *Joe Lang's Old Aunt Jemima Songster,* so its first performer and/or composer may have been neither Kersands nor Grace, but Lang.

The performers of this song, whether black men or white, usually wore drag. In 1889 it was used to brand a pancake mix, and Aunt Jemima gradually became a generic nickname for black women, especially rural ones.

"Bang Away, Lulu," aka "Bang Bang, Lulu," "(My) Lulu (Gal)," "(My) Lulu Lula," "She Is a Lulu," and "When Lulu's Gone"

This dirty crowd-pleaser seems to have been widespread in the United States, Canada, and England by the end of the nineteenth century but for reasons of prudery was published only in censored versions until the second half of the twentieth. Ed Cray offers this undated composite in the first edition of his wonderful collection *The Erotic Muse* (1968), calling it a Southern Appalachian ballad and emphasizing that these verses are just a handful out of hundreds known. Other versions of the song feature (Miss) Rosie or Susie.

CHAPTER VIII: WHEN THE TRAIN COMES ALONG

"When the Train Comes Along," aka "When That Train Comes Along"

A new nineteenth-century American musical form, the Negro spiritual drew on both African and European traditions. "When the Train Comes Along" is a spiritual first published in 1909 (in Howard W. Odum's *Religious Folk-Songs of the Southern Negroes*). The version Blanche hears was collected on St. Helena Island, South Carolina, in 1913 and published in Carl Diton's *Thirty-Six South Carolina Spirituals* (1930). The song appeared in many variations in the 1920s and became popular in white gospel and blues too.

"I'll Eat When I'm Hungry"

The lines Jenny sings here were collected in an untitled three-verse fragment by Emma Bell Miles (1879–1919) in her *The Spirit of the Mountains* (1905). Variations on this floating stanza can be found in "Rye Whiskey"/"Jack o' Diamonds" and "The Cuckoo" as well as "Drunkard's Song," "Drunken Hiccups," and "(Way Up on) Clinch Mountain." Jürgen Kloss, in his tireless investigation of the British/American song lineage that includes "Rye Whiskey," manages to trace versions of the eat/drink quatrain back through Civil War songs ("The Rebel Soldier," "The Rebel Prisoner") to an English play of 1737, Robert

Dodsley's *The King and the Miller of Mansfield;* see Kloss's "From 'Earl Douglas' Lament' to 'Farewell Angelina': The Long and Twisted History of an Old Tune Family," http://justanothertune.com/html/tarwathie.html.

"Who Gonna Shoe Yo' Pretty Little Feet?"

This maverick stanza about parted lovers derives from a mid-eighteenth-century Scots ballad generally known as "The Lass of Loch Royale." Variations on these shoe/glove lines were widespread in nineteenth- and twentieth-century America, sometimes taking the spotlight in composite songs called "Who Will Shoe Your Pretty Little Foot" and "Oh, Who Will Shoe My Foot," but more often turning up in other songs, including "Poor Boy," "Don't Let Your/My Deal Go Down," "Fare You Well, My Own True Love," "The True Lover's Farewell," "The False True Lover," "(Fare You Well, My) Mary Anne," "The Storms Are on the Ocean," "Ten Thousand Miles," and "Turtle Dove."

The version sung in this novel is from "John Henry" (variant E), the famous lament for a heroic black railway man, in *Negro Workaday Songs,* edited by Odum and Johnson (1926).

GLOSSARY OF FRENCH

(in order of use in the novel)

Dors, min p'tit quinquin, / Min p'tit pouchin, / Min gros rojin; / Te m'f'ras du chagrin / Si te n'dors point qu'à d'main
Sleep, my little child, / My little chick, / My fat grape; / You'll annoy me if you don't / Go to sleep till tomorrow

qu'est-ce?: What?
merde: shit (human or animal); exclamation of annoyance
micheton: (literally, "little Michael") prostitute's trick or john
allumeuse: (literally, "she who lights/turns on") cocktease
cigare: (literally, "cigar") penis
l'heure bleue: (literally, "the blue hour") dusk
gamin: urchin, street child
ça va, mademoiselle?: All right, miss?
cuisses de grenouille au beurre noir: frog legs in black butter
mon vieux: my old friend (masc.)
dehors: outside
connard: jerk

bordel: brothel; exclamation of annoyance
chérie, ça va?: Darling (fem.), how are you?
Blanche la danseuse: Blanche the dancer
mac/maquereau: boyfriend of a prostitute
ami intime: bosom buddy (masc.)
Au clair de la lune, on n'y voit qu'un peu: By moonlight, you can't see much
Maman: Mom
quelle salope: what a bitch
la vie de bohème: bohemian life
Courrier de San Francisco: a French-language San Francisco newspaper
con: (literally, "vulva") fool
enchanté: delighted to meet you (masc.)
pantalon: trousers
chacun ses goûts: to each his own
qu'importe: no matter
mon beau: my handsome (masc.)
heureux au jeu, malheureux en amour: lucky at gambling, unlucky in love
petite amie: girlfriend, lover (fem.)
ma puce: my flea; term of endearment
le Cirque d'Hiver: the Winter Circus
les jours anciens: past times
des conneries: bullshit
satané: (literally, "satanic") damn
Français: the French, or Frenchmen
à table, messieurs-dames: come and eat, ladies and gentlemen
Monsieur Loyal: traditional title of circus ringmaster
vous comprenez?: you understand?

Voici la fin de la semaine: / Qui veut m'aimer? / Je l'aimerai. / Qui veut mon âme? / Elle est à prendre.
Here's the weekend: / Who wants to love me? / I'll love him. / Who wants my soul? / It's for the taking.

putain: whore; exclamation of annoyance or surprise
prends-la dans le cul: take her in the ass
chatte: (literally, "female cat") vulva
l'amant de Blanche: Blanche's lover (masc.)
merci: thanks
bisou: kiss
regarde le beau cheval: look at the handsome horse
chut: shh
voilà: there
caca: poo
viens ici, mon gars: come here, my lad
gulli gulli: tickling taunt
putain de merde: (literally, "shit-whore") exclamation of extreme annoyance
mon amour: my love (masc.)
pauv' bébé: poor baby
qu'est-ce que ce sera?: What'll it be?
choucroute: sauerkraut
j'en ai marre: I've had enough
bordel de merde: (literally, "shit-brothel") exclamation of extreme annoyance
patron: boss
foutu: (literally, "fucked") damn
bel ami: boyfriend, boy toy
hein: now (conveying insistence)

Chapeau sur côté, Musieu Bainjo / La canne à la main, Musieu Bainjo, / Botte qui fait crin crin, Musieu Bainjo . . .
Hat on one side, Mr. Banjo, / Cane in hand, Mr. Banjo / Boots that squeak, Mr. Banjo . . .

la vie est trop courte pour boire du mauvais vin: life's too short to drink bad wine
la ville sans honte: the shameless city/town
désolée: sorry (fem.)

Mais il est bien court, le temps des cerises . . . / Cerises d'amour au robes pareilles, / Tombant sous la feuille en gouttes de sang . . .
But cherry time is very short . . . / Cherries of love in the same dresses, / Falling under the leaves in drops of blood . . .

bonne nuit, mes amis: good night, my friends
hou-hou: yoo-hoo
comme il faut: as it should be done
cuisses de grenouille à la poulette: frog legs chicken-style
à bientôt: see you soon
bonne chance: good luck
libre: free (to do)
gratuit: free (in price)
cul: ass (meaning sex in general)
ta gueule: shut your trap
enchantée: delighted to meet you (fem.)
l'une pour l'autre, double paix-paroli, masque, sept-et-le-va: faro jargon

que ça pue: what a stink
va te faire foutre: go fuck yourself
bon voyage: have a good trip
jamais de fumée sans feu: there's no smoke without fire
fille de joie: (literally, "joy girl") prostitute

Mardi i' r'viendra m' voire, / O gai! vive la rose; / Mais je n'en voudrai pas, / Vive la rose et le lilas!
He'll come back to see me on Tuesday, / Hey, long live the rose; / But I won't want him back / Long live the rose and the lilac!

gouine: dyke
ma pauvre: poor thing (fem.)
qu'est-ce que c'est que ça?: What's this?
qu'est-ce qui m'est arrivé?: What's happened to me?
gendarmes: French police
corbillard: hearse
croque-morts: undertaker's assistants
le voilà enfin: there he is at last
un enfant sauvage: a wild child
enceinte: pregnant
mari de convenance: husband of convenience
santé: to your health (a toast)
pommes frites: French fries

Ma chandelle est morte, / Je n'ai plus de feu. / Ouvre-moi ta porte / Pour l'amour de Dieu.
My candle's out, / I've got no more fire. / Open your door to me, / For the love of God.

dernier cri: the last word in fashion